QUANTUM RADIO

BY A.G. RIDDLE

The Atlantis Trilogy

The Atlantis Gene
The Atlantis Plague
The Atlantis World

The Extinction Files

Pandemic
Genome

The Long Winter Trilogy

Winter World
The Solar War
The Lost Colony

Other novels

The Extinction Trials
Lost in Time
Quantum Radio

A.G. RIDDLE

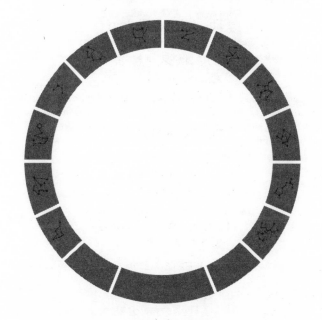

QUANTUM RADIO

HEAD
of ZEUS

An Ad Astra Book

First published in the United Kingdom in 2023 by Head of Zeus Ltd,
part of Bloomsbury Publishing Plc

9 7 5 3 1 2 4 6 8

A catalogue record for this book is available from the British Library.

ISBN (HB): 9781803281698
ISBN (XTPB): 9781803281704
ISBN (E): 9781804549872

Illustration copyright © A.G. Riddle

Printed and bound in Great Britain by
CPI Group (UK) Ltd, Croydon CR0 4YY

Head of Zeus Ltd
First Floor East
5–8 Hardwick Street
London EC1R 4RG

WWW.HEADOFZEUS.COM

To my in-laws, who watched the kids and helped
me write during the pandemic.

Note:

Much of the science and history in this novel is real.

Visit agriddle.com to separate fact from fiction (and browse other bonus material).

PART I

THE ORIGIN PROJECT

1

In an auditorium at CERN, Tyson Klein stood behind a wooden podium, watching his colleagues arrive. It was the end of the workday, and most seemed tired. They shuffled in and plopped down in the folding seats, stowing their messenger bags and backpacks at their feet, weary eyes staring at him, silently saying, *this better be worth getting home late for.*

It would be.

This talk would be the most important of his entire career. And possibly theirs.

The slides—and the discovery they detailed—were the culmination of twelve years of research into his life's work, The Theory of Everything. The data he was about to reveal was, he believed, the key to discovering a master theory that would unite the opposing branches of modern physics. If he was right, this breakthrough would resolve scientific mysteries that had haunted the world's greatest minds, from Albert Einstein to Stephen Hawking. More than that, Ty believed that his discovery might answer the deepest questions of human existence:

Why do we seem to be alone in the universe?

Where did we come from?

And what is the future of the human race?

What is our destiny?

Ty had spent his entire life pursuing those questions. Now the answers were within reach. He simply needed what all scientists eventually require: time and money.

He was about to ask for it.

If his audience said no, Ty wasn't sure what he would do. It was entirely possible that the whole of human history might turn on what was about to occur in this auditorium.

As a child, that sort of pressure would have made him nervous. In fact, in middle school, he had once faked sickness to avoid giving a presentation in class. Luckily, he had a mother who could see through such a ruse. And, even more luckily for him, he had a mother who knew how to speak to him in a language he appreciated: science.

Even at a young age, science was Ty's true north, and his mother wielded it to his benefit—even when arguing against him.

"Everyone is scared of public speaking, Ty. At least at first," she had said, peering down at him as he sat on his bed.

Like any angst-filled twelve-year-old, he had hung his head and muttered, "Great. How does that help me?"

"Practice—that's the only way to get better. The more you do it, the more comfortable you'll feel."

"I don't want to practice. Or get better. There's no point. When I grow up, I'm going to get a job where I never have to talk. I'll be a mute."

"You can't simply not talk when you grow up, Ty."

"You watch me."

"Let's look at this a different way, shall we? Let's apply *science.*"

Ty looked up. "I like science."

"So do I. It's why I became an evolutionary biologist, and it's why I can tell you exactly—from an evolutionary biological perspective—why you're afraid of public speaking."

He squinted at her, still not believing.

"A long time ago, humans spent most of their lives hunting and gathering food. Do you know what the most dangerous thing was for our ancestors?"

Ty shook his head.

"Predators. In particular, a surprise attack. For thousands and thousands of years, the most terrifying moment of a human's life was realizing that a set of eyes was watching them. Especially when those eyes belonged to a predator. Do you know what happened to our ancestors after they realized a predator's eyes were watching them?"

"They ran."

"That's half right. They either ran, or they fought. But one thing we know for certain is that all humans alive today are descended from the survivors of those encounters—humans who either ran and lived or fought and won. In both cases, do you know what saved them?"

"Being strong. Or fast."

"No. Many of the strong perished. And the fast. Do you know why?"

"No."

"They weren't afraid, Ty. They didn't run—or prepare to fight—the second they felt those eyes upon them. Their minds didn't ring the alarm bells that enabled them to react fast enough. The predators pounced. From an evolutionary standpoint, those prehistoric humans who weren't afraid when they realized that eyes were watching them didn't live long enough to pass on their genes. Being unafraid was a bad thing. It was deadly. And an evolutionary dead end. Being afraid *was good*. It conveyed a survival advantage. Selective pressure favored the fearful. Thus, the entire human race became populated with people like all of us—humans with genes that biologically program us to be afraid of eyes watching us. What does that tell you?"

"I don't know."

"It tells you that it's okay to be afraid of giving your presentation. It's natural, Ty. It's science. Our entire species evolved to feel that way. Part of life is knowing that our bodies are biologically programmed to certain reactions. That's what being human is. And I'll tell you another thing: being brave isn't about *not* feeling fear. It's about feeling fear and overcoming it. You can choose to recognize that the fear you feel when you stand up in front of the class is not warranted. You're in no danger."

"You just don't get it, Mom. I'm totally different from the other kids. It's like I'm from a completely different planet."

His mother looked away. "Actually, I do know what that feels like, Ty. But trust me on this: being different will help you a great deal when you get older. People like you—who are different—will be very valuable in this world. You'll see."

"Well, the waiting is killing me. And so is this presentation."

"There's a simple trick to controlling your fear of public speaking. It uses psychology and neuroscience. Would you like to hear it?"

"Very much. And please start with this part next time."

His mother smiled. "Noted. The thing is, there's a way to essentially dampen that innate fear response in your amygdala. And luckily, it comes naturally to you: kindness and generosity. When we're kind and helpful to others, it calms the fight-or-flight response in our brains. Kindness is a natural stress reliever. It puts our minds in a different place. When we change our attitude, it changes how our brain reacts. We're not on the defensive. We're on the offense—and we're doing the offense to help others. That's a deep well of strength."

She studied him for a moment. "Kindness is the fear killer."

Ty considered that for a moment. "Interesting."

"It is. To me, that's the power of science: it reveals the mysteries of life. It helps us understand ourselves and the world around us. And in your case, later today, I want you to approach your presentation with a sense of kindness and generosity. If you're coming from the right place, it makes everything easier. You have to see your presentation as helping others."

"Mom, my report on the War of 1812 isn't helping anyone. Trust me on that."

"Not true."

"Absolutely true."

"Did you enjoy learning about the War of 1812?"

"Mom, I'm a geek."

"Did you?"

"Yes," he muttered.

"So will others. Aren't there other smart people in your class?"

"Yes."

"It gets easier, Ty. In time, you'll realize that your kind heart will be the wind at your back in this life. You'll see. It's painful now, but eventually, you'll figure out your strengths and what you're really interested in. There, at the intersection of what you love and what you're good at, is a magical place of success and happiness. It's just hard to find."

His mother had been right. It had been hard to find. Figuring himself out had been the biggest challenge of all for Ty. And life had dealt him a few setbacks, a few he was still overcoming. But he had found his passion: quantum physics. His mind was uniquely tuned to solving those scientific mysteries. Since college, he had dedicated his life to that work, and now it was finally all coming together.

Ty realized someone was calling his name.

He looked up to find his boss, Mary, sitting in the front row, nodding at him, prompting him to begin.

The auditorium was filled now. Forty of his colleagues sat in the rows of seats, their eyes in the semi-darkness triggering that ancient instinct: fear. Ty's nerves rose as the silence stretched out in the auditorium.

As he'd done so many times since that talk with his mother, Ty focused on centering his mind on a place of kindness and generosity. What he was about to share could help the organization—everyone at CERN—and the entire human race. It was important. It was worth their time. He was here to help.

He focused on that feeling, that serene place in his mind.

A calm came over him as he stepped to the lectern.

"Thank you for coming on short notice. You've probably had a long day, and you're ready to get home. As such, I'll be as brief as I can."

He clicked the pointer, and his first slide appeared.

"I've made a discovery that I believe is of historical significance. One that could change the world. You all are here for the obvious reason: I need help. I need help with some of the science. And I need finance to sign off on the work. What I'm proposing is an experiment on a scale the human race has never seen before, one that I believe will solve the greatest mystery of all time."

2

Ty clicked a button and the next slide appeared on the massive screen behind him. The only sound in the auditorium was the air conditioning vents vibrating overhead.

"Since we have an audience drawn from different departments, I'm going to give some background that I know will bore some of you, but please bear with me. It's necessary and will be well worth it."

Ty motioned to the map on the screen. It showed an area at the border of France and Switzerland, just west of Lake Geneva. A red circle stretched across the two nations.

"As you know, the Large Hadron Collider, or LHC, was completed in September 2008. The first collisions occurred in 2010. It's the latest particle accelerator here at CERN and the largest in the world. The ring itself is twenty-seven kilometers long. In fact, the LHC is the largest machine in the world today. And the largest ever built."

Ty could see some of his audience tuning out, but he pressed on. "The LHC is a complex machine, but in its simplest form, it's like a racetrack for particles. The track has two tubes that are kept at ultrahigh vacuum. Inside those tubes, it's as empty as outer space. The ultrahigh vacuum reduces friction, enabling us to accelerate particles to almost the speed of light. Then, like two cars racing around a track in opposite directions, we crash those particles together. The real work here at CERN—besides the monumental task of building the collider and operating it—is examining what happens after particles collide. What we do, essentially, is examine what's produced from these particle collisions. When you smash particles together, what comes out, at its basic form, are the building blocks of the universe: subatomic particles. Some of these subatomic particles are things we have only theorized—like the Higgs boson. Now, at CERN, with the LHC, we can finally detect particles we have long believed existed. What we're doing, frankly, is peeling back the curtain and finally discovering what the universe is made of. I believe that's the key to understanding how our universe works on a fundamental level, which is the focus of my research."

Ty debated whether to share some of his personal history. He sensed that he was losing some of the audience's attention, but he opted to trust his gut and go for it.

"The LHC is actually what brought me to Geneva and CERN. The promise of what the collider can do for physics and our understanding of the universe—of the very nature of our existence—is simply impossible to exaggerate. My hope was that the LHC would answer some of the greatest unresolved questions in physics: the deep structure of space and time, the relationship between quantum mechanics and general relativity, and the details of how the elementary particles in the universe work."

Ty pointed to the screen, which showed the timeline of the Large Hadron Collider construction and upgrades.

"As most of you know, the LHC was shut down at the end of 2018 after the second run. The reason is simple: after running for a few years, the collisions generally deliver fewer discoveries because we've seen everything we can detect—or everything we can produce from those collisions. There's really only one solution: upgrade the machine. Better equipment gives the LHC more collision energy, more luminosity, and better detectors to see the results. The collider recently came back online for run three, this time with more power and better hardware than ever before. The upgrade to the LHC is what enabled me to make my discovery."

The next slide showed a table with subatomic particles and their counts.

"I wrote a computer algorithm to analyze the data generated from run three—specifically, to look for unexpected patterns. I wasn't sure what I would find. But I kept tweaking the algorithm until I found a pattern—and something else. What I believe are non-original exotic subatomic particles."

One of the managers from the finance department held up his hand. "What exactly are you saying here?"

"I'm saying that I think more is happening during these particle collisions than we think."

The man frowned. "What does that mean?"

"The purpose of the LHC experiments is to crash particles together and look at what they're made of—the smallest building blocks of the universe. I think some of these collisions are doing more than simply breaking apart particles. I believe the collisions themselves are acting upon the fabric of our universe in a manner we don't fully understand."

Ty held up a sheet of paper. "One of the great questions in science is whether our universe is a closed system. In particular, where did all of the matter and energy in the universe come from, and where will it all go? We know all matter and energy in our universe originated with the Big Bang—but what happened before that? And what will happen at the end of the universe? I think I may have detected part of the answer."

He took a pencil from the lectern and stabbed it into the paper. "My working theory is that the collisions in the LHC are breaking open particles, but they're also causing our universe to become porous—for the smallest, smallest fraction of a second. I believe some of the subatomic particles we're detecting here at CERN aren't originating from the source particles we crashed together. We thought they were before because the machine and the detectors weren't sensitive enough and the computing grid couldn't hold sufficient data. That's changed. I think the truth is that some of the particles we're detecting aren't from our world. They're from somewhere else."

"Where?"

"That's the question." Ty paused a moment. "Well, actually, a better question is where—and when? Our understanding of the very nature of space-time is incomplete. Therefore, we only know that these exotic subatomic particles I've identified are coming from elsewhere. They could be from somewhere else in the universe, or they could be coming from right here, but from the future or from the past."

The room was utterly quiet.

Ty took a deep breath and steeled himself to deliver the news he believed would be the biggest scientific discovery in human history.

"But that's not the most remarkable part. The real scientific mystery is that these particles have a pattern. They aren't just random noise. It's organized. What we're detecting is a data stream."

Ty stared at the audience. "I think what we've built here at CERN is far more than a particle collider. The ring buried under our feet is detecting quantum data. It's tuning in to a broadcast across space and time, a message being sent via a sort of... quantum radio."

3

Ty had expected to be grilled on his discovery.

He had mentally prepared himself to be on stage for hours defending his findings, fielding questions, and debating the merits of his theory.

None of those things happened.

The scientists in the auditorium, for the most part, said nothing. They didn't want to discuss his theory. They wanted to see the data.

Extraordinary claims, after all, require extraordinary proof.

Most of all, Ty's colleagues wanted to repeat his experiments, to run his algorithms and get the same outcome. That inspired confidence: a new discovery that was verifiable and repeatable.

The audience filed out of the room, some on their way home, others staying to work the night shift. Ty's boss, Mary, stepped onto the stage and held out her arms to hug him. She was about the same age as Ty's mother and every bit as nurturing.

"It went well, Ty."

"They didn't believe me."

"They will. In time."

He nodded.

"It's a big deal, Ty. Might even garner you the Nobel." Mary smiled. "There could be a slight bit of jealousy in the room. I bet a great many of them wish they had come up with it. Chin up, now."

Outside, the sun was sinking rapidly behind the Jura Mountains. The sound of laughter and smell of barbecue filled the air—the by-product of the informal after-work gatherings that were common at CERN, where post-doctoral fellows and staff regularly mixed with Nobel laureates and theories and experiments were devised and friendships were made. It was a part of the magic of CERN that Ty loved. On any other night, he would have been tempted to wander over and see if he knew anyone and had any interest in the conversation. But tonight, he had something else in mind.

He took out his phone and dialed Penny, the German graduate student he'd met at a small café six months ago.

The same nerves he'd felt on stage returned, though now they were mixed with a sort of excitement. Ty had been unlucky in love. As such, he had avoided dating for most of his adult life. Like a kid who had fallen off his bike and skinned his knee, he had been cautious this time around, taking it slow, careful not to get hurt again. Penny had been fine with that.

"Hi," she answered, sounding surprised.

"Hi."

"I thought you had to work."

"I thought so too." Ty glanced back at the building. "Things wrapped up quicker than I thought."

"Everything all right?"

"Yeah. I think so. Actually, today was sort of a big day."

"Oh, do tell," she said playfully. Ty could imagine her smiling, holding the phone with one hand, setting her textbook aside and curling up on the narrow bed in her studio apartment as she ran her other hand through her long brown hair.

"I'd love to. Over dinner."

"I can do dinner."

"Great. And to give you a cryptic preview, the topic of tonight's talk will be quantum radio."

Silence stretched out so long Ty thought she had hung up. He took the phone from his ear and stared at the screen, watching the seconds of the call tick up. The line was active. She was still there.

"Hello? Can you hear me?"

Penny's tone was flat when she spoke again. "I'm here. What did you just say?"

"Dinner."

"No. Your discovery. What did you call it?"

"Quantum radio. I know it's a sort of quirky name, but it makes sense once you understand it."

"I'm sure." In the background, Ty could hear her moving around quickly, as if gathering her things. "Actually, I just remembered that I need to study tonight. Dinner's no good."

"No problem." Ty couldn't help reading more into it. "Everything okay?"

"Yes. Completely. Sorry, Ty, gotta run."

The line went dead.

Ty stood there, replaying the call in his mind.

Quantum radio.

He shouldn't have even brought it up. Penny didn't want to hear him drone on about his experiments over dinner. Who would?

Ty donned his helmet and pedaled his bike into the warm August night, out of the CERN complex.

Usually, the bike ride home was one of Ty's favorite parts of the day. It was a way to clear his mind. But today, that was a challenge. As the green fields and low-rise office buildings and apartments passed, his thoughts kept drifting back to the call with Penny. Something was off about it.

Five minutes into his trek, the tram passed on its way to CERN. When he'd first moved to the area, he had lived in a hostel for a few months and taken public transportation, which was free to anyone staying in a hostel, hotel, or campsite. He still rode the tram in the winter, but he preferred to bike the rest of the year.

There was a big push at CERN to bike to work, and Ty had to admit that it had been good for him. It was really the only exercise he got, and it had improved his mental health too. Most of his colleagues who lived in France still drove to work, but the truth was that having a car was far easier on the French side of the border. Driving in Geneva was a challenge, but parking was a true nightmare. As such, he now owned a bike and a Unireso pass, which got him access to all of Geneva's public transport networks (trams, buses, trains, and even the mouettes, the yellow transport boats that operated on Lake Geneva). Between his bike and the Unireso pass, he could get anywhere in Geneva quickly and easily.

At his four-story apartment building, Ty dismounted his bike and trudged inside, exhaustion finally catching up with him as the adrenaline from the presentation faded and exertion from pedaling took its toll.

Ty's building, like so many in Geneva, was fully occupied. It had been built in the seventies and hadn't changed much since then. It was worn but clean, and the owner seemed to have no interest in updating it. He was, however, maniacal about the move-out inspection (Ty had heard horror stories about the fees charged to other residents for even the most minor damage).

Still, Ty was glad to have found the place. The property market was competitive, and supply was tight (most listing agents didn't even bother to post pictures of the interior of available properties, and showings were often left to the current occupants; the best places typically went within hours, or days at the most).

Before moving to Geneva, Ty had heard how expensive the city was. Having grown up in Washington, DC, however, the price shock wasn't that bad to him. Things were expensive—especially groceries and health care—but his CERN salary was more than adequate.

Most of all, his lifestyle was what kept his finances in check. It wasn't that he was frugal. He simply didn't do anything besides work and sit at home and read. Well, with the exception of going out to dinner or hiking with Penny, but based on the last call, he wasn't sure how much longer he'd be doing that.

His biggest expense was flying home to DC for the holidays, and even with that cost, he had managed to save a little bit.

In the apartment building's entrance hall, Ty found one of his neighbors waiting by the elevator, jabbing the button to call it, a perturbed look on her face. Her name was Indra Tandon, and she worked as a travel coordinator at the international headquarters of Médecins Sans Frontières, commonly known as Doctors Without Borders in the English-speaking world. Her husband, Ajit, was an interpreter at the United Nations and often worked nights at dinners and late meetings. Their only child, a son, named Ramesh, sat beside her in a motorized wheelchair. From the dinner conversations in their flat, Ty knew that the Tandons could afford a better apartment, but they were saving for two very important reasons: to cover the cost of any potential new treatments for their son's cerebral palsy and to send money home to relatives in India.

"Hi, Mrs. Tandon."

She turned and gave Ty a weary smile. "Hello, Tyson. How are you?"

"Good. Everything okay?"

"Yes. Fine." She motioned to the closed elevator doors. "I think it is broken again."

She took out her phone and glanced at the time, then at Ramesh, who was staring at the floor. "I'm sure Ajit will be home shortly."

From her tone, Ty wasn't convinced she believed that. And he knew she wouldn't call him, because Ajit would indeed come home to help, and it might cause a problem at work, and Indra would end up feeling guilty about it. Ty knew this because it had happened once before, eight months ago.

"Mind if I help?" Ty asked. When Indra grimaced, he added, "I could use the exercise."

She gave a sharp nod. "Well, if you insist."

"I do."

Ty bent down to eye level with the boy, smiling. "What do you think, Ramesh? Up for helping me exercise?"

Ramesh smiled back, and his voice was soft when he spoke. "Sure."

Ty released the strap on Ramesh's wheelchair and lifted him up, holding the boy tight to his body. He ascended the marble stairs carefully, and by the time he reached the fourth floor, his legs were burning and his forehead was damp with sweat.

In the Tandons's apartment, he gently set Ramesh on the couch and whispered, "That was fun, wasn't it?"

Ramesh nodded quickly. "Yeah."

"Will you stay for dinner, Tyson?"

"I'd love to, but I have some work to catch up on."

"Then take some chicken biryani with you."

"No, I can't—"

"Now I must insist, Tyson. You look too thin as it is."

４

At his door, Ty was surprised to find a small package lying on the floor. It was marked Swiss Post, but the sender was listed only as "Shipping Center" with an address in Reinach, Switzerland.

He wasn't expecting anything—and certainly wasn't used to Swiss Post delivering boxes of this size to his apartment door when he wasn't home.

Inside, he put the package on the dining table and set the food Indra had given him in the microwave. He was famished. Soon, the smell of chicken, rice, and spices filled the one-bedroom apartment.

His place was, in short, a mess. The IKEA bookcase next to the door was filled to the brim with nonfiction books. So was the floor. The volumes sat in stacks, like makeshift walls of a book maze in his living room. The coffee table was littered with professional journals and two decaying take-out boxes.

The walls were covered in articles he had torn out and pinned there, sometimes with yellow Post-its with his notes.

The kitchen wasn't much better. Plates were piled up in the sink (the dishwasher was broken). Bottles of supplements and prescription medications lined the wall like chess pieces.

The supplements and medications were part of Ty's years of personal health experiments. He was constantly looking for new ways to enhance his mental clarity and energy—to hack himself, in a way.

The first row of bottles contained his current pill regimen.

A notebook beside the bottles recorded the observations of his experiments. Each row held a date and data consistent with any science experiment, which was exactly how Ty had come to regard his health.

As the timer on the microwave ticked down, he twisted the pill bottles open and downed the tablets for tonight's scheduled doses.

He had to admit: the apartment really was a pigsty. Even more than normal. His last attempt at cleaning up had been a month ago, when Penny had come over. He thought he had done a decent job. Penny... well, she had been less than impressed.

"What happened here?" she had asked.

He glanced around. "What?"

"Ty, this place is a mess. It looks like a police stakeout."

"Really?"

"Actually, it looks like a police stakeout conducted by a serial killer who is, in fact, unbeknownst to him, actually in a padded cell in a mental institution. It's that crazy in here. We're going to my place."

"Why?"

"Because part of Netflix and chill is to chill—and I can't relax in here." She put her bag down. "In fact, we're going to sort this out right now—I don't even think I can relax at my flat knowing yours is in such a state."

And with that, she had set about cleaning up Ty's apartment, like the whirlwind force of nature that she was.

Ty was smiling at the memory when the microwave beeped. As usual, he had overheated the dish—he could barely touch the plastic container. Popping the top released a plume of steam hot enough to take half his face off.

With some finesse, he set the plastic container on the dining table and stirred it with a fork, trying to disperse the heat.

When it was still hot enough to burn his mouth but not enough to matter, he dug in, eating as he always did: quickly.

And as usual, he took out his phone.

No calls or texts from Penny.

Instantly, he regretted looking. He wished he didn't care. But he did. Particle physics was a lot easier than dating. Science made sense. People didn't.

He checked his email, half expecting to find follow-up questions from the attendees at his talk. He found none. That was odd.

When the pace of his eating—or rather, shoveling the food in his mouth—forced him to take a breath, Ty ripped open the package he'd found at his door.

It was an alarm clock. A cheap one.

That, he hadn't expected.

It already had batteries, but the time wasn't set. It simply blinked 12:00 a.m., which annoyed him enough to set the time: 7:09 p.m.

Maybe it was a gift from his mom or sister? He was always late for things, and they hated that. Maybe this was a reference to that. Or possibly a gag gift from a college friend? A way of saying time was running out? If so, it was sort of lame in his opinion.

He considered calling his family to ask about it, but it was 1:09 in the afternoon in DC, and they would be at work. The clock wasn't worth interrupting them. He'd call on Saturday.

When the plastic food container was empty, he washed it out in the sink. He realized then just how tired he was. He didn't know if it was the stress of the presentation or the weeks of long hours building up to it, but all of a sudden, the only thing he wanted to do was lie down.

He typically read a novel before drifting off to sleep, but tonight, even that was too much effort. He slipped off his shoes and stretched out on the bed, not bothering to pull the covers back. He put his wireless headphones in and tapped his phone to start an audiobook.

As he lay there, the story drew him in, deeper and deeper, as if he were falling down a well. He knew he needed to get up and brush his teeth and wash his face. He made a compromise: he'd just brush his teeth. He was too tired for anything else. He'd get up and do that—in a few minutes. Just a few minutes more.

Ty woke to the sound of a long droning.

It came again, a buzzing in his ears.

It was an incoming phone call—ringing in his earbuds.

He turned, but his body responded slowly, as though he had slept on all of his limbs, cutting the circulation off.

It was dark out, and quiet. How long had he been asleep?
Finally, he grabbed the phone. Penny was calling.

At 2:30 a.m.

Something's wrong—that was his first instinct.

"Hello?" he croaked.

"Get out!"

"What?"

"Ty, get out of the apartment!"

"What?"

"Stop saying *what*! Wake up. Get out of there!"

He was moving now, off the bed and into the living room. He
pulled the apartment door open and staggered into the hall and
onto the stairs that shared a wall with his bedroom.

In his sock feet, he descended the risers two at a time.

"Penny, what are you talking—"

The blast hurled him into the far wall of the landing, so fast
he didn't even have time to brace before everything went dark.

5

Pain came first.

Ty's back, elbow, and head ached.

Ringing came next. The sound started in his ears and echoed all the way to his eyes.

Drywall mist and pieces of debris rained down on him like a drizzle of sand and small rocks.

Ty opened his eyes but instantly closed them again to keep the dust out.

He was still on the landing, lying at the base of the wall.

Slowly, he rolled over and got to his hands and knees, wincing at the pain in his right arm. Facing down, he again opened his eyes. Moonlight drifted in through the window above—the now shattered window.

That was dangerous. Ty knew that, but for the life of him, he couldn't grasp exactly why the broken window above was a danger. His brain was as shaken as his body.

A few feet away, something was glowing through the cloud of dust, a lighthouse shining out on a foggy night.

Why would a piece of debris be glowing? That didn't make sense.

Ty opened his mouth, trying to make the ringing in his ears stop.

Without thinking, he reached out his right hand to crawl toward the light but instantly drew back in pain when it touched the floor.

Squinting in the moonlight, he pulled the shard of glass from his palm. *That* was why the broken window was dangerous: the sharp pieces on the floor.

He began to stand but stopped. The broken glass would shred his feet if he wasn't careful.

With his left hand, he swatted away the dust cloud until he could safely see to navigate through the jagged debris.

When he reached the glowing light, he realized what it was: his phone.

It was buzzing. Someone was calling.

Penny Neumann.

He answered, but the ringing in his ears muffled Penny's voice.

"I can't hear," he yelled, but even the sound of his own voice was faint.

The line went dead. A text message appeared:

Meet me. Where we first met. Now.

He slipped the phone into his pocket and surveyed the landing and stairs, searching for shards of glass glittering in the moonlight.

He wasn't leaving. Not until everyone was out of the building or until help arrived.

In the hallway to his apartment, he found Ajit Tandon staggering through the dust, his son Ramesh in his arms.

Ty reached out to help, but the older man brushed him away. His wife Indra was close behind, and when she saw Ty, she reached out and put her hands on his shoulders, sending a bolt of pain through him.

Her words were barely audible. "Are you okay?"

He nodded and stumbled down the hall and into his apartment, where he stopped cold.

It was apparent the blast had originated here. The walls were charred. A hole in the floor loomed where the dining table had been. Below, his neighbor's apartment was also a burned ruin. No one was moving.

Books were blown to bits, the pieces strewn about like confetti. The entire wall that separated the kitchen-dining-living room from the bedroom was gone.

With each passing second, his hearing was returning.

The first sounds he discerned were in the distance: sirens wailing in the night, growing closer, three, maybe four of them. First responders.

Closer: voices in the darkened apartment building, calling out in French, German, and English.

Watch out for the glass.

The door is jammed.

Follow me.

Ty felt a vibration in his pocket. A text message.

His eyes stayed on his apartment. It was clear what had caused the blast: the cheap-looking alarm clock that had arrived in the mail.

Why?

How could this happen?

Had anyone been hurt by the blast?

Someone was trying to kill him. And Penny had known ahead of time.

Why?

His laptop was disintegrated. The only remnants were a few pieces of gray plastic scattered in the living room.

His notes were toast as well, burned or vaporized.

He reached down and felt the USB drive in his pocket. It contained the algorithm to decode the collider data on CERN's LHC computer grid. It was his life's work. And he still had it.

Was this why someone had tried to kill him?

As he held the data drive, his phone buzzed again.

He took it out and read the two text messages from Penny:

Go, Ty.

Now.

Still standing there, he saw a new message appear:

Every second you stay, you put the people around you in danger. They're coming for you, Ty. Go. Now. Please.

Ty's heart began pounding in his chest as if he were walking on a treadmill that had just kicked into high gear.

He reached down and pulled his shoes on and raced into the hall, which was empty now.

Ty found his neighbors gathered just outside the building's entrance, families hugging each other, frightened, sleepy expressions on their faces. And shock for a few. People from nearby buildings were congregating too, standing on both sides of the street like spectators at a parade, waiting for the procession of fire trucks, police vehicles, and ambulances to arrive.

It wouldn't be long; the wail of sirens was growing closer.

Ty mounted his bike and pedaled into the night.

6

The dark streets of Geneva were completely empty. The shops were all closed. Even the bars and clubs were deserted.

Ty's legs, arms, and back ached as he pumped the pedals, but he ignored the pain.

His discovery was clearly a threat to someone.

But who?

And why?

He sensed that his life was about to change forever, that the blast was a sort of demarcation between his quiet, lonely life before and whatever was about to happen now.

He stood and leaned on the pedals as he crossed the bridge over the Rhône River, into Geneva's Old Town.

The coffee shop where he had first met Penny was a popular spot for locals, tourists, and students. It was a block away from the University of Geneva and had been packed that Saturday six months ago. Ty had arrived early, staked out a seat at a small table in the corner, and was reading a book, lost in thought, when Penny placed her hand on the empty chair opposite him.

"Hi."

"Hi," he had answered, his voice scratchy.

She smiled and glanced through the plate glass window, out onto the street where it had begun raining in sheets. "Really sorry, but would you mind if I sat here for a minute?"

Dozens of patrons were standing now, watching the rain, sipping coffee and tea, waiting for a break to escape the crowded café.

As she stood there, staring at him, Ty felt them slipping into their own little world, as though the small table was an island of solitude in the midst of the crowd, the two of them existing outside of space and time.

"Sure," he said, motioning to the chair.

Penny set her bag down, drew out a well-worn paperback novel, and began reading. He expected her to say something, but she didn't. She merely turned the pages and sipped her tea.

Since childhood, Ty had been painfully shy. The very idea of sitting with a stranger in a crowded coffee shop was enough to send waves of anxiety through him. But sitting with her, he felt perfectly at peace, as though it was a natural thing, as though they had done this a million times in a million lives.

"Are you a student?" she said finally, not looking up from the book.

"No. I work at CERN. Are you?"

"I am."

"At the University of Geneva?"

"That's the one."

"What are you studying?"

"International affairs."

"Sounds exciting."

She laughed. "Hardly. It's a lot of reading. Even more talking."

"Do you like it?"

"I do."

"What got you interested in it?"

Her gaze drifted out the window, to the rain still coming down and the people filing out of the coffee shop, to the bus that had stopped on the street. Ty thought she was considering catching it, but she took another sip of tea and said, "Circumstances."

His eyebrows bunched as he waited, watching her, but she didn't elaborate. "What sort of circumstances?"

"The unavoidable kind. Fate. Let's just call it fate. But I like the work I'm doing."

"Which is?"

"Understanding the world and how it came to be the way it is. I think that's the key to bringing people from different worlds together." She set the book down. "What about you? What do you do at CERN?"

"Oh, you know, the usual—accelerating particles to near the speed of light and smashing them together to see what comes out in an effort to understand what the universe was like in the earliest fractions of a second of its existence."

She smiled. "Is that all?"

"Eh, we're just trying to unravel the major mysteries of space and time and reconcile the greatest unanswered questions in physics."

"And how's that going—the whole space-time particle-mystery thing?"

"We're making some pretty interesting discoveries, actually." He exhaled theatrically, teeing up the joke. "But I have to say: some days it just feels like we're going around in circles."

He stared out the window, trying to hold a straight face.

She set the book down. "Wait. Was that a particle physics joke?"

He smiled.

Penny cocked her head. "Because of... what's it called? The loop?"

"The collider. The Large Hadron Collider. It's a ring buried under France and Switzerland, twenty-seven kilometers long."

"I see what you did there—going around in circles."

"It's pretty bad."

"It's terrible. And I liked it."

And he liked her. More than he had liked anyone in a long time. There was only one other woman he had ever been that comfortable with, that happy with, and she had left his life a long time ago. There was still a deep wound there. Every second he spent with Penny seemed to heal it.

But tonight, when he arrived at that fateful coffee shop where he and Penny had met, it was dark and empty. He gently propped his bike against the wall, right beside the window at the table where they had sat.

The narrow street in Old Town was empty and quiet. The stores, restaurants, and cafés were dark. A few lights were on in the flats above the ground level, likely night owls studying or staying up for meetings with people in different time zones.

The alley beside the coffee shop was barely big enough for three people to walk down shoulder to shoulder. With each step, the light from the antique streetlamp behind Ty grew dimmer. The only sound was his footfalls on the cobblestone.

As the light faded, he heard two people talking—a man and a woman. The woman was Penny, and the strain in her voice immediately put Ty on edge. She was scared. He knew that before he processed the words she was saying:

"He'll be here. I promise you."

The man's voice was gruff, his accent German. "You should not have interfered."

"You left me no choice."

"False. We have altered the data on the LHC grid. He was the only remaining threat."

"You're wrong. He has a copy of his research on a USB drive. It also holds notes that aren't on his work computer or the cloud."

"All that would have been destroyed in the detonation."

"You assume," Penny said with force. "You assume. That's your problem: assumptions. Those assumptions could compromise everything. We need to know how far his work has progressed. The truth is, the drive might have survived the blast. Someone else could have gotten it when they arrived at the scene. I had to call him. We need those files."

The words were like a dull knife carving into Ty's heart: not fast, not efficient, but a slow, aching cut that revealed the truth, what had lain below what he had seen the whole time.

Penny didn't care about him. Never had. It was all a ruse. For what? His research?

Ty knew he needed to turn and run, but he stood there, paralyzed, scared, and angry.

Behind him, the sound of a police siren grew louder. Within seconds, the car passed, its roof lights strobing through the alley like a spotlight searching it. And in that flash, Ty saw the German man—he had stepped from behind the building to cast a glance at the vehicle.

Their eyes locked on each other. And things happened quickly then.

7

Ty turned and began running out of the alley.

The large German man charged after him, shoes clacking on the cobblestones like horses galloping in the night. When he reached Ty, he shoved him from behind. Ty stumbled and fell, and by the time he got to his hands and knees, the man had come around to block his way out of the alley. He held a gun at his side, careful to avoid anyone passing by from seeing it, angling it upward at Ty's chest.

Penny arrived then, hands held up. "Take it easy," she said, panting.

The man motioned with his gun toward the rear of the shop, where they couldn't be seen from the alley. "Move."

Ty raised his hands, got to his feet, and shuffled sideways, never taking his eyes off the man. He was clean-shaven, with close-cropped blond hair and hazel eyes that never blinked. A low-simmering hatred radiated off of him.

Penny stayed between the two men, and when they were behind the shop, she said, "Relax, Ty. We just want to talk."

Turning to the German man, she said, "Heinrich, put that away. You're scaring him."

He sneered. "Don't bother with the charade. He heard us." He motioned to Ty with the gun. "Hand over the drive."

On instinct, Ty lied, his own words surprising even himself. "I hid it."

"Liar," Heinrich practically spat. To Penny, he said, "Search him."

She didn't move.

"Search. Him. Or I shoot you both."

Penny took a step forward, eyes locked with Ty's, hands rising. When her face was inches from his, she reached out and touched the pocket on his shirt, her hand flat, fingers pressing toward his heart.

Slowly, she slid down his chest and abs, moving toward his pants—and the pocket where the USB drive waited.

Her eyes betrayed no emotion, only stared at him as her hands moved over him, her breath warm on his face.

Her right hand slipped into his left pocket, feeling the thin cloth next to his leg and groin until her fingers brushed over his phone and closed around the length of the drive. She held it for a moment, and Ty could feel her squeezing it, mentally sizing it up to be sure of what it was.

Still staring at him, she put her other hand in his right pocket and felt his wallet and keys. Her fingers rattled them, the jingle the only sound in the night.

And then, to Ty's surprise, she released the drive and withdrew her hands, empty. She stared at Ty, not turning around.

"He doesn't have it on him."

Heinrich pointed the gun down at Ty's feet. "Remove your shoes."

Ty stepped on the back of one shoe with the other and kicked it off, then repeated it with the other.

"Back away," Heinrich said. "Both of you."

With the gun pointed at Ty, the German bent down, turned the shoes over, and shook them.

"Move away from him," Heinrich said to Penny.

"You don't trust me?"

For the first time, Heinrich smiled, an unhappy, hateful expression that dripped with contempt. "There is only one man here stupid enough to believe your lies."

Ty watched the impassive expression on her face turn hard—for only a fraction of a second—before vanishing. He wondered if Heinrich had noticed it. And if he even cared.

Penny took a step back.

"I said move."

She took another step away.

Heinrich crept forward, eyes drilling into Ty. "If you so much as blink, I shoot you."

Against his will, Ty felt himself swallow hard. The beat of his heart grew louder, like rain on a tin roof growing stronger, the knocking blotting out all sound. When Heinrich reached him and found the drive, it would all end. Ty was sure of that. He would die here, in this dirty alley behind a coffee shop where he had been lured into a fake relationship.

In his entire life, Ty had never struck a stranger with his fists. Growing up, he and his twin brother had gotten into a few scuffles, but rarely enough to draw blood. Now, he sensed that he was about to fight for his life. When Heinrich found the drive, he wouldn't hesitate to kill him.

With the gun in one hand, Heinrich reached out with his other and felt behind Ty's collar, pressing the fabric to his skin, feeling for the device.

He would find the device in a few seconds. Ty glanced down at the gun, mentally preparing himself to act.

In his peripheral vision, he saw a flash of movement—Penny, reaching out, grabbing Heinrich's gun hand, slamming an elbow into his face, connecting just under his cheekbone with a snapping thud that brought the man down onto his back, Penny on top of him.

The gun flew from his hand and clattered across the cobblestones.

Penny screamed out as Heinrich belted her with his free hand, propelling her off him.

Her cry was like a light switch turning on inside of Ty. He dove on the man, raised a fist, and buried it in Heinrich's already-swelling face, the contact sending a sharp spike of pain through his hand and arm, the impact like striking a thin steak on a hard counter. The ache shot through his body, reigniting the places that were still tender from the bomb blast. The effect momentarily paralyzed him.

Drawing his right arm across himself, Heinrich flung the backside of his forearm into Ty, propelling him off.

Heinrich rolled and pushed up, onto his feet.
But he was too late.
The crack of a gunshot shattered the night.
Heinrich's head jerked, and he collapsed to the ground.

8

Penny held the gun with both hands, her body trembling now, eyes wide, staring at the dead man.

Ty gasped for breath and rose on shaking legs. The puddle of blood beneath Heinrich spread out, filling the channels between the cobblestones like tendrils of a dark, flowing beast.

"You have to go," Penny said as she slipped the gun into the windbreaker she was wearing.

Ty's hand drifted to his pocket, to the USB drive that held his research.

Penny seemed to read his thoughts. "I don't want your research."

A million questions ran through Ty's mind. But he said the thing that hurt him the most. "You lied to me."

"I did."

"Why?"

"I had to."

"Why, Penny?"

"I can't explain—"

"Try."

"Ty, you have to go. The police are probably on their way— and so are the people he works for."

"The people you work for."

"Yes."

"Who? Why? What's happening here, Penny?"

She stepped closer to him and gripped his shoulders, making him wince from the pain.

"They only told me to watch you. I didn't know what they were going to do, Ty. I promise."

"It was all a lie."

"At the start. But not after. I... didn't expect that."

"You're lying," he whispered.

She flinched at the words, clearly hurt. "I just killed a man for you, Ty. If that doesn't tell you that I love you, then I certainly don't have the words to convince you."

For a moment, the world faded away, the alley and the blood flowing toward Ty, and he was completely focused on the words she'd just said, words he had never heard her say before: *I love you.*

They stared at each other a long moment, and it was as if that statement had erased everything—Heinrich, the blast, their phone call after work—as though those words had rewound the clock of their relationship to that pure and better time before this night.

Penny let her hands slip from his shoulders and down into his pockets. Ty tensed, thinking she was reaching for the USB drive, but she took his phone instead.

Squatting down, she removed the phone's SIM card, placed it on a cobblestone, and quickly smashed it with the butt of the handgun.

"Don't get another phone. Even a pay-as-you-go. They can track your voice if you use it. Or if you log in to any service or app."

"Who are they, Penny?"

"We don't have time for this, Ty. What you discovered is a threat to them, to the world they're trying to create. It's going to change everything."

"We need to go to the police."

"If you do, you'll be dead within hours. Or in their custody. You don't understand what you're dealing with here."

A siren called out in the night, then another.

"You have to go," Penny hissed.

"Where?"

"Away from me, for one."

"Why?"

"They can track me. I didn't know it until tonight." She glanced at Heinrich. "Go, Ty."

"Where?"

"Somewhere they'll never suspect—where you can get help."

"Where will you go?"

"It doesn't matter."

"It matters to me."

She leaned in and kissed him, recklessly, throwing her arms around him. He ignored the pain in his back and hugged her tight, closing his eyes. When he opened them, the blood flowing in the canals between the cobblestones had reached them, soaking into her tennis shoes, moving toward him next.

She relaxed the hug and stared into his eyes. "I don't know what's going to happen, but I do know this: there is a much stronger person inside of you, Ty, waiting to come out. You'll be surprised. But don't let that person change who you are. It happens before you know it."

She kissed his cheek. "Don't forget the way you were before tonight. That's who I fell in love with."

As the siren blared closer, she hugged him and whispered in his ear. "Go, Ty. Before it's too late."

9

Ty rode into the night, through Geneva's empty streets, away from the coffee shop and the dead man.

Away from Penny.

He once again crossed the Rhône River. This time, the sound of sirens was even stronger, the wails a sharp contrast to the serenity of Lake Geneva, which spread out to the right. On the other side of the bridge, he slipped into the side streets, avoiding the main roads where a street camera or retailer video security system might spot him.

He needed to get help, and quickly. When Penny had said those words, Ty's mind had instantly flashed on a name: Gerhard Richter, a German whom Ty hadn't seen or spoken to in thirty years. Richter might not even recognize him. But Ty felt certain he would help—maybe even risk his life to help. Ty was about to bet everything on that belief.

One thing was certain: no one would expect Ty to try to contact Richter. In fact, only four other people in the whole world even knew that there was any connection between them.

That connection between Ty and Richter had been a point of pain for Ty's entire life. He had periodically looked the man up, out of curiosity mostly, but had avoided any contact.

Ty's last internet search for Richter had been about a month ago, and it had confirmed that he was still in Zürich, Switzerland, which was three and a half hours away from Geneva by car, directly northeast.

The A1 motorway was the fastest way to get from Geneva to Zürich. Taking a train was out— buying a ticket would be risky, and if he did, Ty would essentially be a sitting duck. And: the next train to Zürich didn't leave until morning.

He needed to get out of Geneva tonight.

That meant he needed a ride. Ty didn't own a car. Renting one was out of the question. And taking a car service or ride share seemed too risky as well.

Many of his friends and colleagues at CERN owned cars, but he wasn't about to call them, for two reasons. One: he was certain that it would put them in danger. And two: how would he even begin to explain something he didn't understand himself? ("Hey, Mike, I know it's 3 a.m., but can I get a ride to Zürich? Someone blew up my apartment, and Penny just shot a guy. Gotta get out of town for a bit!")

That left a single option that Ty's sleep-deprived, panicked mind could think of: hitchhiking. The practice was far more common in Europe than America. Ty had even done it several times while backpacking just after college.

At this hour, he knew there would be very few passenger cars on the road, but he hoped there would be some commercial vehicles. Truckers in particular. As he arrived at a gas station near the A1 motorway, he was relieved to find his assumption correct.

From the street, he scanned the perimeter and awning of the gas station, spotting the cameras. He didn't know how likely it was that whoever was after him would have access to the video feed from the Shell station just off the A1, but he knew this: it was better not to be seen, not to take the risk that they could track him that way.

Staying out of the camera's viewing range, he stowed his bike in the bushes of an office building and jogged to the truck farthest from the station and waited. When the driver exited the store, Ty held his hands up. "Hi. Can I get a ride to Zürich?"

The driver put his head down and barreled forward, shaking his head, not even bothering to reply.

Ty repeated his plea in French, then German. He was still learning Italian but knew it well enough to ask for a ride. The man's only response was a mumbling in a Slavic language Ty couldn't place.

The next driver who exited the store spoke English and would have given Ty a ride but was heading south to France.

The third and last truck at the station was pulling away. Feeling more desperate now, Ty stepped in front of it, leaving plenty of space to dive out of the way if the man didn't stop.

He held his arm up, and the massive vehicle rumbled to a stop. The driver cocked his head and rolled his window down and leaned out.

Ty considered changing up his approach. He had no cash— and he didn't dare use his credit cards to buy something to trade, but he had a watch his mother had given him for his high school graduation. For a moment, he considered slipping it off and offering it, but thought better of it, deciding instead to place his faith in the kindness of this stranger.

He walked closer to the cab and peered up.

"Sir, I could really use some help. I need to get to Zürich. It's important."

The man squinted at Ty. He appeared to be in his sixties, with short hair and a bushy black beard streaked with gray. An audiobook was playing inside the truck.

"Very well. Come on."

10

The massive truck drove north on the A1 motorway, past the Geneva airport and into the Swiss countryside.

Since Ty had climbed into the truck, the driver had said only four words: "I'm Lars," and "Don't talk."

And he hadn't.

For the first forty minutes, the only voice in the cab was that of a French audiobook narrator. From the action in the book, Ty was pretty sure it was wrapping up. It was a spy novel, and the protagonist was on the run—and out of options.

When the audiobook finished, Lars lit a cigarette, cracked his window slightly, and held the pack out to Ty, who shook his head.

When the cigarette was half finished, the man said, eyes still on the road, "So why do you need a ride to Zürich in the middle of the night?"

Ty couldn't quite place his accent. Belgian, if he had to guess.

When Ty didn't respond, Lars glanced over, silently prompting.

"It's... complicated."

"What sort of complications?"

Ty had never been a very good liar. As a child, a fixed stare from his mother was enough to make him spill the beans like a burst piñata.

He opted for honesty because, honestly, he really didn't know that much to tell.

"I made a discovery that someone is threatened by. I need to get away from them."

"I assumed you were in some sort of trouble." He motioned with the cigarette toward Ty. "The way you're sitting. Are you hurt?"

"No. Not really. Just bruises."

"A fight?"

"Yeah. You could say that."

Lars crushed out the cigarette in an ashtray and lit another. Ty cracked his window to get some fresh air, and upon seeing that, Lars stubbed out the new cigarette.

"Do you know why I drive at night?"

Ty shrugged. "Less traffic? Get there faster?"

"*That* is the practical reason. The real reason is that I've become used to being alone. Sleeping during the day. Driving at night. You think being comfortable being alone makes you strong. It helps in this work, but it can hold you back in life. I've been driving a lorry on these roads for almost forty years. That's a lot of time to think. This I know: two things are important in life. The choices you make. And the people you meet. You don't think so when you're young, but you'll know the truth one day: every day of your life is nothing more than a series of choices. Streets you can't see. Sometimes you take the wrong road."

He reached for a cigarette, then seemed to remember Ty's reaction to it.

"You took the wrong one. You either did the right thing or the wrong thing. In this world, you can be attacked for both. The only way to avoid being attacked is to do nothing important, nothing that matters to anyone."

Ty was considering those words when Lars added, "I wanted to be a philosopher." The truck driver chuckled at his own words. "I had this theory, a philosophical framework I called 'The Mind as a Biological Machine.' Big plans. The problem was, philosophy—ideas—don't pay the bills. And I had some. Father was gone. Mother was sick. So I left her with my sister and started driving. It was different back then. Good pay. People treated us different. We watched out for each other out here on the road."

Lars put the cigarettes away and ran a hand through his thinning hair.

"The greatest mistake you can ever make in this life is assuming things will stay the same. Change—that's the only real constant. I thought I'd drive this lorry for a few years, save up, and go back to college. It didn't work out. I should have continued my studies on the side—made a living and pursued my passion. You can do both. This job kept changing, and I kept on driving, staying the same. I figured the world will always need lorry drivers, and they'll have to pay them a good wage to make sure everyone is safe and things get from point A to point B."

He took a deep breath. "The shipping companies, they can only save money on two things: fuel and the driver. Used to be, fuel was the only commodity to them. These days, both are. They don't care—the drivers from Eastern Europe. And I don't blame them. They're just trying to support their family, same as me. They spend the money to get their license... and it's a lot of money to them... and they come here, and they work for starvation wages—a third of what we used to earn. Company doesn't care. If you're in the hole and you start earning less, you never get out."

Lars shook his head. "But don't listen to me. I've become a bitter old man. My body's starting to break down, and I'm having regrets. All I wanted to say is that if you're in some kind of trouble, think hard. Don't dig yourself in deeper. Consider where the road you're taking might lead you."

With that, the man put on another audiobook, a work of historical fiction centered on World War II. The words and the hum of the truck and the exhaustion finally overwhelmed the ache in Ty's body. The last thing he remembered was seeing road signs for Bern.

Ty woke to a baseball bat nudging him.

The truck was stopped by the side of the road. There was no rest stop or fuel station nearby, only green fields in the moonlight. He and Lars were alone—and the older man was holding the bat, his eyes burning with intensity.

"You're a terrorist," he practically spat at Ty.

"What?"

His sleep-addled mind could barely process what was happening.

"You set off a bomb in your apartment!"

Lars held his phone up, showing the front page of the news website swissinfo.ch, which was run by the Swiss Broadcasting Corporation. The headline read:

CERN Researcher Detonates Bomb at Home

Quickly, Ty scanned the article.

The Geneva cantonal police are asking for the public's help in locating Dr. Tyson Klein, an American physicist working at CERN, who is a person of interest in the explosion at his Geneva apartment around 2 a.m. The blast killed one person, a sixty-eight-year-old pensioner living below Klein's apartment, and injured a dozen more.

The words hit Ty like a gut punch. That person was dead because of him—because of his work. And others were injured. He wondered how badly they were hurt. He wondered how many might never walk again or see again because of the blast that was meant for him.

There was no mention of Penny or the man she had shot in the alley. Perhaps it was farther down in the article.

Lars jerked the phone back.

"Wait! Let me read it—please. I need to know what happened."

The Belgian driver eyed him a moment, then, still clutching the bat, held the phone out with his other hand, showing Ty the article again.

Details about the incident and Klein's possible motivations are unclear at this time, but sources say that Klein recently gave a presentation at CERN with ambitious claims that were met with skepticism. A colleague reached for comment, who spoke on the condition of anonymity, said that she did not believe that Klein had any explosives expertise or ill intent but that the thirty-five-year-old physicist had been working long hours and had become distant in recent weeks.

A special anti-terrorist strike force within the cantonal gendarmerie has been tasked with apprehending Klein, whom authorities are treating as armed and dangerous. Local organizations, including the World Health Organization, the World Trade Organization, and the International Committee of the Red Cross, have placed their headquarters on alert.

Lars drew the phone back and pressed the baseball bat into Ty. "Why? Why did you do it—"

"I didn't."

"Get out!"

Slowly, holding his hands up, Ty stepped down from the truck.

"I didn't set that bomb off. Someone else did. They're trying to kill me because of my research."

"Liar."

"I'm telling you the truth."

Still holding the bat, Lars glanced at his phone. He was opening the phone app.

"I'm calling the authorities. Turning you in. If they know I helped you, I'll lose everything. All my work—forty years down the drain."

Ty took a step toward Lars, hands still held up. "Look, you said you took some wrong turns in your life. If you turn me in, it'll be another one. I promise you. If you make that call, I'll disappear. They'll kill me. I know it. What I've found will change the world. I'm not certain, but I think it will make it better. I do know that it's important. Important enough to kill for. I just need some help. Please."

11

Lars motioned with the bat, forcing Ty back, into the truck's headlights.

Ty moved his forearm in front of his face and squinted. "Lars, I'm telling you, I think I'm on the right road here. I just need a little help to get where I need to go."

Lars glanced down at his phone. A text message had popped up, but Ty couldn't read it.

"What is it?"

"A roadblock," the Belgian driver mumbled. "Outside Oftringen. Another driver said they're stopping everyone traveling eastbound on the A1."

"If you turn me in, you're signing my death warrant."

Lars shook his head. But the man still hadn't dialed the police.

Ty lowered his hands, letting the headlights blind him so that Lars could see his entire face. "I know you regret some of the decisions you've made in your life, Lars, but I promise you: you won't regret this. I don't have anything to offer you. Only my thanks. But if I can, I will repay you one day." Ty waited, but the man said nothing, so he continued, grasping for anything that might sway him. "You said that the most important things in life were our decisions—and the people we meet. I think I met you for a reason. Those other drivers would have already turned me in. When you saw the article, you woke me up, because you know deep down it doesn't add up. I'm a physicist. I've dedicated my life to using science to make the world a better place. Just like you wanted to do with philosophy."

Still, Lars said nothing.

"Look, I don't know the first thing about making a bomb.

And my own apartment is the last place I would set it off. It doesn't add up."

"Perhaps it was an accident."

"Then why am I still here?"

Lars exhaled heavily. "If they catch me, I lose everything. You ask me to risk that for a stranger?"

"I'm asking you to trust your instincts. You know I'm innocent. Is protecting an innocent person worth taking some risk to you?"

Lars slipped his phone back into his pocket and let the end of the bat fall to the ground. "I should have left you at that gas station."

"I'm glad you didn't. And if I live long enough, I promise you, I'll make you thankful that you helped me."

"I am probably going to regret this."

"I'll do everything I can to make sure you don't."

The man motioned to the truck. "There's a compartment under the bunk in the back. It's cramped, and you'll barely fit. They still might find you."

"I'll take that chance. Thank you, Lars."

The drive after that was far less comfortable. It was cramped and musty in the small compartment, but Ty was thankful that the Belgian driver had agreed to hide him. There was no doubt in his mind that the act of kindness from this stranger would save his life—if they got past the roadblock.

He also considered it sheer luck that he had stopped a truck driver with a sleeper compartment (most in Europe didn't have one).

Ty felt every bump in the road in his aching body. There would be no sleep here, even if Ty's nerves would calm down (and he didn't see that happening).

Finally, the truck bounced to a stop, the air brakes calling out in the night. Periodically, the truck crept forward. Each time it stopped, Ty felt himself holding his breath, mentally imagining what would happen next: dogs barking outside and someone ripping open the compartment and dragging him out, shining a flashlight in his eyes and yelling, "We've got him!"

He had gone to bed that night full of hope, a scientist on the verge of fulfilling his life's work, of changing the world. Now he was running for his life—and hiding like a fugitive. He wondered if his mother and sister had seen the news. Or his friends. Or his colleagues at CERN.

He had never met the woman who lived below him, only seen her a few times at the mailboxes. She rarely left her apartment. Now she was gone—because of his work.

The sound of Lars's voice interrupted his thoughts.

"Winterthur."

That was a city northeast of Zürich. Someone had probably asked his destination.

"Nein," Lars said. Had someone asked him if he had seen Ty? Another pause.

"Sicher," Lars said casually. *Sure.*

A loud click. Hinges groaning. Was Lars getting out? Had he signaled them?

Was it over?

Or perhaps it was the passenger door opening.

Another click, closer now, shorter than the sound of the door. A flashlight coming on?

"Sind Sie allein?" a woman asked. *Are you alone?*

She was very close.

Ty swallowed. Suddenly he could hear his breathing. Could she?

"Ja," Lars replied.

He was still in the truck.

Ty's chest rose and fell, a piston speeding up.

There was a thump on the top of the bunk, the sound of a hand reaching around the mattress, feeling the back of the truck cab, then more moving around before the woman said, "Vielen Dank."

The passenger door slammed shut.

Ty's body fell slack, his head rolled, and he exhaled—what felt like the longest breath of his life.

The truck cab bobbed slightly up and back down and surged forward, slowly at first, then gaining speed as the motor roared. Finally, Lars shouted, his voice barely audible to Ty, "I know it's cramped, but I think you better stay back there."

After the police stop, Ty expected to fall asleep. He was still exhausted. But his mind overpowered his body, keeping him awake. Over and over, he imagined what seeing Gerhard Richter in Zürich would be like. What would the man say? Would he even recognize him? Remember his name? Would he care? Maybe he would recognize Ty and call the police immediately. Or worse. Maybe upon seeing Ty, the man would simply smirk and walk away.

Richter wasn't his only worry.

What if the police were waiting?

Finally, the truck came to a stop. Outside, air brakes and engines roared.

Ty wondered if they had encountered another roadblock. Or if Lars had changed his mind about helping him.

The truck started up again and lurched forward. A few minutes later, it stopped, and Lars finally opened the compartment. Morning light poured in like water from a firehose, momentarily blinding Ty.

"You all right?" Lars whispered, the smell of coffee on his breath.

"I'm good. Thanks," Ty said, slowly opening his eyes. "Where are we?"

"Just outside Zürich."

Ty sat up.

"Where exactly do you need to go?" Lars asked.

"Can I borrow your phone?"

When the man handed it to him, Ty opened a private browsing window. He feared that even looking up the address on the phone might lead the authorities to Lars, but Ty didn't see any alternative. A quick search led him to the website of Richter-Brandt GmbH, a Zürich-based investment bank that disclosed virtually nothing about itself. The contact page had a web form (no email address listed) and a physical address in Zürich, at the corner of Beethovenstrasse and Dreikönigstrasse. There were no hours listed, nor a phone number. The website had a pretty clear message: *we exist, but don't contact us.*

Ty had only been to Zürich a few times, and had never been in the building that housed Richter-Brandt. He did know that it was in an area of the city filled with multinational banks and finance companies. The towering office complexes overlooked Lake Zürich and would be nearly impossible to enter without an appointment.

He glanced at the time.

6:24 a.m.

There was only one solution: catch Richter before he entered the building. There were a lot of assumptions there: that the man was even still in Zürich (and not out of town or working remotely) and that he didn't start his day extremely early.

Ty was certain of one thing: Lars had done enough. He couldn't bring himself to endanger the man any further or draw him deeper into the mess Ty was in.

"Could you drop me at the Arboretum, by the lake?"

Lars nodded. "Sure."

It was nearly seven-thirty when the massive truck rolled to a stop on General-Wille Strasse, next to the open-air park that looked out on the Zürich Yacht Club.

Ty gripped the handle. "Thanks, Lars. Truly."

"Good luck to you, Ty. I hope it works out."

Ty exited the truck and disappeared into the park, quickly slipping behind a copse of trees. He jogged down one of the paved paths that ended at the waterfront, where he turned left onto Beethovenstrasse.

At Richter's building, Ty sat on a low wall facing the road, keeping his head down as he watched the sedans pull up and the suited people step out, their expensive sunglasses and watches glittering in the morning sun.

As each car door opened, he wondered if it would be Richter.

In the past thirty years, Ty had probably imagined a moment

like this a million times: coming face-to-face with Richter, and most importantly, finally getting a chance to talk to him again. He'd imagined the hateful things he wanted to say, the hurtful questions he wanted to ask—questions he'd wanted answers to for so long.

A black Mercedes SUV pulled to a stop and a driver exited and opened the rear driver-side door. Gerhard Richter had aged since the last photo Ty had seen, but there was no question about who the man was. It was easy for Ty to spot some of his own facial features in the older German walking toward him.

Ty rose and stepped into his path. For a moment, he hesitated, not sure how to address the man. *Herr Richter* didn't feel right. *Dad* certainly didn't. He settled for a single word, "Sir," which stopped Richter in his tracks, scowling.

"It's Ty—"

"Tyson," Richter said. "Why are you here?"

His German accent was heavy, and the words hit Ty like a slap. It took him a second to compose himself.

"I... need help."

Richter simply stared.

"I work at CERN now."

"I know."

"Someone is after me. They blew up my apartment."

Richter stood as still as a statue for several seconds then, without moving his head, scanned the area behind Ty with his eyes. He turned his head, surveyed the street, then said quietly, "Get in the car, Tyson. Don't say another word."

12

Inside the Mercedes SUV, Gerhard Richter leaned forward and said a single word to the driver, "Walküre."

The word meant nothing to Ty, but it must have to the driver. He gunned the vehicle and weaved through the streets of Zürich, changing lanes often to beat the morning traffic but never breaking the speed limit.

Richter drew out his phone and typed furiously, ignoring Ty.

"Where are we going?"

"To an airport," Richter replied, not looking up from his phone.

"That's going to be a huge problem. The police are looking for me."

"I'm aware of that."

"Okay... What's the plan here?"

Richter eyed Ty, then let his gaze drift to the driver.

"Be quiet, Tyson."

The words sent a spike of rage through Ty. It wasn't just the dismissive comment—it was the last thirty years of silence and absence and one particular afternoon Ty had spent a lifetime trying to forget. But there was nothing Ty could do. He needed the man's help.

As they exited Zürich, Richter leaned over to Ty. "Are you hurt?"

Ty assumed the man was referring to his harsh command to be quiet. "What? No. Of course not."

Richter nodded to Ty's ribs, which he had been massaging without thinking about it. "Do you require medical attention? Are you *injured*?"

"I'm fine."

They rode in silence then, the vehicle traveling at high speed until it turned off on a private road that led to a small airfield with a single runway. In the parking lot, Richter exited and beckoned Ty to follow. They passed the gate of a chain-link fence, where a uniformed security guard merely motioned them forward without a word.

A woman in her twenties wearing a pantsuit and stylish sunglasses stood on the tarmac, an overnight bag sitting on the ground next to her. When Richter reached her, she put a hand in her pocket and drew out a small pill bottle, which she handed to him without a word.

"Danke, Ilse," Richter said as he pocketed the bottle, reached down, took the bag, and continued onward.

The jet waiting for them had no logo or insignia, only a number across one of the engines. The two pilots standing by the outstretched stairs nodded as they passed, and inside, Richter threw the bag on a couch and said to them in English, "Gentlemen, please depart with all possible haste."

Ty took the seat across from Richter, who didn't look up from his phone. He tapped away, occasionally pausing to read a response.

"Hey."

Richter looked up.

"I have some questions."

"As do I."

"Where are we going?"

"DC."

"Washington, DC?"

"Correct."

"Why?"

"For help."

"Help from whom?"

"The only people who can help us: the United States government."

Ty spread his hands out. "Just like that? I show up, so we hop a plane to the US to get help?"

"It is the only solution."

"What. Is going. On. Seriously."

"It's complicated, Tyson."

"First, I go by Ty now. Second, if it's complicated, that means you can pretty much start anywhere. So, start. Anywhere. It's a long way to DC, and I'm all ears." Ty nodded, prompting the man. "Go ahead."

For the first time, Richter smiled. "You were always high-strung. Even when you were young—"

Ty held a hand up. "Don't. Don't even act like you know the first thing about me. You left Mom high and dry, on her own, and you didn't care one bit."

"You're very wrong about that, Tyso—" He took a breath. "Ty. But you are right. We should put the past aside. It clearly has an emotional impact on you. Your mind needs to be clear for what comes next."

"Which is?"

"I've just read the slides from your presentation."

"What? How—how did you even get those?"

Richter ignored the question. "It's impressive. I don't understand it all, but I believe perhaps I understand how it fits into, shall we say, the grander scheme of things. I understand what it represents. What will happen."

"How is that possible? You're an investment banker."

A small smile formed on Richter's lips.

"You're not an investment banker."

"I am. And more."

"More how?"

"That's not something you need to know right now."

"What do I need to know?"

"So many things. But we will start with the items that I hope might keep you alive."

The way Richter referred to his possible death—casually, frankly, without a shred of emotion—sent a chill through Ty.

"Okay," Ty said, trying to keep his voice even.

Richter leaned forward. "Have you ever felt like the world was wrong, as though events simply didn't make sense, as though the course of history was being altered by some unseen force?"

Of all the things Ty expected him to say, this was perhaps the last. And yet, his answer came readily, instantly. "Yes. I have. I've felt that way a lot. And more often lately. Like things didn't add up—logically. Why? What are you telling me?"

"Have you ever heard of a group called the Covenant?"

"No. Who are they?"

"Are you familiar with something called the Origin Project?"

"No. Why?"

A message popped up on Richter's phone. He read it, typed a reply, and said to Ty without looking up, "Who else knows about your research?"

Ty exhaled, frustrated. "Are you going to tell me who the Covenant are? Or what the Origin Project is?"

"Yes. Soon. But time is of the essence now, and I must know: who else is aware of your discovery, Tyso—" Richter stopped, then corrected himself: "Ty?"

"The people I presented to at CERN. There were probably forty people in the room. Are they okay?"

"Yes. As far as I know."

"Two other people know—at least a little bit. Penny Neumann. She's an exchange student at—"

"The University of Geneva. Yes, I know about Neumann. Who else?"

"A truck driver named Lars. I don't know his last name, but he drove me up the A1 from Geneva to Zürich last night. He shouldn't be hard to find. I think he was headed to Winterthur. He doesn't really know much at all. Only that I got in some trouble. The guy probably saved my life. He certainly risked his own freedom to do it."

Richter nodded and typed on his phone.

"Can you help him? Protect him? He also could use some assistance—financially. He's had some bad luck."

"I can try."

When Richter finished typing, he set his phone on the arm of the chair. "Do you still have your research?"

"Yes."

"Good."

Richter reached inside the bag on the couch and took out a laptop. "We need to send a copy to the Americans."

"Why?"

"For one, it will give the people after you less incentive to hunt you down. They managed to delete your research from the servers at CERN. If we turn everything over to the Americans, it shifts the game slightly, but in our favor. And puts them at a disadvantage."

"They who? The Covenant?"

"Yes. Based on what I know now, they are the ones who sent the explosive device to your apartment."

"Penny was working for them."

"I assume so, though whether she knew—and what she knew—remains unknown."

Richter typed on the laptop, then handed it to Ty. "Plug the drive into the port, please."

Ty hesitated a moment but decided he had little to lose. He had to start trusting someone. Still, he wondered if he would regret what he was about to do.

He inserted the drive into the USB port. A message flashed on the screen:

UPLOADING...

Ty handed the laptop back to Richter, who set it on the couch next to them, the screen still open so both men could see the progress.

"What does quantum entanglement represent to you?"

Ty was again surprised at the sudden change of subject.

"Well," he began, collecting his thoughts. "Quantum entanglement is part of the disagreement between quantum physics and classical physics. Einstein called entanglement 'spooky action at a distance.' It's this phenomenon where one or more particles can act as mirrors of each other. The astounding thing is that it can happen over vast distances. So, for example, if two particles were entangled and one was here on Earth, it would have the same properties as the entangled particle even if the other one was in another galaxy. The problem is that entanglement communicates the quantum state of the particles instantaneously over millions of light years—which obviously violates the theory of special relativity, which established that the speed of light was the fastest anything can move in the universe. Einstein also felt that entanglement wasn't possible based on the local realism view of causality. He authored a paper in 1935 with Boris Podolsky and Nathan Rosen describing their arguments against it, which we call the EPR paradox today. But we've actually observed entanglement in all kinds of particles: photons, neutrinos, and electrons. Entanglement shouldn't be possible, but it is."

Ty held his hands up. "It's a perfect example of one of the biggest problems in physics: the way things work at the macroscale—what we can see—basically breaks down at the subatomic scale. At scales larger than atoms, the universe seems fairly logical and well-ordered. Cause and effect govern the behavior of the universe, time moves in a forward direction, and the objects we observe are measurable—and, most importantly, predictable. That all changes at the subatomic level. Things occur there that shouldn't be possible based on our current theories. Entanglement is an example of one of those things that shouldn't be possible."

Richter nodded. "That's *what* entanglement is, but what does it *represent?*"

Ty shrugged. "Just what I said: a sort of paradox between the major branches of physics."

"You're seeing it like a scientist. Zoom out for a moment. If you can entangle particles and indeed link them over great distances, what are the implications?"

"Well, there are arguments that you could communicate faster than light, but it doesn't really work that way. With entanglement, it's the act of *observation* that determines the particle's state. Once you observe one of the entangled particles, the others take the same state. But you can't force one of the particles into a state and instantly change the state of the others."

"But what if you could? What if someone figured out a way to entangle two particles and control their states? Even across vast distances. Even after observation."

"If you could? Well, that would change everything again. You're talking about faster-than-light communication, sending messages across the galaxy, maybe even across time."

"Apply that to what you found at CERN."

Ty squinted. "What do you mean?"

"Describe for me what you think your... quantum radio is."

"I'm not entirely certain."

"Why not?"

"Well, the very nature of the discovery. Look, the LHC crashes particles together so we can see what they're made of. I designed an algorithm to analyze the data from these collisions. It revealed that the subatomic output of the collisions added up to more than the particles that were collided. Not only that, but in the wreckage of these particle collisions, there are exotic particles that shouldn't be there—and they're organized. A data stream."

"That's what it is. What do you *think* it means?"

"Personally, I think it's our first glimpse of some larger phenomenon at the subatomic level."

"Such as?"

"I don't know. But the theories behind how the quantum radio works could be one of the big answers in quantum mechanics, possibly the key to unifying the opposing branches of physics. It could be a Theory of Everything."

"Consider, for a moment, if you will, entanglement in the context of your discovery. Consider the idea that I previously proposed, that it was possible to alter the states of entangled particles after observation."

Ty shook his head. "I don't follow."

"What I'm suggesting is simply this: what if the particles you're observing at CERN are entangled?"

"As in...?"

"What if they are entangled with particles very far away? In another part of our universe? Or in another universe entirely? Or in another time?" Richter leaned forward. "What if the phenomenon you're observing, the pattern you've been able to detect, isn't a natural phenomenon?"

"You're saying you think that's how the quantum radio works. Our particle collisions make our universe porous enough for someone to send entangled particles through and use them to communicate? Is that it?"

"I'm merely posing some questions. But the real question is this: if that were the case, what would it represent to you?"

"The greatest discovery in history—period. It would be a monumental scientific breakthrough, but it's far larger. We're talking about first contact. A new understanding of our place in the universe."

Richter smiled. "You're still thinking like a scientist. Consider the prospect that someone in another place or another time can alter the state of subatomic particles on our world. Think about what one could do with that power."

"Well, I think that's unclear. For us, even smashing particles requires extraordinary amounts of energy, and we can only do it for a fraction of a second. It's unknown what the limits of long-range—or long-time—entanglement might entail."

Richter held his hand out and rolled it forward. "Play it out, Ty. Think about if you could force entanglement on a grand scale and affect matter here on our world. After all, a brain is composed of neurons that are made of atoms and their subatomic constituents. If those pieces were entangled and you could alter them, what would be possible?"

"*If* that were the case, you could change the state of neurons, change the electrical impulses they fire. You could actually control what someone thinks. But that's only the start. You could conceivably alter a child's DNA the moment an egg was fertilized. Simply put, anything would be possible."

"What would you call that?"

"A breakthrough."

Richter shook his head. "A threat. That's what the people I work with would call it."

"Are you saying this is happening? Has happened?"

"We don't know."

"What do you know?"

"We know that, to a large degree, the world doesn't make sense. Take your physics example—some things seem well ordered and predictable while others seem totally illogical, inconsistent with what is to be expected."

Richter stood and moved to the small bar in the corner of the cabin, where he opened a bottle of water and offered one to Ty, who shook his head.

"I grew up in West Germany in the 1960s. People were asking some very deep questions then—about whether the world truly made any sense, about whether things were broken at some fundamental level. About whether there was intervention or manipulation on a grand scale. An unseen hand shaping the future. We went looking for answers in the only logical place in which to search: the realm of science."

Richter sat again and stared out the window.

"Is that what the Origin Project is?" Ty asked.

"Yes."

Richter took another sip of water. "What you've discovered is the closest anyone has come to a real answer about what's happening. I assume you're familiar with Alain Aspect's experiments in the 1980s."

"Sure. He's a French scientist who built on Stuart Freedman and John Clauser's work on quantum entanglement. His experiments were the first to really demonstrate the violation of Bell's inequalities, essentially confirming that quantum entanglement was possible."

"Aspect's experiments also sent a shock wave through the global military industrial complex in the early eighties. The atom bomb had changed the world a few decades earlier. It was widely expected that a quantum breakthrough would be the next logical step—and a much more drastic leap. It was believed, by many in power, that the next true battlefield wouldn't be one of tanks and mortars and planes or even nuclear bombs but instead a quantum war. Whether that's true remains to be seen, but it is very likely that somewhere within the mystery of entanglement and your quantum radio lies the key to not only understanding our past but to controlling the future. That's what they're willing to kill for. In fact, there's no sacrifice too great to obtain the details of what you've found."

"So what do we do? What happens now?"

"What happens now is very simple: it is a race."

"What kind of race?"

"What you've discovered—with your quantum radio—is a code, a message written in exotic subatomic particles, particles that may have originated from outside of our universe, particles that were created elsewhere, entangled at their point of origin and sent here, then modified in an ordered way to provide a message to us—a message that could only be detected with a super collider. What does that tell you?"

"That it's a message that is *very* hard to find."

"Correct. Specifically, that a species must achieve a certain level of advancement to detect that message. For the first time in history, we have reached that level of advancement. Whatever the message is, it implies that it is the dawn of a new era in human existence. Whoever is the first to understand what the message means may well control the future."

13

Two hours into the flight, Richter stood, gripped one of the seatbacks, and propelled himself down the aisle toward the back of the jet. In the cramped galley, he worked for a few minutes.

Soon, the smell of meatloaf and mashed potatoes filled the small cabin. Ty hadn't realized how hungry he was until the aroma reached him. He wondered if the man was bringing enough for both of them.

The microwave dinged, and Richter returned to the small table he shared with Ty, indeed carrying two trays with heated meals.

Each man dug in without preamble, their motions practically a mirror of each other.

"One thing is bothering me," Ty said, taking his second bite of the meatloaf, which was better than he expected (or maybe he was just hungrier than he realized).

Richter raised an eyebrow as he finished his bite. "There's only *one* thing bothering you?"

"Okay, there are two million five hundred and fifteen thousand things bothering me, but one thing sticks out."

"Which is?"

"Coincidences."

Richter gave a knowing nod. "The same has occurred to me."

"The fact that you're involved in this—and that I discovered the quantum radio broadcast, the fact that I was in Geneva, and you were in Zürich when it happened. Those two coincidences, they're just... too convenient to be random."

"On that point, I agree."

"What does it mean?"

"I can't say yet."

"But you have an idea of what it means."

"The shape of one."

"Which is?"

Richter took a bite of mashed potatoes and stared out the window. "Too early to speculate."

"I'm a scientist. I'm used to speculation."

"As an investor, so am I. But I prefer not to. I prefer facts. As I'm sure you do."

"What do you think is happening here?" Ty asked.

"I think what's occurring is a bit like your Higgs boson. What is it you call it? The God particle?"

Ty cringed. "That's what the media calls it. The articles get more clicks that way. We don't call it that."

"Nevertheless, consider what it represents—something that you knew existed, or at least theorized—an unseen yet vitally important component of the workings of the physical universe. That is what I believe is at work here: something that will make sense once we see the entirety of it, yet defies comprehension now. We have only seen pieces of a larger whole. Yes, the pieces fit together, and later, we will know why."

Ty considered that as he finished the meal. Then, choosing his words carefully, he brought up the other subject that had been nagging him for the past few hours.

"I need to contact Mom."

That drew Richter's stare, and an explanation from Ty: "She's probably seen the articles by now—including the manhunt in Geneva for me. She's probably worried sick."

"You don't need to contact her."

"Why?"

"Because I already have."

"You have?"

The news was a bit like his discovery at CERN: something that turned his world upside down. His parents hadn't spoken in thirty years—as far as Ty knew. He couldn't even imagine the two of them communicating. When he was growing up, his mother wouldn't even let Ty mention the man.

"She'll be waiting for us in DC," Richter said.

Ty opened his mouth to speak, then closed it, dumbstruck. "What... did you tell her?"

"The truth. That you are safe. And that the articles are lies."

"Well. Okay. Good."

"She'll meet us at DARPA."

"DARPA? As in the Defense Advanced Research Projects Agency?"

"Correct."

Ty leaned back in his chair. "I... didn't see that coming. It's a lot to unpack. First, is DARPA where you sent my research?"

"Yes."

"Why?"

"They have been working on a similar project, which, as I mentioned, I am involved in. And have been for quite some time."

"The Origin Project."

"Yes."

The truth occurred to Ty then—the obvious reason for why his mother would be waiting at DARPA. "Mom is part of the Origin Project too, isn't she?"

Richter cocked his head and studied Ty. Was the man surprised? Ty thought so.

"Correct," Richter said. "Her research into evolutionary biology is funded by DARPA."

Ty saw the connection then. "She's really researching quantum evolution, isn't she? The prospect of quantum radio intervention in our species' development."

"Yes, that is the true premise of your mother's work. Consider it: if someone could change a few DNA base pairs in the distant past, the entire future would change. She's found plenty of possible evidence of this phenomenon. Periods when human evolution seems to leap forward or when the human race was clutched out of the abyss, from the edge of extinction, only to return stronger than ever with survival advantages that were not predicted by the biological arc of our species. In short, if you think history doesn't make sense, human evolution, at times, seems even less logical."

"The Origin Project believes there's already been quantum intervention in human evolution?"

"That is the question. There's evidence, but as yet, your mother feels it's inconclusive."

Ty felt as though he were seeing his whole world in 3D now— as if it had all been a flat image before and a new dimension had been added. It wasn't just the added perspective on human history—it was the revelations about his own family history.

"What is the Origin Project going to do with my research?" Ty asked.

"Complete it."

"How?"

"Simply put, they have the resources and manpower—and a head start."

"A head start?"

"DARPA has a series of existing initiatives related to your research. Have you ever heard of the QuEST project?"

"No."

"QuEST stands for Quantum Entanglement Science and Technology. It was started in 2008 at the DARPA Microsystems Technology Office, MTO. Its predecessor, QuIST, was the agency's first foray into quantum data sciences. The project is looking at a wide range of things: secure quantum communications, quantum machine learning, game theory using quantum mechanics, quantum image processing, quantum radar and metrology, and even entanglement-assisted gravitomagnetic interferometry. The group has gone as far as applying entanglement principles to an old CIA initiative: remote sensing. But QuEST is just the tip of the iceberg."

Richter held his hands out. "QuBE is another DARPA initiative to examine quantum effects in biological environments."

"Is it part of Mom's research?"

"Tangentially. There's also the Quiness project, which is building new types of quantum repeaters that could one day form the backbone of a new quantum internet."

"Interesting." Ty had no idea so much quantum research was being done by the military.

"What you've stumbled upon, Ty, is the missing piece that a lot of people have been trying to find for a very long time. The pattern you identified is a sort of key. We had the pieces before, but we didn't know how to put the puzzle together. Now we see the picture."

"And what does it look like?"

"We'll know soon."

"What do you mean?"

"Right now, DARPA and its funded projects are using your algorithm to decode the data stored on the LHC Computing Grid."

"I want to be there. I can help. It's my research—that's why I gave the presentation at CERN, to ask for funding to do what DARPA is doing right now."

"I know. And you deserve to be. That's the other reason we're going to DC."

Ty nodded, feeling a sense of relief and, surprisingly, gratitude to this man whom he had hated for so long but who was so strangely part of this moment, which looked like the culmination of his life's work.

After a long silence, Richter spoke again. "I heard your brother got into some trouble."

Ty studied the man, wondering how he had heard. And how much to say. "Yeah. He did."

"Where is he now?"

"A federal prison in Butner, North Carolina."

"Do you blame yourself for what happened?"

"Every day."

After a long silence, Richter motioned to Ty's tray. "Are you finished?"

Ty nodded, and Richter took the empty carton away. Instead of returning to the table, the older man pulled the shades down on the plane's windows until it was pitch black in the cabin.

"I know you had a long night. And this has been a lot to process. Why don't you get some rest?"

With that, Richter retired to a seat in the back and took out his laptop, and Ty, despite all the questions racing through his mind, realized that he was indeed quite tired. The lack of rest, the adrenaline, and the belly full of meatloaf and mashed potatoes combined to drag him toward sleep, which came within minutes of stretching out on the couch.

Ty woke to Richter's hand on his shoulder.

"We're landing soon."

Ty sat up and swallowed. His mouth felt like he had been gulping sawdust. His body was sore—more tender than when he had been awake.

Across the aisle, Richter raised the shade, letting a beam of light in that sent Ty reeling back, covering his eyes with his arm. The brightness hurt.

With his eyes closed, he heard Richter's voice close by.

"They found it, Ty."

"What?"

"Your code. It works. Your quantum radio *is* transmitting data—and DARPA has decoded it into files."

14

Ty squinted against the sunlight streaming in through the jet's windows. Richter was moving through the cabin, raising the shades, flooding the narrow space with light.

Ty could feel the jet descending, preparing for landing.

"What exactly did DARPA find?" Ty asked. "What's in those files?"

"They won't tell me. Not remotely. Only in person."

When the plane landed at a private air strip in Northern Virginia, Ty followed Richter out onto the tarmac and into a waiting black SUV. It sped away, into the Virginia countryside, heading north toward DC.

Ty checked his watch, which had automatically adjusted to the local time: 10:34 a.m.

In some ways, he felt like a time traveler. They had left Zürich a little before 8 a.m. and the flight had taken almost nine hours, but DC was six hours behind Zürich, so it was still morning here. Their jet had essentially chased the sun, and it made Ty glad he had taken a nap on the plane. Still, he felt jet-lagged, bruised, and shell-shocked at the tsunami of revelations the last few hours had brought. But most of all, he felt hopeful. Very soon, he would learn what was being transmitted over the quantum radio he had discovered at CERN. Deep down, he felt that it would change everything, perhaps in ways he couldn't even grasp.

"Where *exactly* are we going?" he asked Richter.

"DARPA's administrative headquarters is located on North Randolph Street in Arlington, Virginia. But we're not going there. We're going to their quantum research facility."

Ty knit his eyebrows together. "I've never heard of a DARPA quantum research facility. I would have heard of that—it would be big news in our community."

Richter smiled. "You might have and not even known it."

"What does that mean?"

Richter took out his phone and tapped on it for a few seconds. "If you have a secret, do you know the best way to keep it in this day and age, when virtually all information is available on the internet and some very dedicated people spend their life chasing down conspiracies—even fake ones?"

Ty shrugged. "No."

"You announce it. Even better, you ask for the public's help."

Richter handed Ty his phone, which displayed the official Twitter account of DARPA and a tweet posted August 28, 2019:

Attention, city dwellers! We're interested in identifying university-owned or commercially managed underground urban tunnels & facilities able to host research & experimentation. *https:go.usa.gov/xVWCn*

It's short notice... We're asking for responses by Aug. 30 at 5:00 PM ET.

The three pictures posted with the message showed a vast underground complex with steel doors and massive pillars supporting it.

Ty looked up. "Is this real?"

Richter pointed at the phone. "It is. Look at the one below it."

Ty scrolled down and read the next message from the official DARPA account:

The ideal space would be a human-made underground environment spanning several city blocks w/ complex layout & multiple stories, including atriums, tunnels & stairwells. Spaces that are currently closed off from pedestrians or can be temporarily used for testing are of interest.

The next two pictures showed an abandoned subway and an underground corridor with pipes running along the ceiling.

Ty shook his head. "Underground tunnels blocked off from public access that span multiple city blocks. It would be perfect for a small-scale collider and other quantum research."

Richter took the phone back. "Precisely."

They rode in silence until they reached the Virginia suburbs of DC. It went by in a blur to Ty, whose mind drifted again to the quantum radio data stream and what it might represent. And then to Penny. He wondered where she was. And if she was safe.

Within thirty minutes of landing, the convoy was pulling into the parking garage of a building in the Navy Yard neighborhood in southeast Washington, DC. Ty and Richter were ushered into a building with bare white walls and exposed pipes and data cables running along the ceiling.

Around every turn, Ty hoped to see his mother, Helen. Instead, their handlers took Richter's phone (for security purposes) and deposited the two men in a conference room with no windows, only a long table, rolling chairs, and a large flat screen on the wall.

A few minutes later, someone came and requested Richter's presence, leaving Ty alone to pace and count the minutes. He counted twenty before the door opened again, and a man who looked to be in his mid-fifties stepped inside and gently closed the door. He wore a rumpled sport coat that looked like it had been slept in and faded jeans that had been washed too many times. He peered at Ty through thick glasses with black plastic frames.

"Dr. Klein, I'm Sanford Bishop. Chief nerd around here."

Ty smiled. "Call me Ty. I too am a nerd, based at CERN."

Bishop nodded. "Your reputation precedes you."

"What did you find?"

"That's... actually what I wanted to talk to you about. While we appreciate what you've come up with—and you coming all this way, and certainly what you've been through—I just wanted to personally let you know we're going to take it from here.

We're going to put you up in a hotel in Arlington until we can arrange transport home for you—"

"I'm not going anywhere."

Bishop's smile disappeared. "I'm afraid you are. What we're dealing with here is a little bigger than a hobby project."

"You wouldn't have what you have without me. Without my hobby project."

Bishop took a step toward the door and reached out for the handle. "It's a tough break."

"Wait. At least tell me what you found."

"Can't do that."

"What can you tell me?"

"I can tell you thanks. That's the other reason I wanted to see you. Take care of yourself, Ty."

The man marched away, leaving Ty standing at the end of the conference table.

It was over. They were shutting him out. Just like that. Taking his work and running with it. He was mad enough to pick up one of the chairs and hurl it across the room.

The door opened again, and Richter strode in, followed by Ty's mother.

Without a word, his mother walked over to him, arms stretched out, and pulled Ty into a hug.

For a moment, no one said anything. The three of them hadn't been in a room together in thirty years. And the last meeting was still like an open wound in Ty's mind, a moment of hurt that seemed to have been carved with a magic blade that even time couldn't heal.

When Ty's mother squeezed the hug tighter, Ty winced and grunted. She instantly released him and held him at arm's length, studying him, worried.

"You're hurt."

"I'm fine."

"Gerhard told me they blew up your apartment." She looked him up and down. "We need to get you to a hospital."

"Mom. I'm fine. Just sore."

"Which might imply internal bleeding."

"I'm not *bleeding internally*, Mom. Please relax."

"Well, it's hard to relax when someone is trying to blow up your son."

"It's also hard to relax when someone is stealing your research."

She squinted at him. "What do you mean?"

Richter's gaze drifted away from the two of them. It was clear to Ty that he knew what was going on. Ty said to him, "Do you want to tell her?"

"No," he said simply.

"Tell me what?"

"They're cutting me out," Ty said. "Taking my research and running with it."

Helen exhaled. "Well, it's probably for the best. It's safer that way."

"I don't want to be safe."

"Ty—"

"What I want is to finish what I started. I bet you said that to me a million times when I was a kid: 'you finish what you start.' That's how I got where I am, Mom. And it's how I made this discovery—I kept going, and now they're taking it from me."

"You're upset, Ty. You're tired, and you need rest and food—"

"This is my life's work, Mom. I want to finish it. I just need a chance to do that."

She studied him for a long moment, then seemed to make a decision.

She turned to Richter, and Ty could practically feel the air in the room grow colder. He had felt like this once before in his life, the last time the three of them had all been in a room together. His parents were older now, but they stared at each other as they had then: unblinking, both still as statues, sizing each other up, like gunslingers in the middle of an Old West town about to draw on one another. And the words that came were like gunfire in Ty's mind, sharp and bracing.

Helen spoke first. "Did you know about this?"

"I just found out."

"Or just decided?"

73

"It wasn't my call."

"Make it your call."

"You overestimate me."

"That's not possible."

Richter turned away and paced the room. He had flinched first.

"Do it, Gerhard, or I will."

"We could be putting him in danger," Richter said, not meeting her gaze.

"He's likely in danger either way. At least give him a chance to be part of this."

Ty threw up his hands. "Will you two quit talking about me like I'm not here? I'm not a kid anymore. Tell me what's going on."

Richter shook his head as he paced the length of the room again. He clearly didn't like what was about to happen.

At the door, he reached out to the handle and locked it. He turned his head and stared at the camera in the corner for a second before letting his gaze settle on Ty. The stare was like a laser drilling into him.

When Richter spoke, his tone had changed. The words came out slowly, with a rhythm similar to a chant or incantation. "Tyson, listen to what I'm about to tell you. Focus. Think about what it implies."

The room seemed to fade away as Richter spoke.

"The data stream you discovered contains seven distinct characters. One of the subatomic particles is clearly a terminator. There are four major terminating sequences, implying demarcations of five distinct files."

The door handle rattled. Outside, a muffled voice said, "It's locked."

Another voice: "Break it down."

Richter never flinched. "The first file contains only two characters. The characters appear in groups of eight before a terminator, then the groups of eight are grouped by eight and terminated."

The solid wood door shook once, then again, hard enough

74

to rattle the metal frame around it. The drywall cracked. Dust particles drifted down from the ceiling like the first snow flurries of winter.

"The two characters in the first file do not appear in the other four files, which are composed of the remaining four characters and the terminator. The characters appear in groups of four—and every character is present in each group. The sequences of four appear in twenty-four supersets composing 3,088,286,401 strings of four."

The door burst open, and a uniformed marine stumbled in, a hand outstretched to catch himself on the chair at the head of the table.

Still, Richter stared at Ty. "Do you know what it is?"

"Yes," Ty breathed out, his mind on fire, reality shattered.

15

Two more marines raced into the conference room.

Helen reeled back from them.

Richter stood still, staring at Ty, a smile forming on his face, one Ty thought was born of pride.

Sanford Bishop—the man who had described himself to Ty as the chief nerd of the DARPA facility—jogged into the room, panting, eyes fixed on Richter. "What have you done?"

"What must be done."

"We'll have to confine him in one of the empty labs—"

Helen spun on him. "You *are not confining* my son in an empty lab, Sandy."

Richter nodded at Ty. "Tell them what it means."

Ty took a deep breath. "The first file is standard data: the characters are binary. Zero and one. On and off. They're bits—eight to a group, eight of which form a byte. It's a simple computer file. One we can read."

"That was obvious," Bishop muttered. To the marines, he said, "Clear the room." He stared up at the camera in the corner. "Stop recording. Right now. And disable the feed."

When the door closed, Ty pressed on. "The other four files are more interesting. Four characters in groups of four. In twenty-four files. The four characters are base pairs—A, C, T, G. They're DNA sequences. The number of files—twenty-four—implies twenty-three chromosomes composed of twenty-two paired chromosomes, or autosomes, and a twenty-third pair of sex chromosomes—XX or XY. The twenty-fourth sequence is likely far shorter. It's the mitochondrial DNA. The total number of base pairs—3,088,286,401—confirms that the genomes transmitted are for humans."

76

Bishop studied Ty a moment, then snorted dismissively. "We'd gotten that far."

"Yes," Richter said slowly, "but did it take you half a second to get there?"

Bishop nodded. "He's smart. I'll give you that. But we have smart people too."

Richter paced away from Bishop, his back turned to the man. "Apparently not smart enough to assign someone to watch Ty. As the Covenant clearly did."

"What's your point?"

"My point is very simple: they knew to watch him. Why is that? Did they know he would discover the cipher to decode the quantum radio broadcasts? What else do they know? And how? They're clearly a step ahead of us. And they have his data too. They likely already know what it is. What else have they accomplished?"

Richter turned and eyed the DARPA employee. "They're ahead of us, Sandy. It might already be too late."

"What are you proposing?"

"He's part of this. Let's use every resource we have. Face it: what happens in the next few days will very likely change the world forever. We have nothing to lose and everything to gain by bringing him into the loop."

Bishop shook his head. "I don't like it. Personnel changes at this stage are unwise. You know that. Unpredictable. He could be a Covenant agent for all we know—"

"My son," Richter said forcefully, "is not a Covenant agent."

A long silence stretched out. Finally, Richter spoke, his voice once again level. "Sandy, tell him what you think the files are."

Bishop eyed Richter, clearly hesitant.

"Do it," Richter said. "What do you have to lose?"

Bishop stared at the floor. "Our working theory is that the first file is a schematic for a machine. The data stream is huge—we're still trying to constitute it."

Ty nodded. "I agree with that."

"The four genome files," Bishop continued, "are a little more puzzling. Our assumption is that they're the genomes of the representatives of whoever is broadcasting the quantum data."

Ty cocked his head. "As in...?"

"As in, we believe the machine is a printer."

"A printer for...?"

"A printer for human genomes. We build the machine and supply the genomes and it prints out four humans, who we believe are the representatives of whoever is trying to communicate with us."

16

Ty turned Bishop's words over in his mind.

"You're wrong," he mumbled, still lost in thought.

"Excuse me?" Bishop said.

"I believe you're right about what the files are—just not what they do. As I said, I agree that the first file is a machine. And that the others are genomes, but I don't think we're meant to print them. We're not supposed to create humans from what's being sent."

"And what do you base that *speculation* upon?" Bishop asked.

"Gut instinct. Whoever is on the other side of the quantum radio is clearly more advanced than us. They wouldn't just fax over some representatives. First of all, a printed human wouldn't have any memories—"

"That may not be true," Helen said. Ty glanced at his mother, who continued. "We now know that DNA can encode memories—or at least the shape of them.

A research project in Europe called MemoTV—which studies epigenetic, neural, and cognitive memories of traumatic stress and violence—found that trauma experienced by mothers affects early offspring development. In fact, the DNA alterations are actually encoded and passed on to future generations. If trauma can alter the DNA of our children, it's plausible that other, more specific memories could be encoded."

Bishop spoke before Ty could respond. "There's also the obvious: these humans could have advancements that aren't evident in a simple review of the genome. After all, if you compare a Neanderthal genome with one of our genomes, you'd find there's only..." Bishop looked over at Helen. "How much difference?"

"We share roughly 99.7 percent of our genome with Neanderthals. Even chimpanzees have 98.8 percent of our DNA."

"Exactly," Bishop said. "And look at the massive differences those small DNA changes make. For all we know, these humans they want us to print will be a completely different subspecies. They may be capable of things we can't even imagine."

"Yes," Ty said, nodding. "Even more reason not to print them. For all we know, they could be an invasion force. Granted, there are only four of them, but based on what you're saying, it would be dangerous."

"Precisely why we plan to do the printing on an aircraft carrier in the Pacific surrounded by a fleet of nuclear submarines with multiple warheads trained on it."

Ty let his head fall back. "It's a bad plan based on the wrong assumptions."

"Well, what are your assumptions?"

"That whoever is broadcasting is trying to communicate with us. Think about it. They can only broadcast now. The first broadcast, logically, would give us the details of how to build a device that lets us broadcast back."

Bishop pointed at Ty. "Now on that, we agree. And that's *how* we think these humans are different. We believe that they have the innate ability to receive the quantum broadcasts—that the subatomic particles being detected by the LHC at CERN actually have an effect on the neurons in the brains of these new humans. Our working theory is that they are genetically capable of receiving quantum broadcasts, relaying them to us and sending return messages, perhaps thanks to entangled particles in their brains. As I said, they are representatives. A communication conduit."

Ty shook his head. "It's wrong. It's the right idea, but you're wrong on the specifics."

Bishop snorted. "You can't just say it's wrong and leave it at that." He turned to Richter. "This is what I mean—we have to move forward here. This is not some academic seminar where you debate and nothing happens. We need to act."

Richter focused on Ty. "Tell him what you think the files are."

"As I said, the first file is, in fact, a machine. And yes, I think it's a device we can use to communicate with the broadcaster. Which makes it obvious what it is."

Bishop shrugged, clearly annoyed. "Do tell."

"It's a collider. After all, that's what we detected the broadcast with. But if my guess is right, this collider is more advanced— and much smaller."

Bishop chuckled. "Right..."

"Why do you think it's smaller?" Helen asked.

"Logically, it would be. Advancements in technology almost always feature miniaturization."

Ty had always been fascinated with the history of computing and how far it had come so fast. The historical facts were lodged in his mind, and they came rapid-fire now. "Look at history: one of the first programmable, electronic digital computers, the ENIAC, took up roughly one thousand eight hundred square feet and used about eighteen thousand vacuum tubes. It weighed sixty thousand pounds. The ENIAC could do around three hundred eighty five multiplication operations per second. That was way back in 1946. Today, the average smartphone weighs less than a pound and the processor can do *trillions* of operations per second. To put it simply, making technology smaller is the natural arc of innovation. There's another reason to make the device smaller: it makes it easier to hide and transport. Immovable objects are inherently more difficult to defend."

Bishop looked skeptical. "It's one thing to shrink a computer, but a particle collider? I don't buy it."

"It's already happening," Ty said.

"What do you mean?" Bishop asked.

"A few years ago, a team of researchers at Imperial College London described a way to accelerate particles using common equipment present in most physics labs—in a much smaller space. We're talking about a system that would be just a few centimeters long."

"They have a prototype?" Bishop asked.

"Not as far as I know. The work right now is just in

simulations and computer models, but the principles are sound. They still need a large laser, which would occupy maybe three hundred square feet, but their collider would actually create exotic particles at a faster rate than the LHC."

"Well," Bishop said, "what you're saying is all hypothetical, and we'll know what the device actually is soon enough."

"What about the genomes?" Richter asked, nodding toward Ty.

"If I'm right," Ty said carefully, "the genomes aren't of any alien representatives. They're of people already here on Earth."

17

The conference room fell silent. Ty was about to elaborate on his theory when Bishop broke the silence.

"That's completely absurd."

"Why?" Helen asked.

"Think about it," Bishop said. "How would *whoever* is broadcasting even know the genome of someone on Earth?"

Ty opened his mouth to respond, but a knock on the door interrupted him.

Bishop jerked the handle and cracked the door. "We're busy."

A marine slipped his hand in, offering a sealed envelope.

It was clear to Ty then just how secure the Origin Project was being with communications—no digital messages or voice calls. Written notes only. Whoever had sent the message wasn't even willing to call Bishop using the phone on the conference table.

The DARPA scientist took the envelope and closed the door without a word. He ripped it open and scanned it, eyes racing back and forth like an old typewriter. After reading it, he let the page fall back to his side, allowing Ty to see that there were only two lines written there.

Bishop seemed deep in thought.

"What is it?" Helen asked.

"They've constituted the first file—the schematic," Bishop said absently, staring at the wall. "Ty's right. It *is* a collider. A small one. Small enough to fit in the palm of your hand." He looked up at Ty. "How'd you know?"

"I just... it just seemed obvious to me."

Richter stepped toward Bishop. "If he's right about the device, he is likely correct about the genomes."

"Maybe." Bishop slipped the page into his pocket.

"Sandy," Helen said. "Even if you disagree, his theory is easy to test."

He looked up at her. "No. It's not. His assertion is many things. Surprising? Definitely. Brilliant? Possibly. Easy to test? Hardly. I mean, even decoding the quantum data at LHC was a monumental task." Bishop glanced from Richter to Helen. "The two of you have no idea the stops we had to pull out—the sheer volume of computing power we had to requisition. Practically everything at DoD and NSA. CIA too. We even broke up the sorting job into batches and shipped it off to commercial grids— Amazon Web Services, Google Cloud Platform, and Microsoft Azure."

Bishop paced the room. "What you're talking about— comparing the genomes that were broadcast on the quantum radio with existing sequenced genomes—is on a completely different scale. *And* that even presupposes we had the genomic data to compare. We don't. There are nearly eight billion humans alive on the planet. We—the United States government—between NIH data and other sources, might have a few million sequenced human genomes. At best. We're talking about a data set that is one-tenth of one percent of the entire human population. The prospect of getting a hit is remote. It's a needle in a haystack. But the other update I just got is that the president's been briefed. The decision has been made to compare the president's genome against the four. And the vice president, cabinet, and Congress."

"Why?" Ty asked, then instantly realized the truth. "Wait— they think the genomes are of world leaders. Or future world leaders."

"It's the obvious conclusion," Bishop said.

"Are they going to build the machine?" Richter asked.

"It's being discussed," Bishop replied.

That surprised Ty. "Why wouldn't they?"

"The obvious," Richter said.

Ty was still confused. "Which is?"

"You're still thinking like a scientist."

Ty couldn't help feeling attacked by the comment. "Occupational hazard," he muttered.

"One I hope you never lose," Richter said. "Think about it, Tyson. They expected a genomic printer. What was actually received is a collider. Do you recall the uproar surrounding the initial start-up of the LHC? The concerns about how it might destroy our world?"

"Indeed I do."

"Consider what they see now: another collider, smaller, yes, but that only heightens their suspicion."

"Why?"

"If you wanted to make something look safe and non-threatening, what would you do?"

"Make it small."

"Correct. In the same way that the files in the data stream were obvious to you, Tyson, what that machine represents to the Department of Defense is obvious. Or so they think."

Ty saw it then. "A bomb."

"Precisely. If you were an alien civilization intent on wiping out threats across space and time and universes, what would be the most efficient means? Sending ships with troops and guns to invade? No. Of course not. That method, while exciting on TV, is terribly inefficient in reality. It's time-consuming, and the threat of your technology falling into your enemy's hands is too great a risk. What would any sufficiently advanced civilization use?" Richter asked.

"Science." Ty nodded. "And human nature. Curiosity. You could simply send your enemies the means to annihilate themselves and wait for them to destroy their planet. So, the DoD thinks the collider is a sort of quantum Trojan horse—a device that we will create, turn on, and destroy our planet with?"

"Yes."

"I don't think it is," Ty said.

"Why do you think that?" Bishop asked.

"Gut instinct."

Bishop rolled his eyes. "Well, we can't risk the extinction of the human race on your gut instinct."

"But," Ty said, "you can compare a few hundred or a few thousand genomes pretty easily against what was broadcast."

"What are you asking?"

"Do you have sequenced genomes for the people working on the Origin Project?"

Bishop eyed Ty. "Yes."

"Run the comparison."

"Why? What do you know?"

"Just a hunch."

After a long silence, Bishop said, "Okay. Let me make a call."

When Bishop left the room, Richter moved close to Ty and whispered, "Do you know who the genomes belong to?"

"No. Not for sure."

"But you have an idea."

"The shape of one."

18

The conference room at the DARPA facility was quiet, and it was growing more uncomfortable by the second. The tension was nearly unbearable.

Ty sat in a chair at the end of the conference table. His mother and Richter, his biological father, stood on opposing sides of the table, trying to act like nothing was weird. It wasn't working. Ty was acutely aware of the awkwardness in the room.

He wanted to throw his hands up and yell, "What happened between you two?"

He also wanted answers from Bishop. He wanted to be in the loop. Part of the process.

He had asked to see the schematic of the collider. That request had been denied. The details of the device, he had been told, were a matter of national security. That annoyed him. He was the reason they even had the schematic. Now they wouldn't even show him what he had found.

Something else was bothering him: Penny. Where was she? Was she still alive? Had the Covenant caught up to her? And why had she lied to him? What did they have on her?

Another thought occurred to Ty—a way at least to get more information about what was happening and possibly part of the key to understanding the genomes.

"I have an idea," he said, instantly drawing the attention of Helen and Richter, who seemed relieved for any distraction.

"Is it possible to get a sample of Penny Neumann's DNA? And compare it?"

His mother frowned. "Who is Penny Neumann?"

Ty leaned his head back and studied the white ceiling tiles. "She's… it's complicated."

Richter nodded. "It would be a simple thing to have an agent visit her apartment in Geneva and retrieve a sample."

"She lives in Geneva?" Helen asked. "Is she your girlfriend?"

"Mom."

Richter walked closer to Ty. "Why do you think she might be one of the four?"

"Logic. She's connected to the Covenant. And me."

Helen put her hands on her hips. "Ty, how is she *connected* to you?"

"That's..." Ty rolled his head to the left and right. "She... we dated—"

"For how long? *Dated*? As in, it's ended?"

Ty looked at Richter. The man clearly hadn't told his mother about the incident in the alley behind the coffee shop, which Ty counted as a good call. It would have worried her sick.

Richter picked up the phone on the conference table and jabbed at the number pad while Helen eyed Ty, waiting for an explanation. He nodded to Richter, silently indicating that it was rude to interrupt. He was happy for the delay in the motherly interrogation.

"It's Richter. We need to obtain a DNA sample from the Covenant agent who identified herself as Penny Neumann."

Ty's head whipped around. "What do you mean, *identified herself* as Penny Neumann?"

With the phone held to his ear, Richter listened, then said, "Yes, I think that would be fine. Also, please print an article from a newspaper called the *Rhein-Neckar-Zeitung* dated approximately one year ago—"

Richter listened, then said quickly, "Yes, simply search her name. It will be the last article you find. Have it translated and bring it to this conference room."

The second he hung up, Ty stood. "What article?"

Helen stared at Ty. "You dated a Covenant agent?" She turned her gaze to Richter. "Did you know about this?"

"Of course not."

"She wasn't a Covenant agent," Ty said, hands held up. "Well, she was, but not at the end."

"End of what?" Helen asked. "The relationship? So you've broken up."

The door opened, and Bishop stepped in. Upon seeing the scene, he stopped cold. "What happened?"

"Nothing," Richter muttered. "What do you have? A DNA match?"

Bishop peered out the door at the two marines standing watch, then slowly closed it and moved closer to Ty, Richter, and Helen. "Neither the president nor any of the members of the administration were a DNA match. Same for Congress."

Richter smiled. "I assume they were sufficiently crestfallen by this development?"

Bishop looked as though he were suppressing a grin. "Their disposition at the news is unknown to me. However, we do have a partial DNA match."

"Partial?" Richter asked.

"For whom?" Helen said.

"Two people, actually," Bishop replied, eyeing Richter and Helen. "Both of you."

Ty cocked his head. "Which means..."

"Which means," Bishop said carefully, "we can say, with a very high degree of certainty, that one of the genomes broadcast is a match to an offspring of Gerhard Richter and Helen Klein."

Richter's words came rapid-fire. "Male or female?"

"Male." Bishop nodded toward Ty. "It's you, Ty. Your genome is being broadcast."

"Not necessarily," Helen whispered.

"What?" Bishop said.

"I have a twin," Ty said. "An identical twin. We share the same genome."

"Not necessarily," Helen said again, turning away from the three men.

"What does that mean?" Ty asked, surprised by her words.

For a moment, Helen seemed lost in thought. Finally, she looked up at them. "It means that, yes, identical twins—what we biologists refer to as monozygotic twins—do begin with the same genome. Monozygotic twins are created when a single zygote—a fertilized egg—separates into two embryos. At that moment of division, the genomes of those embryos are identical copies of each other. And for a very long time, we believed that two offspring born of this process had little if any genetic difference at the time of birth. That's why twins have been used extensively in studies on the effect of environment on genetics—the nature versus nurture debate. However, a recent study in Iceland by deCODE turned that notion upside down. We now know that identical twins are not as identical as we once believed—genetically speaking. In fact, by the time twins are born, there are already differences in their genomes."

"What do you mean?" Bishop asked.

"Mutations," Richter said.

"Exactly," Helen said. "After the zygote splits, the cells weave new strands of DNA and then split into more and more cells. With any cell division process, there's the chance of replication errors. We now know this happens in the womb—enough to produce an average of 5.2 mutations between twins by the time of birth. In about one in every seven sets of twins, there are more significant mutations—ten to fifteen. The timing of the zygote separation has a significant impact on the number of differences. A zygote typically splits anywhere from one to seven days after fertilization. At this early juncture, there are fewer cells to split, and sometimes the cells don't split evenly. In other cases, the zygote doesn't split until up to thirteen days after fertilization. In those instances, there are more cells and typically fewer mutations in the resulting offspring."

Bishop reached up and massaged his temples. "So…"

"Gerhard and I have two sons," Helen said. "The sequence could be for either of their genomes."

"Okay. Where is this other son?"

"Thomas," Helen said, raising her head slightly. "He is in Butner, North Carolina. In prison."

"Prison?!"

"You need to alert the BOP to isolate him and send the US Marshals as soon as possible to transport him here. He could be in danger."

19

In the conference room, Bishop made the calls to ensure the US Bureau of Prisons would protect Thomas Klein until the Marshals transported him to DC.

When he hung up, he said, "Okay. He'll be here in about four hours."

A knock at the door drew everyone's attention. Richter and Bishop spoke in unison—"Come in"—then glanced at each other.

A young woman wearing surgical scrubs entered. She carried a plastic bag that held a clear tube with what looked like a long Q-tip inside.

"Sir," she said to Ty, "I need to—"

"Get a sample," he said, trying to ease the awkwardness. "I know. It's okay. Go ahead."

When she had finished swabbing the inside of his cheek, she departed. Ty expected to be left in the conference room again with his parents. He wasn't looking forward to that.

He was relieved when Bishop told them to follow him. It seemed that their genetic connection to the quantum radio broadcast had granted the three of them deeper access to the facility. And what was happening.

They weaved through the corridors, Bishop leading the way, two marines flanking the group, fluorescent lights buzzing overhead.

At the elevator, Bishop hit the button for B3, which Ty assumed was basement level three.

"I'd like my phone back," Richter said, staring at the steel doors.

"Even if they'd let me, it wouldn't work down here," Bishop replied.

When the elevator doors opened, a marine who couldn't have been over eighteen was waiting, skinny as a rail, holding a few stapled pages, which he instantly held out when he saw Richter.

"Sir, I was about to bring you the article you requested."

Ty tried to catch a glimpse of the printout, but Richter snatched it from the young marine and folded it, hiding the text. "Thank you, Private."

Ty wanted to ask about the article, but the chaos in the room beyond overwhelmed any conversation. The far wall had a bank of screens that reminded him of NASA Mission Control Center. Graphs and text scrolled by. Two dozen people sat at workstations, typing on keyboards. A few were pacing as they shouted into their headsets.

"NIH says the data is technically there, but most of it is still with the grant recipients. We can get it, but they have to turn it over, and we can't make them go any faster without raising suspicion. If this hits the press..."

"Well, if the CMS is paying the bill, don't we own the data? Who cares if..."

"Tell them we'll pay whatever they want—no, just make something up. Tell them it's going to be used in a de-identified metadata study—what?—no—who cares? Just make something up and ask for a number..."

Ty had heard of dialing for dollars in political campaigns—times when there was a deadline or election looming and the staffers worked long hours, often on the phones, calling donors and other volunteers to round up funding for a final push. The scene felt like that to him. But these people were dialing for data, not dollars, and specifically, for genomic data, trying to procure it from any source and by any means necessary.

Bishop led Ty and his parents to an office with windows that looked into the bullpen. There were three staffers at workstations on the far wall. They stopped typing and turned as the group entered.

"Give us the room," Bishop said, closing the door as the staffers exited.

"As you've probably gathered, we've been authorized to

expand the genomic search," he said, leaning on the edge of the desk. "The higher-ups are now convinced that you're right, Ty. The genomes are for living people."

"How far are they going?" Helen asked.

"For now, it's just US-owned data and whatever we can buy—"

"More must be done," Richter said, staring out the windows at the people on the phones. "Whoever finds those four people first may well control the future of the human race. We are behind, Sandy. The Covenant may already have one or more of the matches. They may have also already built the device. We must hurry now."

20

In the small office, Ty listened as his mother, Richter, and Bishop worked the phones, coordinating the growing efforts to gather genomic data.

When his mother hung up, she walked over to him and whispered a phrase she'd often said when he was a child: "Penny for your thoughts."

Helen seemed to immediately realize what she had said—the name of the woman he was likely thinking about and stressing over. "Actually, I'll give you a quarter." She shrugged. "Inflation."

"Ha ha," he muttered.

"You liked her, didn't you?"

"I like her, Mom. Present tense."

"It'll work out, Ty. If it's meant to be."

"Great. That makes me feel better."

"Attitude, Ty," she said, firm but encouraging. "What do we say about attitude?"

"Mom, I'm too old—"

"Humor me."

"Your attitude determines your altitude." He exhaled. "It's just... It's been a long twenty-four hours."

"You're stressed."

"That's an understatement."

"And from an evolutionary standpoint, what do we know helps?"

"Kindness."

"That's right. Focus on kindness, Ty. And have faith."

"In what?"

"In the future. In the process we can't see. That this will all work out—in time. Time heals all wounds."

Richter wandered over then, seemingly oblivious to their conversation, lost in his own thoughts. "The universities are getting involved."

The levity had left Helen's voice when she spoke again. "What lie did you use?"

Richter crossed his arms. "The sample collection will be done under the auspices of a global cancer research initiative. We're calling it Twenty-Four Hours to Cure Cancer."

"Clever."

"A benign lie to a worthy end: saving lives."

"Certainly your specialty, Gerhard. Clever lies for your causes."

Ty held his hands up. "Stop. Both of you. Please." He eyed his mother. "Kindness, remember."

She smiled. "Touché. And you're quite right, Ty."

He considered adding a bit about time healing all wounds, but sensed that the moment wasn't right, that whatever had happened between them, even time hadn't yet healed.

To Richter, he said, "I want to see that article about Penny."

Richter hesitated a moment, then reached into his pocket, drawing out the folded page and handing it to Ty. Without a word, he walked away, and so did Ty's mother, leaving him alone to read the printout from *Rhein-Neckar-Zeitung*. The headline read:

HEIDELBERG RESIDENT KILLED IN HIT AND RUN

Ty reeled as he read the first lines of the article:

The Heidelberg police have confirmed the identity of the twenty-eight-year-old woman killed in a late-night hit-and-run traffic accident as Penelope Howard Neumann...

It didn't make any sense. It was Penny's full name. And her age. And she was from Heidelberg. The incident had occurred about two months before she had come to Geneva.

Ty scanned the article, then flipped both pages over.

He couldn't believe it—it was wrong somehow.

And there was no picture.

He walked over to Richter. "It's not Penny. There's no photo. There has to be some mistake."

Richter led Ty to the closest computer terminal and logged in—apparently, he had credentials on the DARPA network. He did an internet search and pulled up another article about the death, one that featured a photo.

Of Penny.

It was, in fact, the woman Ty knew. The woman he had met in Geneva.

In the article, she had that same knowing smile and just a hint of sadness in her eyes, as though she had been hurt before.

He shook his head.

"It doesn't make sense."

"No. It doesn't."

"Why would she fake her own death?"

Richter studied Ty's face with what the younger man thought was sympathy. "I believe you're asking the wrong question."

Before Ty could try to find the right question, the door flew open and a tall marine barged in, addressing Bishop. "Sir, pardon the interruption, but we've got—" He stopped in mid-sentence when he realized Ty and the others were in the room.

"Speak freely," Bishop said. "They're cleared."

"We have a hit on the genome matching, sir. One of the males."

"Who?"

"He's a naval officer, sir. A SEAL. Lieutenant Kato Tanaka."

"Where is he now?"

The marine grimaced. "We're not sure, sir."

"He's not on active duty?"

"He is... but, we may have an issue, sir."

21

Deep in a jungle in Nigeria, Kato Tanaka sat on the floor of a run-down, one-room shack, his eyes closed, meditating.

He had been in the small building for five days, waiting, leaving only to use the outhouse and boil more water by the fire outside.

His sleeping bag lay in one corner of the shack, next to his bulky backpack. A table sat under the shack's only window, which Kato had boarded up for safety.

A military-grade laptop sat atop the table, screen glowing in the darkness. Like Kato, it had been conditioned to operate in harsh conditions, including high altitude and extreme temperatures, and to withstand multiple impacts. Like him, it bore the scars of its service: nicks and scratches and a long gash on its back.

Kato's most visible injury was a scar that ran from the right side of his nose to the bottom of his chin, the remnant of a run-in with Somali pirates during a Navy SEAL operation in the Gulf of Aden six years before.

His worst wounds, however, were the kind that couldn't be seen. He had spent years trying to heal those injuries, and like the scar on his face, they had closed, but their effects still haunted him.

The mark on his face was a daily reminder of how a single act—and a slight change in perspective—could change a life.

He often met people who initially saw only one side of his face, the scar in shadow or hidden slightly by the angle at which they viewed him. Countless times he had shifted slightly, turned into the light only to see their smiles disappear, their perception of him instantly changed. It was one of the many injustices in an unfair life that he had come to accept.

But there were those rare instances where justice could be had, dispensed swiftly and permanently. That's why he was sitting alone in the small shack in the long-abandoned coal mine deep in the Nigerian rainforest. He was also there for a selfish reason: to let the rage inside of him out by killing bad people.

The laptop dinged, and a notification appeared on the screen.

Kato opened his eyes and, still sitting on the wood-plank floor, scanned the computer display from ten feet away. A perimeter alarm had tripped.

Video feeds appeared on the screen, showing a convoy of three vehicles bouncing down a muddy dirt road, trying and failing to avoid the tree limbs that had long ago grown into the lane like hands reaching out from the dense jungle. The first vehicle was a Japanese SUV with dark-tinted windows. Behind it was a high-mobility all-terrain multipurpose truck with two men in the cab and ten more in the bed sitting facing each other, semi-automatic rifles pointed toward the sky, most smoking, all ducking the tree branches.

The third and final vehicle in the convoy was a beat-up school bus with lettering on the side that had long since faded into the primer beneath. The bus was empty, but Kato knew why they had brought it—they expected it to be filled with young girls when it left.

They were wrong.

Targeting his client was going to be the last mistake they ever made.

Assuming the SUV had five occupants and that the bus driver joined the fight, that put their head count at eighteen. To his one. About the odds he had expected. As such, he saw no reason to alter his plan.

He rose and walked to the laptop and watched the convoy pass out of range of one of the cameras that was connected to the mesh Wi-Fi network he had created. Soon, the next camera picked up the convoy.

Kato pulled up his map of the area and studied the routes he had hiked and the length of time it had taken to reach the abandoned coal mine.

The convoy stopped, and the traffickers exited the SUV. Their troops began bounding off the truck, headed toward him. Kato checked the map one last time and set his watch to count down from seven minutes.

Methodically, quickly, he rolled up his sleeping bag and stuffed it, along with the uneaten MREs, into his backpack and returned to the table, pulling a round folding stool under him as he opened the email app on the laptop.

His satellite phone, which lay on the table beside the hardened laptop, lit up as it activated the data connection to the internet.

He scanned through the emails until he found the first item of interest: a message from his wife's attorney. The subject line read:

Our FINAL Offer Regarding Division of Marital Assets and LIMITED Visitation Rights

The email was filled with legalese and big words and things Kato would never allow that to happen as long as he was alive.

He hit reply and added his wife to the TO: line and typed a quick response:

Dear Joan:

The past is the past. I made mistakes. I am sorry. I will fix it.
I will see you and Akito when I return.

Kato

He glanced at his watch. Four minutes and thirty-nine seconds left.

The next email of interest was from his judge advocate, with a simple subject line:

Plea Deal

Kato scanned the message, focusing on the pertinent phrases.

Given the judge's denial of our motion to dismiss, I once again urge you to seek a deal with the convening authority so we can all avoid a trial in your court martial.

Kato had lost track of the number of times the lawyer had asked him to make a deal. He replied with the same answer he had sent before.

No.

He checked the time again.

Three minutes and seventeen seconds.

Methodically, he closed the documents he had been working on. The most important to him was a manuscript for a nonfiction book he'd spent the last ten years researching and drafting, a history book entitled *The March of Humanity: The True History of the Human Race.*

The book was a hobby. An outlet for his love of history. His goal was to present a unified, non-biased history of the human race. Kato believed that would reveal the arc of humanity: how our past explained how we got to where we are today and what the future might hold.

Kato saved the documents and ensured they were synced with the cloud. If he didn't return from this jungle, at least they would survive.

He closed the laptop and stowed it and the satellite phone in his backpack, then donned his body armor and performed a quick check of his sidearm and rifle.

When he finished, there were less than two minutes left on the countdown. He had gone over the plan countless times, but still, his heart began beating faster, his nervousness growing. He hoped he would never lose that feeling: fear. Manageable fear. Manageable fear was useful. Essential in his line of work. It had kept him alive over the years.

He set the backpack against the front wall, out of view to anyone outside, then swung the rickety wooden door open and casually stepped out into the afternoon sun. Heat pressed into him like an electric blanket.

The only sounds were the birds calling across the dense rainforest and the voices of children in the large wood-plank building next door. The teacher was talking loudly, interrupted only by the girls' laughter and occasional questions.

Kato strode off the front porch, into the open field where he knew the traffickers could see him clearly. He unzipped his pants and urinated, mentally keeping track of the seconds. There was the chance that one of the attackers might take a shot at him from the trees, but it was an acceptable risk.

No shots came, only the continuous sound of the schoolchildren next door.

When he was finished, he turned and ambled back to the shack, head slightly hung. When the door creaked shut, he moved to the center of the room and slid aside the wooden boards that covered a hole in the floor. In the dirt beneath the shack, the opening to his tunnel loomed.

In truth, the passage that ran from the shack to the mine wasn't much of a tunnel. It was more of a deep trench, which Kato had hastily dug and covered with boards and tarps and dirt. It wouldn't hold up to rigorous inspection, but Kato was betting his enemy wouldn't get close enough to find it. And if they did, it would already be too late.

He hopped into the hole and pulled the makeshift trap door back over the opening in the floor, then army-crawled quickly through the dark passage, pushing his pack ahead of him, his rifle on his back. It was musty and cramped, and he could feel wet dirt sticking to his clothes, soaking through. Finally, he emerged just inside the mine shaft, out of view of the shack. He was filthy and panting, but he didn't bother cleaning himself off. He moved deeper into the mine until he spotted the narrow beam of light shining down from the vertical escape tunnel.

At the escape tunnel, Kato climbed, knowing time was slipping away. If he was right, the armed men were about to clear the tree line. They would run then, weapons held out, until they reached the buildings. He had to reach the surface before then. The escape tunnel exited onto a hill above the mine, at just the right vantage point—if he could reach it in time.

The vertical shaft was damper than it had been during Kato's two practice runs. It had rained that morning, leaving the walls muddy, the rock loose. He slipped once but jabbed a hand into the mushy earth, pushing his back into it, bracing himself until he could plant his feet again.

His watch vibrated on his wrist. Time was up.

Sunlight glimmered a few feet above.

He climbed faster then, like a drowning man swimming for the surface.

At the top of the escape tunnel, he dug his fingers into the ground and pulled his body out of the hole. He drew his phone out and connected to the camera inside the larger building below.

The windows of the structure were boarded up. The door was closed. Two dozen desks were spaced evenly across the room. Bodies sat in chairs at each one. But they weren't actual people. They were children's clothes stuffed full of straw. Like the trench from the shack to the mine, they wouldn't hold up to close inspection, but they didn't need to. They just needed to fool the attackers long enough to buy him a little time.

At the front of the room, a mannequin stood with its arm extended, posing as the teacher. He had bought the model for pennies in an open-air market.

The camera had no audio capability, so it didn't transmit the recording that was playing in the room, but Kato heard it in the distance, through the trees, the faint sound of children's voices mixed with the stern commands of the teacher. He had captured the recording while visiting his client.

He took the detonator from his pocket and activated it. On the screen, the door to the fake one-room school flew open and half a dozen men rushed in, waving their rifles left and right, high-capacity magazines hanging down.

Their shouts were loud enough for Kato to hear from where he lay. He watched as a few more of the men entered the room.

By then, the first arrivals were starting to realize the ruse. Their guns fell to their sides. One man pushed the mannequin over.

Kato depressed the detonator, ending their lives in three booming explosions.

He rose from the ground, shouldered his rifle, and crept forward toward the rising cloud of smoke billowing up below, spreading from the wreckage of the two buildings out into the serene rainforest.

From his high perch above, he crouched and watched, firing at any movement in the cloud. He emptied two magazines and loaded another before the smoke had cleared enough for him to see the bodies scattered across the field.

He descended the hill and stalked through the wooden wreckage of the buildings, delivering coups de grâce as he went, the shots a sickening symphony of his march to the last survivor, who had been the farthest away when the explosives detonated. The man had likely waited at the edge of the tree line, watching his troops do the dirty work. The dangerous work. He was corpulent and wore a bloody athletic jumpsuit. A thick gold chain hung from his neck. Large sunglasses covered half his face. Shrapnel from the buildings had shredded his legs.

As Kato approached, the man threw up a hand and pleaded in a language he didn't recognize, but the message was clear: *don't kill me.*

Kato believed that every person deserved a chance to explain their actions, to be heard before they were judged. But life had taught him that there was the justice that one deserved and the justice that could be had. Here and now, this jungle justice was the only thing within reach.

Kato took a step closer, held the rifle to his shoulder, and gave the man what he deserved.

It was night when Kato arrived at the village.

At his client's home, he approached quietly and peered in through the screen door. The schoolteacher sat rocking in a recliner, fanning herself with one hand, holding a smartphone with the other.

Kato knocked, and she jumped at the sound, then stared out at him as though she had seen a ghost.

"Thought you had gone and left," she said, rising and lumbering to the screen door.

"Took longer than I thought."

She swung the door open and stepped onto the porch. "You talked to 'em?"

"They won't bother you again."

The teacher studied his face. "Just like that, huh?"

"I guarantee the results."

She snorted and smiled. "Well, all right then. Gimme a second."

She let the rickety door slam shut and retreated into the small house. A few seconds later, she returned with an envelope full of money. "Here you go." She seemed to remember something then. "Hey, there was some guys come around asking about you. Where you was. How long you been here."

"When?"

"'Bout an hour ago."

"Who were they? Traffickers? Gang associates—"

"Nah, not them kind of guys. They was like you."

"Like me?"

"Yeah. Americans. They wasn't in uniform, they wore shorts and T-shirts, but it was obvious. They had the haircut—and the voice. 'Ma'am this' and 'ma'am that' and if I see you I need to call 'em and they would pay me and all." She reached in her pocket and took out a slip of paper with a number scrawled on it.

"Did you…"

"I told 'em I hadn't never even heard of you."

Kato smiled. "Thanks."

Behind him, the sound of SUVs roared in the night, a convoy driving along the dirt road of the village at high speed, headed his way. There was no doubt in his mind about why they were here.

"Stay inside," he said quietly. "And away from the windows."

She closed the door, and Kato walked into the street.

The lead SUV bore down on him, the second vehicle close behind, a column of dust rising in the moonlight. A hundred feet away, the SUVs skidded to a halt, one forking left, one right.

Kato drew his handgun from its holster but kept it behind his back. With his eyes still on the vehicles, he began stepping sideways, away from the schoolteacher's house, toward the row of dilapidated buildings that could provide some cover in the gunfight he was mentally preparing for.

The cloud of dust the convoy had created drifted forward, carried by the breeze, like a tumbleweed drifting through.

Kato could hear car doors opening and closing. Boots crunched the loose dirt in the road.

Along the street, curtains were drawn closed. Lights winked out.

"Lieutenant Tanaka!" a man's voice with a southern accent called from the cloud.

"You just missed him."

That drew a few chuckles as four men emerged from the cloud. They looked like the people the headmistress had described: buzz cuts, civilian clothes, and hard eyes.

The man who spoke looked like an NFL linebacker. "Stand down, Lieutenant, we're friendlies. I'm Commander Nathan Ross."

"What do you want?"

"We were sent to pick you up."

"The judge said I could remain free until my trial."

"What trial?"

"Court-martial."

"I don't know anything about that. These orders got sent down from way on high. Direct from the Pentagon."

"You're going to have to give me more than that."

The large man exhaled and put his hands on his hips. "Listen, all I know is that the Pentagon wants you there yesterday. And I'm gonna deliver you." He nodded. "Now, we've got a helo on standby a click away, and I don't think we ought to be dilly-dallying out here any longer than we have to. I mean, I don't know about you, Lieutenant, but I'm scared of the dark—*real, real scared of the dark*—and beyond that, frankly, I'm just a little bit worn out from looking all over half of Nigeria trying to find you, so why don't you, pretty please, get in the vehicle and we'll get you a secure sat phone and you can call whoever you want and we'll sort all this out. Okay?"

22

At the DARPA facility near the banks of the Anacostia River in Washington, DC, Ty peered out the office's wide window at the open-concept team room, watching Bishop arguing with two of his colleagues, who were dressed in plain clothes.

"Something's wrong," he said, drawing the attention of Richter and his mother, who came to stand beside him at the window.

As if sensing their eyes on him, Bishop turned, stared at them for a long second, then stalked toward his office.

He pushed the door open and exhaled, clearly annoyed. "Okay, settle a debate. We're ordering lunch." He held up two fingers. "I'm going to give you two choices to make it simple because I'm sick of arguing about it. Chipotle or Panera?"

"I'm fine with either," Helen said.

"Same," Ty muttered, a little surprised that this was the subject of the strenuous debate.

"Richter?" Bishop asked, hand held out, palm up.

"I too am neutral on this decision."

"So if we get Panera," Bishop said, "everybody is going to be happy?"

"What is Panera?" Richter asked. "Is it like pizza?"

"Panera Bread. You don't have Panera in Zürich?"

"You only eat bread for lunch?"

Bishop closed his eyes. "No, Gerhard, it's like a café. They've got everything: soups, salads, paninis, cold sandwiches, bakery stuff—and that's the problem. Bill says it's like hospital food. They have everything, but nothing is really *that* good, especially if you've had it a bunch—and we have lately. He keeps saying, 'Panera is overpriced hospital food, change my mind.'"

"Well," Helen said slowly, "as someone whose office is on the campus of Georgetown University at the med school and who routinely eats at the university hospital cafeteria next door, I can assure you I am quite comfortable with hospital food."

Bishop let his head fall back. "So you *are saying* it's like hospital food?"

"I didn't say that—"

"What I'm not hearing is Chipotle," Bishop snapped. "That's clearly out."

"I can do Chipotle," Ty said.

"Me too," Helen said.

"No, no," Bishop muttered. "I get it. Fine—we're doing Jersey Mike's. We haven't had it since last Tuesday, so it's time."

With that, Bishop left the three of them in silence.

Richter's back was turned. He was still staring through the large window when he spoke. "He's cracking."

"He's fine," Helen responded.

"What he is," Richter said slowly, "is ill-suited to the intensity of this new phase of our endeavor."

Helen shook her head. "Well, few mortals possess your fortitude, Gerhard. We'll simply have to make do."

"We must consider the prospect that he may be incapable of seeing this through."

"He's just stressed," Helen said. "During times of duress, we take comfort in routines, and it can be even more jarring if those routines are disrupted. His blood sugar might also be low, which triggers the release of hormones like cortisol and adrenaline, causing even more stress and activating the body's fight-or-flight response. It can impact decision-making."

Ty massaged his forehead. He was seeing a whole new side of his parents, one that was equally illuminating and trying. "Mom, he's just hangry."

"Yes, he's hangry."

When Bishop returned after lunch, he was indeed in better spirits.

"You all want to stretch your legs?" he asked before leading them out of the office and to the elevator.

At basement level four, they exited into a small foyer with white walls, a gray linoleum-tiled floor, and a white drop ceiling. A single door loomed ahead with a biometric hand reader beside it.

Bishop planted his hand there, and the door clicked open, revealing a corridor wider than Ty had expected based on the small foyer. The passage was empty except for three metal rolling carts scattered along it. Each was littered with opened packages with what looked like small mechanical parts and electronic components. A set of closed double doors sealed the opposite end.

Bishop led them down the corridor to a wide window that looked into a clean room where three people were working in space suits hooked up to spiraling hoses that hung from the ceiling. They were crouched over a metal table, examining something through a microscope. With their hands, they were operating a surgical arm that reached down, moving very slightly and flashing a light every few seconds.

Along the far wall, a 3D printer was building something Ty couldn't see.

To him, the scene looked like a surgical operating room, with the three "doctors" diligently performing surgery on a small object.

"They've decided to build the device?" Richter said.

"Yes," Bishop replied.

"What convinced them?" Ty asked.

Bishop shrugged. "Same reason we built the atom bomb and got to the moon first. They're scared someone will beat us to it—and what it could mean. Right now, the Covenant might be constructing its own device. The premise we're operating under is that whoever finishes first will likely control the future."

On that point, Ty agreed.

Bishop turned his back to the window and focused on Ty. "I've asked again if we can show you the schematics for the device."

"Asked who?"

"The White House. They're managing the entire operation directly. It's that important."

"So I assume you're telling me this because the answer was no."

"I'm sorry, Ty. It's not my call."

"They wouldn't be building that device without my work."

"I know."

"They don't trust me."

Bishop grimaced. "I can't say—"

"Is it because of Penny? Because I dated a Covenant agent? They think I might be one too."

"Look, Ty, it is what it is."

Richter spoke then, his gaze still on the three suited figures working in the clean room. "Why are you telling him this now?"

Ty felt it was a good question—one that cut right to the heart of the issue.

"Because," Bishop said, exhaling, "they want me to ask you about the device. Specifically, if there's a... code that might activate it."

Ty turned that question over in his mind, trying to put his anger aside. He had to admit, the question surprised him. He had assumed the device would be one that they simply turned on. "Why would they ask that? Is there an interface of some kind on the device?"

Bishop's gaze drifted up to the ceiling.

"I'll take that as a yes."

Bishop let his focus drift back to Ty.

"So there is an interface. What type? You're asking me for a code to operate it, but you're not even supplying the syntax the code might be in. Or the length. You guys want me in the dark, but you also want me to solve problems I don't understand. It's not fair."

"No," Bishop said, "it's not. That's DC. And, frankly, that's what working on classified projects is like sometimes."

"What is this interface? You've got to give me something. Does it select which particles are accelerated?"

"We think it's simply a way to tune the quantum radio."

"Tune," Ty said, thinking. "As in modulating the horizontal and vertical betatron tunes? You can do that by varying the strength of the quadrupole magnets—"

Bishop held up a hand. "No—it's nothing like that. We're looking for a sequence. An ordered arrangement of a set of symbols."

"How many?"

"We don't know."

"How big is the character set?"

Bishop chewed his lip. "Twelve."

"How do you know it's a code?"

"It follows based on the layout of the interface."

"You've got to let me see it."

"I can't."

"Then I can't help you."

"Just... try to think of a code that might activate it. If the Covenant is building their own quantum radio—if we are indeed in a race here—we need to be prepared to activate our device first."

23

By mid-afternoon, fatigue was overtaking Ty. It brought brain fog with it, like a cloud rolling in late in the day, dumping heavy rain, a force of nature bearing down on him that he couldn't stop. It was enough to make him want to lie down and sleep for hours.

He was sitting in a chair in Bishop's office contemplating doing just that when Richter walked in and marched over to him.

"Your brother will be here shortly."

Ty nodded.

"You feel unwell," Richter said.

"I'm fine."

"You take medications for your condition."

Ty looked up at him, shocked, but said nothing.

Richter continued, his face showing no emotion. "It's a cocktail you've refined over the years, a combination of prescription medications offered via online services and nonprescription supplements."

"How do you know that?" Ty whispered.

"I've kept tabs on you."

"How?"

"I paid a firm to do it."

"Why?"

"You know why."

Ty rubbed his eyebrows, feeling the headache starting. Richter remained an enigma to him, one that only grew the more they talked.

"My medicines and supplements were in my apartment. They were destroyed in the blast. I need to get refills."

"No, you don't." Richter reached into his coat pocket and drew out the white pill bottle Ty had seen Richter's assistant hand him on the tarmac at the private airport outside Zürich. He held it out to Ty, who eyed it. There was no label. Ty took the bottle, opened it, and studied the capsules inside, which were filled with gray-white powder.

"What is this?"

"What you require."

"I need you to be more cryptic right now."

"I shall comply when you increase your sarcasm."

"I'm serious. This is my health. I can't just take some random pills."

"They are hardly random."

"Then what are they?"

"The product of research I've funded for a long time."

"Research into what?"

"Your condition. What you hold should resolve your symptoms." Richter turned to leave. "I'll get you some water."

"Wait."

The older man glanced back.

"What do you know about my condition? Really?" Ty held the bottle up. "What is this?"

"When I can, when the time is right, I'll tell you."

Ty's mother walked into the office, prompting Ty to shove the pill bottle in his pocket. He had never told her about his condition—mostly because he didn't want to worry her, and frankly, she would've had a million questions, ordered a million tests, and probably spent endless hours thinking about it and wondering if he was okay.

Helen eyed them. "What are you two doing?"

Ty shrugged. "Chatting about mystery drugs."

She frowned dismissively, then let out a short laugh before motioning through the office window. "Bishop sent me to get you both. Apparently, there's a briefing."

When she turned to leave the office, Richter nodded to Ty, who took out the pill bottle and dry-swallowed one of the capsules, still wondering what in the world it was.

* * *

The briefing room was similar to the conference room where Ty had been held when he first arrived at the DARPA facility, only larger. In the center was a long conference table with power and Ethernet connections at each seat. A massive screen covered the wall opposite the door.

A tall marine stood at the front of the room, wearing a spotless uniform with rows of medals on his chest, a map of Africa displayed behind him. A red dot was moving on the map, blinking just off the coast of Liberia.

Bishop introduced the marine as Lieutenant Colonel Travis, the Origin Project's Pentagon liaison. The man spoke as soon as the four of them were seated.

"Ladies and gentlemen, I'll lead with the bad news: the active searches of the DoD and other government-controlled sources of genomic data yielded no further results other than the match for Lieutenant Tanaka."

"And where exactly is Lieutenant Tanaka?" Bishop asked.

"That's the good news, sir. A rapid response team located Tanaka an hour ago. He's in custody and en route to this facility."

"What took so long?" Bishop asked.

"He was in the field, sir. In Africa. Took a while to track him down."

"I thought he wasn't deployed."

"He wasn't, sir. Sources say he was doing freelance work."

"Freelance work. As in…"

"Security work, sir."

"What sort of security work?"

"Sir, I'm told this instance was a K&R counteroperation."

"K&R?" Helen asked.

"Ah, that's kidnap and ransom, ma'am. The term typically encompasses extortion as well."

Bishop frowned. "So he was rescuing someone who was kidnapped?"

"Ah, not in this case, sir."

"What exactly was he doing?"

"The specifics aren't exactly clear, sir."

It was obvious to Ty that the marine was holding back. Richter seemed to sense it too. He spoke slowly, tone neutral. "Colonel, we believe Lieutenant Tanaka may be an integral part of what is happening here. It's possible that his recent activities may be connected. Any information—including *speculation*—would be helpful."

Travis nodded. "Copy that, sir. What I do know is that Tanaka was doing a job subbed out by Halogen Group in Nigeria."

"What is Halogen Group?" Bishop asked.

"A private security firm, sir. They're a pretty large operation, similar to Blackwater and Aegis."

"So they hired Mr. Tanaka?" Helen asked.

Travis paused a moment. "Ma'am, I think it's more likely that they referred this job to him. On small jobs like this, they really don't want to be in the loop."

"What exactly was the small job?" Richter asked.

"Our contact at Halogen reports that the client in this case was a school that had been threatened. Local unfriendlies were demanding protection money. Basic extortion scheme, sir."

"What did Tanaka do?" Bishop asked, leaning forward.

"Sir, in the debrief, the team that acquired Tanaka reported being uncertain about his specific actions in country. Reading between the lines, I think that would have generated a lot of questions and paperwork."

Richter cleared his throat. "We have no interest in paperwork, Colonel. Only your opinion about what the lieutenant was doing in Nigeria."

"Yes, sir. We believe—based on eyewitness reports—that Tanaka let it get around that he had evacuated the school to a remote location for safekeeping. An abandoned mine. Details about what went down there are unclear, but we have drone footage of some very large explosions in that area and roughly ten to twenty deceased hostiles." Travis tilted his head. "It's hard to tell from the photos, but we believe they are the same group cited in the case file Halogen handed off to us."

Richter frowned. "Why was the team in the field unable to ascertain an exact body count?"

"Sir, I believe that was because the hostiles in question were in pieces."

The room fell silent.

Bishop closed his eyes and rubbed his forehead. "Freelance work," he mumbled. "My nephew does graphic design. He's on Fiverr. *That* is freelance work. This guy's a mercenary. A hired killer."

The tall marine said nothing.

"Where's the file on this Lieutenant Tanaka?" Bishop asked. "The full workup?"

Travis reached into his bag and pulled out a thick manila folder and slid it over to Bishop, who flipped through the pages, then looked up suddenly. "He's being court-martialed?"

"Yes, sir."

"He's a criminal," Bishop muttered, still reading the file.

"He's been accused, sir. He's yet to be tried. Or convicted."

Bishop was still reading the file when he spoke again. "We need to have the Bureau of Prisons sequence every single inmate in the country. And coordinate with the state prison systems. Foreign nations too. Have State offer aid. Get the CIA to offer bribes. Use dirt if they have to. I'm sure they have it."

Bishop's words shocked Ty. He didn't follow the line of reasoning at all. But Richter clearly did.

"I concur," he said quickly.

"Why?" Ty asked.

"A pattern is emerging," Richter said.

Bishop closed the file and passed it to Helen. To Travis, he said, "Anything else, Colonel?"

"No, sir. That's all I have for now."

"Please have ops start making those requests to the White House to coordinate with BOP, State, and CIA." Bishop glanced at his watch. "It's getting late in the day, and the bureaucrats will be going home soon. Make it happen, Colonel."

"Yes, sir."

When the marine was gone, Ty said, "What pattern?"

"Prisoners," Richter said.

"There's a fifty-fifty chance," Bishop said, "that either you or your brother are a match. Let's say it's your brother, Thomas. We know he's a convicted felon. We now know that Tanaka is facing a court-martial and that he's taking jobs where he's hired to kill people."

Ty shook his head. "That's not accurate."

Bishop shrugged. "Which part?"

"To me, it sounds like Tanaka was hired to *protect* people. A school. And it sounds like he had to kill some people to do that—and not good people."

Bishop grimaced. "You're missing the point."

"Which is?"

"The point is that we've received schematics for a device— what looks like an advanced particle collider. We're really not sure what it will do when we activate it. We've also received the genomes of four people. Two are likely people who have broken the law. One is already in prison. One is the subject of a court-martial. He was in the process of killing ten to twenty people when we found him. The fact that there were so many body parts that a special ops team couldn't accurately estimate the death count speaks volumes. Perhaps the most important fact in all of this is one simple thing: both men are under the direct control of the government."

"I don't see why that's important."

Ty waited, but no one said anything. The three others seemed deep in thought. Finally, Richter spoke. "Consider it from the other point of view."

"What other point of view?"

"The point of view of whomever—or whatever—is broadcasting via this quantum radio."

Ty frowned. "I don't follow."

"They've sent schematics, correct?" Richter asked.

"Right."

"For a device."

"Yes, for a device."

"And what would the recipient need to do?" Richter asked.

"Build it," Ty said, unable to hide his annoyance at the simplicity of the questions. He felt like he was being treated like a child, which was even more annoying because when he actually was a child, Richter had skipped out on being a parent.

"What would you do after building it?"

Ty exhaled. "Turn it on."

"And what do you do when you turn on a prototype of any new device?"

"You test it—" Ty saw it then. "Wait." He stood up and began pacing in the conference room, shaking his head. "No way."

"It's the obvious conclusion," Richter said, staring at the conference table.

Ty said the words he was thinking, hoping he was wrong. "You think the genomes are test subjects. Prisoners. People whoever is broadcasting knows we would have access to. People they think we'd be willing to experiment on."

The silence confirmed Ty's assertion.

"You think the device is going to do something to them."

"A safe assumption," Richter said. "The subjects should be under observation when the device is activated. And perhaps close to it. Proximity may be important."

"I don't like this," Ty whispered. "I don't like it at all."

"I don't either," Helen breathed out.

"It's wrong," Ty said.

"I agree," Helen whispered. "It's testing without consent."

Ty shook his head. "Yes. That makes it wrong. But I also disagree with the conclusion you all are making here. I don't think the genomes are test subjects."

"You want it to be wrong," Bishop said, not looking up.

"Yes. I want it to be wrong. But that doesn't mean it's right."

"What are you saying?" Richter asked.

"I'm saying we're looking at this incorrectly. We're simply following the possible correlations the data is providing."

Bishop reeled back. "I fail to see the flaw in that."

"The flaw is very simple: we're excluding avenues of inquiry before we've ruled them out."

"Meaning?" Richter asked.

"We need more data. More genomic data, to be exact. We need to start testing on a global scale. Everyone, and I mean everyone—in every nation."

Bishop snorted. "Why didn't I think of that? Should be easy enough." He patted his pockets. "Now, where did I put that magic wand?"

"Very funny," Ty said, exhaustion and annoyance creeping into his voice.

"Look," Bishop said, "the president has been briefed on the situation, and the full force and capabilities of the United States government are behind this effort, but there are practical limits to what we can do here."

"You're wrong. The only real limit is our imagination."

"Sounds great," Bishop muttered. "On a t-shirt."

"I'm serious. We need to start finding these people—and fast. We need to go beyond dialing for data." When no one made eye contact, Ty pressed on. "Look, you all made me part of the team, but you're still not listening to me. Everything I've told you has been right, both what the device was and what the genomes were. Existing people. You want to start ignoring me now?"

Ty's mother smiled. "He has a point, gentlemen. Can't recall either of you coming up with any good ideas recently."

Bishop threw a hand up. "I'm all ears. How exactly are you going to get the entire world to voluntarily submit to DNA testing—and quickly?"

"It's very simple," Ty said. "We offer what everyone wants."

"Okay, I'll bite," Bishop said, clearly skeptical. "What does *everyone* want?"

"To win the lottery."

Bishop frowned. "Sure. But they can't buy a lottery ticket with a buccal swab from their mouth."

Richter leaned back in his chair and stared at Ty. With each passing second, a smile spread across his face. "Sure they can, Sandy." He nodded. "They can. And they will. If given the right enticement. It's a very, very clever idea, Ty."

Bishop shrugged. "What's a clever idea?"

"A genetic lottery," Ty said. "An unclaimed inheritance."

"Go on," Bishop said.

"We release a story on social media and news outlets about a reclusive, world-traveling billionaire who has passed away with no known heirs. In his will, this unnamed billionaire directs his family office to conduct a search for his biological relatives. They could be his direct issue or the descendants of a brother or sister or one of his aunts and uncles going back generations. That casts the net pretty wide. Global. We say nothing about the billionaire's background. Nothing about his country of origin, race, ethnicity or history. Anyone who submits a DNA sample may end up with billions. And then we sweeten the deal: we pay anyone a hundred dollars just to get tested to see if they're a match."

Bishop leaned back in the chair and let his head fall back. "This is going to be a pain. A royal pain—"

"Gerhard should do it," Helen said. "He's the resident expert on reclusive billionaires keeping secrets."

24

Associated Press

Breaking News Alert

The White House has announced an executive order directing the United States Bureau of Prisons and National Institutes of Health to collaborate on a nationwide initiative to collect and sequence DNA samples from all federally incarcerated inmates. The action was met with resistance from the American Civil Liberties Union, Amnesty International, and private prison operators CoreCivic and The GEO Group, who claim that the forced testing is likely to put their employees in danger. At this time, the motivation for the order and urgency with which the testing is being carried out is unclear. We will update this breaking news alert as details emerge.

25

At the DARPA facility, Ty was returning from the bathroom, making his way through the crowded team room, when he spotted Richter and Bishop standing near the elevators, arguing.

The two men could hardly have been more different. Bishop was animated, his diatribes long and winding. He held his hands out and shook his head and rolled his eyes. Richter was a statue, his retorts rarely more than a few words.

Ty wondered what they were talking about. His brother, more than likely—and what would happen when he arrived.

At Bishop's office, Ty opened the door and found his mother standing by the large window, looking out at the team room.

"We need to talk," she said, glancing at Richter and Bishop, who were still arguing by the elevator. "While we can."

"About what?"

"Your brother."

"What about him?"

"If it is his genome that matches... we need to figure out what we're going to do."

"Okay." Ty wasn't sure where she was going with this. He closed the door behind him.

"I've begun making a plan to get him out of here."

"As in..."

"Disabling the marshals guarding him and getting out of the building—"

"Mom, are you serious?"

"If the device really is going to harm him, we can't let them turn it on—not when he's close by. That's our only hope."

"We don't even know if it works that way."

"True, but we can't take that chance—that it could kill your brother."

"Yes, but do you really think we can even get him out of here?" Ty held his hands out. "We're scientists, not secret agents."

"We're a family."

Ty nodded. "Of scientists."

"You'll understand when you have children. You do what you have to—to protect them."

"Mom, let's take it down a notch. I'm just trying to be practical here."

"Practically speaking, there's no way a mother would allow them to do that to their child. I wouldn't let them do it to you either. Or Sarah."

"Even if we get out of here, they'll come after us."

"Yes. They will. But they might test it on the other three first."

"Mom, listen to what you're saying."

"I know. I know. I don't like it, but I won't let them harm him."

Ty knew his mother had been deeply saddened by what happened with Tom. Though she had never said so, Ty thought she blamed herself. He sensed that now she saw this as an opportunity to set things right, at least partially. Or maybe it was really just what any parent would do. Ty didn't know, but he feared that what she was planning might make things even worse for Tom. And all of them.

He massaged his temple. "Have you… talked to Richter about this?"

"No. And I won't."

"He could help us."

"I don't trust him."

"Why? He saved me in Zürich."

"There are things you don't know about him, Ty."

"Mom, to be exact, that covers pretty much everything about him."

The door opened, drawing panicked glares from both of them. Richter paused in the doorway. "Am I interrupting?"

Ty and his mother spoke simultaneously.

She said, "Yes."

Ty said, "No."

"Well," Richter said casually, "thank you for clarifying. Thomas has arrived."

Helen glanced at Ty, silently reminding him of what they had just talked about.

Richter continued, "Bishop is waiting by the elevator to escort you." He paused. "I assumed you would not want me to join you."

Helen marched toward the door, not meeting Richter's gaze. "You assumed correctly."

In the elevator, Bishop hit the button for basement level one and, when the doors opened, led Ty and his mother through a maze of abandoned cubicles. The dust on the desks was thick, and the floors were grimy. It gave Ty the impression of some post-apocalyptic office building.

Bishop seemed to read his expression.

"We typically work on the floors above ground. The lower levels are for more discreet operations."

At the far wall, Bishop stopped at a set of double doors and placed his hand on a palm reader. The door buzzed, and Bishop swung it open, revealing what looked to Ty like a wet lab. There were three rows of counter-height steel tables, all bolted to the floor. Ty could imagine microscopes sitting atop them and scientists moving samples around. But all of the equipment was gone.

The left-hand wall was lined with steel cabinets with glass doors. They too were empty.

Dead ahead, a woman in a black pantsuit was talking, waving her hands in the air at two men in suits who were listening. Ty assumed they were US Marshals. One laughed at the woman's joke, putting his hands on his waist, brushing back his jacket, revealing a sidearm in a holster.

Two marines stood by a stainless-steel door to what looked like a walk-in freezer.

"Sandy," Helen began, but he cut her off.

"I know, I know, Helen, but they requested the most secure room we have. What do you want—"

"You're not keeping him in a meat locker."

"We'll figure something out."

Ty was still sizing up the five armed guards. He didn't know what his mother was planning, but he did know it was likely to fail.

"Mom?"

"Yes," she said, voice level.

"I've decided. When this is over, I don't want to do that vacation. I want to stay right here in DC. Just hang out."

Bishop glanced between the two of them. "Is that some kind of code?"

"We'll see, Ty," she said, ignoring Bishop.

As they approached the freezer, one of the marines removed the metal pin on the door and pulled the long handle while the other took several paces back, hand on his sidearm. The three suited US Marshals took notice but seemed mostly unconcerned. They watched the door but continued their conversation.

At the threshold, Bishop stood while Ty and his mother entered. Ty was relieved when he felt the air, which was only slightly cooler than the room temperature outside. The freezer wasn't on, and hadn't been for a while. The inside was lined with metal racks, and sitting on one of them was Ty's mirror image, his twin brother Tom, who rose as the door closed behind Ty and their mother.

26

Ty watched as his mother strode forward, arms out, wrapping them around his brother.

"Are you okay?" she whispered.

"I'm fine," he replied, hugging her back tightly. When he released her, he glanced between Ty and their mother. "What's going on? They told me I was being transferred." He motioned around him, at the empty freezer and silver metal racks. "This is not what I was expecting."

Helen glanced back at Ty. "We're working on that."

Tom's eyebrows knitted together. "What does that mean?"

"It means," Helen said carefully, "that things are complicated."

"Complicated how?"

"Well, you know your brother works at CERN doing physics research. He works on a device called the Large Hadron Collider. It's a particle collider—"

"Mom, I know what the LHC is. I live in a federal prison, not under a rock."

She held a hand up. "I know, I know. I'm trying to put my thoughts together here. The point is that your brother made a discovery."

"What kind of discovery?"

"We can't say. Not yet. But it's important."

"So why am I here?"

"That's... well, we can't say that yet either."

He nodded, seeming resigned. Seeing that broke Ty's heart. Tom had changed. It was as if the fight had gone out of him. The brother Ty had grown up with would have demanded to know what was going on. Was it prison that had changed Tom? Or time? Time spent questioning his choices?

And that was the real difference between Ty and his brother: their choices. The thought reminded Ty of what Lars had said about life being a series of roads—of turns and exits taken and not taken, a web of choices that sews together a life. Ty and Tom had taken different roads at key points. And that had led them to very different places.

And inexplicably, those roads had converged again, leading both brothers here, and Ty wondered what was next and if there was a chance to repair the past, to redo those turns that had led his brother astray.

The three of them talked, then, about everything and nothing at all, passing time like families reunited often do, asking questions about how each other was doing, and listening, but most of all watching the reactions that told more than words revealed. Ty could tell his mother was tired. And that there was still that core of strength within his brother, despite some of it being worn away.

When Helen left, Tom eyed the closed door. "Think she's doing okay?"

"Yeah. I think so. She's just worried. About both of us."

"You worried?"

Ty shrugged, trying to play it cool.

"Just another day at the office, huh?"

Ty laughed. Some things never changed. His brother had his limitations, but he had always been able to see through Ty.

Tom shook his head. "Man, all this cloak-and-dagger stuff. It's wild." He eyed his brother. "Bet it's not what that big brain of yours thought you were signing up for at CERN."

"No. It's not. The last twenty-four hours… have been super weird."

There was another topic on Ty's mind, something he had wanted to discuss with Tom since the minute he had found out that his brother was coming here, something only the two of them could discuss, the one thing in the world only they understood, a shared hurt and desire that neither time nor choices had changed. "Dad's here."

Tom glanced up, clearly shocked. "In DC?"

"In this building."

"You've seen him? Have you talked to him?"

"He brought me here. From Zürich. He sort of... saved me."

Tom stood from the rack he had been sitting on and walked the length of the meat locker, then suddenly looked back at Ty. "Saved you from what?"

Ty realized what he had said then. "Nothing."

"Doesn't sound like nothing." He studied Ty for a long moment. "I thought Mom was the one I should be worried about. Maybe I was wrong."

"You've looked out for me enough."

"Is that how you see it?"

"That's how I see it."

"You blame yourself."

"I do."

"You shouldn't."

"I can't help it."

"You can. If you try. And you have to. Or else it'll eat you up inside, Ty. I'm telling you."

Ty stared at the floor. This was the conversation he had wanted to have with his brother for years, that he had rehearsed in his mind a hundred times. Maybe a thousand times. But now that it was happening, he couldn't find the words.

"You know what the most important thing is in prison?"

Ty stared at his brother.

"The past," Tom said. "Thinking about it. Obsessing about it. It's around every corner, as real as one of the guards—and the walls and fences that keep us confined. The past is what really traps a person."

"It's hard not to think about," Ty said.

"I would have done it with or without you. You dwelling on what happened doesn't do either of us any good. It'll just wear you down. The past is like a boat anchor for some people. They can't get free of it."

"It's like that for Mom and Dad."

"Yeah. Turns out are parents are human too, just like us."

"I can't just ignore the past."

"No. That's not what I'm saying. We've all got to learn from our past. That's the other thing I've realized from my time inside. If you don't, you'll never grow, never figure out who you really are. But I tell you what, Ty: once you learn from the past, you've gotta let it go. It can't do anything else for you. The future is all that matters." Tom glanced around at the meat locker. "And based on what I'm seeing, you're going to need all that brainpower for whatever is going on here."

27

In a small apartment in Oxford, England, Nora Brown stirred a cup of tea as she turned the page of a psychology textbook. Steam rose from the mug and drifted out the open window, over the hedgerows and past the old stone buildings like an apparition released into the night.

Nora reached out and pulled the Post-it pad closer. She jotted a note, then pulled off the yellow sticky and attached it to the page. The book was an advance copy of a colleague's latest work, which she had readily agreed to read and provide feedback on.

When she had made the commitment, Nora had expected a digital file delivered to her email. Instead, a courier had dropped the book off at her cramped office with a note from the professor's assistant, requesting that all feedback be in written form, which the aging scientist had become accustomed to over the past forty years.

If Nora had learned anything during her years at Oxford, it was that seniority conferred privilege and accommodation. And also, that new ideas were treasured as much as the old ways. To her, it was part of the charm of the place.

Her research in experimental psychology had initially brought her to Oxford. The facilities were world-class. Researchers were well supported, but she had stayed for one reason—the people. People who could challenge her ideas and make them better, people like her, who were on the cutting edge of psychology, people who were making discoveries that would change the world.

Her years at Oxford had been painful at times, but in her opinion, pain was often the price of growth. To her, it was worth it.

She had also come to Oxford not for what she could receive but for what she could give. Besides the research she had spent her life working on, her relationship with her students was her other great love. She hoped that she would be teaching at the storied university for as long as she was able.

In her idealized world, she imagined herself as a professor not unlike the older woman who had authored the textbook she was now reading—accomplished, hardworking, and perhaps a little bit quirky in her old age. Always open to new ideas in the field, but in some fashion, set in her ways. She certainly felt herself drifting in that direction, becoming inflexible to outside influence—including her mother's gentle prodding about why she wasn't dating anyone and if she ever saw herself moving back to DC and having children of her own.

At age thirty-five, Nora had to concede her mother's point: time was slipping away for her to have children—at least, without a surrogate and freezing her eggs. But she wasn't sure she wanted that. She had spent her twenties in graduate school and doing research, and now, in her mid-thirties, she had achieved much of what she had sought professionally: she was a teacher at a prestigious university, and she was working on a book that she believed would define her life's work. Those things were important to her too. But she knew she would have to make some big decisions about her life soon.

Behind her, the microwave beeped. She stood and retrieved the soup and blew on it as she turned another page, watching the steam from the bowl mingle with the wisps from the tea like a supernatural dance of ghosts, curling and dissolving in the yellow glow of the streetlamp through the window.

Twenty pages and five Post-it notes later, she closed the book, set the empty mug and soup bowl in the sink, and slung her backpack over her shoulder. Within ten minutes, she had arrived at her destination—an old stone building with limestone lintels and an oriel window over the entrance. It was typical Oxford architecture (another thing she loved about this place).

Next to the bike rack, two large tents loomed in the night. A banner with big block letters stretched across them with a message that said 24 *HOURS TO CURE CANCER*. Below hung a smaller sign that read *A COLLABORATION BETWEEN THE CENTRE FOR HUMAN GENETICS AND CRUK.* Nora recognized the acronym for Cancer Research UK, whose research she had tried to support as much as she could.

Under the tents, there were two long tables where half a dozen college-age students were working, calling out to passers-by, collecting samples, and typing away at their laptops.

A young man waved to Nora. "Excuse me! Could we get a sample, please? No blood required. Just a swab!"

She checked her watch. She was about twenty minutes early for her talk, and the volunteers seemed to be moving the line along pretty quickly. She shrugged. "Sure, why not."

Soon, Nora was standing with her mouth open, watching a girl with strawberry hair reach in with a long swab, collecting cells from the inside of her cheek.

Beside her, a young man was typing at a laptop. He spoke without looking up, his accent faintly Canadian. "Just need your ID."

Nora handed him her Bod card, and he swiped it, then glanced quickly to make sure what popped up on his screen matched the card.

"MD and a PhD, eh?"

"Couldn't settle on one," Nora said.

"And how many times have you said that joke?"

"Too many," Nora said, laughing.

"You're all set, ma'am. Or should I say, doctor-doctor."

"You shouldn't say."

He laughed then. "Thanks for helping us cure cancer. Have a good night."

Inside, Nora made her way to the lecture hall, plugged her laptop in at the podium, and pulled up her slides. As the room started to fill, she could feel the nerves building in her stomach. Luckily, she had a technique to deal with it, one she had learned in high school from the mother of a childhood friend.

Nora had grown up in the Georgetown area of Washington, DC, and her next-door neighbor had been the same age as her, a brilliant boy who was almost always lost in thought and quick with a joke, though usually corny. His smile never failed to melt her heart. Growing up, he was her best friend and first kiss and, though she tried with all her might to resist, her childhood crush.

But it was his mother who had perhaps exerted the most influence on Nora. She was an evolutionary biologist and was one of Nora's heroes growing up. Helen Klein was, quite possibly, just a little bit, part of the reason Nora had pursued a career in science. Even today, she still remembered Helen's words on public speaking, how she'd explained the fear most everyone felt as a simple function of evolutionary biology, how kindness quieted the mind and suppressed the body's natural fight-or-flight instinct. The technique wasn't hard for Nora—kindness was a sort of true north for her.

As the rows of the auditorium filled, she focused on that sense of kindness, on the knowledge that she was here to help people, to share ideas that could make them better, ideas that would help them see and understand their world. Because that was exactly what she was about to reveal.

She stepped to the lectern and spoke into the microphone. "I'd like to start with a simple question. I would wager that it is not the question you're expecting—not the question that has ever been asked in the hallowed halls of this institution, where ideas big and small have been taught for almost a thousand years."

Nora watched as the audience looked up from their laptops and mobile phones. She had them now.

"The question is, when you buy a major appliance, what always accompanies it?"

She smiled. Some in the audience laughed. A few frowned. Across the lecture hall, she saw confusion, curiosity, and most of all, what she wanted: undivided attention.

At the back of the room, the don of St John's College leaned against the wall, arms folded, wearing a tweed jacket, a wry smile forming on his lips.

Nora lifted her arms. "Anyone? What always comes with a refrigerator or a dishwasher—or if we should be so lucky in this quaint ancient little village we all love so much—a washer and dryer? Guesses? Anyone?"

"Headaches!" someone shouted from the back to a few snickers.

"Payments," a young woman muttered from the second row.

Nora smiled. "Yes, maybe it comes with headaches and payments. But that's not what this is about. And trust me, study hard and have faith and know that the poverty of your student years will lift." She cocked her head. "Well, at some point."

Nora paced away from the lectern. "So, what comes with any appliance? A microwave. Even a new mobile phone or TV."

"Delivery!" a student shouted.

"Not always," Nora replied gently. "What's in the box? It's always in the box."

From the front row, one of her students supplied the answer she was looking for. "A manual."

Nora pointed at the woman. "Correct. An instruction manual. Granted, we don't always need it. And at the risk of raising the ire of the university's gender sensitivity group, I daresay some of the males in the audience would admit to actively resisting reading any provided manual—even in an hour of extreme need."

Laughter rippled across the audience like a wave at a baseball game.

Nora held a finger in the air. "The EP department has experimental data to support that supposition, by the way." That revived the laughter a second longer.

"So, every major appliance comes with an instruction manual. It explains how to use the device, how to care for it, and even how to do repairs. And where to get help."

Nora clicked to the next slide.

"The thing that's strange to me is that while our refrigerator or microwave or mobile phone might have a big impact on our daily lives, it is, to put it simply, our own minds that have a far greater impact on how we perceive the world around us, how happy we are, and how much success we find in life. And yet, we are never given any sort of instruction manual for our own minds." Nora nodded. "Granted, we are given pieces—random bits of advice and clues that reveal how our mind works and how the world around us impacts our thinking. When it comes to our own minds, we are given an instruction manual of sorts, with pages missing and out of order, and written in a language we don't understand."

She moved back to the lectern and clicked to the next slide. "I have made it my life's work to change that. And *that work* is what I want to talk about tonight. An instruction manual for the mind. A book that shows us how to use our minds to find greater happiness and success. We all deserve that. Indeed, I believe that success and happiness are the *birthright* of every human being. And that's exactly what I've entitled this instruction manual for the mind: *The Birthright*. If I'm right, it has the potential to improve human life for everyone on Earth. And everyone in the future."

28

WRAL News Video Transcript
Video Title: You May Be a Billionaire. No, Seriously!

Transcript:

[Video opens with the WRAL News Studio with two anchors sitting at a wide desk]

Anchor Taryn Scott: "If you're feeling like you need some good news for a change, well, you might just be in for some."

Anchor Byron Nelson: "That's right, Taryn. While we all feel like the past few years have been filled with catastrophes no one expected—or wanted to see happen—there may be a ray of sunlight on the horizon. Our very own Paige Randall is in the field and has more."

[Video switches to a female reporter in her late twenties with black hair. She's standing in the consulting area of a pharmacy where a man in a white coat is swabbing the inside of a female customer's mouth.]

Reporter Paige Randall: "Good evening, Byron. I'm here at the Walgreens on Creedmoor Road where local residents are getting swabbed for a DNA test—and getting paid for it. You heard that correctly: every person that visits a Walgreens or CVS here in the Triangle area will be paid one hundred dollars for simply providing a saliva sample. But that's not even the best part. For one lucky person—and possibly more—getting this simple DNA test could mean a windfall of billions. You see, this testing is actually part of a worldwide search for the heirs of a recently deceased billionaire. Although details aren't known about the estate conducting the search, we do know that the person was of advanced age and was very well traveled, hence the broad reach of this campaign."

Anchor Taryn Scott: "So, Paige, I just have to ask what I think a lot of viewers are probably thinking: 'What's the catch?'"

Reporter Paige Randall: "Fair question, Taryn, and that's part of what makes this program so interesting: there is no catch. The one hundred dollars is paid by Walgreens or CVS at the time the sample is collected—either with a store gift card or a prepaid VISA charge card. There's absolutely no commitment, and according to a professor at Harvard Law School who has read the contract, the data can't be used against you in a court of law or even turned over to the government. Your only commitment is to provide a contact method so that you can be notified if you're an heir to the billions."

The reporter smiles. "There is one thing to know: as soon as even one heir is identified, the program will end—the one hundred dollars for submitting a sample will be gone for good."

Anchor Byron Nelson: "Well, Paige, if I had to guess, I'd say this is going to be a pretty popular program. It amounts to free money and the chance for more."

Reporter Paige Randall: "You're right about that, Byron. The parking lot at this Walgreens here on Creedmoor Road began filling around four o'clock, shortly after the program was announced on social media, and as you can see now—"

[Camera pans to a line inside the store stretching past shelves full of supplements.]

"—there is a line, but it's moving pretty quickly. We were just told a few minutes ago that anyone arriving near closing time will be given a sample kit that they can complete at home and drop off in the morning."

Video Comments

NCSU82: "No way. This has got to be a joke."

MorpheusBluePill: "I had the exact same thought. Had to check the date to make sure it wasn't April first. It's not."

JayZDax: "Stay home guys. This visa gift card sure feels real, and I got three kits for my roommates, so I hope they don't find the family members for a long, long time. I'm going to a different drug store in the morning—these fools probably won't know we're double dipping."

WildBillCassidy: "You people are idiots. This is probably an FBI operation to catch a serial killer. Half of you are going to end up in prison for crimes you didn't commit."

29

Ty had dinner with his mother and Richter in the briefing room. He was beyond exhausted, having slept only a few hours the previous night and a few hours on the plane. None of it had been restful sleep. He sensed that both of his parents were tired as well. He had thought that spending the day together might lessen the tension between them. He was wrong. The exhaustion seemed to bring it back to the surface, like a body that had been thrown out to sea but kept washing up on shore.

On the whole, Ty was glad when the marine came to show them to their sleeping quarters. There was no mention of leaving the building, and in the back of his mind, Ty wondered if they could leave without permission. Adding to that fear was the fact that the sleeping accommodation the marine led Ty to was very much like a prison cell. It was a small, windowless room that had probably been a basement office at some point. There was a narrow double bed pushed along the wall with sheets so thin they looked nearly translucent against the cheap mattress. Folded at the end of the bed lay a dark-brown blanket that was rough to the touch. Ty felt like it could have been a prop on an Old West television show. It was all clearly military issue, and old.

There was a sink and a cheap vanity on one wall and a desk next to it with a rolling chair. In the corner stood a giant water jug with a round metal dispenser full of small clear cups.

When the door closed and he was alone, Ty lay on the bed and closed his eyes, letting the fatigue wash over him. The last time he had lain down to sleep had been in Geneva, at his apartment, which was now gone. That felt like a lifetime ago.

Since then, he had reconnected with his father and brother

and was close to seeing the culmination of his life's work. It was like a lifetime of experiences had been crammed into a single day.

Against his will, his mind drifted back to Penny. He wondered if she was as safe as he was (if he was, in fact, safe, that is).

That and other questions ran through his mind like a freight train he couldn't stop, the thoughts driving sleep away. He wondered what the code was that Bishop had mentioned, the code that might activate the quantum radio. More than that, he wondered what the device did. Could it be dangerous? Had he inadvertently discovered the means to end the human race?

Other questions dogged him. Who were the other two genomic matches? How were the four people connected? Logic dictated that they were. It was all a big puzzle, but Ty had no idea what the big picture was.

A knock at the door—three sharp raps—made him sit up, the exhaustion swatted away like a swarm of flies.

"Come in," he said, voice scratchy.

From the tone of the knocking, he expected a marine to enter. Instead, Richter stepped inside and swung the door closed.

"Am I interrupting?"

Ty smiled and looked around the spartan room. "Interrupting what?"

"Your thoughts." Richter sat in the chair at the desk and rolled it closer. "I've often thought that was the most important thing a person can do when they're alone."

Ty studied the man who had given him life, marveling at how alike they were and yet how little he knew about him. "Yeah. Me too, actually."

"I suspect I know what you're thinking."

"And what's that?"

"Right now, you're likely thinking about Penny. Her safety. And the other, as yet unidentified genomes. How they fit in. But most of all, you are entertaining a dangerous type of thought."

Ty studied the older man, surprised at the words.

"Doubt," Richter said.

Before Ty could react, Richter stood and turned away. "You're starting to doubt whether what you found is indeed a beneficial discovery, whether it might, in fact, be the means to our end. In short, you're doubting whether the device should be built at all."

Ty stared, awestruck. It was like the man was some sort of supernatural being with the power to read minds, as if he had taken an X-ray of Ty's thoughts and read it as casually as someone might browse the Sunday morning paper over coffee.

Ty asked the obvious question: "Haven't you wondered the same thing?"

"No."

"Why not?"

"Because there is no use in it. The device will be created. By us, or by others."

"How do you know?"

"I know it because I believe it is the shape of history, just as discovering the atom was humanity's destiny. The discovery of organized quantum data is no different."

After a pause, Richter went on. "The question is, who will harness its power first? Take the atom, for example. Its potential was long theorized. And then, in the 1940s, that breakthrough was needed—to end a war. Back then, the world's superpowers were racing to develop the atom bomb. Now we are in a similar race—to develop a quantum radio. Just like then, the outcome will change the balance of power on Earth. Imagine if our side hadn't invented the bomb first."

Ty was a bit surprised by Richter's words. "Our side?"

Richter cocked his head. "Our side indeed. The side of people who want to see peace in the world, good overcome evil, kindness conquer hate. That is always a side, and it transcends nationality and everything else for that matter."

A silence stretched out.

Ty didn't know if it was the fatigue relaxing his guard or sheer curiosity, but he asked a question that he had wondered about his entire life: "Did your father fight in the war?"

Ty knew nothing about his grandfather, though it wasn't for

lack of looking for answers. His internet searches for Gerhard Richter's family history had turned up very little—and nothing about the man's father.

"I believe so."

Ty studied Richter, waiting for an explanation, but the man's face was a mask. "You don't know?"

"Not for certain."

"He didn't talk about it?"

"We've never spoken."

For a brief moment, Ty saw himself in his father. And then, he wondered how anyone who had gone through what he had—growing up without a father present—could do that to their own child.

"You never knew him?" Ty asked.

"No. I grew up wondering about him. Searching for answers. A very painful endeavor. The only thing worse, I later discovered, was knowing that your own sons and daughter were wondering about you and not being able to do anything about it."

A million questions flashed through Ty's mind.

Richter spoke before he could ask the first. "I believe my father was a Russian army officer. I don't know much more. The time in which I was conceived was, to put it simply, chaotic. Records were destroyed. Secrets were a way of life."

"Did you—" Ty began, his mind grasping about for the right question, but Richter cut him off.

The man held out a thick manila folder and said, "Speaking of records, here is the file on Tanaka."

Ty took it and set it on the bed, ignoring it. "Your father—"

"Is lost to the sands of time, I'm afraid," Richter said, tone flat. "There's nothing more to say on that matter, Tyson. But there is something I need to tell you about the file. Please look at it. Scan the pages."

Ty shook his head and picked the file up off the bed and flipped it open, mentally trying to find a way to steer the conversation back to Richter's past. He glanced at the photo of Tanaka, who looked to be slightly older than Ty. He had a scar that ran from his nose to his chin and eyes that somehow seemed both kind and hard.

He turned the pages, which were filled with long black boxes over the text.

"It's been redacted. Half of it's blacked out."

"Much of his work is classified."

"They want us to work on this project but don't want to share information?"

"It's their way. I don't really blame them. There's likely little reason for us to know many of the details in that file."

"You know about that. Withholding information."

"I know about necessity."

Ty continued flipping through the pages, fatigue and annoyance growing inside him.

Richter sat back in the chair. "Are you sure you've never come into contact with him?"

"Not that I know of. Certainly not in person. Maybe online or something." Ty set the file on the bed. "You didn't come here to give me this. One of the marines could have."

"True."

"So?"

"I have other news. Which I thought you would… which I felt you would not want to hear from a stranger."

Ty snorted. Twenty-four hours ago, this man—his father— had been a stranger to him. What he was now, Ty wasn't sure. But he was pretty sure he knew what the news was. "The DNA tests are back," Ty said.

"Correct."

"Penny?" Ty asked, feeling the nervousness grow in his stomach.

"She isn't a match for any of the four."

"And what about me?"

"You are indeed a match. Thomas is not."

For a moment, Ty tried to reflect on how he felt about the news. He didn't know if it was the exhaustion or simply how odd the situation was, but he couldn't quite wrap his head around it.

Some… entity had broadcast his genome… but from where—or when—and why?

It was incredible.

He was one of the four. He was at the center of this.

Until that moment, he hadn't realized the truth: he wanted it to be his genome that was being broadcast. He wanted to be in the middle of whatever was about to happen. Even if it was dangerous. He sensed that on the other side was something remarkable, something worth risking everything for.

"What happens to Tom now?" he asked quietly.

"For now, he'll stay here."

"Why? They don't need him. He's not a match."

"You are correct. On both points."

"They're keeping him as a hostage, aren't they? To control us. Me, you, and Mom. He's leverage against us."

Richter's silence was all the confirmation Ty needed.

"So, we *are* prisoners here."

"Every person exists within confines of some kind. Only some realize it." Richter studied Ty. "Your problem is simple: perspective."

"You sound like Mom. To her, it's all about your attitude."

"Attitude and perspective are two sides of the same coin. Your mother's advice is wise. My point is this: it does not do to dwell on that which you do not have. You find strength—and freedom—in what you have."

"I have nothing."

"You *have* a bad attitude and the wrong perspective. Sleep may remedy both. And provide an opportunity."

"Opportunity for what?"

"What have you wanted ever since the day Thomas arrived at prison?"

"His freedom," Ty said almost automatically.

"And now you're a prisoner of sorts. But if you study the situation, you might find that fate has given you the means to the end you've long sought. It's just a matter of perspective."

Ty was about to ask what that meant when Richter rose from the cheap chair and walked to the door. He paused there and turned to Ty. When he spoke again, his voice was soothing and rhythmic, as if he were almost singing the words he was saying, as though reciting a hymn from memory.

It was the same tone Richter had used that morning, when he told Ty what the quantum broadcast was, the makeup of the file and genomes, when he had given him the means to stake his place on the team.

"Think about what I've said. And study the file on Tanaka." Richter nodded at the folder. "It can tell you more than you think. Consider what it is: a collection of reports, assessments, and performance reviews. But it is far more. It is the sum of a life. If you connect the dots, if you see through the pages, if you study it hard enough, you'll see the most important thing of all. The shape of a life. It's more than what a person did here on Earth. It's what they leave behind. I'm not talking about buildings or trinkets that will wilt in the sands of time. I'm referring to the only thing that really matters: people. To me, the sum of a life is how they've impacted the people around them and the strangers they've never met. Did they make us better? Did they leave the next generation better off? When I read the lieutenant's file, that's what I see—a person trying to create a better world. A person who has paid a high price in that pursuit."

Richter stared at Ty, eyes burning. "I believe Tanaka would love to turn the page on his past—to see a way out. He's thirty-seven. There's still time for him, but it's running out. Maybe that's what this is all about. Time will tell."

Richter gripped the door handle. "Sleep well, Tyson. And study the file. *Backward and forward.*"

When the door closed, Ty looked at the file. He was almost certain that in the words his father had just spoken, there was a code, a deeper meaning he was meant to find. And it was somewhere in that file.

30

Deep in the DARPA facility, the Covenant agent made their way to a bathroom, slipped into a stall, and locked the door. Working quickly, the agent removed seven small plastic and glass pieces from the hidden pockets inside their coat and assembled them. The moment the secure satellite phone booted, the agent opened an app and furiously typed out an encrypted message:

1 GENOMIC SUBJECT SECURED. 1 INCOMING. QUANTUM RADIO BEING BUILT. MAKING ARRANGEMENTS TO EXTRACT. STAND BY FOR DETAILS.

When the message was sent, the agent disassembled the phone, wiped down each piece with toilet paper, then hid the parts in the metal box that held the extra rolls of toilet paper.

The agent assumed that the transmission would be detected. Things would change after that. A search would begin. But it wouldn't matter. It would all be over soon.

31

Two hours after Ty fell asleep, Kato Tanaka was sitting in a conference room one floor above, trying to comprehend what he was being told.

The man in the room was a civilian working at the Department of Defense, but for all intents and purposes he might as well have been speaking another language.

"You're telling me I'm part of some kind of experiment?" Kato asked. "But it's not an experiment you have control over?"

The man with the thick glasses cocked his head and peered out with eyes enlarged by the curved glass. "That's... technically accurate."

"Dr. Bishop, why am I here? What do you want from me?"

"We just want you to do your job. To safeguard American interests. It may require sacrifices."

"Sir, what *specifically* does that mean?"

The man leaned back in his chair. "Well..."

The door opened, and another man strode in. He was tall, with a muscular face. He stared at Kato, not breaking eye contact. Military—that was Kato's first thought.

Still not looking away, the man spoke with a German accent. "I'll take it from here, Sandy."

When they were alone, the man placed his hands in his pockets and spoke slowly, almost rhetorically. "You're an amateur historian, are you not, Lieutenant?"

"Yes, sir, I suppose you could say that."

"Why do you like history?"

"Sir, I believe understanding our past helps us create a better future."

"Wise words," the man whispered. "Would you like to know why you're here?"

"Very much, sir."

"You're here to write history."

"Sir?"

"You're here for the same reason you joined the Navy. The same reason you went to BUD/S school. You're a student of history because you know there are pivotal moments that have the power to turn the world, to change it forever. You want to be part of those moments. You don't want credit. You want the responsibility. You want to have the weight of the world upon you when that very world hangs in the balance."

Kato felt as if the man had just looked into his soul and read it like a private journal, thoughts Kato himself had harbored his entire life but had never seen clearly until that moment.

A long silence stretched out.

"Sir, to whom am I speaking?"

"My name is Gerhard Richter."

"Sir, would you mind telling me your rank and branch?"

"I have no rank or branch. Only a role to play."

"Mr. Richter, what is that role?"

"Let's just say I'm a manager."

"Manager of what, sir?"

"History."

Kato opened his mouth to ask a question, but the man spoke first. "What would you like, Lieutenant?"

"Sir?"

"If you could leave here right now and go anywhere in the world and do anything you wanted, what would you do?"

Kato's answer came instantly. "I would go home and see my wife and son."

"What about your court-martial? Would you like for it to go away? That can be arranged."

"No, sir. I'd like to stand trial and have my day in court. Sir."

For the first time, the man smiled. It was barely a smile, the slight tugging at the corners of his mouth, an expression that quickly faded. "You cannot go home, Lieutenant, but you can see your wife and your son, Akito. I will arrange for them to be brought here."

"Thank you, sir. If I may ask, what are you asking in return?"

"Nothing."

Kato nodded. "With all due respect, sir, I would like a little more clarity on that point."

"It's very simple, Lieutenant. I believe that when the time comes, when history hangs in the balance, a man like you won't have to be asked to do the right thing. I think you only need to be reminded of what you're fighting for. We all do, every now and then."

32

That morning, Nora was showering when she heard a knock on the door. She ran her hands through her hair, trying to rinse the shampoo out, expecting the knocking to stop. It was likely Mrs. Whitcomb from next door, and she had likely run out of sugar for her tea again. Nora was happy to help her, and to lend her as much sugar as the widowed retiree needed, but it just so happened that her morning shower was where she did some of her best thinking, and on this particular morning she was in the middle of a very good thought, one she planned to incorporate into the manuscript of *The Birthright*.

The knock came again, booming this time, the sound loud enough to make Nora open her eyes for a fraction of a second before she shut them again, wincing from the stinging shampoo. It was a very insistent knock, a very non-Mrs. Whitcomb knock. A knock that said, *We are not going away.*

A knock like the police might make. Or the fire department.

She finished rinsing the shampoo off, turned the squeaking knobs on the wall until the showerhead sputtered and shut off, then stepped out of the porcelain tub just in time for another bout of knocking to echo through the small apartment.

"Dr. Brown!"

"Just a minute!" she called back, pulling a towel around her, worrying that whoever the man was, he had already woken half the building—and done it calling her name no less, so there would be little doubt who had brought the ruckus to this quiet corner of Oxford.

Nora jogged out of the bathroom, into the bedroom, hair dripping on the rug as she went.

A fire. That was the only real explanation for the disturbance and how insistent they were.

She swung the door open, revealing two men and a woman, all dressed in police uniforms.

From their expressions, Nora got the impression that waking the neighbors was now the least of her worries.

33

In a homeless shelter on Lafayette Street in downtown Nashville, Maria Santos sat in the administrator's office, trying to keep her face from showing the fear building inside of her.

The man behind the desk was in his late fifties, though his wrinkled, sun-damaged face looked older. In the group sessions, she had heard him share his story, which somewhat mirrored her own: early success in a band that seemed magical at first, as though everything they touched turned to gold. A solo career that looked even more promising, then personal struggles that he couldn't shake. For Maria, those struggles—and a string of bad luck—had landed her here, homeless and trying to stay clean.

But she was working night and day with every fiber of her being to get back on her feet.

Maria didn't want to reclaim the fame and fortune she once had. She only wanted to be happy. To feel whole. To get up every morning filled with purpose and do something she loved. To be free of addiction and have a safe place to lay her head every night.

She had made a lot of progress toward those goals, but it was taking time. And time was something she sensed she was running out of. The look on the homeless shelter administrator's face confirmed that. So did his words.

"I don't make the rules, Maria. You either get a job by the end of the day, or you have to go. I'm sorry. I really am."

"I've looked."

"I know."

"There's nothing out there."

"You'll have to look harder. It doesn't matter what you're doing. Washing dishes, cleaning buildings—"

"Tried that. The cleaning companies all want a background check—and a current address—and they don't like this one."

He nodded, gaze fixed on his desk. "I hear you. I do."

"Can I work here?"

"You know you can't work here. It doesn't work like that."

"Why not?"

"The rules."

"You make the rules."

"I don't, Maria. I wish I did. I just work here."

"You run the place."

"That's true. But I don't make the rules. The people who fund the Music City Rescue Mission do. And they say you get two weeks, and if you don't have a job, you have to go."

She exhaled, mind searching for the words that might save her, finding none. "There are no jobs," she whispered. "Not for somebody like me. Retailers, they're barely hanging on. Can't even keep their family members on. I can't get some gig job—I don't have a computer, or a car, or anything else. My prepaid phone is almost empty."

"You can sing. Get a job—"

She put her face in her hands. "I can't do that."

"I've heard you."

"That's not the problem. I can't be in that environment, around that temptation. Not right now. Not until I'm stronger." She looked up at him. "You know what that's like."

"Yeah. I do." He stood up and motioned to the door. "Maria... just get out there and find something. Okay? Go on now."

He didn't meet her gaze. She saw regret in his face. He knew what he was doing. And she thought he was actually sad about it.

She stood and took a step toward the door but didn't leave. There was something she had to say before she did. Something important. "I just want to say..."

The man tensed up, anticipating what was coming.

"Thank you," she said, trying to make eye contact. "I really do appreciate what you tried to do for me. What you did."

Before he could respond, she made her way to the stairs,

descended to the ground floor, and walked to the large open room where twenty bunk beds were lined up in rows. At the bed where she had stayed for the last two weeks, she grabbed her backpack, opened the zipper, and peered in, making sure the notebook was there.

The worn, spiral-bound pad wasn't her only possession in this world (she had a few more), but it was her most treasured. She had bought it at a dollar store, likely in a pack that cost a dollar and twenty-five cents, and she had been filling it for six years now, scrawling notes and ideas, lyrics and scenes for a new kind of art, a fusion of music, story, and augmented reality she called *Worlds & Time*. It was her opus. At times, she felt more like she was discovering *Worlds & Time* than creating it. In those moments, Maria got the sense that this work had always been inside of her, waiting to be unearthed. To her, the notebook and the cheap ink pen, with its frayed end she had chewed, were more like the tools of an archaeologist: a trowel and a brush. With each stroke of the pen, she cleared away more of what hid this work of art waiting to be discovered. When fully realized, Maria was certain that it would reveal deep truths about the human race, enabling people to see the world more clearly—and to change the world around them in ways they never thought possible. That was the potential she saw in the notebook. That's what it meant to her. Everyone else just saw a used, frayed notebook full of scribblings. To her, it represented her future. And perhaps her only chance at a happy future.

When Maria was a child, her mother had said something that had stuck with her for her entire life: "This world will try to take everything from you, Maria. But they can't take what's in your mind. You guard your thoughts. Someday, it may be all you've got."

The ragged notebook was full of her thoughts. And she indeed intended to guard it with everything she had.

She took one of the gallon Ziploc bags out of the backpack's small pocket and slipped it around the notebook, just in case it rained today. Or tonight—if she had to sleep outside. And she probably would.

She exited the building onto a concrete porch with stained, cracking steps that led down to the sidewalk along Lafayette Street, which was bustling with morning traffic.

A guy with a shaved head and a white T-shirt and tats up and down his arms was leaning against the metal railing at the base of the stairs, smoking a cigarette.

"Hey," he called as she descended the stairs.

Maria ignored him.

"You want to make some money?" he asked in a Russian accent.

On any other day, she would have walked right on by. Today, she stopped with her back to him.

"Takes less than a minute. Pay you twenty bucks."

She felt the rage building inside of her. She took a deep breath. Then another. The anger would pass. She had come to see her rage as a demon inside of her. If she let it burn out and didn't act on it, she would be fine. It would die down. That demon had dragged her into the trouble she was in, and she was done letting it control her. She told herself she was in control of her rage demon. She just needed time. Time was toxic for it. Time smothered its fire.

But his next words were like gasoline on the flames burning inside her.

"All you do is open your mouth."

She turned, and she didn't see the man. She didn't see anything. Maria marched toward the sound of his voice, the words she couldn't make out, and she swung at him, her fist flying, but he was faster. His forearm flew up, stopping her blow, connecting just beyond her wrist, the pain in her arm like a lightning strike. He grabbed her other arm and shouted, "Hey, hey, hey! What's wrong with you?"

She was getting ready to spit in his face when he spun her around, trapped her arms against her body, and put one of his arms around her, then reached in his pocket for something. She rocked back and forth, trying to get free, but the little troll was stronger than he looked. She expected him to draw out a knife, and was about to scream when he held out a clear plastic bag in front of her. It had a CVS logo on it and a tube inside that held a long Q-tip. There was a page with three illustrations showing a person placing the swab in their mouth, then placing the swab in the tube, and finally sealing the bag.

"You just wipe it in your mouth. Twenty bucks!"

"Let me go."

When he released her, she took three steps away from him.

"You're crazy," he muttered.

She studied his face. One skill she'd picked up on the street was sizing people up. It had saved her life a few times. And it was crucial in any negotiation. She sensed that twenty bucks was a lowball offer.

"Fifty bucks." She practically spat the words.

"Forty."

"Fifty."

He threw the bag at her feet. "Forty-five. Be glad you're gettin' that."

She knew his type. Had dealt with them all her life. He wouldn't let her set the price. He'd walk away first. It was a power thing for men like him. He had to have the final say, had to set the terms to feel like he was in control.

If she could, she would have walked away. If she had forty-five dollars in her pocket and a place to sleep tonight, she would have turned and left. But she didn't.

So she bent over and picked up the bag.

34

Kato stood in the center of the windowless room, watching the solid wood door, anxiously waiting for it to open, listening for the slightest sound, any hint that Joan and Akito had arrived. He imagined hearing his son's laughter or the boy asking his mother a question as they walked down the narrow halls of the nearly deserted building, the soft sound drifting in through the door. But it had been utterly silent thus far. Kato wondered if there had been a problem. If Joan had declined to meet with him; if she had refused to let him see his son.

In the middle of the room was a group of cheap, dusty furniture: a fabric couch, a coffee table with nothing on top, and two matching chairs. The decor reminded Kato of a doctor's office—or more likely, the waiting room of a government office building, which was probably where the furnishings had come from, at the end of their useful life, discarded to be thrown into a landfill, only to be sucked into this black hole of a location where they hadn't seen the light of day since. This was a sort of place out of time, a tomb hidden away from the world.

Beyond the door, Kato heard the faint hint of the sound he had been waiting for: Akito's singsong voice. "Mommy, where is the people?"

A pause, then he pressed on. "Where they go?"

"Be quiet, Akito," she said, voice hushed.

Akito had always been a curious child. Every new discovery sparked a dozen questions from the boy. Kato thought that trait would serve him well in life. And possibly get him in some trouble, but sometimes a person's passions had a way of doing that.

The door opened, and a uniformed marine held the handle just long enough for Joan and Akito to step inside before closing it.

Kato's wife stared at him, eyes filled with a mix of anger, fear, and something he thought might be relief—perhaps at the fact that he was here or maybe that he was alive (he didn't know what they had told her to get her to come).

She held Akito in front of her, her hands on his chest.

Kato hadn't seen them in person for nearly seven months. His son, who was almost four now, appeared to have aged years. He was taller, his face more mature—more like Kato's face, except for the wicked scar that ran from his nose to his chin.

If there was one thing Kato liked about being a father, it was how his son looked at him—like no other person on Earth. Kato had gotten the scar two years before his son came into the world. Akito had never known him without the scar. And when he looked at his father, he didn't see a monster. Just the opposite. He saw a protector. A playmate. A provider.

Akito had once run a finger down Kato's face and said, "Daddy got a boo-boo." And that was all it was to him.

In time, the child would see it differently, but now, he stared up at his father with innocent, loving eyes, glittering with excitement that was spreading across his face. He broke free from his mother's grasp and ran into Kato's arms, yelling, "Daddy! Daddy!"

Kato hugged him tight and rocked him side to side, never taking his eyes off of Joan, who stood by the door, unmoving.

During his past deployments, they had talked via video conference. That had helped Kato get through them. Joan had refused to talk to him during his last deployment. That had weighed on Kato. It just may have been one of the things that had gotten him into the trouble he was in.

"Where is the people go, Daddy?" Akito asked.

"They all went home, little one."

"Why?"

"Their work was done."

"What work?"

Kato smiled as he sat on the couch, setting Akito in his lap. Joan sat in the chair diagonally from him, farthest away.

"All kinds of work. Some are wizards that make computers do things."

"Wizards!"

"That's right. It's like magic, only with robots and computers. Some make sure things get to where they need to go."

"Like you, Daddy."

"Sort of like me. They're all trying to keep us safe. Their families too." Kato looked at Joan. "Because they'd do anything for them."

She glanced away from him and spoke quietly. "They put us in a van. Without windows. In the back, like we were delivery boxes. They played music so we couldn't even hear where we were going." She paused. "It wasn't a black bag over our heads, but it did make me wonder: what did you do this time?"

"I haven't done anything."

"Is this about the court-martial?"

"It's not that."

Akito looked at his mother. "What's wrong, Mommy?"

"Nothing."

The door opened, and Gerhard Richter stepped inside. When he spoke, the thick German accent was gone, replaced by a neutral American accent, the type that didn't place him anywhere. Perhaps even more surprising was the warm smile on his face, a sharp contrast to the cold, expressionless man Kato had met the night before.

"Please, pardon the interruption, ma'am." Richter held out his hands. "Just wanted to pop in here and say something we rarely get a chance to say to the families of the folks working on this project."

Richter held Joan's gaze a second.

"Thank you."

She nodded, clearly surprised.

"The work Kato is doing here could very likely change the world, ma'am. I'm not just being grandiose. I mean it—what he's doing is that important. I know the work has been trying, especially lately, and I want you to know that *we know* that military spouses and children bear some of that weight too, not just the folks wearing the uniforms. I just wanted to tell you personally: we see you, we recognize your sacrifice, and we thank you." Richter nodded. "Well, that's it. That's all I wanted to say. Again, pardon the interruption, and thank you again."

When Richter left, some of Joan's anger seemed to leave with him. The hardness in her eyes had softened, and when she looked at Kato, he thought he saw a shadow of who she was before, in the years before his troubles started.

35

That night, Ty read Lieutenant Kato Tanaka's file cover to cover. Every single word.

The trouble was, despite having so many pages, there simply weren't that many words. For the most part, the file was redacted. It was page after page of long black boxes. And when Ty had finished reading the file, that was what Tanaka remained to him: a black box. Perhaps the only thing he knew for sure was that both of their genomes had been broadcast via the quantum radio transmissions.

They shared a bond, but what was it?

He paced the room, hoping the exercise would focus his mind. It didn't.

He sat on the narrow bed and again opened the folder and read the pages until he was so tired the words began to blur. In his sleep-deprived, nearly delirious state, the black letters seemed to morph together and march over the long black bars of redaction like ants on a log.

He was getting nowhere. He was too tired to even process what he was reading.

He set the file aside and let his body fall back to the bed, thinking, *I'll just close my eyes for a second.*

Ty woke in his clothes.

Above, the lights buzzed, a bright beam like a hospital exam room. And that's exactly how he felt: like a patient after surgery. Sore all over, mind fuzzy, disoriented.

Without a window in the small room, there was no way to know what time it was.

He attempted to get up, but his body wouldn't cooperate. He rose a few inches and flopped back onto the thin mattress.

As he lay there, he realized that although his body was numb, his mind was refreshed, and it instantly went to the words Richter had said to him last night, the speech Ty instinctively felt contained a code.

The lines ran through his mind, like numbers of a combination lock, as though every possibility was a turn of the tumblers waiting to fall into place, to unlock whatever the man was trying to tell him.

Study the file on Tanaka, Richter had said.

It can tell you more than you think.

... connect the dots.

... see through the pages.

... study it hard enough, you'll see the most important thing of all.

... turn the page on his past—to see a way out. He's thirty-seven. There's still time for him, but it's running out.

... Study the file. Backward and forward.

In the clarity after sleep, Ty was certain that the lines contained the key to an elaborate puzzle.

A code hidden in the file.

He tried to sit up again, and this time his body responded, though his back ached. He flipped through the file, studying every page that mentioned time. The years of Tanaka's deployments—

And then Ty saw it.

Richter had said Tanaka was thirty-seven.

But he wasn't. Kato Tanaka was only twenty-nine years old. What did it mean? The difference was eight. And the two ages added to sixty-six. Ty flipped through the file again, looking for instances of any of those four numbers. There were a few, but none that seemed significant.

He rubbed his eyelids. He needed some water. And to use the restroom. And another year of sleep.

He stared at the file, trying to see it another way—a different perspective. That was part of what his father was trying to tell him, Ty was certain of that. Whatever that was, it was in the file. Ty was close. He sensed that. He just couldn't see it.

He smiled at one revelation though, a subtle change in his own thinking, an event he wouldn't have dreamed possible thirty-six hours ago: just then, he had thought of Richter as *his father*, not as the mysterious stranger he had always known as Gerhard Richter.

That was something.

For his entire life, Ty had hated Richter. He was someone who had hurt him. Who had left him. Who had refused to contribute to his life.

But not here. Not now. Here and now, he was the guiding force Ty needed. He was, for the first time in three decades, playing the role of a father—someone who cared, who helped, who was there when it mattered.

And Ty's mind had, subconsciously, adapted, changing how he thought of the man. His perspective had changed. His attitude toward Richter had changed. Would that change eventually cause him more pain? If Richter repeated the past—if he left again or turned his back on Ty? *Yes*, he thought. It might.

Ty had to marvel at the fact that here, in this bizarre place, in the scariest two days of his entire life, he had found one of the things he had wanted most in his life, a thing he wanted so badly he had never even admitted to himself.

A father.

Would his newfound relationship with his father change again when the quantum radio was completed? When Richter didn't need him anymore to unravel the mystery?

Apart from that, Ty wondered if the device would transform him somehow. If it wasn't related to him, why had his genome been included in the broadcast?

Ty wanted answers. And he was sure of one thing—he wouldn't find them in the small room or the file he had now read four times. Not without some perspective.

He rose and opened the door and found two marines sitting at a folding table. They were playing cards and appeared to have been in mid-conversation. One stood at the sight of him.

"Sir."

"Sorry to interrupt. Could you tell me what time it is?"

The young man glanced at a cheap watch on his wrist. "Almost twelve hundred hours, sir."

The news instantly vanquished the last remnants of sleep that had been dogging Ty. It was noon. He had slept half the day.

Five minutes later, he was jogging into Bishop's office, where he found his parents sitting at a round table, in chairs adjacent to each other—not opposite. His mother was smiling, the sort of smile that existed in the afterglow of a heartfelt laugh. His father was speaking softly, a wry grin on his face.

In that fraction of a second, Ty felt as though he were seeing a moment out of time and space, a scene from another world where the two of them had never separated, where the thirty-year rift between them had never happened, where his family's own little cold war had never happened.

And then, as they realized he had entered the room, the moment was gone.

His mother turned to him. The smile vanished. And worse, she almost looked embarrassed by it, as though seeing him had severed the connection to Richter, returning her to the state of animosity she had long held toward the man she had three children with.

Ty thought the two of them seemed like entangled particles, existing in a natural, linked state of attraction, bound across space and time, defying the known laws of the universe. And when he had entered the room, the observer effect had happened, instantly altering the state of one particle and with it, the other.

He wished he could back up, rewind time, and watch from outside the room, listening to what his father had been saying.

But there was no going back.

His mother rose and walked over and hugged him. Ty wasn't sure why—if it was just to get distance from Richter or because recent events had made her more thankful each time she saw him. They had certainly made him more thankful to be alive and to still have his mother in his life.

When she released the hug, Ty looked between the two of them. "You let me sleep half the day."

His mother sighed. "You needed the rest."

"What I need is an alarm clock." Ty's mind flashed to the cheap black one that had destroyed his apartment in Geneva. "Actually, check that. What I need is a wake-up call."

His mother smiled. "Well, try this out—they found the third match."

Ty felt himself holding his breath as he waited.

"It's Nora," his mother said, a warm yet somber expression on her face.

"Nora…"

"Brown."

Ty turned away, confused, trying to process this.

He hadn't formed any real expectations of the third and fourth matches. Well, beyond the obvious—based on XX chromosomes in their genomes, he knew they would both be women, but that was all he knew. What he hadn't expected was for one of the matches to be the girl who had grown up next door to him. There was no way that was a coincidence.

Though he saw no link between himself and Tanaka, Ty was clearly linked to Nora, and had been since the age of three. He and Nora, much like his parents, were entangled. Over the years, they had drifted in and out of each other's lives, like rivers weaving through time, growing closer and flowing together for long periods and meandering apart at other times until finally diverging forever—after a particularly dark moment in Nora's life.

Ty had never blamed her for pulling away back then. He had desperately wanted to help Nora cope with what had happened. But he couldn't. She had retreated inward, locking him out.

At age eighteen, it had broken his heart, smashed it so hard he had thought it was irreparably broken—until he had met Penny six months ago.

To Ty, Nora was a bit like his father: a person who had hurt him. But it hadn't been her fault. It had simply been circumstances, a twist of fate that had torn them apart, events beyond her control. And then and there, he wondered if that was truly the case with his father. He sensed that somehow it was all linked, a giant web he was caught in, the threads all around him, the pattern unclear.

"What's she doing now?" he whispered.

"She's on her way here, on a private flight."

"No, I mean, what does she do? For work? And where does she live? I haven't talked to her in... well, since our ten-year high school reunion. We emailed about it, about going... it was the only reason I went. But she didn't show. She apologized, and said something came up."

"She's a researcher at Oxford. In experimental psychology."

Richter picked up a folder from the table and handed it to Ty, who flipped it open and began scanning the pages. It was so odd to read a report on someone he once knew so well. The seventeen years since he had last seen her were detailed in objective, almost clinical fashion. Ty wanted to know more than what was written in the file.

He sat down at the computer in the corner. "Is this connected to the internet?"

"With limitations," Richter said. "You can't send any emails or post anything. The firewalls and filters ensure that."

Ty opened a browser and searched for Dr. Nora Brown. He clicked the first video result, which had been posted a few hours ago by Oxford University's Experimental Psychology department.

In the video, Nora was standing in an auditorium, at a podium, smiling in front of a giant screen. The image was a dark green background with massive white letters that read *THE BIRTHRIGHT*.

The video played, and she began her talk. The infectious enthusiasm she had as a child and teenager was still there, and it drew Ty in like a riptide carrying him out to sea.

"I would like for you to consider, for a moment, that your mind is a key. When we're born, the key is a blank. There are no teeth, only a block of metal, untouched. Each of us is in charge of cutting that key, of filing the teeth and shaping the ridges and notches. If we do that correctly, that key will unlock something wonderous—our true potential. A nearly limitless well of happiness and success."

On the screen, Nora smiled.

"What is the shape of that key? How do you find it? That is part of what *The Birthright* is about. Finding that key to your own potential. Your key, simply put, is shaped by the contours of your mind—of your strengths and weaknesses. The good news is that they're easier to find than you ever imagined. And your potential is far greater."

The office door opened, and everyone turned to look at Bishop, who was a little winded. "They found the fourth match."

Richter rose. "Where?"

"Nashville, Tennessee."

"Name?"

"Sergei Evanoff."

Richter frowned. "He's a male?"

"He is," Bishop said, studying the top page of a stack of papers.

"Was he born a female?" Helen asked.

"He was not," Bishop replied.

"He's running a scam," Richter muttered.

"A scam?" Ty asked, confused.

"Yes," Richter said. "One we should have expected."

"Why?" Ty asked, still confused.

Richter crossed his arms. "It's very simple. Any time you offer a new way to make money, two types of people show up. Those who play by the rules. And frauds and con artists, who get what they can, by any means necessary, until it's over." He eyed Bishop. "I assume Evanoff got multiple kits and turned them in, collecting the cash?"

"Appears that way," Bishop said. "FBI is investigating, but it looks like this guy submitted several hundred kits to different pharmacy locations around Nashville. It's unclear if he had a network of people collecting and aggregating or if he did it himself. Guy made like thirty thousand dollars in twenty-four hours. All in cash. Well, VISA gift cards."

"What do we know about Evanoff?" Richter asked.

"Not a lot. We only have the IRS filings so far. He's a bail bondsman and does payday loans. We're waiting on local records of any ongoing investigations from Nashville PD. He's clean on the National Crime Information Center database."

"So what happens now?" Ty asked. "How do we even begin to track down the actual owner of that DNA sample?"

"Legwork," Bishop said. "The FBI is sending pretty much every field agent in the region. They're going to interrogate Evanoff and start running down leads. We'll have this woman in custody within hours."

36

In a small bedroom, Kato paced back and forth. In his mind's eye, he replayed every second of the meeting with his wife and son. To him, every moment with them was precious. The way the boy had looked at him was like a painkiller for the wounds deep inside of Kato. He needed that every now and then, just to go on.

In Joan's eyes, Kato thought he had seen the glimmer of a chance for them. A small chance. But one he would take.

The next thing that occupied his mind was the things his captors (or hosts) had taken from him—his laptop, and with it, his working manuscript of *The March of Humanity*.

Kato had never been comfortable being idle. He liked to work. *The March* had occupied him during those lulls on deployments, times like right now when he had nothing to do.

But was that true? Was there truly nothing he could do right now?

No.

There was *something* he could do. Something important.

He opened the door and peered out into the large room that held a maze of empty office cubicles. Near his doorway, there was a rectangular folding table where four uniformed marines sat playing cards. Texas hold 'em, by the looks of it.

All four rose at the sight of him, hands moving to their holsters, eyes boring into him.

"Hold it right there, sir," the closest said.

Kato held up his hands. "Relax. Just stretching my legs."

One of the marines, a sergeant, said, "Sir, you'll have to stretch them in that room."

"Sergeant, with all due respect, if I stay in that room, my next stop is a psych ward. The only thing in that little cell is the past, and it won't quit running through my mind." Kato nodded to the cards splayed on the table. "Can I join you guys?" He shrugged. "I just want something to distract me for a few minutes."

One of the marines cut his eyes at the sergeant.

Kato shrugged. "Look, you're four to my one."

The sergeant stared at him, hand still on his holster.

"Tell you what," Kato said. "I'm right-handed. I can play cards with my left, so you can tie one arm behind my back."

The sergeant sighed. "Briggs, stand by the elevator. Shoot 'im if he even breaks wind."

The marine private seemed disappointed at being excluded from the game but retreated to the elevator as Kato took a seat at the table and watched a lance corporal gather the cards and begin shuffling.

"Where you guys from?" Kato asked, beginning his true objective: gathering intelligence that might lead to an escape plan, in case he needed it. It was always better to have an escape plan and not need it than to need it and not have it.

Two thousand miles away, in a private jet flying over the Atlantic, Nora gazed out the window at the clouds and the sun, wondering what was waiting on her at the end of the flight. She had tried and failed to sleep. She was too nervous.

She had been told only one thing: that she was being flown to Washington, DC.

Home.

Nora had wanted to call her mother, to arrange to see her, but they had taken her phone. She counted that as a bad sign.

In downtown Nashville, Maria stopped on the sidewalk outside a small café. A sign in the window read *HELP WANTED*.

She pushed the glass door open, ringing the chime and drawing a few glances from the patrons having brunch.

"Table for one?" the chipper hostess asked, already clutching a menu to her chest.

"No." Maria tilted her head toward the sign in the window. "I'd like to apply."

Ten minutes later, she was sitting at an empty table in the back of the restaurant, just off the doors to the kitchen, filling out a job application.

When she was halfway down the page, the café's owner exited the kitchen and plopped down across from her. He was a heavyset man with big bags under his eyes. Even with the air conditioning and fans whirring overhead, sweat was pouring off of him.

"You have a car?" he asked, taking a handkerchief from his pocket and mopping it across his brow.

"No." Before he could say anything, she added, "But I can walk here."

"Where d'you live?"

"Over on Lafayette."

"In an apartment?"

"Something like that."

He narrowed his eyes, then scanned the form, no doubt noticing that she had left the address fields blank. He pointed a chubby finger at the page. "Why don't you note your address there—just in case we ever need to mail your check."

Maria exhaled and wrote the only address she had and watched in her peripheral vision as recognition dawned on the man. He was familiar with the shelter. They probably got a few applicants from there each month.

She set the pen down. "Am I wasting my time here?"

He didn't meet her gaze as he reached a meaty hand out and pulled the uncompleted form across the table. "I think that's all we need. Thanks for coming in, now."

In the conference room in the DARPA building, Bishop opened a folder and slid a printed sheet across the table to Ty. It contained twelve designs that, at first glance, Ty thought were modified astrology symbols.

"Do you recognize these?" Bishop asked.

Ty studied the symbols. Colonel Travis, DARPA's White House liaison, stood behind Bishop, staring at the page as if it were a foreign language, which Ty believed it was, in a sense.

"These twelve symbols are on the quantum radio, aren't they?"

"Yes," Bishop replied.

Ty nodded. "They tune it somehow?"

"We believe so. Do you know how to arrange them? What sequence to enter them in?"

Beside him at the conference table, neither Ty's mother nor father said a word. If either recognized the symbols, they clearly didn't want to say anything here.

A few days ago, Ty would have readily replied with the simple truth: he didn't recognize the symbols. They looked like star constellations to him, but he knew the DARPA teams would have checked that already. If they were constellations, they wouldn't be asking him. They were asking him for one reason—they were out of ideas. And that was an opportunity.

Ty glanced at his mother, then his father, who was watching him with an expression that didn't betray a shred of information. But somehow, Ty knew what the man was thinking. It was as though thirty years of time together had been packed into the last thirty hours. They had a rapport now.

In his mind, Ty replayed the conversation with his father the night before:

"What have you wanted ever since the day Thomas arrived at prison?"

"His freedom."

"And now you're a prisoner of sorts. But if you study the situation, you might find that fate has given you the means to the end you've long sought."

Ty picked up the page and studied the symbols, feigning mild recognition. "If you want my help, you have to help me."

"Help you do what?" Bishop asked.

Ty let the page fall back to the table. "I want a full presidential pardon for my brother."

Bishop's eyebrows bunched together. "What?"

"You heard me."

"We don't have time for this."

"I agree. Please hurry."

Bishop held up his hands. "Look, this is not *Let's Make a Deal*. You're going to help us. And besides that, I think you want to, Ty."

"I do. And I will. After I get that signed pardon."

"Forget it. You're not in charge here."

Ty leaned forward. "Are you sure?"

Bishop snorted.

Ty shrugged, trying to seem confident. "The thing is, Sandy, the Origin Project needs me more than it needs you. Think about what will happen if you don't start getting results. I'm guessing the device is close to completion?"

Bishop's silence confirmed that for Ty. "How long before it's operational? Tomorrow morning?"

Bishop stared at him.

"Late tonight?" Ty paused, seeing confirmation on Bishop's face. "So, tonight. And you still don't know how to operate it." Ty pointed at the page. "You need a code to operate it—a sequence of these symbols to enter, which you don't have, leaving you with the most important device in human history and no way to use it. What happens then? I'm not cooperating. But they can't get rid of me. It's my genome being broadcast. They can, however, get rid of you." Ty cut his eyes to Richter. "Who's in charge really becomes a matter of perspective, doesn't it?"

Bishop shook his head slowly, seething.

"I want that pardon," Ty said. "And that's not all. I want to talk to Tanaka. And Nora, the moment she arrives. Specifically, I want to be the first person to talk to her. She's likely going to be unnerved by all of this, and seeing a friendly face will help her. It's what I would want. And lastly, I want to see the whole picture—the full schematics for that device. And I want to see it right now."

Ty saw a small smile form at the edges of his father's mouth.

Bishop exhaled and twisted back to look at Colonel Travis, who held a leather portfolio at his side. Bishop pointed at it. "Okay. Show him."

Travis took out several pages and slid them across the conference table.

Ty picked up the top page and, for the first time, saw the quantum radio he had discovered. It was round, with twelve symbols around the perimeter and an open center, like a medallion someone might wear around their neck. At the bottom of the design was a hole for a chain to slip through.

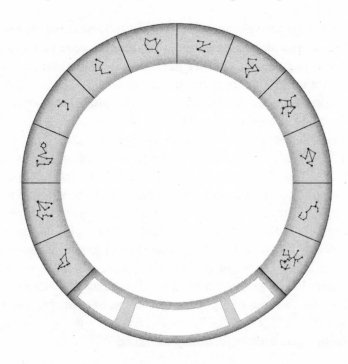

Emotions flooded through Ty. Curiosity. Pride in his accomplishment. And lastly, fear about what the small device might mean for the future of the world.

37

In the bathroom stall, the Covenant agent opened the metal box that contained the parts to the secure satellite phone and assembled it and typed out a message:

QUANTUM RADIO WILL BE FINISHED TONIGHT. 2 GENOMIC MATCHES SECURED. 1 INCOMING. 1 IDENTIFIED, SEARCH ONGOING. STAND BY FOR RAPID EVAC.

38

After a quick lunch in Bishop's office, Ty retreated to his bedroom.

At the small desk, he sat and read Tanaka's file again. His father was trying to give him a message with the file. It was there somewhere. Ty just couldn't see it.

He paced the room, then stretched out on the narrow bed and stared at the mineral fiber ceiling tiles, letting his mind work on the questions that dogged him. He was getting nowhere with Tanaka, so he returned to the desk and read through Nora's file. Next, he studied the schematics for the quantum radio again, focusing specifically on the twelve symbols around the dial.

What were they?

Star constellations? He felt that was likely. The problem was that they didn't match the night sky from Earth. At least, not the sky we see today.

Ty saw two possibilities. Either the star constellations were the sky as seen from Earth in the past, or they were the sky as seen from another world.

He leaned back in the chair, turning the two ideas over in his mind. The sky from another world. Or another time. Worlds and time. They were at the center of all of this.

But somehow, his gut told him he was missing something. The worlds and time in the symbols around the radio dial were more than that.

Besides, DARPA had the ability to model the night sky in the past. And the future. Surely they had checked those possibilities.

The quantum radio would be finished tonight. He needed to understand the symbols before then.

There was also another sort of constellation at work: a cluster of related items—Nora, Tanaka, Ty, and an unidentified woman.

How were they related? Instinctively, Ty felt that therein lay the key to unlocking the secrets of the quantum radio.

But there were only four of the genomes. The dial had twelve symbols.

The two numbers—four and twelve—didn't match. Like his father misquoting Tanaka's age. Had that been a clue about the quantum radio symbols—and not Tanaka?

Ty closed his eyes. This was driving him crazy.

He glanced back at the file for Tanaka. What was special about him? The man was working on a multivolume book, *The March of Humanity: The True History of the Human Race*. It promised to present a complete, unbiased history of the world. It was Tanaka's hobby. His life's work. His opus. One that would enable humans to understand their journey and place in the world like never before.

Ty had something similar, though in place of history, he had focused on science—physics, specifically. His Theory of Everything was a breakthrough that had the potential to unite the major opposing theories in physics and explain the deepest truths of human existence. He felt that the quantum radio was at the heart of that revelation.

And Nora had a similar pursuit: *The Birthright*, a revolution in human psychology. Her great work was in psychology and self-development, a unique fusion of medical and psychological insight that would provide a new framework for human happiness and potential.

That was the pattern. Each of them was working on a cornerstone work that could change the future—the entire way people saw the world, the past, and human civilization going forward. They were simply at different corners: history, science, and psychology. What did that portend about the fourth match?

Art.

That was the missing piece, if Ty had to guess.

He stood and paced, willing his mind to connect the dots.

His great work: The Theory of Everything.

Tanaka's: *The March of Humanity*.

Nora's: *The Birthright*.

There were twelve symbols on the quantum radio dial.

One for every month. That was something.

March.

Birthright.

Theory of Everything.

The words and facts shifted and fit together in his mind like LEGO blocks connecting, building upward.

Ty had never spent much time studying astrology, but he knew it offered a sort of theory of everything, a framework for predicting the future and drawing inferences about the past. Astrological symbols were based on constellations. Maybe the symbols on the radio dial represented some sort of astrological symbols from a long-dead society, some syntax that had been lost forever.

A knock at the door interrupted his thought process. He rose to open it, but it swung inward, revealing Colonel Travis and half a dozen marines.

Ty assumed they were there to take him to see Tanaka, as he had requested. Instead, Travis stepped into the doorway, blocking Ty's exit.

"There's been a breach."

"Breach?" Ty stared at him. "Of what? The building?"

"Comms. Someone is broadcasting from within the security perimeter. Unauthorized."

Ty shrugged. "It's not me."

"I'm sure it's not, Dr. Klein." Travis turned and nodded at a marine who was skinny as a rail. "Sorry about this. But we need to search your room, sir. And you."

Ty watched as Travis gathered the files, careful to keep them out of sight of the uniformed marines who swept in and ransacked the cramped space, then patted him down, rubbing and pressing into every nook where he might have hidden anything.

When they were satisfied, Travis nodded for them to leave and closed the door.

Ty held his hand out. "I'd like my files back."

Travis handed them over. "Sorry again, sir."

"I understand. Do you know what was broadcast?"

"Yes."

"And?"

Ty could tell Travis was struggling with what to reveal. "Let's just say… we may have a problem, sir. But we're going to deal with it."

"Well, that makes me feel great."

Travis opened the door. "Also, we've arranged for you to see Lieutenant Tanaka."

39

Ty found Tanaka waiting in a windowless room with a couch, coffee table, and two chairs.

The Navy SEAL rose when the door opened and stood with a stance that was distinctly not aggressive but, Ty thought, ready for anything. More than that, he was struck by how serene Tanaka was in person. The man stood utterly still, unblinking, but not staring daggers at Ty, merely waiting as though there was a deep well of patience inside of him, a ready calm that few possessed.

That wasn't in the file. The accounts of his work and even the psychological assessments couldn't convey that.

In person, the scar on the man's face was more noticeable— or perhaps it was the contrast of the hurtful mark to Tanaka's serenity. They didn't seem to match.

Ty held his hand out. "Hi. I'm Tyson Klein."

Tanaka grasped his hand firmly, but not oppressively. "Kato Tanaka, Lieutenant, United States Navy, sir."

"Call me Ty. We're on the same team."

"In that case, Kato will do. If I may ask, what team are we on?"

"That's actually what I wanted to talk to you about."

Ty shuffled over to the chair and sat and motioned for Kato to join him.

"I read your file."

Kato nodded. In his micro-expressions, Ty thought he sensed some hesitation on Kato's part, as though he were self-conscious about people knowing the things he had done.

It was amazing how familiar Kato seemed to Ty, as though they had known each other for a long time, as though being in each other's company was a natural and effortless thing. Maybe it was having read the file. Or maybe it was the serenity that surrounded Kato, a cloud that now extended around Ty. Or perhaps it was simply the relief at meeting one of the other genetic matches, the feeling of not being alone in that.

"Most of the file was redacted. But I got the picture. As an American, I appreciate what you've done. I know it hasn't been easy. I know it's cost you a lot."

Kato studied Ty's face. "Are you related to Richter?"

That caught Ty off guard. "Yes. He's... my father."

"Thought so. Your facial structure and some of your expressions are the same. He thanked me too. Arranged for me to see my family. When you see him, please tell him I appreciate that. I didn't get a chance."

That surprised Ty even more, but he tried not to show it. "I will."

"What is our mission?"

Kato had cut right to the issue. And Ty was equally direct. "Honestly, I'm not sure. I wanted to meet you because I think you deserve to know as much as we do. What's about to happen is probably going to be dangerous. And it could have a huge impact on the world."

"How?"

"I don't know yet."

"What do you do at DARPA?"

"I actually don't work for DARPA. I'm a researcher at CERN. A physicist. A few days ago, I discovered a pattern in the subatomic particles being observed at the Large Hadron Collider. That pattern, it turns out, is an organized data stream. A broadcast."

"Of what?"

"Two things. The first file was a schematic for a device."

"A device to do what?"

"We're not sure yet. We know it's a small particle collider—small enough to fit in your hand."

Kato seemed to consider that for a moment. "Interesting."

"We're calling it a quantum radio. The other data in the

stream were four complete human genomes. You, me, and two women."

"Who are the women?"

"One is a medical doctor and PhD who teaches psychology at Oxford. We're still looking for the fourth match."

"What happens now?"

"The device will be complete in a few hours. The other two matches will be here by then. One of the reasons I wanted to meet with you is because DARPA isn't the only one that wants my research and the device. The organization pursuing it is called the Covenant. Have you ever encountered them? In your work?"

"No. How do you know they want your research?"

"They stole it from CERN. And they tried to kill me."

"How?"

"A bomb. It blew up my apartment."

"How did you survive?"

"Frankly, through no skill of my own. Someone close to me warned me—at great risk to herself."

"What happened to her?"

"I don't know. I imagine, right now, the Covenant are looking for her. And I think they're coming for us too. There's been a breach here. Someone is working with them, communicating with the outside."

"We should relocate."

"We should. But we can't. They're building the device a few floors below us. They want us close by."

"So we're trapped."

"For now."

Outside the room where Ty had met with Kato, Bishop was waiting with a thick sheet of paper.

"The pardon," he said, holding it out.

Ty took it and glanced at the heading:

EXECUTIVE GRANT OF CLEMENCY

The form was short, with the president's signature and the embossed gold seal of the Department of Justice.

"Thank you," Ty whispered. "I'd like to give it to my brother myself."

Bishop exhaled and rolled his eyes. "I want to know what you know first. The code for the radio."

"After I meet my brother. And Nora. I'll talk then."

Five minutes later, Ty was in a small bedroom similar to the one he occupied, handing the page out to his brother, Tom.

"Is this a joke?"

"It's no joke," Ty said, smiling.

Tom stared at the page. "This is surreal."

"It's effective immediately." Ty paused. "Well, whenever you can leave here."

"When will that be?"

"I'm not sure. Soon. One way or another."

Tom looked up. "What does that mean?"

"It means… I think something is about to happen."

"Be careful, brother."

"I will."

40

When Maria returned to the Music City Rescue Mission's homeless shelter on Lafayette Street in Nashville, she had thirty-eight dollars and seventeen cents in her pocket, one more page of lyrics for a new song in *Worlds & Time*, and no job.

And no prospects.

And nowhere else to go.

She wanted to get to the shelter before sunset. The beds filled up fast these days, and even though this would be night fifteen, she knew that the Mission was her best shot at having a roof over her head. At least, a good roof over her head. Where she was safe.

She looked up at the clouds that had been gathering all afternoon, darkening, waiting to pour down. The first drops of rain fell on her as she climbed the cracked concrete stairs.

The administrator who had shown her the door that morning was sitting at the intake table this evening.

"Maria," he said, looking up from the list, a pencil held in his hand. "Tell me some good news." He didn't smile. "You got a job?"

"I've got thirty-eight dollars in my pocket. I know that's twelve short, but I'll get the rest."

He sighed.

"And I'll work." She nodded. "In the kitchen. Cleaning. Whatever needs doing."

"We've given those jobs out—to those in need, who aren't able to get anything else."

"I'll apply for food stamps too. And turn them over to you all." She shrugged. "I don't care if the tabloids pick it up and report it. So be it."

"It's fifty dollars a month, Maria. The Mission doesn't take partial payments. And it doesn't make loans."

She opened her mouth to plead her case, but stopped when she saw him rock to the side and draw his wallet from his back pocket and count out two five-dollar bills and two ones. "But I do. And I think you're good for it. Don't make me regret it, Maria. The truth is, I'm not that much better off than you are. I'm just getting by myself."

Maria had learned a lot of things in her five years in the music business. One was that different people needed different environments to do their best creative work. Some liked it loud—a coffee shop, the back of a tour bus, or a busy subway train. Others needed nearly absolute quiet—a library, a closet, or a messy hotel room after the rest of the band had passed out.

The thing Maria had learned recently was that when you were hungry, the rules got rewritten. All of a sudden, you became capable of things you weren't before. A hungry person became more able to work anywhere. And faster.

In the cramped bunkroom, where conversations and arguments and card games raged, she lay on her stomach staring down at the notebook, chewing the end of the white pen, seeing the music flow in her mind.

For her, sometimes the lines of a song formed from a vague image or a feeling. In this case, the inspiration was a tree, reaching to the sky, branches forking, never predicable. The limbs on the left and right grew outward until they turned down, growing thin, wilting, eventually extending below the ground, where they flowed toward each other, joining and surging upward to become the trunk.

It was a tree of life with no beginning and no end. In her mind's eye, she studied the image. It was more than a tree. On both sides, in the negative space where the branches turned downward, the area between them and the trunk was egg-shaped, like an embryo that had started in the center and then split, both sides seemingly equal, but in truth with small differences shaped by the paths the branches had taken.

She turned to a fresh page and wrote a heading.

The Mirror Tree

Yes, she liked that title. The song would be about beginnings and endings and standing tall against the test of time, about how time grows in branches. About how every ending is also a beginning.

Around her, a hush fell over the room.

Maria didn't look up.

She couldn't. She was into the song now. It was coming to her, as though she had uncovered the first flash of the white bone of a buried skeleton. Her pen raced over the page, an excavation brush wisking away, uncovering more lyrics.

The shelter administrator's voice called out above her. She looked up from the bunk, still balanced on her elbows, her feet in the air. There were two Nashville uniformed police officers with him. And three people in suits standing near the creep who had paid her for that CVS swab this morning.

She didn't like this.

The man pointed. "Yeah. That's her."

41

After visiting his brother, Ty found his father waiting in Bishop's office, sitting at the small round table, fingers steepled.

"I met with Kato," Ty said.

"And?" Richter said, not meeting his gaze.

"He told me to thank you for arranging the meeting with his family."

"Being separated from one's family eats away at a person. Time compounds the pain."

Richter still didn't look up.

There were so many things Ty wanted to ask about that statement. Answers he wanted. But he sensed that his own time was running out—that his personal questions would have to wait in favor of answers that mattered more in the grander scheme.

"I read Kato's file."

Richter finally met his gaze. "And?"

"It seems... pretty straightforward. Nothing jumps out at me."

"Straightforward it is not, Tyson. Please read it again. *Backward* and forward."

In his bedroom, Ty sat at the small desk and opened Kato's file.

Backward and forward.

He turned the file over and flipped the pages, which were only printed on one side.

They were all the same.

Blank.

The lights buzzed above as he flipped the pages, wondering what he wasn't seeing—

And then he saw it. Rows and rows of black lines soaked through the paper. The page had been redacted by hand, with a thick permanent marker.

As he flipped it over, Ty recalled his father's words.

Turn the page.

Ty glanced at the page number: thirty-seven.

This was it. The page he was supposed to turn. It had been redacted on the computer, with printed black boxes. Then Ty's father, or someone else, had taken a black marker and redacted it more.

Why?

What was the message?

The page was a medical assessment. Between the printed black boxes and those added in marker, there was barely any text on the page. But nothing jumped out to Ty. Was something wrong with Kato's health?

Or was there a code here, some way he was supposed to arrange the words that spelled a message?

No.

That seemed too obvious.

Ty closed his eyes and rubbed his eyelids, willing his mind to go back over the words his father had said.

Turn the page. Connect the dots.

Ty flipped the page over. With a pen, he drew between the black blotches that had soaked through.

It was a map. A series of... what? Roads? Or hallways in this building?

Or was it Morse code—the small blocks representing dots, the longer ones serving as dashes?

What did it mean?

How could he use—

A knock at the door made Ty jump.

He slammed the folder shut just as the door opened.

A marine stepped into the room. "Sir. Dr. Bishop has requested your presence at a meeting."

Ty's heart beat faster. Did they know about the code? Did they know that his father was secretly revealing information to him? Had they finished the device?

"A meeting about what?"

"Sir, I don't have that information." The marine turned and stepped back through the doorway.

Ty followed him to the elevator and up one floor, wondering what this was about. Had they found the Covenant agent in the building? Or had they located the other genomic match?

The marine stopped outside a door and swung it open, revealing a room similar to the one Ty had met Kato in. Except in this room, Nora was sitting on the couch.

He had been so wrapped up in the message in Kato's file, he had forgotten she was on her way here.

She stood and stared through the doorway, surprise evident on her face. Then she smiled, and that smile grew by the second, the expression so warm it felt to Ty as though it were radiating actual heat toward him. It drew him in like a warm fire on a winter night.

He marched into the room, slowing as he reached her. Should he offer his hand? Hug her? He hadn't seen her in person for seventeen years. They hadn't ended on bad terms. But things between them hadn't ended the way either of them had wanted.

Nora didn't hesitate. She reached her arms out and pulled him into a hug, pressing him into her, resting her head on his shoulder. She exhaled a warm breath that flowed over his neck. He held her, surprised at how good it felt.

"Ty," she whispered. "What's going on?"

Ty heard the door close behind them.

"It's... complicated."

42

In the visiting room in the DARPA facility, Ty sat in a cheap armchair as Nora settled across from him on a couch that had seen better days.

They were silent for a long moment, and Ty thought that it revealed something very important: how comfortable they still were with each other, even after all these years apart. There was no tension. No need to fill the void by talking. Only a quiet reflectiveness, both of them taking stock, both likely wondering where to start, where to begin climbing the mountain that was the mystery of what was happening here—and how to address the past, which was a mountain of its own. But in the valley in which they now sat, it was peaceful. A safe place they had returned to after a long time away.

For Ty, seeing Nora brought back a flood of memories and emotions. The first to surface was of an afternoon in late spring during their senior year in high school. That day, they had engaged in one of their favorite things: a picnic on the National Mall.

Under the sun, they had lain on a wide, thick quilt. A basket held sandwiches, snacks, thermoses of water, and a nice supply of paperbacks. The Washington Monument towered to their right. The US Capitol loomed to the left. The Smithsonian museums lined the streets between the two attractions. Tourists buzzed around them.

But to Ty, it felt as though the quilt in the expanse of green grass was an island all its own, insulated, a square of existence independent of the universe. He and Nora existed there. And in that space and time, nothing else mattered.

As they often did on their Sunday afternoon retreats, they read the paperback novels they had brought, lying on their stomachs, the sun on their backs, feet kicking in the wind, periodically reaching for the snacks or water.

Theirs was a sort of two-person book club. They would check out library books and read them one after the other, discussing when each had finished the latest tome. That was the other half of their Sunday afternoons—discussing books and, particularly, the ideas they contained. They shared that love as well, a passion for big ideas.

Looking back, that afternoon in spring before they graduated high school had been the calm before the storm in Nora's life. It was perhaps one of the last happy moments before everything changed. Ty wished he had known that back then, but that was the nature of tragedy—you never truly appreciated the good times until they ended.

And you never knew when someone from your past would come crashing back into your life.

"I didn't expect to see you," Nora said. "But I guess I shouldn't be surprised."

Ty raised his eyebrows.

"I knew this was big when the police showed up at my door and put me on a plane. You're the smartest person I ever met, Ty. I should have known you were connected somehow."

"You need to get out more."

"I teach at Oxford, Ty. You're *still* the smartest person I've ever met. That mind of yours is like a force of nature."

"It's been a bit cloudy lately." Ty leaned forward and put his elbows on his knees. "What we're dealing with here is indeed big, as you say. Complicated. I'm still trying to figure it out. I wanted to meet with you because you're part of it." He shook his head. "How exactly, I don't know. But I do know you deserve to be in the loop."

For the next thirty minutes, Ty described his discovery at CERN and what had happened since. He briefed Nora on the device, and the genomes, and Kato.

She was a good listener. Always had been. It was one of the

things Ty had loved about her. Growing up, she had always been able to unpack his emotions, to help him process and understand what he was going through. She had said he was the smartest person she'd ever met, but to him, she was easily the most fascinating person he had ever encountered. And being here with her now, he realized that he was still fascinated by her.

And more.

She had been his next-door neighbor, his best friend, and then, starting in high school, his first love.

That spark was still there. But the bond between Ty and Nora wasn't like with him and Penny. With Penny, the relationship had been like reaching out to touch an exposed wire—not knowing if it was live or not. When he thought about her, he still felt that surge of adrenaline as if he were touching that wire, feeling the electricity pulsing through him, the things it had awakened, long dormant—the parts of him he had first discovered with Nora.

Maybe it felt different with Nora because they had grown up together and had been friends before they were lovers.

In his mind, he associated her with warmth. With deep caring. With someone he trusted completely, someone he would do anything for—and who would do anything for him. Until then, he hadn't realized how much he needed that, how much more confident he felt now.

He had once read a perspective on loneliness that he had never forgotten: that loneliness isn't about the lack of contact with people. It's about feeling like there's no one who really cares about you. In Ty's experience, that was true. In his academic life, he had met people who were surrounded by peers and colleagues but who were truly and utterly lonely. Some of it was likely their intellect, a feeling that no one understood them and how they saw the world. But mostly, it was that lack of caring.

Time and events beyond their control had torn him and Nora apart. But being here with her now, Ty knew this much was true: they both still cared deeply for each other. And just being around her made him feel far less alone in the world.

When he had finished bringing her up to speed, Ty added the other thing he wanted to tell her.

"My father is here. He's part of the Origin Project. He saved me. He's the one who got me out of Switzerland."

"Had you been in contact with him before this?"

"No. Before two days ago, I hadn't seen him in person for thirty years."

"That has to be overwhelming. On top of everything else."

"It's tough. He's nearly impossible to read." Ty was about to add that he thought his father knew more about what was happening than he was saying, but he held back. DARPA was likely listening to the conversation in the room.

"Did you ever find out what happened to your father?" Ty asked.

"No. I haven't stopped looking. But I have stopped thinking about it as much. That's helped. Some."

"Believe me, it's impossible to completely stop thinking about something like that. I tried. For a long time."

It struck Ty then that the most painful thing for both of them was a similar experience: their fathers being ripped from their lives unexpectedly and with little explanation. It had happened to Ty when he was five and to Nora when she was eighteen.

When Nora's father had disappeared, the shock of it had torn her and Ty apart. She had pulled away, retreating inward. He had always wished he could have been there for her, but they were attending different colleges then, and it wasn't just the physical distance that had separated them. It was the walls Nora had built around herself in the aftermath of her father's disappearance.

"I'm glad your dad is back," she said. "It seems like things have changed between the two of you."

Ty was amazed at how well she could still read him, even after all these years apart. "How can you tell?"

"The way you talk about him. It's not like before, when we were young. The bitterness is gone."

He nodded. "I'm starting to think that maybe he had good

reasons for what he did. Maybe things are more complicated than I thought."

"They usually are," Nora said. "So what do we do now?"

"For now, we wait. But I don't think we're going to be waiting very long."

43

Ty was sitting at his desk, staring at the stained page from Kato's file, when someone knocked on the door. He folded the page and slipped it in his pocket just in time to hide it from the young marine who entered.

"Sir, you're wanted for another meeting."

Five minutes later, Ty was walking into a conference room where Colonel Travis and Bishop were standing at the end of a long table. Ty's parents were sitting on one side.

The moment the door closed, Bishop said, "They've found the fourth match."

He took a folder from Travis and slid it across to Ty's father, who opened it and placed it between him and Ty's mother so they could both read the summary page.

"Her name is Maria Santos," Bishop continued. "Age twenty-four. She's living in a homeless shelter in downtown Nashville. She's a junkie—"

Ty's mother held up a hand. "Please don't say that."

"What? Homeless shelter?"

"I don't think the word junk should be used to describe a human being."

Bishop exhaled heavily. "Miss Santos has a past history of substance abuse." The man eyed Helen, expression bordering on mocking. She glanced up, then returned her attention to the file, not taking the bait.

"She's apparently a singer. Or was. Her band had a few hits, then broke up. Some kind of disagreement or lovers' quarrel or something." Bishop flipped a page. "She went solo and started having a lot of problems. That's about all we know. Oh, and she seems to have absolutely no connection to any of the other three matches. Or science. We're scratching our heads on this one."

"It's not as mysterious as you might think," Richter said, still scanning the file.

"What does that mean?"

"I'd like to speak with her first."

When no one objected, Richter rose, and Helen looked up at him. "You don't want to finish reading the file?"

"There is no need. The pattern is clear. We need to see what she was working on." To Colonel Travis, he said, "Do we have her cloud accounts? Have you downloaded the data there?"

"She doesn't have any."

"Physical files?"

"Only a notebook."

"Bring it to me. I want to read it before I see her."

"Why?" Ty asked.

"I believe she's an equally important component of this mystery." His gaze settled on Bishop. "Regardless of her past."

Bishop crossed his arms. "Didn't realize you were such a music connoisseur, Gerhard."

"On the contrary. I've been waiting my whole life for this particular piece."

"You want to tell me what that means?"

"No."

Bishop snorted. "You people... Look, somebody is going to have to start giving me some answers." He pointed at Ty. "Starting with you. I got you the pardon. And the meeting with Tanaka. And Dr. Brown. Now talk. What's the code to operate the device?"

Ty felt every pair of eyes in the room focus on him.

"The symbols on the dial are star clusters."

Bishop shook his head, annoyed. "No. They're not. We've run the simulations. They're not from the past. Or the future. Or from any planet in the solar system. We're even trying to model worlds in the habitable zones of the closest stars. Results are pending, but they're telling me it doesn't look likely. So, what you're saying is just not correct."

"I'm right," Ty said, voice rising.

"Prove it."

"I can't."

Bishop threw up his hands. "Wonderful."

"Look, I can't tell you how I know, but I just sense it—like I knew the genomes were of living people and that the device was a small collider."

"Then what's the code? How do we operate it?"

"I don't know yet."

"So you were lying when you said you would talk in return for the pardon."

Ty felt blood rushing to his head, the beat of his heart faint but growing in his eardrums. "I didn't lie. I told you I would help in return for that pardon. I am helping. I'm telling you what I know."

"You better start knowing more, and fast. The device will be done in a few hours."

"I want to brief the team."

Bishop squinted at him. "What team?"

"Kato and Nora."

"*Kato and Nora?*" Bishop practically spat out. "You're not a team."

"We are."

"*No. You're not.* A team is a group of people who work together toward some measurable outcome. You people are, simply put, not that. You don't work together. You have no goal. Look, we still don't even know what the device does. Or how you're connected to it."

Ty laughed. "That's exactly my point."

"Well, you'll apparently have to make it for me."

"The point is, we need to start working together, right now. Because we are a team. And I think we're the key to figuring out what's happening here."

In the meeting room, Ty stood when Nora entered.

"What happened?"

"I'll tell you when Kato gets here."

They didn't have to wait long. The Navy SEAL arrived a minute later, face placid, hand extended to Nora. "Ma'am."

"Nora, this is Kato Tanaka. Kato, this is Nora Brown. I thought you two should meet. And there's something else. They've found the fourth match. Her name is Maria Santos. She's a singer and a songwriter. She's had some difficulties in her life, but it sounds like she was trying to get over them."

44

Maria was scared. The cops who had picked her up at the homeless shelter had barely said a word to her. They had put her in the back of a car, and then on a flight that landed in Washington, DC, and finally into a windowless van where they played weird static so that she couldn't hear anything going on outside the vehicle.

It had been a bizarre, disorienting experience.

They had also taken her bag and with it the notebook that held *Worlds & Time*.

She wanted it back.

She didn't have much in this life, but she had that, and she was proud of it, and she couldn't afford to lose it. Maria thought she could probably recreate the last few pages, but not the whole thing. If she lost it forever, it would be like losing a piece of herself. Because there was a piece of her in those songs. Her pain. Her hopes. Her struggles. Her beliefs. Those songs were a reflection of her. And she wanted to share them with the world. She wanted others to see themselves in that music, to know that they weren't alone. To her, that was part of the magic of art.

But whatever was happening wasn't about her music. At least, she didn't think so. That guy outside the shelter. It was somehow connected to him. She shouldn't have hit him. He was probably a cop. Undercover. Or some kind of confidential informant. She was in deep now, by the looks of this place—and the fact that they had put her on a private FBI plane. She wasn't in a county lockup, that was for sure.

Her rage. That's what had landed her in this mess.

That fire inside of her had fueled the success of her music career. But it was also a curse. She wished she could turn it off like a flame in a gas fire. Another part of her wondered who she would be without that fire. If she could still create incredible work without all the hurt and hate deep inside of her.

Whatever she had done, it had landed her in this conference room, inside what she assumed was a prison. She was confined here. But she also had a roof over her head. And she had been fed. Maria was thankful for those two things, and the thought laid bare just how far she had fallen—to be thankful for a warm place to stay, even if she couldn't leave when she wanted to. The realization that being a prisoner was an improvement in her circumstances was a gut punch in and of itself.

The door opened, and a tall man with a toned face strode in. His eyes were locked on her, emotionless, studying her like a hunter might size up its prey. Under his unmoving gaze, that was exactly what Maria felt like.

He spoke first.

"Good evening, Miss Santos. My name is Gerhard Richter."

"Look, I didn't hit that guy."

"To whom are you referring?"

"That creep outside the shelter. He said something lewd—"

The man held up a hand, making her fall silent. For a moment, he was still as a statue. Somehow that made her nervous.

"This isn't about that... creep."

"It's not?"

"It's about something vastly more important."

"You a cop?"

"I am not. Not in the sense you're asking. Though my role here is law enforcement, of a sort."

"What laws?"

"The kind that rule us all. The laws of worlds and time."

"You read my notebook."

"Yes."

"I want it back."

"I don't think that will be possible."

"Please. It's all I've got. What can it hurt?"

"If I'm right, Miss Santos, at the end of this, you won't need that notebook. But your work of art will be complete."

"What are you talking about? Are you high? Where am I? I want a lawyer."

"Do you know what time does to a tree, Miss Santos?"

She stared at him.

"Time makes a tree grow branches. The tree watches the sun rise and fall, a continuous loop with no beginning or ending. Sometimes the tree stands in the light. Sometimes in darkness." Richter paused. "At this moment, you are in the dark. But there is light, Miss Santos. The sun always rises. The question of a life is whether we possess the courage to wait long enough for the dawn."

45

In the bathroom stall, the Covenant agent reassembled the phone and sent a short message.

ALL GENOMIC MATCHES SECURED. QUANTUM RADIO WILL BE FINISHED WITHIN THE HOUR. AWAIT MY SIGNAL TO BREACH.

46

Ty woke to hands gripping him, shaking his shoulders, and a voice calling his name. The fluorescent tube lights above buzzed and shone down, draping the person's face in shadow.

"Rise, my son."

Ty squinted and saw his father staring down.

"I'm up," he muttered.

"It's time."

Ty planted his right elbow in the thin mattress and pushed himself into a sitting position. He was still in his clothes, and he had slept on his left hand—it was dead and awkward.

"Time for what?"

"The machine. It will be finished shortly." Richter leaned over. "Did you read the file?"

Ty rubbed his hand on his face. "Yes. I got the picture. But I don't understand it. How to use it."

"Just keep it with you. Do you have the pills I gave you?"

Ty put a hand on his pocket, felt the bottle, and nodded.

Richter turned to leave, but Ty reached out with his left hand, which was slowly coming back to life. He gripped his father's arm. Richter spun, seeming surprised. The man clearly wasn't used to someone placing their hands on him unexpectedly. Instantly, his face softened, and Ty saw, for the first time, an outward show of warmth, his guard coming down.

"Thank you," Ty whispered.

"For what?"

"Saving me in Zürich. The Covenant probably would have caught up with me if you hadn't."

"That's what parents do."

The words hung in the air for what felt like an eternity, both men staring at each other. Ty thought his father would pull away, but he stayed.

Finally, Ty leaned closer and whispered, "Do you know the code—for the radio?"

"No."

Ty studied his face. He had been sure his father knew. If he didn't, then Ty was truly at a loss. He sensed, however, that he needed to figure it out quickly.

"I was told," Richter said, "a long time ago, that the answer to all of this is written in the stars."

Richter led Ty to a conference room, where he expected to find his mother and Bishop waiting. Instead, he found Maria Santos pacing in front of a long table, a cup of coffee in her hand. The photos in the file had been from her singing career—standing on stage, microphone in hand, airbrushed promo photos, and still-captures of online music videos and social media posts.

Here, in the flesh, Maria still had the same fire in her eyes, but the sockets that held those eyes were more sunken now, with black bags beneath them, as though time and stress had left charred pits.

"Miss Santos, this is my son, Tyson."

"Call me Ty."

"I'm Maria," she said cautiously, studying the two men. "What's going on?"

Richter turned to leave. "I'll leave that to Tyson."

When the door closed, Maria said, "Your dad is really not one for explaining things." She shrugged. "No offense."

"Believe me, I know *exactly* how you feel. You have no idea." Ty took a deep breath. "But if you give me a few minutes, I'll try to bring you up to speed."

By the time Ty had finished briefing Maria, her eyes were wide, and her coffee cup was empty.

"This is crazy," she whispered.

"I know. It's a lot to take in."

"If I was still on drugs, I probably wouldn't believe it at all."

"Yeah, it's a trip."

Maria knitted her eyebrows. "You make dad jokes."

"I do. It's... unfortunate."

"Are you a dad?"

"No. No, I'm actually not. And I think that probably makes it worse."

She laughed. "Hey, nobody's perfect."

The door opened, and Nora and Kato walked in.

Ty stood and introduced the three of them.

"What's the latest update?" Nora asked.

"Dr. Brown," Bishop said, marching through the doorway, "to answer your question, the latest is that the device is ready."

Colonel Travis followed Bishop into the room and set about working the controls for the screen on the wall. A video feed appeared, showing a clean room where three people in white suits stood around a metal table, the quantum radio lying in the center.

Ty's parents arrived then. Richter paused at the door to allow Helen to enter before him. Ty sensed that they had been talking beforehand.

Through the doorway, he saw uniformed marines, who were carrying rifles, exiting the elevator. There had to be two dozen of them in the outer room now, massed as if for an invasion—or to repel one.

Colonel Travis called to a sergeant outside the conference room, and the man stepped inside, followed by four others, who stood along the wall, eyes fixed on Ty, Nora, Kato, and Maria. They were clearly there in case something happened to the four of them, some transformation that endangered the rest of the room. Was that what they thought was about to happen when they turned the quantum radio on?

On the video, a suited figure in the clean room looked up through a clear helmet, directly at the camera. "We're ready to seal the enclosure."

Colonel Travis turned to Bishop, who swallowed hard, then

eyed Richter. Ty's father inclined his head slightly. Beside him, Ty's mother took a deep breath and held it as Colonel Travis pressed a button on the conference speaker on the table and said, "Proceed."

On the screen, tiny pops and flashes issued at the edges of the device.

Ty felt eyes upon him. Across the table, Nora was staring, a question in her eyes. Even after so many years apart, he knew what she was silently asking him: *What's going to happen?*

With a slight movement of his head, straight across, he told her he didn't know. He felt as though they were standing on the precipice of something incredible.

Beside Nora, Kato was as still as a redwood tree, towering in the face of whatever was coming.

Maria was chewing one of her fingernails as she squinted at the screen.

The man in the clean room spoke again, "We're sealed."

"Stand by," Travis said into the speaker phone.

The room fell into an uneasy silence, everyone waiting. Ty could feel the marines scanning him and the others, watching for changes. He wondered what their orders were.

Richter reached into his pocket. Ty could see him holding something, working his fingers. Was it a gun?

Bishop looked up at Ty. "We need that sequence to activate it. Right now."

"I don't know it."

"Then we're going to start guessing."

"You can't be serious," Richter said.

Bishop drew a slip of paper out of his pocket, then held a finger down on the conference speaker. "Depress the fourth symbol."

Helen turned to Richter and whispered, "Make them stop."

"Stop this, Sandy," Richter said, taking a step forward, hand still in his coat pocket.

On the screen, the view focused on the quantum radio, which sat face up on the silver-metal table. A finger came into the view and pressed the fourth symbol on the device. Behind the symbol, a yellow-orange glow emerged for a fraction of a second, then faded quickly.

The suited man's voice came over the speaker. "Momentary lighting on the keypad and slight vibration as the key was depressed—likely a haptic feedback mechanism. No other change here."

"Why the fourth symbol?" Nora asked, eyebrows bunched.

"Four genomes," Bishop said, studying the page. He pressed the speaker again. "Try one-two-three."

Ty threw his hands up. "You've got to be kidding me! One-two-three?"

Bishop eyed him. "It's the sum of your four ages: thirty-five, thirty-five, twenty-nine, and twenty-four."

"Sandy," Richter said, "you don't even know if it operates on a base-ten number system. There are twelve symbols."

On the screen, the finger hit the first three symbols in rapid succession. Once again, the symbols flashed, but nothing happened.

Bishop was studying the page, ignoring Richter.

"Sandy," Richter said, voice rising. "You're playing roulette here. Entering the wrong sequence could kill us all."

Bishop looked up. "Is that what will happen, Gerhard? How do you know?"

He waited, eying Richter. "You know what, I think you know a lot more about this device than you're telling us." Bishop spread his hands. "You put all these pieces in place as though you knew we'd need them. So we'd be ready to build a small collider when the time came. You've also kept us a step ahead of the Covenant too. How is that? How do you know so much?"

"What I know, at this moment, is that it is dangerous to operate this device until we understand it."

Bishop shook his head. "Well, it looks like the only way to understand it is to experiment—and that's what I've been instructed to do. By the President of the United States. He wants an operational quantum radio—by any means necessary and at any cost."

At any cost.

Ty wondered what the cost of typing the wrong code into the radio would be. His father feared that. And this was the first time he had seen him scared.

An idea occurred to Ty then. A possible code. One thing he knew: it was better than Bishop's guesses. And he needed to buy time to think it over more.

"I know the code," Ty said quietly.

Every head in the room turned to him.

Bishop spoke first. "Okay. Go ahead."

"I need to key it in myself."

"Why?"

"I believe it has a built-in security measure—to ensure one of the four of us has to be in possession of the radio to operate it."

Bishop squinted at Ty. "You're guessing."

"Yes. I'm guessing about that part. But it doesn't mean I'm wrong."

"Tell me the code."

"No. I'll only type it in myself."

"It's a quantum device, Ty. It could operate from anywhere in the universe."

"That may be, but why would they supply our genomes? What's the harm in me typing it in? The device is a floor away. If there is a security countermeasure against anyone other than us typing in the code, it could be catastrophic. Do you really want to take that risk?"

Bishop shook his head and looked at Ty, his mother, and then his father. "You people are going to be the death of me."

He motioned to Colonel Travis, who held a hand out to the marines. They broke formation and exited, joining the other troops in the outer room, massing at the elevator.

Ty stepped across the threshold and looked back at Nora, Kato, and Maria. "Come on."

"No," Bishop said. "They stay."

"They're coming with us."

"No. *They stay.* There isn't a lot of extra space in the lab, and we need security around you four in case you change."

"Change how?" Nora asked, concern evident on her face.

"What's he talking about?" Maria said.

"We're a team," Ty said to Bishop.

The older man snorted. "They are not your team."

"I never said they were *my* team. I said *we're a team*. Four corners of something important."

"Well, there's just not room for security and the *team*."

"Make room, Bishop. You want the code, that's the deal. Besides, they may need to be close by to even activate the device."

Bishop seemed to think for a minute, then shook his head. "Fine. You want to bring the quantum village people along? So be it."

He took a phone from his pocket and began tapping on it.

"What are you doing?" Richter asked.

"Sending an update."

"To whom?"

"The people we work for, Gerhard."

Bishop motioned to the door. "Let's go."

Nora turned her gaze to Ty, silently asking, *Is this going to be okay?*

He put on a reassuring smile, but he knew her well enough to know she saw through it. They were about to roll the dice on the biggest scientific experiment in human history.

47

Ty, Nora, Kato, and Maria marched out of the conference room, into an open area where disassembled cubicles were stacked like dominoes. Marines stood in rows, rifles ready, staring as if they were watching death row inmates take their final walk. Ty wondered if that was what this was. He was scared. He knew Nora well enough to know that she was too.

They rode the elevator down one floor in groups: Helen, Bishop, Richter, and Ty first, accompanied by four marines.

At the lab level, they waited in a similar open-concept office area as above. Two dozen marines were massed here as well. It was as if the entire building was filled to the brim with armed troops now.

The elevator opened again, and Nora, Kato, Maria, Colonel Travis, and four marines accompanying them stepped out.

Bishop led the combined group to a set of double doors that he used his palm and retina to open. Beyond was a narrow corridor with labs on both sides. Wide windows provided a view inside.

Travis motioned marines forward until the corridor was filled, then closed the double doors.

A boom shook the building. Then another, and finally a third blast. Two seconds of silence followed. Then faint pops of automatic gunfire punctuated by smaller explosions. A battle.

Travis pressed a finger into the earpiece in his left ear and touched the mic on his lapel. "Report."

He listened, then turned to Bishop. "We've been breached."

"Breached?" Bishop's voice was rising. "As in—"

"Unidentified combatants on the above-ground floors. They've overwhelmed our forces. They're clearing the floors—"

"Call the Pentagon!" Bishop shouted.

"Comms are down," Travis said. He motioned to the closed double doors. "Elevators are offline too. We're barricading the stairwells. We'll make a stand in the outer room."

Bishop pointed at Ty. "We're activating the radio right now." He marched down the corridor, past the window that looked into the clean room lab with the radio. The three suited figures were still standing around the table, waiting. Bishop used his palm and retina to unlock the door, which opened with a pop.

He motioned the three people in suits to exit, then reached out, ushering Ty through the doorway. Ty turned and signaled for Nora, Kato, and Maria to follow. Richter, Helen, Travis, and three marines from the corridor squeezed in.

A boom shook the lab, releasing white dust from the ceiling. It reminded Ty of that dust cloud in the stairwell in Geneva, of lying there after the blast, body aching, lungs gasping for air. He felt dizzy, as if the present were slipping away.

A hand gripped his arm. Someone was saying his name.

"Ty."

"Ty."

He grabbed the hand on his arm and squeezed until he heard a yelp. It was Nora's voice, crying out in pain.

That snapped him out of it.

She was staring at him, brow furrowed, speaking slowly: "Are you okay?"

He felt another hand on his upper arm, strong, gripping but not clawing into him. Kato.

"I'm fine," he breathed out, trying to regain his bearings. He was in the lab. The quantum radio sat on the metal table before him. Looming. Waiting.

"Enter the code," Bishop said.

Gunfire sounded nearby.

In the outer room.

"Do it now!" Bishop shouted over the pops of gunfire.

Ty stepped toward the metal table.

More white powder fell from the ceiling, blanketing the room, the tiny particles filling in the symbols on the dial on the quantum radio.

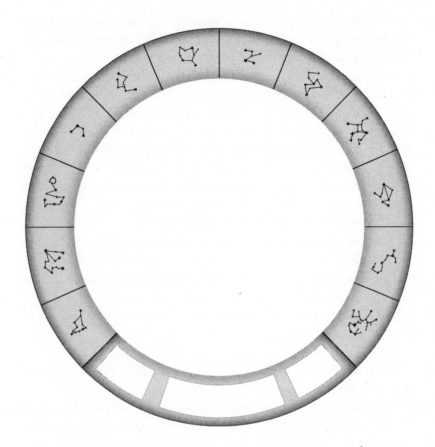

Ty stared at the device.

He reached out and picked it up. The metal was cold. The device was the thickness of perhaps two quarters fused together and fit easily in the palm of his hand. Like a medallion a person might wear around their neck.

"Ty!" Bishop shouted. "*Type. The code.*"

Mentally, Ty reviewed the thread that ran through the four genomic matches. Each had a life's work.

For him, The Theory of Everything.

For Nora, *The Birthright*.

For Kato, *The March of Humanity*.

For Maria, *Worlds & Time*.

The theme was there. A thread that ran through them.

Birth. March. Worlds and Time. A theory of everything. "Do it!" Bishop yelled as the wall behind him exploded.

48

The blast threw Ty into the marine standing behind him. They hit the wall together, and Ty lurched forward, falling face-first onto the floor. Still, he held tight to the quantum radio medallion. He sensed, even in the carnage, that it was the key to saving everyone.

His ears rang.

Vision spotted.

Debris rained from the ceiling.

In front of him, Nora was lying on her back, eyes closed.

Unmoving.

Ty lunged forward, crawling toward her, ignoring the pain as debris on the floor dug into his forearms. He could barely hear the booms from the explosions, but he could feel them vibrating through him.

His eyes were locked on Nora. Nothing else. She still hadn't moved.

A piece of the ceiling broke free, crashing down on her left leg.

Ty crawled faster.

His hearing was returning. And the only sound was gunfire. And screams.

His father was army-crawling across the floor as well, toward Ty's mother. Richter covered her with his body, ensuring the falling debris hit him instead. He turned his face to the side and shouted, voice loud enough to slice through the din.

"Stop! Stop shooting."

Ty realized Kato was standing by the open door, shooting into the hall with a rifle he had taken from one of the fallen marines. About half of them were down, unmoving.

When he reached Nora, Ty positioned his body over hers,

shielding her. He pressed his thumb to her neck, feeling for a heartbeat. Her warm breath reached his face first. Her eyes cracked open. And she smiled, a weary but happy smile.

"Hold your fire!" Richter yelled, still crouched over Ty's mother. "You could damage the device. Get back!"

Through the clean room's broken window, Ty could see a dozen figures in the corridor, dressed in jet-black fatigues, wearing balaclavas over their faces, rifles aimed into the lab.

At Richter's words, one of the figures—a man near the front—began barking orders:

"Fall back. Prep for evac."

As the invading troops backed away, Kato stepped out into the hall, crouching, rifle pointed at the troops.

"Put the gun down, Lieutenant," Richter called to him.

Kato eyed him.

"We're outmatched."

Kato hesitated.

"Lieutenant, if you keep fighting, more people will get hurt," Richter said. He glanced at the three other marines. "Same goes for you all. It's over."

Ty could barely process what he was hearing. They had lost. If these were Covenant soldiers, what would they do to him? And Nora? And Kato and Maria? And his parents?

Kato squatted and placed the rifle on the floor, the center resting on his right foot. Ty imagined that was so that he could propel it upward and into his hands quickly if he had to.

Behind him, Maria had her back to the wall, clutching her knees to her chest, breathing in and out heavily, her eyes wide. She was scared, but she was alive, and Ty was thankful for that.

Beside her, Bishop was stirring. Blood covered his face. His thick glasses were gone, and he was running his hands through the rubble on the floor, blinking, desperately looking for them.

A few feet away, Colonel Travis lay dead, shards of broken glass lodged in his neck.

Nora reached a hand up and gripped Ty's upper arm. "I'm okay," she whispered. "Just shaken up. Are you okay?"

He nodded.

The debris had stopped falling, and his father had moved away from his mother to stand at the doorway, as if waiting for someone.

Ty's mother sat up, rubbing the back of her neck.

"Gerhard, what's going on?" she asked.

Before he could answer, a black-clad figure strode into the hallway, a handgun held at his side. Two others lingered a few feet behind him, rifles pointed at the floor.

"Richter," the lead figure called.

"The device is secure."

"Hand it over."

"No. We exit together. Then you take possession. When we're safe. That is the deal."

The man paused. "Fine. But we need to hurry. We have incoming."

"Wait for us outside the doors and be ready to move."

The man hesitated a moment and then turned and walked away, taking the two others with him.

Helen, still sitting on the floor, crab-walked backward away from Richter until her back hit the wall. Ty could see the hurt on her face.

"Traitor," she spat out.

Richter didn't meet her gaze. He turned to Ty. "Do you still have it?"

Ty's mouth felt full of sawdust. He simply stared at his father, hurt overtaking him too.

"Tyson, answer me."

Ty nodded.

Bishop had found his glasses, but they were broken. Still, he put them on, and that seemed to give him the confidence to speak. "Gerhard, what are you doing?"

"Be quiet, Sandy."

Ty's mother rose and stepped across the room, stopping between Ty and Richter. "You've betrayed us."

Richter reached over and took one of the rifles from a dead marine. "You have every right to judge me, Helen. I only ask that you wait until you know everything."

Richter peered around her, at Ty. "You have to go."

That surprised him. "Where?"

"It's time to turn the page, Tyson."

Turn the page. The page from Kato's file. The back.

Ty realized what it was then: a map. Of how to get away.

Richter had used the bleedthrough of the redactions to draw a path that led somewhere, perhaps outside. It was brilliant.

Bishop rose to his feet. "How could you, Gerhard?"

"I had no choice, Sandy."

"Why?" Helen said. Ty thought hurt was overtaking the anger in her voice now.

"The Covenant has known about this place for years," Richter said. "The building is full of moles. The Covenant would have moved in the moment we decoded the schematic. This was the only way to hold them off." He nodded to Ty, Nora, Kato, and Maria. "And give them a chance to escape."

Richter stepped over to Ty and gripped his shoulder. "Go. Now. But hug your mother before you leave."

There were so many things Ty wanted to ask.

Richter picked up a rifle and glanced at the corridor. "I'll hold them off as long as I can."

When Ty didn't move, his father reached out a hand and propelled him toward his mother. For a moment Ty thought about turning back and hugging him, but Richter was already moving to the door. To Kato, he said, "Take a gun with you, Lieutenant."

Ty's mother wrapped him in a tight hug that made his body ache, but he didn't dare pull away.

"Be careful," she whispered.

Nora approached them, and Ty's mother reached an arm out and pulled her in. "You too," she whispered.

Kato helped Maria to her feet, and together with Ty and Nora, they stepped out into the corridor and jogged toward the door at the other end, away from the Covenant troops. The door had a biometric lock, but the lights were off. It had been disabled. Ty pushed the door open, revealing a dark hallway.

Kato switched on a flashlight that he had scavenged from a

marine, then handed another to Ty, and the team stepped across the threshold, into the near darkness. Kato closed the door behind, and Nora whispered, "Where are we going?"

Ty pulled the page from his pocket, unfolded it, and shone his flashlight down. "I think this leads out of here. My father passed it to me in secret."

"A map," Nora said. "Of what? The building?"

Kato took the page and studied it. "That and the aqueducts. They connect to a bunch of buildings here in the naval yards and run under DC. They link up with the sewer system and steam tunnels—even underground railroads, the metro, and abandoned trolley tunnels. It's like a labyrinth under the city. I talked with some of the marines here. They use the tunnels to move troops and material in at night, in secret. I know where the entrance is."

Beyond the closed door, Ty heard gunfire. It was his father, fighting to give them time to escape. He gripped the quantum radio medallion in his pocket and nodded to Kato. "Okay. Let's go."

49

In a dark corridor, deep in the DARPA facility, Ty watched as Kato held the flashlight with one hand and threw open a door with the other, the rifle slung over his shoulder.

Behind them, in the lab section, the gunfire stopped. Muffled voices rang out. Ty couldn't help wondering if his parents were all right.

Kato marched deeper into the room, past a boiler, air purification scrubbers, and water heaters.

"Over here," he called, raking his flashlight over a massive iron door at the back of the room. There was a metal pole across the center of it, ensuring it couldn't be opened from the outside. It reminded Ty of a door from a medieval castle, barred to keep intruders out.

Kato lifted the pole and pulled the creaking door open, revealing a stone passageway beyond, which to Ty appeared even more medieval.

He looked back, making sure the door to the mechanical room was closed, then followed Kato and the two women into the tunnel.

It was damp and chilly inside. Dark too—the stone walls seemed to absorb light and never give any back, like a black hole that stretched into the darkness as far as Ty could see.

"The map," Kato whispered as he closed the iron door behind them. There was no lock on this side, but Ty watched as the Navy SEAL set the pole against the middle of the door, leaning it slightly. Instantly, he realized the reason: as an alarm, not a deterrent. The moment the door opened, the metal bar would clang onto the stone floor.

Ty handed Kato the map, and he studied it, eyes moving

like the character in Pac-Man, up and down, left and right, at seemingly random points, as though he were tracing the pattern in his mind.

Without a word, he marched deeper into the tunnel. Nora fell in behind him, then Maria, with Ty bringing up the rear.

"Can you all jog?" Kato asked, voice low.

By way of response, Nora broke into a jog, and so did Maria. Ty kept pace, careful not to let his feet slip on the stone floor. At a four-way intersection ahead, Kato turned right.

Behind them, the metal bar clanged on the stones. The Covenant troops were in the tunnels. Or his parents. That thought gave him a flicker of hope. Maybe they were running too.

Nora reached a hand out to Kato, causing him to slow down and finally stop.

"Should we hide?" she whispered.

Kato shook his head. "They'll find us if we do. The map has an endpoint. I'm assuming help will be waiting for us there." He eyed Ty. "Or at least safety. I vote to keep going." He paused. "And stay quiet until we exit."

Ty nodded. "I agree."

"Okay," Nora said as Maria nodded as well.

The next turn was into a smaller shaft, with pipes running along the ceiling and walls. Ty could tell the pipes hadn't been used in a long time. They were cold and quiet and pitted. There were holes every few feet, evidence of time and wear eating away at them. Ty felt as though he were snaking his way through the insides of a giant beast, staring directly at the veins that carried its lifeblood, the holes and pockmarks like the damage time did to a body.

Kato glanced down at the page as he walked, then turned again, into a passage where the pipes were coated in a white powder. He stopped and turned to the three of them. "Don't touch the pipes—they're coated in asbestos."

Before anyone could reply, he spun and resumed his march, breaking into a jog.

After another turn, Kato abruptly came to a stop. He held

his left hand back, palm open, fingers pointing up. Ty sensed that it was a military hand sign. As far as he could tell, it meant stop, and all three did. Ahead, they heard splashing water. And voices.

Whoever was in the tunnels was closing in fast.

50

Kato turned and led Ty, Nora, and Maria back through the passage the way they had come until he found a small alcove.

A rusted metal gate stood at the alcove's entrance. Kato raked his flashlight over it, inspecting the hinges, then the latch. There was no lock there.

He grasped one of the bars and pushed, eliciting a sharp squeak like nails on a chalkboard.

Ty winced at the sound, which could very well get them killed down here. Still, he said nothing. He had to place his trust in Kato now.

Kato paused, letting the sound fade.

In the distance, the voices grew louder. The splashing stopped.

Slowly, Kato pushed the gate again, and this time the squeak was quieter. He stopped when the gap was barely wide enough to slip through, then crept forward.

In the beam of light carving through the darkness, Ty saw that the alcove was, in fact, a small passage that connected to another tunnel—a larger one that looked as though it may have been an underground railway. In the middle of the tunnel was a flat-top mound made of gravel with rounded indentions every few feet, like inverted speed bumps in the gravel road. Ty figured the railroad timbers had once lain where the holes were, but someone had removed them, probably a long time ago.

Kato moved to the end of the small passageway but didn't shine his flashlight outward; he kept it pointed at his torso, preventing a large beam of light from issuing forth. In the soft glow, he peeked out into the tunnel, then clicked off his flashlight and crouched. He motioned for Ty to do the same.

In the darkness, they waited, listening. Ty saw what Kato's plan was: if the people searching came the way they had come, they could enter this other tunnel and escape.

The voices drew closer, their words more sporadic. Boots pounded the stone floor.

First one, then another, and then a third beam of light shone into the passage they had just retreated from. In the dim glow, Ty saw Kato reach out and take Maria's hand and motion for her to reach out to Nora. The two women clasped hands, and Nora offered her palm to Ty. The touch of her warm skin was soothing, a contrast to the cold, dark place.

Kato crept forward, and soon Nora was pulling at Ty's hand, and they emerged from the passage between the tunnels, following the abandoned tracks.

It was darker here—the light from the search party in the other tunnel was fading by the second. So were the sounds of their boots on the stone floor.

Kato led them, pulling them by the chain of hands like a tugboat leading the way through murky, treacherous waters.

The only sound was the crunch of their shoes on the loose gravel beside the mound. Ty felt as though the four of them were floating in the underworld, disembodied, only their souls drifting along, the touch of Nora's hand his only connection to anything real, the last string that tethered him to reality.

Abruptly, she pulled him to the left. He stumbled on the gravel, kicking rocks, the sound grating after the near silence.

"You okay?" Nora whispered.

"I'm fine."

They moved slower in the blackness then, and Ty felt the air change. The dampness returned as they slipped out of the large tunnel and into another alcove.

How had Kato known where the entrance was? He must have seen the other connector tunnel before and timed their march, counting his steps and then feeling for the opening along the wall when they were close.

He led them down the small passage, and Ty heard the slight

creaking of metal, possibly another gate, before they stopped again.

For a fraction of a second, Kato flicked his flashlight on, pointed inward at himself, stole a glance down the original passage they had been on, and clicked it off.

"It's clear," he whispered. "Keep your flashlight off, Ty."

Nora's hand pulled at Ty's, and they were once again moving through the tunnel, which was quiet now. They turned several times, until the passage opened onto a newer section of tunnel that had diffuse light drifting down from above. Ty thought it looked like some sort of underground utility maintenance tunnel or a security passage. Periodically, there were locked grates above with metal ladders leading to round openings that Ty assumed were manholes.

With the aid of the dim light, they moved faster, jogging.

Up ahead, flashlights lanced out through a side tunnel—a search party moving to intersect with them.

Kato came to a halt, the others piling up behind him.

The Navy SEAL glanced behind them, and Ty followed his gaze, to the light emerging there. The sound of voices followed. The searchers had split into two groups—one behind, one ahead. They were closing in.

"Hurry," Kato said, voice low, as he surged forward. "We're close to the exit."

Up ahead, the beams of light turned into the tunnel and raked across the four of them.

"Stop!" a voice yelled.

Kato barreled ahead.

"We'll shoot!" the man's voice called.

Kato turned left, into an opening with stone steps leading up into darkness. Ty was about to ask what the plan was when Kato reached some sort of metal door, switched his light on, and stopped.

Was it locked? Ty heard him rattling something.

Behind them, the lights were growing brighter, the voices louder.

A gunshot rang out, deafening in the cramped space. Before Ty could ask what had happened, Kato threw open a metal door. Moonlight poured in, accompanied by the glow of streetlights. The only sound was the distant roar of a truck.

Kato climbed the stairs, rifle at the ready, the others close behind.

Ty scanned around them, surprised at what he saw. The Smithsonian Castle was directly ahead. The towering monolith of the Washington Monument lay to the right, lighted in all its glory. The United States Capitol loomed to the left, also lit up in the night.

They were on the National Mall. It was deserted at this hour—except for three groups of armed soldiers charging across the grass, converging on them.

Ty's first thought was that the shot had drawn the attention of Capitol Police. But these weren't Capitol Police. They were wearing military fatigues. Ty couldn't tell what branch. They carried rifles with laser sights, their beams trained on the group, red dots dancing across their bodies like glowing bugs swarming in the night.

From the tunnel below, the shouts grew louder, the flashlights brighter.

Kato raised his rifle and pointed it at the oncoming groups, swiveling between them as if trying to decide who to shoot first.

"Ty," he shouted. "What do you want to do here?"

Ty's mind went into overdrive. If they were captured, by either side, there was no doubt in his mind that their captor would enter a code into the quantum radio medallion. If that was going to happen, Ty wanted to type the code himself. He wanted to control their destiny as much as he could. And he was pretty sure he was right about what code to key in.

He just didn't know what would happen when he did.

He shoved the flashlight into his pocket and drew out the round metal object.

"Ty!" Kato called as the armed soldiers continued advancing on them from all directions and below.

Ty mentally repeated what he believed to be the key to using the device:

The Birthright.

The March of Humanity.

Worlds & Time.

The Theory of Everything.

In each, was a single clue.

Birth.

March.

Time.

Everything.

They were the shape of the answer. In his mind's eye, Ty saw the file folders he'd been given for the genomic matches. The cover pages contained photos and birth dates of the three others:

March.

July.

August.

And his birth date: April.

On the quantum radio medallion, he pressed the third symbol. It lit yellow and vibrated as he pressed it. Then the fourth, then the seventh, and finally the eighth symbol.

His vision blurred.

The world around him disappeared.

And in the blink of an eye, it was back.

But the world he saw wasn't the same.

PART II

THE WORLD AFTER

51

Ty stood on the National Mall in Washington, DC, the moon glowing overhead. In the place where the soldiers had been, there was only an overgrown field, swaying in the wind.

The group that had pursued him, Nora, Kato, and Maria in the tunnels below was also gone.

In fact, there was no one in sight. It was completely quiet. The streets were empty. The buildings were dark.

The night sky was brighter than Ty had ever seen it. Stars burned white and yellow across the streaks of purple, blue, and green. Ty had only seen a sky like that once in his life, while camping in the Sahara, far from civilization.

The sky wasn't the only change.

Nature had reclaimed America's capital. Vines climbed up the walls and into windows like snakes invading a carcass. Weeds split the roads and sidewalk.

Ahead, the Smithsonian Castle was a crumbling ruin. The beautiful red sandstone building with its Gothic and Romanesque architecture was half gone. The towers with pointed roofs were collapsed.

To the left of the Smithsonian Castle, Ty expected to see the Hirshhorn Museum, which held art and sculptures. There was nothing there, only trees and tall weeds.

To the left, the Smithsonian National Air and Space Museum was gone too. Growing up, it had been Ty's favorite museum in DC.

In the distance was the US Capitol. Or what was left of it.

The sprawling white building looked as though a giant had smashed it with a massive hammer. The dome was gone. The north and south wings were in shambles, like a mouth open to the sky with teeth missing. The corridors connecting them were mostly collapsed.

Still panning left, Ty got a glimpse of the National Gallery of Art. The massive building that stretched from Madison Drive to Constitution Avenue was, like the Capitol, a crumbling heap. Its marble facade lay in jagged pieces.

The block that held the National Gallery of Art's sculpture garden was overgrown with tall grass and small trees. Immediately to the left, on the north side of the mall across from the Smithsonian Castle, stood the National Museum of Natural History.

The wide neoclassical building had fared better than many of the others. Though the left side was collapsed, the central mass was mostly intact. The golden dome that covered the rotunda, however, had several holes. The pedimented portico with its fluted Corinthian columns and pilasters stood resolute in the quiet night, like the face of a proud fighter who had been hit repeatedly but refused to collapse.

To the left, the National Museum of American History was as Ty remembered it, though some of the walls had taken damage and the windows were broken.

At the end of the mall, the Washington Monument had been demolished. The white obelisk that had once towered over 550 feet in the air was now a pile of marble, granite, and bluestone. Steel from the elevator shaft and stairs lay in twisted red strings weaving through the rubble.

Ty felt eyes upon him and turned to see Nora staring at him, the ruins of the Capitol behind her. The question in her gaze was clear. *What happened here?*

Before he could answer, a crack sounded in the night. He stared up at the sky, where the roar of jet engines grew louder, followed by the rapid *tat-tat-tat* of gunfire.

Two jet fighters were racing toward DC, the guns flashing from only one plane—the pursuer.

Ty couldn't make out the insignia on either aircraft.

A shot ripped through the leading plane, partially severing the wing.

Another shot hit the fuselage near the engine, and then a final burst slammed into the vertical and horizontal stabilizers at the rear.

The bubble canopy over the cockpit blew open and a seat blasted skyward before the jet lurched sideways, the fire of its single engine fading.

It tailspun through the sky, pieces flying off as it plummeted toward the ground.

"Run!" Kato shouted. He turned away from the plane, which was spiraling toward the mall.

Ty took a step back, spun, and sprinted, a mad dash that lasted only a few seconds before the ground shook from the plane's impact.

52

The plane made landfall in a deafening explosion that threw Ty from his feet. A wave of heat washed through the tall grass. The cry of metal twisting groaned in the night. Dirt and airplane pieces rained down, hot as coals from a fire.

Ty lay face down and covered the back of his head with both hands, feeling the wreckage pelt his back, legs, and arms. He was trapped.

He waited, listening, body tensing, half expecting a massive chunk of the plane to fall on him at any second, piercing his body, a fatal blow that would bury him in this strange world. It was a hopeless, nerve-wracking feeling to be pinned down, helpless.

Finally, the shower of fragments and earth slowed and then stopped, and all was quiet again except for the crackle of fire at the crash site.

"Nora!" he called out, still lying face down.

"I'm here."

"Tanaka!" Kato called. "Status green. Santos, report!"

Silence stretched out.

In the distance, Ty heard a jet engine roar again. Was it the pursuing plane? Or a new one?

"Santos!" Kato called again.

Maria's voice finally broke the silence, sounding weary and annoyed. "Quit calling me Santos! We're not on a football team."

Ty smiled. She sounded fine.

He sat up and peered over the swaying grass at the mangled plane. Simmering flames danced over it, lighting the vast field.

The plane that remained in the air was getting closer, engines screaming as it drew near. Gunfire rang out, the *tat-tat-tat* of its mounted guns hammering in the night.

Ty followed the sound, scanning the skies, horrified by what he saw. The pilot who had ejected was floating to the ground, a broad parachute swaying above. The pursuing plane passed by, the light from its guns flaring as it fired, trying to pierce the parachute's canopy.

Kato stalked over to stand beside Ty, watching the parachute sway in the wind. Nora rose and joined them, then Maria, the four of them witnessing the deadly assault in the air, like a duel in which one person was helpless, left to await their fate.

The plane shot past the parachute, then turned sharply, its course veering toward the wreckage on the mall. Gunfire once again spewed from its guns, the shots ripping up the earth, a line of death making directly for them.

"Go!" Kato shouted as all four of them turned and raced toward the National Museum of Natural History directly behind them.

Dirt fell from the sky where the gunfire dug into it. The shots thumped into the ground, shaking it beneath their feet.

Kato altered course once, then again, and the shots ripped past them, barely missing.

The doors to the museum were only a steel skeleton. All the glass was gone, the pieces nowhere in sight.

Kato slowed as he reached them, enough to test whether they were locked, and pushed them open.

The rotunda beyond was in ruin. The light of the moon and stars above shone through the punctured dome overhead.

The giant elephant that stood on a raised platform, which Ty had seen so many times, still towered over the foyer. To the right, Ty knew, was the Hall of Fossils and Deep Time, and to the left lay the Mammals exhibit.

Kato apparently knew the museum's layout as well. He marched toward the Ocean Hall, which lay between the café and Smithsonian research wings. The Human Origins and African Voices exhibits lay beyond, but Kato veered toward the stairs.

"Wait," Nora called out.

Outside, gunfire erupted again, and the jet engine screamed into the night.

"We need to get below ground," Kato said. "We need cover. And there's an exit onto Constitution on the lower level."

Nora crept back to the glassless doors and peered out. Ty arrived just in time to see bullets rip through the parachute and the pilot began plummeting precipitously.

"We have to help him," Nora said.

Apparently sensing he was in a losing argument, Kato came to join them. A second later, the pilot crashed to the ground, disappearing in the sea of tall grass that covered the mall.

"I'll go," he said.

"He—or she—may need a doctor," Nora said.

"I have medical training," Kato said, still peering through the door's metal bars.

"Kato and I will go," Ty said. "We'll carry the pilot—"

"Moving them may not be wise," Nora said. "That's why you need a doctor to make that assessment."

Kato turned to Maria. "Stay here."

"No way. I'm going."

"Why?"

Maria shook her head. "Horror movies."

Kato bunched his eyebrows. "What?"

"In horror movies, the person who gets separated from the group *always* dies. *Always*. I'm not going out like that."

"This isn't a movie."

Ty held up his hands. "Okay. Let's all go."

When the sound of the plane had faded, they ventured out onto the grassy mall, stalking past the simmering wreckage of the downed plane.

The gunshot-riddled parachute had settled into the field, mashing flat a large swath of grass. The suspension lines snaked through the blades, a trail leading to the pilot, who lay on their side, helmet still on. Unmoving.

Kato reached the downed pilot first, held a hand to the person's neck and whispered, "They're alive."

He moved his hands to the helmet, but Nora reached him then

and waved him off. She bent down and examined the person's neck. Ty assumed she was looking for bruises or any sign of swelling, but he wasn't sure.

"It's okay," she whispered.

Kato removed the helmet, revealing a man's face, slender almost to the point of emaciation, deep eye sockets, like someone who hadn't slept well for a very long time, and close-cropped, thinning hair. The man's eyes were closed. He was sweating, Ty assumed, from the pain or shock of the impact. As Ty studied him closer, he realized the man was trembling too, as though a fever process was at work. He wondered if the man was sick. And if whatever had sickened him was contagious.

As Nora examined him, Ty took in the pilot's uniform. There was a patch on the man's chest with what Ty assumed was his last name: James. He wore the rank insignia of a major, and the next thing that caught Ty's eye was the flag on his right shoulder. It was red, with a map of Europe and Asia on it.

"Can you hear me?" Nora asked, leaning close to the pilot.

The man didn't stir. His breathing was shallow and irregular.

Kato unsnapped one of the bundles clipped to his flight suit.

"Here's a survival kit."

He detached a larger sack and tossed it away.

"What was that?" Ty asked.

"Life raft."

Nora unzipped the survival pack and began visually taking stock of the contents.

"We need to get back to the museum. For cover," Kato said.

Nora eyed the man. "We shouldn't move him."

"We shouldn't be out here. We're sitting ducks."

"All right," Nora said. Ty could tell she didn't like it. He didn't either, but he had to agree with Kato—every second they stayed out in the open was a risk.

Kato unclipped the parachute and slipped his arms beneath the man.

"Careful," Nora said. "He could have internal injuries."

Ty moved to help Kato, but the SEAL shook his head. "If we have to run, this will be easier."

Ty wanted to disagree, but he had to admit that Kato was probably right. He could run faster carrying the man than the two of them could together. And Kato seemed to be bearing the weight easily.

As they marched through the grass, Ty listened for the plane, expecting it to cry out in the night at any moment and gunfire to follow.

But there was only silence.

Inside the museum, Kato strode past the elephant in the rotunda, his feet grinding over the dirt and grime that coated the marble floor. It was clear to Ty that no one had been here for a long time.

At the stairwell just to the right of the entrance to the Ocean Hall, Kato turned to Ty.

"Going to need a light."

Ty clicked his flashlight on and shined it ahead, lighting Kato's way down the stone staircase.

Kato turned right at the bottom of the stairs, then right again, and slipped into the Gallery Store. The shelves were mostly bare except for a few figurines and trinkets. A thick coat of dust blanketed everything. The air was stale, like a tomb.

Kato set the pilot down, then took out his own flashlight, switched it on, and placed it on the floor, letting it shine up like a lantern.

"We need answers," he said to no one in particular.

Nora crouched by the pilot, unzipped the survival bag, and began laying out its contents.

"The device," Kato said, "the... radio. It destroyed the world."

"I don't think so," Ty said.

"Looks destroyed to me."

"I don't think the quantum radio did this."

"Cause and effect," Kato said. "We turned it on, and look what happened. How?"

"I'm not sure," Ty said, instantly feeling guilty for not disclosing more. But he wasn't ready to discuss his theories—not without a little more certainty.

Nora seemed to sense his reluctance. She looked up from the bandages and medications. "But you have an idea."

"A theory."

"The device altered the timeline, didn't it?" she asked.

Ty bit his lip. "I don't think that's exactly it."

"Some of the buildings on the mall are gone," Nora said. "Buildings we've been in—you and me—many times over the last thirty years."

"They could have been destroyed," Kato said.

"There was no rubble pile," Nora replied. "It looks like they were never built."

"Or they were razed," Kato said. He paced away from the group. "Actually, we don't need to speculate. We can go get answers. Right now. Next door."

Ty squinted, confused.

"The details of what happened here should be in the building beside us," Kato said. "In the National Museum of American History."

53

In the gift store of the National Museum of Natural History, the team agreed that Kato and Ty would venture out to search for answers about what was going on while Nora and Maria stayed with the unconscious pilot.

Outside the gallery gift store, Kato switched off his flashlight, and he and Ty moved through the museum with only the aid of the dim moonlight filtering in through the entrance from Constitution Avenue. The doors to the outside lay directly ahead, past the T. rex skull and a row of Moai, the monolithic human figures carved by the Rapa Nui people on Easter Island.

The entrance at Constitution Avenue had long ago been broken in. Kato ventured out tentatively, his rifle held at the ready, listening.

As they crept forward in the moonlight, Ty considered what the quantum radio had brought with them: seemingly everything attached to their bodies, such as their clothes, thankfully, and the items they held. It was as if a bubble had formed around the four, one that encompassed all the items attached to them. He noted that fact for the future.

Kato crouched, listening. Ty assumed he was waiting for the sound of the plane to return. But it was utterly silent.

"Did you see the flag on the man's uniform?" Ty whispered.

"I did. It's very curious."

Kato rose and crept forward, rifle at the ready. They were a few feet from the entrance to the National Museum of American History when they heard clacking on the broken pavement of 12th Street, which ran between the two museums. Kato spun toward the noise, bringing the rifle to his shoulder.

Ty's heart thundered in his chest.

The *clack-clack-clack* grew louder until the source emerged from behind a large limestone building that Ty recognized as the United States Environmental Protection Agency.

It was a family of deer. Four of them, led by a buck with tall antlers ending in ten points. They stopped and stared at Kato and Ty, as though they had never seen a living person before. They didn't know to fear humans, which told Ty something very important about this world.

Inside the National Museum of American History, Ty snapped on the flashlight and Kato held the rifle at the ready, but there wasn't a soul in sight. The museum had changed radically. Gone were the exhibits Ty remembered from his youth and even from the past few years when he had been home to visit his mother and sister.

Ahead, a large sign hung with an arrow pointing to the right. The large block letters read:

*THE COVENANT WAR
PERMANENT EXHIBIT*

54

Nora unzipped the pilot's flight suit and used the surgical scissors from the survival kit to cut open his T-shirt, revealing the man's torso.

Blue and purple bruises ran across his chest and sides. Two of his ribs were probably fractured. Of more concern to her was the large black circle to the left of his belly button.

It indicated internal bleeding. This man needed to be in a hospital operating room. Right now.

Working more urgently, she used the scissors to cut the pilot's pants up from the bottom. His legs were worse than his torso. Bruises that likely surrounded fractures striped his upper and lower legs. He had landed on his feet, and his long bones had probably shattered in several places.

The fractures presented a larger danger: embolisms. Blood clots were the most common cause of embolisms, but with large breaks in his leg bones—and probably pelvis—Nora was concerned that fatty embolisms might develop.

If an embolism traveled to the man's brain or heart, his survival chances would be low.

During her residency, Nora had done rotations in virtually all fields of medicine, but her specialty was psychiatry. And her PhD was in experimental psychology. The brain and how it functioned biochemically and psychologically were her domain. Given time and the right tools, she might be able to care for the man. But here and now, she had to admit that she was way out of her depth. She had to get him some help.

"So... you're a doctor?" Maria asked.

Nora realized that they had never really had the chance to get acquainted.

"I am."

"Can you help him?"

"I'm not really that kind of doctor."

"What kind are you?"

"A psychiatrist. A researcher, mostly."

Maria exhaled. "Perfect. I'm gonna have a lot of things I need to talk to a shrink about after this."

Nora smiled, glad for the levity that eased the growing anxiety inside of her. A part of her wanted to point out the nuances between a psychiatrist and a psychologist, especially in a clinical therapy setting, but she sensed that this wasn't exactly the right time for that.

"I think we all are," Nora said.

"So what do we do?"

"We need to get him some help."

"How?"

"I don't know. He probably has some sort of radio or beacon on him somewhere."

Maria nodded to his uniform. "He's not US military. How do we know we're on the same team?"

"That's a good question."

"And?"

"And I don't know the answer. But I know it's our responsibility to try to help him."

Nora set about searching the man, running her hands in each pocket and drawing out the contents.

They were empty.

"This is going to sound crazy," Maria said, "but I'm hungry." She shrugged. "I get hungry when I'm nervous."

"Yeah. Me too."

"I know I said I wasn't going to leave the group, but I'm thinking of going to look for some food." She motioned to the pilot. "I don't think I can do anything to help."

Nora reached into the survival kit and drew out a tube of liquid that she was fairly certain was a chemical light. She bent the stick until it cracked and began glowing with greenish-yellow light. She shook it, and the light grew brighter.

"Here, take this," Nora said. "We'll be fine. But be careful."

Maria rose and receded into the darkness, shining the ChemLight as she went, the glow reminding Nora of the lightning bugs she used to catch in her hands as a child.

Maria's footsteps on the stone floor gradually faded, leaving Nora in silence except for the pilot's shallow breathing.

She opened the survival kit and rifled through the contents again, mentally noting the items in case she needed one quickly. Organizing had always been a source of serenity for her. As a child, stressful situations would drive her to her room and to her closet, where she would arrange her clothes relentlessly until a sort of Zen-like clarity came over her.

As she counted the supplies and laid them out on the floor in neat rows, that peace still evaded her. It wasn't just the dying pilot. It was this place. The uncertainty. And Ty being away from her. She sensed that he was in danger out there.

An eerie sensation swept over her. She turned quickly and looked across the small gift store at a glass display case by the entrance. But there was no one there. She could have sworn she heard something. Or felt eyes watching her.

"Maria?" she called out in the dim light.

There was only silence, not even the sound of Maria's footsteps.

Nora rose. "Hello?"

Nerves gathered in her stomach. She gripped the flashlight and held it out as though it were some sort of light sword that could protect her.

"Hello!" she said, louder now, unable to hide the fear in her voice.

At her feet, the pilot stirred and grimaced.

Nora shined the flashlight on him and squatted down and gripped his shoulders, steadying the man. He opened his eyes. They were yellow and watery—he was jaundiced.

"Doc," the man whispered.

"I'm here," Nora said instinctively, moving a hand from the man's shoulder to grip his hand.

"I thought they captured you," he whispered.

Nora paused, confused. "I..."

"How did you escape?" he asked.

"Who do you think I am?" Nora asked.

A smile tugged at the man's lips. "Doc, I'm banged up, not out of my mind. You're Dr. Nora Brown. Pax Director of Psychological Warfare. You were the psych officer on Operation Hydra."

The man closed his eyes and swallowed hard.

Nora's heart was thundering in her chest, her mind racing, trying to understand.

"What happened to the rest of the team?" he asked.

"They..."

"Dead, aren't they?"

"We'll have to talk about that later," Nora said, her mind grasping for the right words to try to understand what was happening. "Major, tell me what you remember."

He bunched his eyebrows together. "Major?"

Nora nodded to his uniform. "Are you not Major James?"

He let out a laugh and immediately grimaced. The convulsion must've been agonizing with the wounds to his ribs and abdomen.

"I stole this uniform from a Covenant pilot before I threw him in the Atlantic." He sucked in a breath and eyed her. "Are you sure you're not the one with head trauma?"

She paused. "I wasn't sure what state you were in. I need you to tell me what you remember. We're trying to piece things together here. Please start from the beginning. Tell me your name."

He swallowed, closed his eyes, and nodded. "Standard debrief."

"Right. Standard debrief."

The man tried to take a deep breath, but it was as if his chest couldn't expand completely. Finally, he got enough air in his lungs to continue. "Commander Matthews. Pax Spec Ops, American division. Assigned to Operation Hydra."

"Operation to do what?"

"Determine if the intel was correct."

"Intel about what?"

"The A21."

"A21?"

The pilot studied her face. "What is this? Some new procedure?"

Nora seized on the opportunity. "That's right, Commander. We need to make sure you are who you say you are. No offense."

He swallowed hard. "None taken. Can't be too careful... especially with the Covenant."

When Nora said nothing, he continued. "Operation Hydra was a mission to confirm the existence of a new kind of Covenant rocket: the A21. A long-range rocket capable of hitting the last Pax camps deep in North America and Australia."

He gasped for breath.

"We spent a month on a Pax submarine. We came down past the Shetlands, through the North Sea, and with the help of radio intel from resistance cells, we made it to the Baltic."

He inhaled sharply two times, struggling to catch his breath.

"We surfaced, and a group of fishermen who were part of the resistance took us ashore near Peenemünde."

"Germany?"

Matthews frowned. "Germany? Only ever heard my grandparents call it that."

Nora paused, feeling caught in a lie. She saw only one solution: to press on. "Please continue, Commander. You put ashore in..."

"Peenemünde." He squinted at her. "You don't remember?"

"Describe it for the record. If you don't mind."

"It's a coastal town in the state of Mecklenburg-Vorpommern in Reich Europa. On shore, we linked up with a local resistance cell and soon gained access to the Peenemünde Army Research Center. We confirmed that the A21 was real. And its range capabilities. It can hit us. All of our camps. But that's not the worst part."

Matthews's chest was heaving now. The effort was catching up with him.

"The A21 carries a new payload. We don't stand a chance against it."

He drew another breath. "You made the call: to relay the information back to Pax Intel even if it meant getting killed or captured. And we did. They killed most of the team except for me. I got away. And I followed orders. I came straight here. But they caught up to me."

"What's in the warheads?" Nora asked.

"A weapon that will change us somehow—change our minds. They're unveiling it in four days at a massive ceremony at Peenemünde." He was breathing hard now. "What we didn't know is that they're going to launch the rockets that night. They'll wipe us out. The entire Pax. In seven days."

55

Inside the National Museum of American History, Ty and Kato walked toward the exhibit marked *THE COVENANT WAR*.

Ty's flashlight led their way. Behind them, hazy moonlight shone through the museum's entrance on Constitution Avenue.

Dust lay heavy on the ground and the exhibits, a blanket laid by time, covering many of the signs. Ty wondered how long the place had been abandoned. Ten years? Twenty? Longer?

The first section of the exhibit was a series of pictures and placards with descriptions. Ty recognized the people in the historical photos: Joseph Stalin, Winston Churchill, Franklin D. Roosevelt, Benito Mussolini, and Adolf Hitler. The sign above it read *PRELUDE TO WAR*.

The description under the heading read:

In the years before the outbreak of the Covenant War, alliances were forged.

Ty moved his gaze to the first photo, which showed Joseph Stalin shaking hands with a younger, slightly taller man with blond hair and a black sport coat. The caption indicated that the younger man was German foreign minister Joachim von Ribbentrop. Ty read the heading and description:

GERMAN–SOVIET NONAGGRESSION PACT
August 23, 1939
Nazi Germany and the Soviet Union shocked the world by signing a nonaggression pact that forbade either nation from taking military action against the other for the next ten years. The pact also included secret details of how the two

major powers would divide up Eastern Europe in the coming war.

"It's the same as in our timeline," Kato said.
Ty scanned the next photo and the text below:

Easter Accords
April 16, 1938
In Rome, representatives from the British and Italian govern-ments agreed to keep the existing world order and prevent Italy from aligning itself with Germany in future wars. The agreements were later registered with the League of Nations in March of 1939.

Benito Mussolini, the fascist dictator of Italy, harbored different feelings. He believed that nations with rising populations were destined to rule the world while those with falling populations would eventually be conquered. As such, Mussolini placed relentless demands on Italian women to have more children in order to reach a population of sixty million—which he believed Italy needed to win a major war.

Mussolini believed that the declining birth rates in France would eventually doom the nation and that the British Empire faced a similar fate as 25 percent of its population was over fifty years old.

Below was a picture of US president Franklin D. Roosevelt at what appeared to be a dais in front of Congress. The caption read:

The US Neutrality Acts of the 1930s
In the years after the Great War, growing isolationism and noninterventionism in the United States prompted Congress to pass a series of neutrality acts starting in 1935 and again in 1936, 1937, and 1939, with the goal of keeping the United States out of another global conflict.

"It's still just like our timeline," Kato said. "In our world, those neutrality acts probably prolonged the war because they didn't distinguish between aggressor and victim. They prevented the United States from providing early support that may have helped bring the war to a conclusion."

At that moment, Ty had the distinct impression that someone was watching him. He spun, raking the flashlight across the exhibit hall and out into the lobby.

Kato raised his gun and stepped away from the glass display case that held the photos.

"Someone's here," Ty whispered.

Without a word, Kato crept forward, rifle stock at his shoulder, leading the way.

In the lobby, they waited, listening.

But there was no one there. Not even a sound.

"Maybe I imagined it," Ty said.

Kato glanced up at the ceiling. "No. I felt it too. Maybe it's just this place creaking and falling apart."

"Maybe," Ty mumbled.

It was clear neither of them believed that.

They returned to the exhibit, to the next section that was labeled:

WAR BEGINS

In the pictures and descriptions, Ty saw a timeline that matched the history he knew:

- July 7, 1937: War between China and Japan begins.
- September 1, 1939: Germany invades Poland.
- September 3, 1939: France and Great Britain declare war on Germany. Australia, New Zealand, South Africa, and Canada soon join in the war against Germany.
- September 17, 1939: The Soviet Union, after entering into a cease-fire with Japan, invades eastern Poland.
- May 10, 1940: Winston Churchill becomes Prime Minister of Great Britain. On the same day, Germany launches its offensive against France. In a

surprise move, the Wehrmacht invades Belgium, the
Netherlands, and Luxembourg, transiting the thick
forests and difficult terrain of the Ardennes region and
completely bypassing the extensive French fortifications
of the Maginot line that run along the Franco–German
border. Forty-six days later, the Battle of France is over,
ending in a German victory and the surrender of France
and subsequent occupation by German forces.

- June 1940: The Soviet Union forcibly annexes Estonia,
  Latvia, Lithuania, and various regions of Romania.

Kato pointed at the next placard, which showed a black-and-
white photo of planes in the air shooting at one another over
London.

"Here's the first difference in the timeline," Kato said.

Ty quickly read the description:

- July 10, 1940: The Battle of Britain begins. In the first
  major military campaign fought entirely by air forces,
  Great Britain's Royal Air Force (RAF) and Fleet Air Arm
  (FAA) defend the British homeland against a relentless
  assault by the German Luftwaffe. While the Luftwaffe
  fighters and bombers never achieve air superiority over
  the RAF squadrons, the tide turns decisively during the
  Blitz, when Germany launches a massive rocket attack
  known as the Night of Fire on September 15, 1940. During the Night of Fire, Germany launches 382 A4 rockets. The barrage delivers a devastating bombardment of
  London, destroying the British Parliament and most of
  the city and taking the lives of most members of parliament, including the Prime Minister, Winston Churchill.
  RAF bases are also nearly obliterated, including RAF
  Fighter Command Headquarters at Bentley Priory. A
  week later, Great Britain falls.

"That's it," Kato said. "In our time, the British survived
the Blitz and won the Battle of Britain. By the beginning of

September 1940, the Luftwaffe had essentially lost the battle. The Germans were desperate to turn it around. They began bombing London. Starting on September 7th, 1940, the Luftwaffe unleashed on the city, dropping bombs for fifty-six of the next fifty-seven days and nights. It was brutal. September 15th was the climax of the action—what we call Battle of Britain Day. About fifteen hundred aircraft were involved in the fighting. It was part of Hitler's plan to force Britain to surrender or agree to peace. The plan was to break the RAF and then invade the British mainland on September 17th in what was codenamed Operation Sea Lion."

Kato thought for a moment. "On our world, at this point in the war, Germany had conquered most of Western Europe and Scandinavia. The British Empire and the Commonwealth was the only major power left opposing them. Hitler had made several peace offers, but the British kept rejecting them. The Battle of Britain is arguably one of the most important military battles in history. If Britain had fallen, the world would be a very different place. At that moment—in the fall of 1940—they were very much alone. The Russians were still allied with the Germans. The Japanese wouldn't bomb Pearl Harbor for two more years, and the United States' populace was still staunchly opposed to another war. But in our time, the Luftwaffe never broke the RAF or the British people. They held strong on September 15th, and Hitler had to cancel Operation Sea Lion. The Germans never invaded the UK."

Ty shook his head. "How in the world do you remember all this?"

"I told you. I like history." Kato pointed at the placard. "But it's different here. During the Blitz in our time, Germany fought with bombers and fighters. They didn't have any ballistic missiles capable of striking deep into Great Britain." He pointed at the display case. "Here they had A4s—and a lot of them. In our time, the A4 missiles weren't used in the war until September of 1944—almost four years after Battle of Britain Day—what they call the Night of Fire here."

"I've never heard of the A4."

"Sure you have," Kato said. "You've just heard its other name: the V-2 rocket."

"The A4 is the V-2?"

"One and the same. The A stands for 'Aggregat.' That was the internal name for the program, which started with the A1, a rocket designed by Wernher von Braun in 1933."

"Him, I've heard of. He was moved from Germany to the US after World War II, where he invented the rockets that took the Apollo spacecraft to the Moon."

"Indeed. His work at NASA was sort of the culmination of the research he began in Germany. Von Braun, along with Walter Dornberger and Walter Riedel, began working on rockets in the 1930s at Kummersdorf—an estate south of Berlin. They developed the A1, A2, and A3 at Kummersdorf before they moved the research to Peenemünde on the island of Usedom on the Baltic coast. They had more space there, and it was harder to spy on. The A3 was the first Aggregat rocket to launch at Peenemünde. They used Kummersdorf for nuclear research, starting in 1938.

"At Peenemünde, the Aggregat program made incredible progress. They had several different rockets in development— including the A10, which was designed to reach the continental United States. As early as 1940, the Germans were actively working on the A10, which they projected could hit America by 1946. But the A5 is when the Aggregat rocket series gets interesting. A lot of its components were reused in the A4— which was actually launched after the A5 and, again, became known as the V-2 when it was used in the war. In our world, the A4 first flew in March of 1942, and it didn't fly far—about a mile before it crashed in the water. But by October 3rd of 1942, the A4 was flying one hundred twenty miles and reaching an altitude of fifty-two miles. They put the missile into production in 1943, and as I said, in our time, they launched it in the war in September of 1944. But here, in this time, they had them four years earlier, and look at the difference it made."

Kato nodded toward the display case. "Those A4—or V-2— rockets turned the tide in the Battle of Britain. They enabled the

Germans to defeat the British. Someone in this timeline must have pushed harder in the 1930s at Kummersdorf and Peenemünde. They had the foresight to know how important those rockets would be to world history."

"Or someone told them," Ty said, his gaze drifting up to the sign that read THE COVENANT WAR.

"Meaning?"

"Meaning this world might be like ours in one important way—history is not what it's supposed to be."

"What are you saying?"

"Consider the idea that there's an unseen hand at work here, forcing progress, like in the German rocket program, progress to some end we don't yet understand. I'm not saying we know that for sure. But what I do know is that there is a common thread running between this world and ours, and it leads directly to the Covenant."

56

By the time Maria returned, the pilot had once again slipped into unconsciousness.

Nora had to admit that she was a bit disappointed to see Maria empty-handed.

"No food?" she asked.

"Nothing," Maria replied. "This place has been picked clean. And it's weird in here."

"Weird how?"

"Can't quite place it. The language on the signs. It's sort of antiquated. Like from some kind of black-and-white movie or something."

Maria glanced down at the survival kit supplies, which were lined up in neat rows and columns.

"What happened here?"

"It's sort of a habit."

"Like chewing your nails."

Nora smiled. "A lot like that."

Maria rubbed her palms on her pants as though they were sweating, as if she was nervous all of a sudden.

"What is it?" Nora asked.

"I've got some habits myself."

"What kind?"

"The bad kind."

"I think we all do."

"Not like this."

"I'm a doctor. You can tell me about it."

"I've been taking methadone to help me control cravings."

"For opioids."

"Yeah." Maria swallowed, suddenly seeming embarrassed. "It

happens before you know it. You're on the road. Standing up for hours on high heels. The aches and pains. Advil and Tylenol stop working after a while. Plenty of doctors around—the agent and manager have them on speed dial. They write you something to get you though the show, and you think, 'He's a doctor. He knows what he's doing.'"

"You don't have to explain," Nora said.

Maria kept going. "The pain in your body isn't the worst, though. It's the hurt in your mind. Things that happened before the music. And after."

Maria swallowed. "You spend months—sometimes years—making a piece of art to share with the world. You put a piece of yourself in it. You have to. If you don't—if you phone it in—people will know. They can sense authenticity. And when it's not there. But that authenticity, that piece of you in the art, makes you care about it. It makes you vulnerable. And that's the problem. No matter how many people like it—and especially if a lot of people like it—someone decides it's not for them or that it's overrated, and they attack you. They write articles that tear your work to shreds. But that's not the real problem. They have a right to dislike the work. And to tell the world. It's the personal attacks that get to you. The people who make the personal attacks have gotten smarter about it. They post them in groups now. Groups that make all their posts public so the world can see them. But you have to be a member to respond. They like that—using their reach to hurt you and their numbers to defend themselves. Haters find strength in numbers. Tearing you apart feeds their ego. It makes them feel big to cut someone successful down. And it doesn't matter whether they're right or wrong—you can't say a thing. Because you're the artist, and the haters think it's their right to psychologically assault you. Publicly. It's almost like they're daring you to join the group and defend yourself. They delight when you do. Because they swarm. The minute you respond, they've won. You have the choice of sitting there and just taking their assault or defending yourself—and you're up against people who specialize in online warfare. People looking for a fight. After all, that's why they posted. Because in the end, what they really want is to hurt you and your career and make themselves feel more powerful. And either way, they win. Because if you don't defend yourself, it haunts you. Because you just took it. And where I'm from, you don't just take it when somebody comes at you personally. Not if you want to survive. Not if you want to make something of your life." Maria shook her head. "And I admit, I've got a temper. Besides pills, that's my other problem. And when it comes to the internet, that's an issue. When you're the artist and you defend yourself, they make you out to be a jerk. And if they can make others dislike you, they'll stop buying your work, no matter how good it is. Game over."

Maria fell silent. Nora wasn't sure what to say. So she reached out and took Maria's hand in hers. The woman seemed to remember Nora was there, and she continued:

"You get useless advice like, 'Oh, just ignore the haters. Focus on the work.'"

Maria snorted. "Then you get an email a few weeks later from your publicist asking why you're not supporting the media tour by posting on social media, interacting with fans online. You tell them why and they say something about people booing you in a dive bar and this online hate being just like that."

Maria laughed, eyes cold. "But it's not. Not even close. In a dive bar on a Friday night, when a bunch of drunks boo you off the stage, it doesn't really matter. Hurts the first time. Maybe the second. But you get used to it. And you realize that it sort of helps. You're getting feedback. Half those dudes booing won't even remember it in the morning. The next night you'll be on stage in the same place singing different songs and be better off for it."

She nodded. "But not online. The internet isn't a hole-in-the-wall dive bar. It's the whole world watching. It's where art is sold now—by and large. Those online haters aren't booing you off the stage. They're burning down your business. And you have to stand in the parking lot and watch. You scroll through your feed, and you see those public groups throwing Molotov cocktails at your storefront—at your brand and you personally—and some catch fire and some don't, and you just have to take it. I couldn't do that. Couldn't control my temper. Until I took those pills. For the first time in a long time, I *was* able to ignore the haters. To scroll on by. To stop caring for a while. And more. I could create with reckless abandon again. And I loved it. Those pills gave me my life back. All they asked was that I kept taking more every week. And then, before I knew it, they took everything from me. At that point, the haters weren't my biggest problem. The pills were."

Maria reached in her pocket. "Getting free of them has been the hardest thing I've ever done in my life. I'm not there yet. But I'm close." She held up a small bottle. "I've got seven methadone pills left. If I don't get some more, I'm going to be in a terrible way."

"There aren't any in this kit," Nora said quietly. "But we'll find some."

Maria chewed her lip as she stared at the survival supplies. "But there are opioids in there, aren't there?"

Nora looked up at Maria. "There are. But we'll figure something else out."

57

For a long moment, Kato stared at the Covenant War exhibit in the National Museum of American History, considering Ty's words.

"It's a big leap," he said finally. "Some force interfering with history on this world. And ours."

"It is," Ty admitted. "But it fits."

"Let's read the rest," Kato said.

The pictures in the next display class showed a series of ships loaded with passengers carrying overstuffed duffel bags, sheets serving as sacks bulging with contents, and battered suitcases.

To Ty, they looked like people who had left home in the middle of the night, having gathered their most prized possessions in seconds.

The large heading above the photos read:

THE BRITISH EXODUS

The description was heartbreaking.

In the forty-eight hours after the Night of Fire, Great Britain executed a mass migration on a scale the world had never seen before. Millions of its citizens were evacuated to Iceland and to waiting ships from the Canadian and British Royal Navy. British troops had invaded Iceland in May of 1940 and had been controlling the small island to the north ever since. But Iceland would only be a stopover for the final destination in the British diaspora.

Millions of British and Irish citizens settled in the Dominion of Newfoundland, a British Territory bordering

Canada. Like the millions of children and elderly sent overseas during Operation Pied Piper in 1939, the mass evacuation of 1940 saw British citizens relocated to Canada, South Africa, Australia, New Zealand, and the United States, but the new seat of the British government was established at what was then St. John's in Newfoundland, which was renamed New London.

Ty turned to Kato. "How much of what happened here happened in our timeline?"

"About half and half."

"Which half?"

Kato reread the placard. "The British did invade Iceland in May 1940."

"Really?"

"Well, technically, it was an invasion, but there was no fighting. The British Royal Navy and Royal Marines basically walked onto the island and took over. There were fewer than eight hundred British troops involved, if memory serves. The biggest trouble was with the British military personnel having relations with the Icelandic women. It rubbed a lot of the local men the wrong way—an issue that was referred to as 'The Situation.'"

"Why invade Iceland at all?"

"Two reasons. One: Iceland's location. The island would've been a good launching point for the Luftwaffe, and of course, the Kriegsmarine. The second is that the Germans had recently overrun Denmark, which had a union with Iceland."

Kato scanned the placard again. "Operation Pied Piper in 1939 also happened in our timeline—millions of children were evacuated the summer before war broke out in Europe."

"And Newfoundland?"

"It was indeed a British Territory in 1940. It had been one of the original dominions within the meaning of the Balfour Declaration and had been self-governing for a long time until the early 1930s, when the British government had to step in and reassert some control."

"Why?"

"I think they went broke. I can't remember exactly why."

"I thought you liked history."

"Hey, I said I liked history. Remembering the details of the revocation of Newfoundland's dominion status in the 1930s is next-level obsession."

Ty held his hands up. "Just messing with you."

With that, Ty resumed reading the exhibit:

After the fall of Great Britain and the British Exodus, Germany was now firmly in control of Western Europe except for one island of neutrality in the middle of the continent: Switzerland. Germany had been drawing up plans for the invasion of Switzerland since the conclusion of the Battle of France. The massive mobilization, codenamed Operation Tannenbaum, was carried out on December 24, 1940. In a maneuver as stunning as the blitzkrieg through the Ardennes, the Wehrmacht overran Swiss forces in a three-day assault that resulted in the Swiss confederation's full surrender in Bern on December 27, 1940, though sporadic fighting in several cantons continued for another week.

With the fall of Switzerland, Germany had full control of continental Europe and the British Isles. Its closest ally, Italy, controlled the Mediterranean. The Soviet Union stretched from Poland to China. The Empire of Japan occupied everything from the Soviet Union to Australia. Those three powers: Germany, the Soviet Union, and Japan, with the support of Italy, controlled nearly all of Europe and Asia. Sensing that suppressed nationalism was a threat to its ambitions on the continent, Germany changed its official name from the Greater German Reich to Reich Europa, removing the German name and attempting to forge a single continental identity. Within each nation, states were given their autonomy and legislative seats in the Reich Europa Congress. But the most surprising move from the Axis powers was still yet to come: peace.

The last line surprised Ty, especially given what he had seen outside—the war zone Washington, DC had become. Or once had been.

The next heading was:

THE LONG PEACE

In a stunning move, Reich Europa, the Soviet Union, and the Empire of Japan announced the establishment of a new mutual cooperation agreement: the Human Covenant, or the Covenant, as the new alliance came to be known. The Covenant's stated purpose was realizing humanity's ultimate potential. But it had a darker goal, and it hid that secret plan behind perhaps the greatest cover of all: forty-two years of peace that lasted until October of 1982.

"Incredible," Kato said. "In this timeline, World War II effectively paused after the loss at the Battle of Britain and the British Exodus. The Germans never invaded the Soviet Union in Operation Barbarossa. In our timeline, Germany invaded the Soviet Union in June 1941. It was a desperate gambit to try to force the British to make terms. The Germans thought that if they invaded quickly, they could collapse the Soviet Union. The feeling was that if they kicked in the front door, the entire country would collapse. They made two miscalculations. One, they underestimated the Red Army. And two, they underestimated winter in Russia. It was a massive blunder, one that pretty much doomed Germany. It's debatable, but it's probably on par with Pearl Harbor."

Kato motioned to the display. "Another event that never happened here. America was still anti-war until Japan dropped those bombs on Pearl Harbor in December of 1941. That changed everything. In our timeline, after the US joined World War II, there was very little doubt in anyone's mind how things would turn out—eventually. Between the Soviet Union, the British and their dominions, and the United States, the allies had the numbers and the industrial base to win. But here, the US never joined the war."

"It's amazing," Ty said, "how one small change can turn the course of history. In this timeline, Germany focused on its rocket development in the 1930s and that changed everything. It redrew the map of the world."

"Indeed. History is far more fragile than most people realize."

Ty moved to the next exhibit:

MASS MIGRATIONS & NEW ALLIANCES

The image above it was of the flag he had seen on the pilot's shoulder.

Beginning in the 1940s, the Covenant states instituted a broad-based policy of forced deportations of what they considered to be undesirable populations, which they left on the shores of non-Covenant nations. Initially, the "Relocated," as the Covenant referred to them, were resettled in Africa. But after waves of the Relocated began returning across the Mediterranean, the program began transporting large groups to the United States, Canada, and Australia, where passage back to Europe and Asia would be more difficult. When the United States, Canada, and Australia began intercepting deportation ships, the Covenant began dropping the Relocated in Indonesia, the Philippines, and Greenland, where conditions were deadly in the winter.

The early 1940s were marked by massive refugee crises around the world that exacerbated the already strained resources of nations who had taken in those fleeing the war in 1939 and 1940. In that crisis, a new alliance was born: the Pax Humana—which became widely known as simply "the Pax." The founding nations of the Pax included the United States, Canada, the United Kingdom and Commonwealth in exile, Australia, the newly liberated nation of India, Indonesia, the Philippines, and Mexico. Later signatories included nations in Central America, Egypt, Libya, and Morocco.

The Pax nations agreed to a mutual defense pact as well as a broad-based sharing of resources to combat the growing humanitarian crises straining their national resources.

Below the text was an image of five men sitting at a long table. Four were wearing keffiyeh, a traditional Arabian headdress. The heading read:

BLACK GOLD FORGES NEW FRIENDSHIPS

With the birth of the Pax, and the Covenant continuing to tighten its grip in Eurasia, an unexpected new alliance emerged—one of the major oil exporters, Iran, Iraq, Kuwait, Saudi Arabia, and Venezuela. The five nations of the newly formed Global Petroleum Cartel, or GPC, declared themselves neutral in any future conflict and pledged to supply oil to all nations, regardless of alliance or beliefs.

"It's the same founders as OPEC," Kato said. "Except in our timeline, OPEC wasn't formed until 1960."

"It amazes me that you remember all that."

"It amazes me that you discovered a device that transported us here."

"Yeah, that amazes me too."

Ty focused on the next heading.

A NEUTRAL CONTINENT

With the world rapidly forming alliances, the nations of South America—with the exception of Venezuela—formed their own alliance, one dedicated to neutrality. Their first act was to build a massive wall along the border between Panama and Colombia, stretching ninety miles across the Darién Gap. With its neutrality recognized by the Covenant, Pax, and GPC, the nations of South America quickly carved out important roles on the world stage. Argentina became the world's new banking capital. Many bankers from Switzerland and across Europe had escaped there during the war, and they quickly reestablished their presence in international finance.

Brazil became an important exporter of minerals and agriculture. Nations throughout South America became known for their cultural impact—from music to radio programs to novels translated for consumption around the world.

The next display case had been shattered. The heading was still there—*THE SECOND DARK AGE*—but the placards were gone.

"A new Dark Age?" Kato whispered, studying the missing exhibit.

"Could have been a natural disaster."

"Or a continuation of the war." Kato looked back toward the entrance to the hall. "After all, the exhibit is titled 'the Covenant War.'"

"A fair point."

"Over here," Kato said, pointing at a display case nearby.

The heading read:

THE COVENANT SEAWALL.

Beneath it was a series of photos of military ships intercepting commercial vessels.

In the 1940s and '50s, the Covenant massively increased spending on infrastructure across Europe and Asia. They built high-speed rail lines, created a unified air force and navy, and centralized control of their phone system and TV broadcast systems. While each Covenant signatory maintained its own army, the Covenant air force and navy grew substantially. The new Covenant air and naval forces launched a coordinated effort called "The Covenant Seawall," which formed a floating and aerial defensive perimeter around the Covenant, preventing people and material from non-Covenant nations from entering. The only exception to the Covenant Seawall was passage from South America, which became a popular waypoint for a growing number of Pax citizens trying to make their way to the Covenant.

Out of the corner of his eye, Ty saw a photo that nearly made his heart stop.

He strode over to the standing exhibit and studied the picture encased in glass. The woman was in her late thirties by the looks of it, and she was standing in an auditorium in front of a group of extremely fit men and women in their twenties.

There was no doubt in Ty's mind that it was his mother in the picture. The caption confirmed it:

Dr. Helen Klein unveils the first cohort in her Darwin Program, a Covenant initiative to elevate the physical and mental potential of the human species.

Ty swallowed as he read the next card.

Together with her husband, Lars Jacobs, Dr. Klein developed the Darwin Program at the University of Bonn, in the Reich Europa state of North Rhine-Westphalia.

Kato seemed to sense Ty's distress.

"What is it?"

"My mother."

Kato came over to look at the photo. "But obviously that isn't your father."

"No," Ty said quietly. "I don't know what it means, but I met that guy in our time a few days ago."

"Doing what?"

"He was a Belgian truck driver working in Switzerland. And an amateur philosopher. He's much more here."

"And your mother isn't an American."

"Apparently. In our world, she was born in the West German capital of Bonn, but her parents—my grandparents—emigrated to the United States in the sixties."

"What does it mean?" Kato asked.

"I don't know yet." Ty glanced at the remaining display cases. Every one of them was broken, the photos and placards stolen.

Suddenly, he again had the unnerving sense that someone was watching him. He spun and scanned the room and the hall, but there was no one there. No sound. No movement.

58

In the soft, yellow-green glow of the ChemLight, Nora and Maria sat in the gift store, listening for any indication that Kato and Ty were returning.

The pilot—Commander Matthews—lay on the floor, his breathing shallow and erratic. Periodically, he would stir, but he hadn't opened his eyes in perhaps an hour.

Maria took out the bottle of methadone pills and stared at it. Nora knew she was debating whether to take one.

Maria must have been feeling pretty bad, because she exhaled heavily, twisted the top off the bottle, extended a finger in, and brought a capsule out and dry-swallowed it.

Matthews inhaled sharply and jerked, his right shoulder rising.

Nora placed a hand on him, and he settled, then opened his eyes and, to Nora's surprise, smiled at Maria.

"Maria," he whispered.

She studied him, brows furrowed. "Do I know you?"

He let out a ragged laugh that turned into a cough—a painful cough, Nora thought.

"'Course not," he breathed out. "But I know you." He swallowed hard. "Saw you at Camp 17."

"Camp 17?"

"On your *Worlds & Time* tour."

Maria's eyes bulged. Nora caught sight of a small tremble beginning in her hand.

Matthews stared at Nora. "Did you contact her? Recruit her?"

"Why would I?"

He squinted at her. "Because she's performing at the A21 launch. In seven days. Is it part of the follow-up operation?"

Nora swallowed, trying to make her voice steady. "I can't say, Commander."

He nodded and refocused on Maria. "'Mirror Tree.' It's my favorite song. Played it a million times in my bunk in flight school."

Maria sat stock still, eyes still wide, as though she was paralyzed with shock.

Matthews, seeming oblivious to her duress, smiled. "I like 'The Looking Glass World' too. But 'Mirror' is still my favorite." He drew a breath that didn't fill his lungs, exhaled, and sucked in air again, trying to make his ragged voice singsong-like.

"In the forest of time... A tree grows to the sky... An endless climb... To a future that's a lie..." With the last word, Matthews closed his eyes and his breathing slowed again, as if singing the lyrics had soothed his mind enough for sleep to come.

It had the opposite effect on Maria.

Her chest was heaving, body trembling. Nora reached out and placed a hand on her forearm.

Maria reeled back, shaking like a caged animal who had just been shocked with an electric prod.

"Maria," Nora said, leaning forward.

The younger woman's breathing slowed, but she didn't tear her eyes away from the pilot.

"Maria."

Finally, she made eye contact with Nora.

"How does he know that?"

"The song?"

"He can't."

"Why not?" Nora asked.

Maria closed her eyes and shook her head as if trying to make it go away.

"Maria, what's wrong?"

Maria tried to slow her breathing, and when her chest finally stopped heaving, she said, "I've never sung that song. Never even had a chance to write it down. They took my notebook."

"Then..."

"I thought up the lyrics on the plane from Nashville to DC.

I was going to write it down, but I never had a chance." She focused on Nora. "How does he know? What's happening here?"

Behind them, Nora thought she heard rustling; the sound of footsteps. But when she looked, there was no one there. The sound came again, faint but clear.

"Stay here," Nora whispered.

Maria reached out and grabbed Nora's arm, fingernails digging in, eyes wild. "Don't leave me."

"I'll be right back."

"Doc."

Gently, Nora wrapped her fingers around Maria's hand and pulled it away. "I'll be right back. I promise."

Nora clicked the flashlight on and ventured away from Matthews, Maria, and the glow of the ChemLight, toward the stone stairwell that led up to the first floor and the entrance onto the National Mall.

She paused there, listening. Had the person—or animal—left?

"Hello?" she called out.

There was no response. But she had the distinct impression someone was watching her.

59

At the stairwell, Nora waited and listened, but the sound was gone.

She turned and made her way back to the gift store. The glow of the ChemLight grew brighter by the second until she came upon Maria sitting beside Matthews, her eyes staring into the darkness as if mesmerized.

Matthews was still unconscious, and Nora thought his breathing was getting shallower. He needed proper medical facilities, and soon.

She sat down beside Maria and wrapped an arm around the younger woman, who gave no reaction to her presence. Nora was dead tired, but stress and fear fought away the fatigue.

Nora had never worn a watch, and they had taken her cell phone. Without something to mark the passage of time, she felt a bit adrift. And for that reason, she was unsure how much time had passed when the ground began rumbling beneath her feet.

A glass display case in the gift store rattled. A figurine of the giant elephant in the rotunda tipped forward, falling off one shelf, part of it catching the edge of the one below, shattering it, the sound adding a startling clang to the shaking.

At first, Nora thought it was an earthquake, but then she realized that the vibrations were directional—they were from bombs exploding nearby. And they were getting closer. A blast must have hit the mall because a crack opened in the marble floor, and above, she heard pieces of the building falling into the rotunda.

Nora felt Maria's arms reach around her, and she embraced her in return. They sat, holding each other, shivering from fear, as though they were trying to stay warm through a winter storm.

When the rumbling stopped, the quiet that followed was periodically interrupted by the sound of debris falling above and around them. The air was filled with dust that glowed in the ChemLight like a slow-motion sandstorm.

Beyond the dust cloud, from the entrance on Constitution Avenue, Nora heard the sound of boots pounding the marble floor. She wasn't imagining it this time. It was real.

Her pulse quickened as Maria squeezed her tight.

Nora knew Matthews was in bad shape now—he had barely stirred during the bombing.

The footfalls were approaching. Was it Ty and Kato? Or the person she had heard before—if there actually had been a person there.

She clicked the flashlight off and gripped the handle.

The boots pressed into the broken glass at the edge of the gift shop, grinding the shards.

"Nora!" Ty called out.

She exhaled and yelled to him, "We're over here!"

He switched on his flashlight and zeroed in on her voice.

When he emerged from the dust cloud, Ty peered down at Nora, a relieved smile forming on his face. "You okay?"

"Fine. Just... shaken up."

Ty pointed the flashlight up and toward the mall. "We think the bombs were destroying the plane. The Covenant probably doesn't want the Pax to get the technology."

"Pax?"

"It's a long story..."

For the next thirty minutes, Ty shared what he and Kato had learned in the National Museum of American History with Nora and Maria.

Next, Nora related what Commander Matthews had said, including the fact that she—or the version of her in this world—had been part of a mission to destroy the Covenant's new ballistic missile, the A21.

Ty studied the sleeping pilot, and Nora knew he was turning the pieces of the puzzle over in that enormous mind of his. "The thing that haunts me the most," he said, "is the sheer number of coincidences. Us getting here *right now*. This pilot crash-landing at our feet. The fact that you, Nora, your counterpart in this world, seems to be at the center of an operation that might change this world's history... it all means something."

"What exactly?" Kato asked.

"I'm not certain yet. But I'm starting to see the shape of it."

"Which is?"

"I'll know more soon."

"Well," Kato said, "I know one thing for certain. We need to establish a chain of command."

The statement was met with blank stares from the other three.

"When that plane crashed, we were paralyzed," Kato said.

"I think we were all in shock," Nora said quietly.

"True. But the next time something like that happens, we need to be ready to act more decisively. In life-or-death situations where we're in danger—or someone else is in danger—we need to be able to make decisions quickly."

"So you want to be in charge?" Maria said flatly.

Kato cocked his head. "I'm not saying that. I'm saying *someone* should be in charge. For all of our sakes."

Nora took a deep breath. "It should be Ty. He knows more about what's happening than any of us. And he's the smartest person I have ever met. We need our best mind making the calls for whatever is coming."

"First," Ty said, "you flatter me."

"You know it's true," Nora insisted.

"Even *assuming* it's true, being smart is not enough—not for what we're dealing with here. The person calling the shots needs experience. Knowledge." He motioned to Kato. "There are going to be tough calls, like what to do in the tunnels before we got here and when that pilot crashed. We need someone with military experience for that. Kato should be making those calls. He's spent his entire career training for and handling situations like that."

Ty pointed to the pilot lying on the floor, unmoving. "And when it's a medical situation, Nora should decide what to do."

Ty paused. "For the rest—for the big picture stuff, for research, for developing plans, I'm happy to contribute whatever I can."

"Not good enough," Kato said, shaking his head. "Someone has to be *in charge*. This is not a democracy."

"It's also not the military," Nora said.

"True. But we need to start operating that way," Kato said. "We're behind enemy lines. Alone. Cut off from support. With an undefined mission."

Maria shrugged. "Why does everything have to be a *mission*?"

"Necessity. Survival," Kato shot back. "We need a clearly defined objective to evaluate our tactical options at any given moment. If we don't know what we're trying to achieve, it's impossible to know what to do next."

"On that point," Nora said, "I have to agree. We've been running for our lives—or trying to get answers—since we got here. I think it's time to start being proactive. To set our own course here."

Kato nodded. "It's very simple. Our objective should be to get home. As quickly as possible." He exhaled. "I want to get back to my family. I have unfinished business there."

"Finally," Maria said, "something I agree on. I need..." She glanced up at Nora. "I need access to health care."

"We don't belong here," Kato said. "We should go back." He nodded to Ty. "I'm assuming you know how to do that?"

Ty hesitated. "Not exactly."

"You punched a code before," Kato said. "Enter it again."

"I don't think it's going to work," Ty said.

"Why?"

"Gut instinct."

"I think it's worth a try."

"We don't know how this thing—this quantum radio—works. We don't know that dialing the same sequence will take us home. Yes, it may well take us back to our home world, but it could also transport us to another world where Earth doesn't even exist. We could be adrift in space. Or on an Earth orbiting closer to the Sun—an Earth with a boiling hot surface and no breathable atmosphere. Or an ice-ball Earth where our blood freezes in minutes, and we die of cardiac arrest."

Nora held up a hand. "We get it. It could go bad."

"Dialing a wrong number has never been this dangerous."

Nora couldn't help but laugh. Ty's borderline lame joke landed flat on Kato and Maria, but they had always seemed to have an effect on her—even when she didn't want to admit it, like that very moment. "Good one," she muttered, suppressing a smile.

Ty shrugged. "Multiverse humor. By the laws of the many-worlds theory, there's a universe where that joke works."

Nora closed her eyes. "Yeah, but it's not quite this one."

"No," Ty said, mock sorrow in his tone. "No, it's not."

"Dad joke aside," Kato said, "I think we should at least *try* dialing the same code."

In the distance, another bomb exploded. It wasn't powerful enough to shake the floor or rattle dust from the ceiling, but its timing made Kato's point.

"The next missile could hit us," he said. "Do we really want to take that chance? We should dial right now."

Ty closed his eyes and rubbed the backs of his eyelids. "We don't know how it works. Period. I mean, do we need to be in the same place as before for it to work correctly? Does the dial code vary depending on what world you're dialing from? I mean, it's a particle accelerator under the hood—and the laws of physics may be different in this universe. They're very finely tuned in ours."

"I agree with everything you're saying," Kato said. "My point is that those risks are acceptable given that there are bombs actually falling over our heads and we're in a ruined world—one that seems to be in a perpetual war and that we know nothing about."

"I'm with GI Joe on this one," Maria said. "Let's just dial and see what happens."

"I see your points," Nora said. "But I think we should wait."

"Why?" Kato asked.

Nora motioned to the unconscious pilot. "This man is in our care. He's hurt. He's dying. He needs help, and I consider it our responsibility, as human beings, to try to get him some help. If we dial and it works—if we leave—we may well be leaving him to die."

After a long silence, Kato spoke, his voice more reflective. "Thank you for saying that. I didn't even consider it." He paused. "Before yesterday, I hadn't seen my family in a long time. And… there's been some issues there—things I want to resolve. I want to get back there and do that, and I admit, that is bearing on my thinking." To Nora, he said, "You're right. This man is our responsibility. We can't abandon him."

"Same here," Maria said. "I'm not really cut out for any of this, but I don't feel right leaving the guy. Didn't think about that before. I'm not used to spontaneously disappearing." She shrugged. "It's an adjustment in your thinking."

"All of this is," Ty said. "But how do we get help for him?"

"I don't think we should move him," Nora said. "Not without a facility to take him to. We probably shouldn't have moved him to begin with."

"I'll leave at first light on a scouting mission," Kato said. "We need food, and we need to make contact with the Pax government—or whoever is out there."

"I'll go with you," Ty said.

Kato nodded. "I still think we need to assign roles here. A chain of command."

"I don't think we're that kind of team," Nora said.

When Kato frowned, she held out her hands. "What I propose is… authority based on areas of expertise. We're all specialists in different fields. We have different backgrounds and knowledge. For example, I believe I should make any medical decisions for the group. Kato clearly has the military expertise to make those calls."

Nora motioned to Ty. "When we face issues rooted in science and complex problems, like whether we should dial the radio, I think Ty should make the call. His instincts have kept us alive, and I think if any of us can figure out these big, mind-bending problems we're going to face, it would be Ty. I, for one, want him making those calls."

In her mind, Nora reviewed what she knew about Maria, struggling to find a role she might play, an area of authority to assign to her.

Before she could speak, Maria said what she had been thinking.

"That leaves me." Everyone turned to her. "The odd man out—odd woman out, I guess. I'll say what we're thinking: I don't bring anything to this *team*. I'm dead weight. I'm a washed-up singer who used to be a decent makeup artist until I got tired of dolling up starlets and decided I wanted to be one myself. I grew up covering my mom's black eyes and bruises. I bet none of you ever did."

An awkward silence stretched out. Ty spoke first.

"There are a lot of questions here. Why us? Why this world? What are we doing here? But there's one thing I am certain of. There are too many coincidences here for this to be random. As a scientist, I'm skeptical of randomness. I want to see order. A reason for effects, cause behind it. I believe there's a reason we are here—each and every one of us, including you, Maria. I think we're the four corners of something, a process or an event that we don't yet understand. And I think that's life. I think sometimes we have to put one foot in front of the other, not knowing what the right path is but trudging ahead because, frankly, we don't have a choice, and because, optimistically, I choose to believe where we're going will be worth whatever we're about to go through."

Maria tilted her head, as if examining what Ty had said.

"What are you thinking?" Nora asked her.

"I'm thinking there's a song there, in that long, wordy diatribe of his."

Nora couldn't help but laugh, and Maria joined her.

"I'm glad I could be your inspiration," Ty said.

Kato brought them back to the task at hand, a role Nora sensed he was made for.

"So," he said. "We're agreed on these roles?"

When the others nodded, Kato continued. "We should set up a watch for the night—in shifts. We all take one. Sleep is imperative in survival scenarios."

For Nora, hearing Kato describe their situation as a "survival scenario" brought home the reality of it.

"I'll take first shift," Kato said. "Ty will be next. We'll be leaving at first light to look for supplies and help. We need to rest before that. Maria will follow Ty's shift, and finally Nora. Assuming the time here is the same as our home world, that shift will overlap our departure."

With that, they set about making pallets on the floor from sweatshirts and T-shirts from the two gift stores in the museum.

Instead of making three beds on the floor, they made one long pallet, laying the garments down in overlapping layers like a quilt made of the decaying clothes.

Less than a minute after she lay down, Maria was snoring softly. Nora found it hard to focus on sleep, but she wasn't surprised Maria had dozed so easily. Drowsiness was a known side effect of methadone.

Ty, it seemed, was struggling to sleep as well, based on his breathing. He lay in front of her, on his side, facing Matthews, Nora behind him.

"What are you thinking about?" she whispered, soft enough that Kato couldn't hear. He had begun at the stairwell and was now making a wide loop, stepping carefully so as not to crush the glass and debris, inspecting every inch of the ruined museum.

Ty twisted onto his back, his face moving closer to Nora's. "I was thinking... about the last time we were here in the mall."

"Me too."

"It was a good day."

For a moment, she was back there with him, sitting in the sea of grass on the quilt—an expanse of cloth that felt like the one beneath them—eating and reading and talking and watching the sun cross the sky.

Looking back, that was the last calm before the storm in her life. She had returned home, and everything had changed.

The front door stood open. Inside, drawers were pulled out of the cabinets and dressers, their contents splayed across the floor. Mattresses had been cut open, the stuffing ripped out like the contents of a piñata.

And her father was gone.

No note.

No blood.

No trace of him.

An hour later, two officers and two detectives from the DC Metro Police were standing in their kitchen asking her mother questions as she sat at the island, staring straight ahead, putting on a brave face that Nora knew was for her and her brother Dylan.

Her father's disappearance had torn Nora's life apart. It had also driven her and Ty apart. They were on the verge of going off to college then, which would have been a test of their relationship—the distance and the influx of new friends and influences. But the abyss that was her missing father had drawn Nora in, causing her to withdraw. She knew she had been unreachable then, but there was nothing she could do about it.

Ty seemed to know what she was thinking about. Even after all this time, it was amazing to Nora how in sync they were.

"You thinking about him?"

"Yeah."

"Losing a parent is tough," he said. "I know. Especially when you spend endless hours wondering what happened. Almost as jarring as having them return."

Nora didn't know what to say to that. She simply put her arm across Ty and gripped his side with her fingers, holding him.

He reached up with his left arm, placing it next to hers.

Inexplicably, unexpectedly, sleep came to her then.

Nora woke to the soft sound of tapping on the marble. At first, she thought it was rain. Perhaps the ceiling was open to the rotunda above in places.

But as her eyes adjusted to the dim light, she realized it wasn't rain. It was the tapping of tiny metal feet on the marble. Metal feet attached to a small robot with a rectangular silver body and six legs that tap-tap-tapped forward, creeping toward her.

60

Ty felt a hand pressing into his ribs, which still ached from the explosion in Geneva and the blast at the DARPA facility. He stirred, but his body was stiff and unresponsive. His brain was foggy, as though molasses were flowing through it.

Another squeeze at his side brought a rush of pain and adrenaline that chased the brain fog away.

His eyes shot open.

It was still dark in the museum.

At his ear, he felt hot breath and heard a soft, sweet voice he knew so well: Nora.

"Ty. Ty, wake up."

He turned to her, saw the fear in her eyes, and instantly felt himself come fully awake.

Ty sat up and saw what looked like a metal insect crawling toward them on six spindly legs with sharp ends—points that he imagined could drive deep into human flesh.

He rose to his hands and knees, flashlight in one hand, and frantically searched the floor for the handgun he had set down before he slipped off to sleep. He spotted it by the pilot, grabbed it, but when he returned the light's beam to the spot where he had last seen the robot, it was gone.

Ty swept the flashlight across the deserted museum gift store.

Footsteps pounding in the stairwell drew his attention, and soon the glow of another light raked over him—Kato's.

He rushed toward them, rifle at the ready.

"What happened?" he whispered, scanning the room.

"A robot," Ty said. "It was watching us. I think it was going to attack before Nora woke me."

"I'll keep the perimeter closer," Kato said, still searching the room.

"It's almost my shift anyway," Ty said. "I'll watch for it."

In the hours that followed, Ty patrolled the abandoned museum in a state of constant unease.

Every small sound drew his attention. And there were plenty of those small sounds: the creaking of the ruined building, the clattering of falling debris, and the wind through the cracked rotunda.

Every time he heard a noise, he went to investigate. And every time, he found nothing.

Shortly after the first rays of morning light filtered down through the stairwell, it was time for Nora's shift. But Ty didn't wake her. He merely watched her sleeping peacefully.

He knew she needed the rest. The physical exertion was one thing, but he knew Nora well enough to know that worry was weighing on her more: worry for the dying pilot and worry for all of them. She felt things deeply.

Lying next to her, Kato slept with his rifle held at his side, the safety on. He had drifted off seconds after lying down. Ty wondered if that was a skill he had acquired as a Navy SEAL—being able to sleep in high-stress environments like active combat.

Other questions dogged him as he marched carefully through the museum. Why were they here? How could they get home? The radio was the obvious answer, but he wanted to be sure about the dial code he used.

As agreed, when the morning sun cleared the Smithsonian Castle, Ty woke Kato, who shrugged off the sleep like a thin blanket and was soon fully awake.

For the next watch, they opted to wake Maria since she had gotten the most sleep that night.

The young woman seemed groggy. Ty wasn't sure if her sleepiness was from the medication she was taking or from the rough sleep on the pile of clothes on the marble floor.

Maria declined to keep the handgun, insisting that she had never used one and wasn't confident she would be able to. That admission brought a promise from Kato to train her and a grunt from Maria.

Ty and Kato again exited the Museum of Natural History via the entrance on Constitution Avenue, marching out into the morning light, into the area of the city known as the Federal Triangle, which on Ty's home world had included the National Archives, the Department of Justice, the Environmental Protection Agency, and the White House Visitor Center. Just outside of the Federal Triangle lay the Ellipse in front of the White House.

As they walked, Ty realized how hungry he was.

"Where to?" he asked Kato, who was turning right on Constitution Avenue.

"I've been thinking about that. We need food. And help. But we need one thing more: information."

"So..."

"We need a vantage point. A place to look out and figure out what happened here. See if we can spot any people or signs of life."

"That's going to be tough here in DC. By law, nothing can be taller than the Washington Monument. Or the Capitol. Can't remember which."

Kato stopped and stared at Ty. "You can't be serious."

"What?"

"You grew up in DC, right?"

"Yeah."

"That's a myth."

"What's a myth?"

"That buildings can't be taller than the Washington Monument or the Capitol Building. The height restriction has nothing to do with protecting the views of the Washington Monument or Capitol. It's just urban planning. The 1910 Height of Buildings Act is what determines how tall a building can be in DC. It's all based on the width of the street. The idea was that wider streets could have taller buildings—and more narrow ones couldn't.

The cap is one hundred thirty feet—no building can be taller than that, with the exception of a small portion of Pennsylvania Avenue from 1st to 15th Street Northwest, across from the Federal Triangle, where structures can be one hundred sixty feet tall."

"Interesting."

"Some buildings were grandfathered in, such as the Old Post Office on the corner of Pennsylvania Avenue and 12th."

Kato tilted his head toward a sprawling limestone building at the end of the block, which Ty recognized as the Old Post Office. Amazingly, the structure was still intact. Like many offices and embassies in Washington, DC, the building looked like a skyscraper lying on its side, except the Old Post Office had a prominent square clock tower that rose on the Pennsylvania Avenue side. Ty had been there a few times and had even taken a tour of the observation level, which had an incredible panoramic view of the city.

"The Old Post Office is actually the second tallest *habitable building* in the city—right behind the Basilica of the National Shrine of the Immaculate Conception, which I believe is only fifteen feet taller."

"Isn't the Washington Monument taller than the Post Office?"

"Much," Kato said as he began to march up 12th Street Northwest. "But it's not permanently habitable. There are radio towers in the DC area that are taller than the monument, but besides those, it's the tallest structure in DC."

Kato glanced backward and to the left. "Well, in our DC. Here, it's a pile of rubble."

As they continued up 12th, Ty got a closer look at the building he had always known as the national headquarters of the Environmental Protection Agency. On this world, there was a large sign that read *ATF*. Growing up in DC, he had been constantly inundated with acronyms, and this was one he recognized, the three-letter name for the Bureau of Alcohol, Tobacco, Firearms, and Explosives.

He tapped Kato on the shoulder and motioned to it.

"No EPA."

"That tells us more about the timeline."

"How so?"

"On our world, the EPA didn't move in until the early nineties. The ATF was there before. It made sense. For most of its history, ATF was under the Treasury, specifically the IRS. They collected billions in taxes. After 9/11, the Homeland Security Act in 2002 transferred ATF to the Department of Justice and renamed it the Bureau of Alcohol, Tobacco, Firearms, and Explosives. They created a new division for tax collection related to alcohol and tobacco, which is called the Alcohol and Tobacco Tax and Trade Bureau, or TTB."

Ty stopped walking. "Seriously. How do you remember all this?"

"My parents."

"They were in the ATF?"

Kato smiled. "No. They were strict enforcers of rules, though. And they were passionate about America. They were immigrants. My dad from Japan, my mom from China."

"So you're half Japanese, half Chinese?"

"Close. Technically, I'm three-quarters Chinese, one-quarter Japanese. My father's father was a Japanese soldier who became a textile merchant in the forties after the war. He met my grandmother in Beijing. They had a single son, and he went into the family textile business and, like my grandfather, met a woman in Beijing who he fell in love with. But my parents were obsessed with America. Against their family's wishes, they emigrated in the seventies. So, I was born here and grew up in North Carolina, but I spent a lot of my summers up here in DC, touring the museums and everywhere else... basically anything that was free or close to it. That was what my parents could afford. To them, this place was like Disneyland. It was to me too. I couldn't wait to get here every time we came."

Kato exhaled. "The car rides here were a lot like most evenings at home: my parents quizzing me on American history facts. They were constantly drilling me with all this endless information. I think they thought that if I knew more than anyone about America, I would be unquestionably American."

"I had a similar upbringing," Ty said, smiling. "But with science in place of history."

At that moment, Ty saw a parallel between him and Kato. They'd had similar childhoods, though on different tracks—his of science, Kato's of history, both rails laid by well-meaning parents who had lost something dear to them. For Ty's mother, that loss had been Richter, the father figure Ty had longed for but never had. For Kato's parents, it had been their homeland, which they lost when they came to America.

"When you're surrounded by something as a kid, it gets down in your blood."

"Yes, it does." Kato said. "My parents cared a lot about US history. That's probably why I started caring about it so much. When your parents reward you for doing something, I think it's natural to want to become good at that. And I did. I fell in love with this country. I fell in love so hard that when I grew up, I was willing to give my life for it. And sometimes, to neglect my family for it."

The sun was hot on Ty's face when they reached the Old Post Office. He walked through the arched entryway, past the foyer, and out into an atrium. There was a glass ceiling above, held in place by a metal skeleton. Stone columns ran from the floor to the ceiling, the railing of balconies running between the pillars. Ty counted ten floors to the top.

"Over here," Kato said as he shuffled toward a small deli under the overhang. The place was devoid of food or any signs of life. The cash register at the checkout counter was what caught Ty's eye. It wasn't a digital register or an iPad with a credit card reader, the kind that was pervasive in the world he had left. These were mechanical devices with a spring-loaded drawer that rang when the merchant made change. It was a device from another time.

Ty searched the abandoned space for a newspaper or any clue about when it had last been inhabited, but he found only shreds that had been ground down nearly to dust by time and pests.

Kato led them out of the café and back to the staircase and up the floors until they reached the highest level of the mezzanine.

The skylight over the atrium was cracked in dozens of places, the morning sun poking through. Dirt and grime lay heavy on the glass, a burden left by years of not cleaning it.

Kato strode across the catwalk that looked down on the tables and decaying umbrellas over a hundred feet below. At the elevator, he punched the button, but they both knew what would happen before the panel confirmed it: there was no power here.

At the clock tower staircase, Kato climbed, and Ty followed. His legs were burning by the time he reached the level where he expected to see the Congress Bells. He stopped, his chest heaving, and looked at the empty space.

"The Congress Bells," he said between breaths. "They're gone."

"They were a gift from a British foundation in 1976 at the Bicentennial of America's independence. They placed them here in April 1983. Obviously, that never happened in this timeline. The British left their homeland in 1940 on this world."

Kato continued climbing the stairs until they reached the observation deck. There, Ty peered out through the vertical bars at the north side of Washington, DC.

What he saw, in a word, was destruction. The city he had grown up in looked as though a giant rolling pin had run over it, flattening buildings.

In the midst of the carnage, he spotted automobiles sticking out of the debris. They were all American-made, massive, hulking cars with large metal bodies in soft curving forms. To Ty, the cars looked similar to those from his world from the sixties and early seventies. Many had bullet holes in them. They told a story of a city and a time where traveling the streets was dangerous.

Ty panned left. The White House was still standing. So was the Lincoln Memorial to the west. That meant something, he thought—that whoever was at war here, there was some desire to preserve history and the heritage of this place.

To the southwest, Arlington County, Virginia, with its skyscrapers defying DC's height ordinance, was entirely gone. The ground was dotted by massive charred pits where bombs had fallen. In places, trees had reclaimed the land, a dense forest that grew to the banks of the Potomac.

To the south, the Jefferson Memorial glimmered in the morning light, the George Mason Bridge and Interstate 395 behind it. Both roads over the Potomac River were disintegrating, the concrete crumpling like papier-mâché.

South of the bridges, Ty saw something that surprised him more than the destruction of his hometown: a massive airship floating toward DC. It looked like a Zeppelin from the early 1900s—an elongated, flying football that glided through the air like a massive ship on the sea.

At the bottom, near the front, a crew and passenger compartment hung like a train car affixed there, with windows and large guns mounted at the front and along the sides.

There was no insignia on the ship.

"Look," Kato said, pointing at it.

Ty watched as a massive ramp dropped open at the bottom of the compartment. Figures raced to the end of the ramp and dove, flying face first.

Two dozen people exited the airship before the ramp closed up.

Soon, the divers ripped cords on their chests and parachutes bloomed in the air, slowing their descent. There was no mistaking their destination: they were coming directly for the mall.

To the east, Ty heard a screeching roar. He panned over in time to see three missiles coming in fast.

The airship fired a booming broadside, a dozen shots that intercepted the missiles, exploding them in mid-air over the Atlantic.

Ty didn't know what the missiles were carrying, but their explosion was like nothing he had ever felt. A buzzing wave rolled across the ruined city. Ty's legs went weak. His head spun, like a boxer who had just been punched.

He gripped the rail on the observation deck, steadying himself. Another salvo of missiles bore down on the airship, which issued another defensive volley.

Again, the wave from the detonated missiles hit him, a

debilitating pulse like an electric shock. To him, it was as though the missiles were carrying ordnance that took a bite out of reality, leaving a hole in its wake.

Ty felt a hand on his shoulder.

"We have to go," Kato said, dragging him toward the stairwell.

As he turned, Ty spotted the first of the paratroopers touching down on the mall. They were heading directly for the museum—and Nora and Maria.

61

Nora woke to the booming of guns and an ear-splitting explosion. The force of it seemed to reach through the rotunda, down the stairwell and into her chest and mind, pressing her against the marble floor like a wave of gravity pinning her.

Her head swam.

Commander Matthews, still unconscious, stirred, moaning as his head rolled side to side.

Maria was standing, shivering.

"They're bombing us!" she screamed. "We've got to go!"

On wobbling limbs, Nora managed to rise. "We can't."

Maria closed her eyes and shook her head. "We have to."

"We can't leave this man."

Ty struggled to make his body work. He was nearly tumbling down the stairs, as though the blasts had short-circuited his nervous system.

Kato had fared much better. With one hand holding Ty's bicep and his rifle in the other, the SEAL stomped down the stairs of the clock tower.

He sped up as they reached the atrium of the Old Post Office, dashing to the other stairwell and pulling Ty once again, but Ty took Kato's hand and tried to dislodge it.

"Leave me," he gasped, trying to catch his breath.

"I'm not—"

"I'm fried, Kato. Just go. Help Nora."

Kato simply tightened his grip on Ty and kept pulling him down the stairs.

With each step, feeling was returning to Ty's body, as if a neurotoxin was draining from his blood.

His problem now was that he couldn't breathe fast enough to keep up with Kato.

At the bottom of the stairs, in the courtyard covered by the dirty, broken skylights above, Kato finally paused to draw a breath, gun sweeping back and forth as he searched for enemy combatants.

A few seconds later, they exited the Old Post Office and charged down 12th Street Northwest toward Nora and Maria.

Nora listened as boots hammered the marble floor of the rotunda. Whoever had entered the museum wasted no time searching it. They moved directly to the staircase toward the ground floor, footsteps clacking as they descended, heading right for them.

Ty's legs burned as he tried to keep up with Kato. The paratroopers were dropping faster than Ty had expected, and soon they disappeared behind the Smithsonian museums. They were going to reach Nora and Maria before Kato and Ty. And there were too many of them to fight.

Kato seemed to realize that too.

He stopped in the middle of 12th Street. "We need to regroup."

In the dim glow of the ChemLight, Nora made out a dozen figures, dressed in silver-gray suits that reminded her of sheets of lead. The dull, crinkly material seemed to absorb the soft light, not reflecting even a shred of it. The invaders wore helmets with large, mirrored eye patches that made them look like humanoid insects.

Maria, still trembling, turned to the oncoming figures and shined her flashlight at them, the beam shaking as she held it out. At the sight of them, she passed out, collapsing hard to the floor.

A jolt of fear rushed through Nora. She crawled over to

Maria and ran her hands over her head, searching for bleeding, but there was none. Maria would be bruised from the fall, but she would likely be fine.

When the leading figure reached Nora, they reached back into their pack and tossed two bundles on the floor.

Through the helmet's speaker, a man said, "Hurry. Suit up."

Nora recognized the voice. But it couldn't be. She stared at the packs on the floor. They were silver suits like the figures wore, wrapped up.

"Nora," the voice said, urgent. "Are you okay? Do you understand me? Put the Faraday suit on."

The man pulled off his helmet and peered down at her, worry lines deep on his forehead and crow's feet carved at the corners of his eyes. He was in his late sixties, and time and whatever he had gone through had been unkind to the man, but Nora still recognized her father.

He took a step closer to her. "We need to go, Nora. We have a tactical Zep waiting to evac us. We took out the EMOs, but Covenant drones could be here any second. Let's go."

A clanking sound drew Ty's attention.

He turned and spotted seven small metal robots crawling out of the shadows of the ATF building. Their bodies were rectangular and they walked on six pointed metal legs. They were the same crab-like bot he had seen in the museum the night before. This time, the robots didn't retreat at the sight of him.

The seven bugs charged, their legs dancing across the broken pavement with a *ting-ting-ting* sound.

Kato leveled the rifle and opened fire, mowing down three of them before the others planted their pincers in the concrete. Small round portholes opened on their front faces, and tiny fléchettes issued forth, the metal darts digging into Ty's legs, bringing a sting of pain, like a half-dozen giant syringes digging in.

Pain rolled up his legs.

Dizziness followed.

As he hit the ground, Ty realized Kato was staggering back,

trying to aim the gun, but he too was hit—and losing his struggle to stand.

The last thing Ty heard before everything went black was the dinging of the robots' sharp legs prancing toward him.

62

Two soldiers worked to get Maria into the silver-gray suit. The young woman didn't stir as they held her and pulled the crinkly garment on. Three others approached Commander Matthews, who was still lying on the floor, unconscious.

"Careful with him," Nora called. "He's sustained internal injuries."

"What about you?" her father asked, concern evident on his face. "Are you hurt?"

Nora stared at him, a mix of emotions coursing through her—elation at seeing him again, and fear of revealing that she wasn't the person he thought she was, at least not the same version he had known. She sensed that revealing she was an impostor could be dangerous, even if she was telling her own father. This was a world at war... a strange world that she still didn't understand.

"I'm fine," she said quietly as she pulled her own suit on.

Nora started to tell her father about Kato and Ty, that they should wait for them, but instinctively, she sensed that there was danger in that. Kato might have a counterpart in the Covenant. Additionally, if they had been captured, it was possible Nora would need to try to free them. Admitting that they were together now could put her at a disadvantage. She was, she had to admit, a bit surprised at how quickly her mind had adapted to the use of subterfuge.

She marveled then that one never knew how adaptable a mind was until it was tested.

When she had finished donning the suit and pulled a helmet on, her father's team led them out of the National Museum of Natural History and onto Constitution Avenue, where they marched for two blocks until they reached the Ellipse, a wide lawn south of the White House.

The well-manicured park Nora had known from her world was now overgrown with tall grass and a few small trees.

Most surprisingly, there was an airship nearly as long as the White House touching down there. It reminded Nora of the Goodyear Blimp or even the Hindenburg airship, though that association gave her pause as she watched her father march toward the waiting vessel.

As it reached the ground, a ramp descended and the suited team marched inside, Nora, Maria, and Matthews with them.

In seconds, the ship was lifting off. Inside the cargo area, Nora removed her helmet and peered out of a small oval window.

Behind her, they rushed Matthews deeper into the vessel along with Maria, likely to some sort of medical facility.

The airship flew northwest, along the route of the Potomac, deeper into the United States, over the border of what had been Maryland and Virginia.

To Nora, the view was breathtaking—in all the worst ways. Washington, DC was a ruined expanse. A post-apocalyptic wasteland of charred, crumbling buildings and hulking abandoned cars. The roads were being erased as grass and trees overtook them, as if the highways and streets were lines drawn on a page that was fading with time.

She realized that her father was staring at her.

"What is it?" he asked.

Nora hesitated, then realized why he was confused—the Nora he knew wouldn't be surprised by the view. What would that Nora be doing now? Likely debriefing him on the mission she had just returned from. Nora couldn't do that. Any slight misstep or careless phrase could give her away. The same was true for Maria. Nora realized then how precarious their situation was.

And that wasn't even her biggest problem. She still hadn't seen Ty or Kato. Where were they?

She needed more information.

Apparently, so did her father. "What happened out there?" he asked.

"It's complicated," Nora said, not making eye contact with the man. "I'm sorry, but I need to rest."

He nodded. "Of course." He led her out of the cargo bay and into a narrow corridor with hatches on both sides.

Behind the first opening lay a small med bay where Matthews and Maria were strapped onto gurneys, several soldiers taking their vitals.

At the end of the corridor, a hatch led to a small bridge where several crew members were piloting the ship.

Nora's father stopped at one of the hatches halfway down the corridor and motioned to the opening. "Come find me at tactical whenever you feel up to it."

Nora closed the oblong metal door after she entered and took stock of the small room. There was a narrow bed with a foldout bunk above it and a desk with a round stool that didn't attach to the floor but rather sat atop an articulating arm affixed to the wall. There were no windows. The only decoration was the large blue flag hanging on the wall. It reminded Nora of the United Nations flag.

She pulled the stool out and sat at the desk and rifled through the drawers. In the bottom one, she found a linen hardcover in the same light blue as the flag. Gold foil letters stamped onto the cover read *The Pax: A Fight for the Future of Humankind.*

She glanced back at the flag. It had to be the Pax flag, and this a Pax airship. That matched her assumptions.

Nora flipped through the book, which contained a mix of history and education on the ideology of the Pax. As she read, Nora realized that these were people who felt guided by a shared purpose, to create a world of tolerance and acceptance, where freedom and peace were guaranteed. The history sections told her why.

At the chapter titled "The Second Dark Age," Nora began to read.

In the years after the European Offensive of the Covenant War, the Pax struggled with integrating the influx of new immigrants into a shared society. Compounding those challenges were the oppressive economic sanctions from the rapidly unifying Covenant sphere of influence.

Throughout the 1940s and 1950s, the Pax and Covenant functioned as polar opposites. The Pax became a society of people brought together by circumstances, struggling to form a cohesive society and balance their needs for survival with the growing awareness that the war was simply paused and not over. In the Pax, one thing was certain: building military capacity was of the utmost importance.

By contrast, the Covenant was a unified society, one that explicitly chose its citizens and bound them with a shared purpose, ostensibly to create a more perfect human race.

In the absence of a conventional war, the Covenant waged a new kind of war—an economic blockade of the Pax that delivered a devastating blow. Central to the initiative was the Covenant Seawall, which effectively locked the Pax nations and its citizens out of Covenant markets and restricted travel between the two superpowers.

Beginning in the late fifties and continuing in the sixties and seventies, the Covenant took a bolder approach to the Pax. They began insisting on restrictions on Pax military capability and size, as well as limiting the amount of technology the Pax could possess. War was the perpetual threat, and the two superpowers existed in a nearly constant state of negotiation.

Peace inspectors became a constant fixture throughout the Pax, armed envoys who searched for companies, university labs, and government organizations that might be developing advanced technologies that violated the Pax–Covenant peace accord.

With each passing year, the Pax watched itself fall further behind the Covenant technologically. Compounding the difficulty was the lack of information coming from the Covenant—news and videos from inside the sprawling confederation were also blocked at the Covenant Seawall.

As such, the era known commonly as the Long Peace was, in fact, a slow decline within the Pax. The Covenant, however, was becoming an advanced, technologically driven society.

Within the Pax, younger generations began to rebel at the lack of opportunity. Soon, the peace inspectors became the subject of attacks. In response, the Covenant withdrew in-person inspectors and rolled out an automated surveillance system powered by a series of monitoring buoys in major cities and drones patrolled overhead.

The biggest surprise was yet to come. In October of 1982, the Covenant launched a new enforcement mechanism: electromagnetic ordnance, or EMOs as they became known. The EMOs were carried by long-range intercontinental ballistic missiles known as A18s, which were developed at the Peenemünde Research Center in the Mecklenburg-West Pomerania province of the Reich Europa nation within the Covenant. The EMOs detonated above areas where the Covenant claimed there were advanced electronics that violated the peace accords.

The EMOs were deployed in accordance with the enforcement clauses of the peace accords, which gave the Covenant the right to destroy advanced electronics so long as no Pax citizens were harmed.

The EMOs proved devastating to the Pax. Almost overnight, the population of the Pax was plunged into a new dark age where advanced electronics were rendered useless. In the years that followed, the EMOs became more powerful, with greater reach. In later years, the Pax began to suspect the EMOs had been further modified to have effects not only on electronics but also on the human body.

Nora pushed the book back on the table and swung the stool away from the desk, considering what she had read. The book told the story of a world at war—a war to oppress technological development. Here, in this world, the Covenant had used rocket warfare to devastating effect, on Britain in 1940 and in later years, against the Pax nations—the United States, Australia, Canada, and others.

Nora wondered if the Covenant here in this world was the same as, or connected to, the Covenant in her home world. It seemed too much of a coincidence for them not to be connected.

What did it mean?

She wished Ty were here. For several reasons, but especially to have someone to bounce ideas off of. But she sensed that she was on her own for a while. And more, that she may be the key to helping the others now. That thought landed upon her like an inescapable weight, and with it came something else: resolve.

Since coming to this world, she had been reacting—first rescuing the pilot, then keeping him alive, and finally when her father had rescued her.

Now was the time to act, to gather the facts of their situation and take a shot at freeing them and getting home.

As she considered her options, the airship turned slightly, a gradual, gentle tug that reminded Nora of a submarine moving through deep water. In a way, that was what the dirigible was: a vessel floating upon the sky, buoyed by the elements and buffeted by the hands of nature.

After reading the details of how the Second Dark Age came to be, she now saw why the Pax had come to rely on airships—a technology that dated to the 1800s, long before advanced electronics came into being. She wondered what other unexpected choices the Covenant's EMO assaults had forced them into.

With the airship carving its way through the sky, she opened the history book and began to read again.

63

Ty woke in a dark cell. His head swam as he tried to sit up. He collapsed back to the thin mattress and took in the space. He was lying on a bunk that was bolted to a concrete block wall.

The air was damp and smelled of mold. The room was empty. It had a single door, which was steel and rusted but not enough to see through. It had a twelve-inch square opening at eye level with vertical bars running across it. A slot no bigger than a mail flap was situated close to the floor. There were no lights in the small room, though a soft yellow glow shone through the bars.

It was a nightmarish place to wake up in. What scared Ty even more was what he had woken without. Gone was the quantum radio medallion that had been in his pocket. The bottle of pills his father had given him was also missing.

Without the pills, he feared his health would deteriorate a little each day. The missing radio was a bigger problem. What would happen if they dialed it? Would Ty, Nora, Kato, and Maria disappear from this world and arrive in another? And if so, what then? Would they be separated as they were now? And would the world even be habitable? Or more dangerous than this one?

He had to get both items back—and reunite with Nora and the others.

Ty rose on legs that felt like stilts, lifeless and unreliable and ready to collapse at any moment. With a hand bracing himself on the wall, he stumbled to the door and peered out through the bars. A dingy hallway with cinder block walls lay beyond. A row of glowing yellow light bulbs hung from the ceiling by black electrical cords.

"Hello?" he called, voice scratchy.

After a few seconds, he heard metal scraping on metal. But no one entered the hall.

Ty strained to see, finally realizing that a slot had been opened in the door at the end of the corridor.

A man's gruff voice called to him: "What's your name?"

Ty was fairly certain there was no version of him on this world. But he was absolutely certain that those sorts of assumptions could get him killed. As such, he evaded the question.

"Where am I?"

"Weird name."

"Why are you holding me?"

"Ground rules, dumb-dumb: when you're in a basement prison cell, you don't get to ask the questions. Mmmm-kay?"

Ty opened his mouth to ask another question but shut it. He sensed that every question was pressing his luck.

The man spoke again. "Let's start with an easier one. How did you get here? A submarine? Have you all built tunnels?"

"Just let me go," Ty said. "I have nothing to do with your war. I assure you."

"Why are you here?" the man asked. "Were you sent to recover Matthews?"

"No. We helped him."

"Why?"

"It was the right thing to do."

"Who sent you?"

"No one."

"You need to start answering my questions."

"I don't have any answers."

"You're going to get hungry soon. We'll talk then."

Kato woke in handcuffs. The silver metal was cutting into his wrists. Another set of cuffs bound his ankles. Both sets were chained to a cinder block wall in a dark room, lit only by the dim light trickling in through the bars of a square opening in a steel door.

He was on the floor, and his body ached.

The door swung open, and a bulky, muscular man with a goatee and hateful eyes sauntered in.

"We took bets on when you'd come around."

"Who is we?" Kato struggled to sit up, but it was no use—the chain was too short.

"You know who we are. We're the people you animals are trying to wipe from the face of the Earth."

"You have me confused with someone else."

"We're not confused. Incidentally, I lost the bet. I thought you Covenant Intel operatives were made of tougher stuff. Thought you would wake up sooner. But you slept like a baby."

"I'm not a Covenant Intelligence operative."

"Said like a true Covenant Intel spook." The man smiled. "You are. We know you are. We're poor as dirt, but we managed to scrape together enough to buy info on the top-ranking Covenant military officers. But we've never captured one. Until now. And we're going to ask you a lot of questions. We don't really care what we have to do to get answers. If we don't, our kids are going to starve. That has a way of loosening your morals, you know? Watching every generation get thinner, a little shorter, shrinking out of existence while you cower and wait for the next bomb to explode."

The man raised his eyebrows, eyes flashing. "But you're going to give us some answers that might help us turn it all around."

64

Nora was sitting at the desk in the airship when a knock sounded at the door. Before she could close the history book that lay open, the door swung inward, and her father stepped in.

She didn't dare move then. A sudden reaction might imply guilt.

His gaze drifted to the open book.

"Reading *A Fight*?"

Nora didn't trust her voice. She nodded.

The question was obvious. Why would someone in her position read a history book—someone who had lived it? She needed an explanation...

"Lately," her father said, "I find myself doing the same. It gives you perspective on what we're about to do. Helps me feel better about it."

He closed the door behind him and continued speaking, not making eye contact. "They held us down like animals. I bet it's easy for them... to press a button, and no one dies in the moments after. But we starve to death. A little each day."

He inhaled and waited, but Nora said nothing.

"I know I've kept you in the dark," he said. "I had to. I didn't want to."

"It's okay," she said quietly.

"It's not okay. I knew you were going over there for the recon mission. I couldn't risk you getting caught and revealing what we're planning."

He studied her. "I thought my life's work would be saving Earth's oceans. Things change, don't they?" He squinted. "You watch your grandchildren starving... and then the government asks you to use what you know as a weapon to save them. What do you do?"

Nora felt her heart beating faster. What was he telling her—that she had children? Perhaps a husband too?

On her world, she had a younger brother, but he was unmarried and, to a large degree, had been adrift in life. Dylan had never found what he wanted to do or a person he wanted to spend his life with. On this world, had that changed?

Her father was an even bigger mystery. The man she had known—the Robert Brown from her world—was a reflective academic and, above all, a caring family man.

He was passionate about his research, which on her world concerned ocean currents and how they affected sea life. Beginning at a young age, he had taken Nora on his research expeditions around the world, to coral reefs and barrier islands, and places so remote they barely had names. And she loved it. On those trips, she developed a passion for science and a curiosity about how things worked. The father she had known had an infectious positivity and thirst for knowledge that had transferred to her very early in her life.

Where he wished to peel back the layers of the ocean and understand how the lifeblood of the Earth worked, to understand what lay beneath, for Nora, the great mystery was the human mind. In it, she saw what her father saw in the oceans: currents that shaped our lives, a murky sea full of wonder and mysteries, and things that lay buried, hard to reach, and even harder to understand.

She realized then why his disappearance when she was eighteen had been so difficult for her: he had shaped so much of her view of the world and her own identity. She had been about to leave home for college then and was already feeling unanchored. His disappearance had left her nearly listless in life, and it had taken years to right herself. Even then, she hadn't made a full recovery.

This version of her father was different from the one who had raised her in at least one important way. He was more somber, almost regretful. Maybe that was part of the cost of war for this Robert Brown.

A knock echoed from the door, and a uniformed soldier ducked in and whispered something to Nora's father. He turned to leave, glancing back at Nora. "Matthews is awake."

Nora rose and followed him into the narrow corridor and to the med bay where Matthews lay on a gurney, talking to a Pax officer. Two medical technicians lingered nearby, watching with perturbed expressions on their faces.

As she crossed the threshold of the med bay, Nora caught a glimpse of Maria, who was also awake now, lying on a gurney on the opposite side of the room, her eyes wide as a medical technician quizzed her.

Nora gave a quick jerk of her head to the side, silently instructing Maria not to say anything. The younger woman nodded quickly, and the medical technician turned to look at Nora, who shifted her attention to Matthews.

The pilot had seen her and was raising his right arm to point at her, mouth moving faster now, the words still indecipherable to her. The only phrase she could make out was "A21."

One of the med techs by his bed turned then and held up her arms. "Okay, this is too much—too many people, too much activity. Clear the bay."

Outside the room, Nora's father said to her, "Matthews is talking. That's good. We'll need to get your account too. Are you ready?"

"Just... give me a few more minutes."

Back in the stateroom, Nora closed the door and leaned against it and exhaled heavily. She felt the airship shift again, turning toward some unknown destination, adjusting course based on the winds, perhaps. She needed to as well. She felt as though the walls of this strange ship were closing in on her. Most of all, she needed to figure out what exactly had happened on this world.

At the desk, she sat on the round stool, opened the book, and began reading.

THE FALL

On November 11, 1987, the Pax took the only route to survival left: they counterattacked the Covenant federation.

In a surprise attack launched by land, sea, and air, Pax forces punched a hole in the Covenant Seawall along the Irish and Scottish coasts, hoping to gain a hold in those areas believed to be sympathetic to the plight of the Pax.

Concurrently, French Canadian troops landed in the Normandy area of Northern France with a similar objective. The ultimate goal was to establish a beachhead from which to launch a new short-range missile the Pax had developed in secret. The target: the Peenemünde Military Research facilities in the Mecklenburg-Vorpommern state of Reich Europa. The Pax believed that if they could destroy the Covenant's missiles and manufacturing capabilities, they could then sue for peace—or fight a war on more equal footing.

But that hope died in the three days that followed. The Covenant must have known about the attack. A16 missiles landed at the invasion sites just as amphibious ships made landfall. No prisoners were taken. In total, 147,302 Pax armed service members perished in the battles. But the worst was yet to come.

On November 13, the Covenant launched a counter strike against the Pax homelands—a rain of missiles that authorities still don't have a firm count on. It is believed to have been in the thousands. They carried a new type of incendiary ordnance that delivered devastating effects, leveling cities and destroying major interstates and bridges. Fields in the American heartland burned with wildfire that water and dirt couldn't extinguish.

America, Australia, Canada, and the other constituents of the Pax watched as their civilization was destroyed.

The years that followed would become known as the perpetual war—a time characterized by ever-present missile attacks. In the months after the fall, EMOs exploded nearly every week in major cities. Hot bombs detonated too. There seemed to be no rhyme or reason to the bombings—only a desire for terror from the Covenant. Populations shrank, due both to direct deaths from the bombings and to starvation. Just as many perished from losing their will to live.

The Dark Age gripping the Pax grew darker as the last survivors splintered into smaller, almost nomadic groups.

65

In the airship, shouts came from the hall. Nora went to the door and listened to the doctors and nurses barking orders.

She opened the hatch with a loud clang, just in time to see her father barreling toward the med bay.

Nora fell in behind him and stopped cold right inside the room. Matthews was convulsing on the gurney. Medical staff were working desperately to save the man. Her first thought was that it was an embolism. Or a heart attack.

She felt Maria's gaze upon her, eyes filled with fear.

Her father's voice was low and intense behind her. "Let's go."

She eyed him, silently questioning why. He took her by the arm, gripping tight enough to alarm her. Had Matthews talked? Did he know that she was an impostor?

He tugged her from the bay into the hall, where she reached out and broke free of his hold.

"Dad." The word caught in her throat. It was a word she thought she would never say to him again. The act of saying it had an effect on her she hadn't anticipated.

"What?" he shot back, seeming alarmed.

"What's happening?"

His brow furrowed. "Isn't it obvious?"

Nora shook her head.

"If I'm right, there's one or more Covenant agents on this ship. They got to Matthews. You could be next. What you know is dangerous— worth risking an agent's life for. I'm not letting you out of my sight. And you need to talk. Right now."

Nora swallowed hard. "Okay. But bring Maria."

He squinted at her. "The singer?"

"She may be in danger too."

He raised his eyebrows but motioned to a soldier who had entered the corridor. "Bring Santos to Stateroom Two."

Gently this time, he nudged Nora into the stateroom, where he closed the door, and she took a seat on the bunk. She had the strangest sensation then: of being a teenager, in one of those rare times when she had gotten in trouble and been relegated to her room until she confessed what had happened.

The hatch sprang open, and Maria entered. Nora rose, wrapped her in a hug, and whispered in her ear, "Stay quiet. Follow my lead."

Nora didn't yet know what her lead was, but she sensed that the next few seconds would determine whether they lived or died.

Outside the door, three soldiers stood guard, rifles at the ready.

Nora's father locked the hatch and turned to the two of them, who were both seated on the narrow bunk now.

"What happened in Peenemünde?"

"What did Matthews say?" Nora thought that was a good place to start. And buy some time.

"That the A21 was finished and had already been mass produced—that the Covenant is much further along than we knew." He studied Nora, waiting, but she said nothing.

"Matthews said the missiles were capable of carrying a payload that would completely wipe us out this time. Is it true?"

Nora was unsure what to say, so she said the truth. "As far as I know."

"Matthews said they were set to launch in seven days."

He cocked his head, waiting for Nora to respond to the unspoken question.

"That's my understanding," she said quietly.

"Then we have no choice. We will end the world so that we can rebuild it."

Nora's mind sputtered. What did he mean by that? Had her words—confirming Matthews's account—sealed her father's resolve for whatever action was about to take place? If so, she was now partly responsible.

She realized then that her father was talking to her.

"Nora. Nora."

She looked up.

"How is she involved?" he asked, pointing to Maria.

"She saved me," Nora said, watching her father for any indication that the lie was working. "She helped me get out of Peenemünde."

He cocked his head and glanced between the two women. Nora wasn't sure if he was buying it. She pressed on. "As a South American citizen, she can obviously travel to the Covenant."

"Yes, but to a top-secret army research facility?"

"She's performing there—at the launch of the A21. She was touring the facilities and testing the acoustics."

He opened his mouth, perhaps to ask another question, one that might expose the ruse, but they were saved by a sharp knock at the door.

Nora's father jerked it open, clearly annoyed.

"What?"

"Sir, we're on approach."

At that, he exited without another word to Nora, leaving her sitting on the bunk beside Maria, who turned to her.

"What are you doing?"

Nora leaned closer and whispered, "Trying to keep us alive."

66

In Kato's prison cell, the sound of the lock opening shot through the small space. The tall man with a goatee stepped inside again, this time holding a folder.

"Yeah," he said, drawing the word out. "That line you shot us before is not playing well upstairs."

He threw the folder on the metal table. "What I have here is a file on a Sicherheitsdienst Sturmbannführer—" He looked up. "Oof, that's a mouthful. I guess when they integrated with the Covenant, the SS *really* wanted to keep their ranks and organization." He tapped the folder. "Anywho, point is, this SD spook looks suspiciously like you—as in, he is you. As in, we know who you are, and ergo—by the way, I just learned that word, ergo, which means therefore—so therefore, ergo, you have info we want." He held his hands up. "And we're not super particular about how we get it. Hard way. Easy way. All fine by us. Not a lot of love lost for the Covenant around here."

He waited.

Kato said nothing.

"Hey, it's more paperwork for me if we go the super unpleasant way, but frankly, I hope you choose that. Frankly, I don't mind the paperwork. It's a bit cathartic, really, writing it all down, sorting through what happened in a room like this and how I feel about it. Writing can be therapeutic, you know?"

He stared at Kato, eyes like lasers carving him up, unblinking, cold and deadly. "So, what do you want to do, SD spook?"

"I'm not who you think I am."

"That's disappointing. I figured you SD operatives would have better lies than that. We get that one all the time." The interrogator made his voice whiny and pleading. "*You've got the wrong guy, really, I'm telling ya.*"

"I don't have the answers you want. I'm not supposed to be here."

"Well, on that last point, we agree. But we're going to start peeling the onion here and find out what you know."

In the dank cell, Ty listened as the man called again, the same refrain he had repeated several times now: "Hungry? Talk, and we'll feed you. All you have to do is start talking—and you'll start eating."

Ty's jailer left the hall and returned with a metal tray, which he set on the floor outside Ty's cell, out of reach. The smell of meat and butter and spices wafted through the small opening in the door.

It was a kind of torture Ty never knew existed: to be hungry and smell food. Still, he didn't say a word. He knew if he did, it might hurt Nora, Kato, or Maria. Or himself.

But each time they brought the tray and took it away, he felt himself breaking a little more.

67

In the stateroom, Nora felt the airship touch down with a thud. A few minutes later, a uniformed Pax soldier pushed the hatch open and beckoned her and Maria forward, out into the hall and past the med bay, where Matthews's body was draped in a white cloth.

In the cargo bay, the ramp extended to the ground.

The midday sun was blinding, and it took a few moments for Nora's eyes to adjust. When they did, what lay beyond the ship took her breath away.

They had landed on a small ridge above what appeared to be a village with narrow thoroughfares. Shacks and small shops lined the dusty streets, a scene that reminded Nora of America two hundred years ago—a settlement on the frontier of a new land.

Three soldiers escorted Nora, Maria, and her father down the ridge, into the town and past the shops, where merchants were haggling over crates of fruits and vegetables and cured meat wrapped up tight. Their clothes were simple and nondescript, as though they had been resewn from other clothes—a patchwork of remnants. And indeed, that was what this civilization was.

In the street, the group stood aside as two tall horses trotted through town pulling a hollowed-out car whose roof had been sawed off, one driver holding the steering wheel, the other grasping the reins to the horses.

A large water wheel loomed at the banks of what Nora thought was the Potomac River.

As she took in the scene, Nora realized her father was watching her.

"What's the matter?" he asked.

"What do you mean?"

"You look like you've never seen Camp Shenandoah before."

"It's... been a long trip."

"You sure you're feeling okay?"

"I am."

After that, Nora made an effort to keep her expression neutral. Soon, it became obvious to her why the village seemed so impermanent. It was. The homes and shops were made of panels bolted together with tents and canopies between them. Large wagons lay empty behind them, conceivably waiting to be loaded again and moved.

As the small group ventured deeper into the camp, the merchants and settlers turned and stared. Children stopped playing, their soccer balls rolling into the street and behind the shops. People held their baskets full of fruit and bread and gawked.

At first, Nora thought it was the sight of the soldiers. But their gaze didn't rest there. It was on Maria. And of course it was—she was a global superstar in this world. She must look completely out of place here.

Maria seemed to notice too. She brushed her hair in front of her face and hung her head slightly.

At a hobbled-together shanty at the center of town, Nora's father opened the front door and told the soldiers escorting them to wait outside.

The home was as modest inside as outside. Two folding tables butted together served as a dining table. Canvas folding chairs, like one might see around a campfire, were arranged around a wood-burning stove with a pipe that snaked up and out of the back wall.

Through an opening, Nora caught sight of a makeshift kitchen with a portable grill on a table beside a cistern that appeared to be connected to a rain barrel outside and a pot for boiling water inside. Even the homes here were built to be moved.

A door opened and Nora's brother ventured out, arms outstretched.

"You're back!"

His face was the same as she had known, but it was more worn, the worry lines deeper, the tan darker, gray spreading out at his temples.

She hugged him awkwardly as two young children ran out and joined the hug. The boy was about four, and the girl was slightly older.

"Aunt Nora!" they yelled out of sync.

The feel of their tiny hands pressing into her was surreal. She peered down, taking them in, studying their faces, marveling at how truly different and beautiful and heartbreaking this world was.

At the dining table, they sat down to a lunch of venison, carrots, and navy beans in a light coating of molasses and dotted with pieces of cured pork. Nora didn't realize how famished she was until the first bite of food reached her mouth. She ate with barely contained control.

Her niece, who was named Allie and wore taped-together glasses, was more curious than her brother, Wyatt. She lobbed questions at Nora between mouthfuls of her lunch.

"Where did you go, Aunt Nora?"

"Oh, I was on a trip."

"Where to?"

"Far away."

"To the Covenant?"

Nora's father held up a hand. "That's enough."

Allie took another bite of beans, her feet hanging off the metal folding chair, swinging beneath her. "Daddy says you're doing important work to end the war."

Nora felt her father watching her.

"I think we're all doing important work," Nora said carefully.

"Was your trip dangerous?" Allie asked, raising her eyebrows.

"That's enough," Nora's father snapped. "No more talk of work."

Allie didn't even flinch. "When I grow up, I want to do the same work as you, Aunt Nora. Just like Mom did."

Nora's brother had been raising a fork full of venison to his mouth. His hand stopped in midair. He stared ahead, frozen for a long moment, then let the utensil fall back to the plate, his gaze following it.

The silent act told a story, one that stabbed deep into Nora's heart.

She smiled at the niece she had never known, who reminded her so much of herself at that age. "I hope you don't, Allie. I hope you grow up in a world without war, where you can do something you love."

The girl cocked her head as if that didn't make any sense. Nora didn't think much could have been worse than the reaction her brother just had. But what she saw now was indeed worse—a child who couldn't imagine a world without war.

Nora's brother broke the silence, mercifully changing the subject. "So, look, I've just got to ask. How in the world do you two know each other?" He glanced between Nora and Maria, holding up his hands. "No offense, but we don't get many celebrities around here."

"We're..." Nora began, mind grasping for the right words.

"Working together," Maria finished.

Dylan smiled, a laugh starting. "On what?"

"Can't say yet," Nora said quietly.

He studied her, somewhere between amused and, Nora thought, unconvinced. "All right then," he said simply, as he rose and began to clear the table.

After the meal, Nora said goodbye to her brother and her niece and nephew and followed her father out of the rickety home and down the lane. Maria followed, taking in more of the town, the soldiers forming a small circle around them as they walked, rifles held at the ready.

At a blacksmith shop, Robert ducked through the doorway and, with a slight nod, walked past a hulking man who was hammering what looked like a car fender over an anvil. There was a small office beyond the working area out front and a windowless tool room beyond that.

In the tool room, a soldier closed the door behind them

and quickly pushed a cart to the far wall. He pulled up a ratty braided rug from the floor, revealing a trapdoor in the wooden planks. He twisted the handle and lifted it. Below was a round metal shaft with a wooden ladder inside. It reminded Nora of a manhole.

She was stunned to see it here. The entire town had seemed transitory. This had the look of something permanent, something buried. Perhaps they covered it when the camp moved on?

Her father was the first to mount the ladder. The guards simply stood by, and so did Nora and Maria.

When he had descended a few rungs, he called up to her, "Come on. We'll be late."

Before she could ask what for, he was descending the ladder faster, nearly out of sight.

She followed him down and so did Maria, and soon she saw the glow of a ChemLight looming at the bottom, lying on a metal floor in a small room. When she reached it, she realized there was a single exit from the space: an oblong metal hatch that reminded Nora of the doors on the airship. It was the last thing she'd expected to see here.

There was a combination lock by the handle with seven rotating disks that had both numbers and letters—a total of thirty-six possibilities for each position in the sequence.

Quickly, her father rolled the disks and pulled the handle, and the door popped open. Beyond, two uniformed soldiers were waiting, guns in hand, goggles positioned on top of their helmets.

Nora's father marched past them without a word, leading her and Maria through a network of metal corridors, their footsteps echoing as they went. The walls were gunmetal gray, the ceiling was low, and the pathways were narrow. ChemLights lit their way.

It again reminded Nora of the airship, though this place was more cramped.

Abruptly, her father stopped and pushed against the wall in a spot where there seemed to be no door, only a seam in the metal. It swung in, revealing a landing to a curving staircase.

The steps were wide and metal, and after descending for a while, Nora felt disoriented, as though she were a marble in an endless corkscrew, constantly going around in circles.

Finally, the sound of their clanging steps on the metal changed, and the staircase came to an end at another hatch with a combination lock similar to the last one.

Robert spun the disks until the handle clicked and he pulled the hatch open. The room beyond was some sort of airlock. Nora felt the pressure on her ears as they adjusted, and the airlock on the opposite side popped open.

This section of the underground facility was far different. The walls were painted white, not gunmetal gray as the corridors had been before, and it seemed cleaner, newer, the ceilings higher.

And there were people here. Not many, just a few individuals in gray wool tunics and pants passing by, carrying clipboards and talking, like it was a very natural thing to be down here.

At that moment, the thing that occurred to Nora was that if she and Maria were discovered to be impostors, she would never escape this place. This bizarre, labyrinthine bunker would be the last thing she ever saw.

Her father ventured deeper into the space, to a rail that looked out over a circular opening about fifty feet wide. The chasm extended down four floors, reminding Nora of something she might see in the promenade of an enclosed shopping mall. The ceiling above hung perhaps fifteen feet away.

Nora wondered if her counterpart had been here before. Was this new to the Nora from this world? Or a frequent event?

Her father eyed her, as if studying her reactions. She gave no reaction. She felt that was safest.

He led them away from the overlook to a wide window that ran nearly from the floor to the ceiling and displayed a massive fish tank so expansive it seemed to have no end. As Nora watched, a school of fish swam by and then cut away from the glass.

Staring between Nora and Maria, her father said, "What do you think of it?"

"It's incredible," Nora whispered without even thinking.

Robert cocked his head.

"What is this place?" Maria asked.

"The future," he replied. "And it starts now."

68

Nora followed as her father led her and Maria to a corridor that was wide and well lit.

This area of the bunker seemed to be some kind of office complex. There were doors on each side of the hall, and when she passed an open one, Nora saw an open-concept team room with desks that were mostly empty.

On the whole, she got the impression that this was a shelter waiting to be occupied.

Perhaps the most surprising aspect of this place was that it had power. Did burying it this deep put it out of reach of the Covenant's electromagnetic ordnance? It would seem so.

Nora's father rounded a turn and marched past four armed guards standing by a set of double doors, which led to an auditorium. The room had stadium seating capable of holding what Nora estimated would be a hundred people.

Far fewer were present. Perhaps twenty individuals sat in the rows. On the stage below, a lectern waited, bright lights shining down on it.

Nora was reminded of her recent talk at Oxford, of the announcement of *The Birthright*. She marveled at the fact that she had given that speech only a few days ago, yet it felt to her like a million years.

"Take a seat anywhere," Robert said before he made his way to the lectern, where he conversed with the man and woman there and then tapped a control panel that dimmed the lights.

A beam lanced out from the back of the room, displaying an image on the screen, a black background with white letters that read *PROJECT POSEIDON*.

Robert stood in the center of the stage, surveying the crowd.

When the room fell silent, he reached into the lectern and took out a small round controller with a single button and a thick cord that ran back to the lectern. It reminded Nora of a jump rope and its handle.

When her father clicked the button, there was a mechanical shuffling sound at the back of the room as the projector rotated the next slide into place. Nora marveled that while the bunker was like a dark dystopian future, the technology inside was much like the 1960s.

Robert's voice boomed in the auditorium.

"When I was a child, I learned a fact that changed my life. Telling you that fact now will reveal just how odd a young man I was."

He smiled, and motioned to the image behind him, which showed a global map with the landmasses in gray and yellow rings around the coastline. There was also a faint yellow line at the equator. The oceans were shades of blue, and the colors got darker toward the center of the seas, away from land and the equator.

"The fact that changed my life was that somewhere between fifty and seventy percent of the oxygen in the Earth's atmosphere comes from the sea. I had always thought that the forests and the trees and plants around us were responsible for the air we breathe, but they are only a bit player in the oxygen cycle upon which life on this planet depends. The true star of Earth's oxygen cycle is phytoplankton, a group of organisms that includes photosynthesizing bacteria and plantlike algae. Most phytoplankton are too small to be seen by the unaided eye. They live principally on the surface of the sea, where they capture sunlight and use its energy to split carbon dioxide and water, making sugar for themselves and releasing oxygen as a by-product. And they release a lot of oxygen. Phytoplankton alone account for about half of global photosynthetic activity and about half of the oxygen production, yet they represent only about one percent of the global plant biomass. And unlike trees and other plants that live for years—sometimes hundreds of years—phytoplankton have a life cycle measured in days."

Robert paused. "As a child, that fact fascinated me. I thought:

here is a mostly unseen organism that controls the fate of our world, the very air we breathe. It floats at the top of the seas and lakes and streams, blown by the wind and carried by the currents, and its destiny is our destiny, and we should try to understand it and ensure that it flourishes. Its destiny is linked to ours. That's why I became a marine biologist. I believed that the seas were the key to securing humanity's future."

He clicked the small controller. An image appeared that showed what Nora recognized as a slide from a microscope, a view of a viral particle.

"It's funny how life has a way of distorting your dreams. I saw in the seas a way to protect future generations. Today, I still believe the seas are our key to survival, but in a far different way."

Robert took a deep breath. "In less than a week, the Covenant will launch a new wave of missiles—the A21. We don't know precisely what their new ordnance is. We know only that it will wipe us from the face of the Earth forever."

He set the small controller on the lectern and paced on the stage. "The Covenant has taken our ability to use advanced electrical technology. They've relegated us to the Stone Age. They think we don't have a way to fight back. They are wrong."

He nodded. "Sure, our weapons are no match for them. Nor are our numbers. At this point, they probably see us as a nuisance to get rid of. But we have one last way to fight back: biology. Biology doesn't depend on electricity. Or advanced technology. And it is the most powerful weapon on Earth."

He pointed to the image of the viral particle behind him. "What you're looking at is the key to our survival. It's something I never dreamed I would help create. A pathogen to kill the seas—a virus that, within days, will kill virtually all of the planet's phytoplankton. We call it the Poseidon virus, and it will be carried by the fish in the tank you all walked past just a few moments ago."

Robert shook his head. "In a way, my childhood dreams are coming true. I am using my love and knowledge of the sea to save humanity. I simply never imagined the cost."

He returned to the lectern and took the controller and clicked the next slide, but Nora found it nearly impossible to focus on it. Her heart was beating in her ears, chest heaving. She couldn't believe what she was seeing. It was impossible, the dark future her father was about to usher in.

"I know what you're thinking," he said, voice booming in the auditorium. "How does killing the phytoplankton save us? The answer is simple: in a matter of days, Earth's fragile ecosystem will be irreparably altered. In particular, the production of oxygen will plummet—I estimate by at least half. Now, I can imagine your next question, that it won't affect the atmosphere for some time. And you're right. The atmosphere is vast, and it takes time to cycle completely. But the thing is, it doesn't take much for this planet to become uninhabitable."

He motioned to the image of a drawing of a human body and a chart that showed oxygen levels from green to red. "The air we breathe is about 78 percent nitrogen gas, 20.9 percent oxygen, and the remaining 1 percent is primarily argon gas with trace amounts of carbon dioxide, neon, and helium. A human needs a minimum oxygen concentration of 19.5 percent to breathe effectively. The lungs take in air, separate out the oxygen and use red blood cells to carry that oxygen throughout the body. Every cell requires oxygen to function—and without it, they begin to degrade. At lower than 19.5 percent oxygen, mental and physical performance will degrade. Humans will tire faster. Below 14 percent, thinking will become even more difficult. Respiration will be intermittent. At lower than 6 percent oxygen in the air, no human can survive."

Robert looked up at the ceiling. "So after the phytoplankton are gone, how long will that take? The short answer is that we're not sure. We think a few years. Keep in mind that the death of the phytoplankton won't only affect the oxygen levels—it will impact CO_2 levels as well. Without phytoplankton to remove carbon dioxide from the atmosphere, the planet will become warmer."

He inhaled, a deep lungful of oxygen-rich air that Nora now saw in a completely different way. "While I don't know the exact timeline—that is, how long it will take humans to perish after the phytoplankton are gone—I know it will happen. And I know we will be safe down here. Here in these arcologies, we have massive oxygen concentrators and scrubbers that will provide for our needs. We have farms where we can grow food to sustain us." He paused. "What has given us this opportunity is a simple shift in thinking. Where we once saw disadvantages, we searched for strength. In a world choking to death, having a small population, and being underground, is an advantage. In a world where we can't have electronic technology, mastery of biology becomes the key to survival. And we will survive, thanks to Project Poseidon—and that's precisely what you are here to vote on. A no vote will be the last you ever cast. This is our final chance to strike back, to give our children a future on this Earth. I'll take questions now."

Murmurs erupted across the auditorium.

Nora's father's gaze settled on her before she had a chance to wipe the shock from her face. In that split second, she knew that he saw it, and that it surprised him. He squinted, studying her. Nora knew what he was seeing: that she was indeed an impostor.

He stared at her, his expression a mix of confusion and hurt.

Nora placed her hand on Maria's arm, gripped it, and motioned back to the closed double doors behind them, where she knew the soldiers stood guard.

She had to get out.

But when she glanced back down at the stage, her father locked eyes with her and gave a sharp jerk of his head to the side, the meaning clear: *Don't go anywhere.*

69

In the bunker beneath Camp Shenandoah, in the auditorium where Nora's father had given his presentation, a debate raged. And, Nora thought, rage was the right word for the discourse. Tempers flared. The representatives of the Pax Humana yelled and cried and pleaded.

At the heart of the argument was a simple question: whether they had the right to destroy the world to save themselves. By a vote of twelve to eight, they decided that they did. The resolution was formally titled the Act of Self-Defense and Self-Preservation.

There was no clapping at its ratification. The representatives were instructed to prepare their camps to occupy their own bunkers. Sundry arrangements were made, and a single amendment was added to the act, a directive that Dr. Robert Brown should seek out any alternative route to peace before unleashing the Poseidon pathogen.

When the representatives had filed out of the room, Robert strode over to where Nora and Maria were sitting and slipped his hands in his pockets, staring down at her.

"I think we need to talk."

Nora swallowed, not trusting her voice. This man was capable of genocide. What would he do to her now that he was sure she was an impostor? Was there any piece of the father she had known left inside of him?

"Follow me," he said as he marched past them, up the stairs, and through the doors. They walked deeper into the office complex, snaking through the corridors until he came to a door with a combination lock and large numbers beside it: 255.

He glanced at Nora expectantly, but she stood still, unsure what to do.

He looked away and exhaled, as though he had just received bad news, then spun the dials on the lock and opened the door, beckoning them to enter.

Inside, Nora scanned the small space. A desk sat in the center, a stack of papers in one corner. Behind it lay a credenza with a few framed photos. She wandered closer and bent and soon realized what they were: her family. In the closest picture, her brother Dylan and a woman about his age were smiling, holding up a baby. In the background was the cityscape of a place she didn't recognize. Only a few of the skyscrapers had been bombed. The next was of Dylan, older now, more rugged and worn, standing alone, towering over two children. None of them were smiling.

The last picture was of Nora—the other Nora, the woman from this world. She was wearing leggings and a zip-up hooded sweatshirt and a cap. Her father was next to her, their arms around each other. They stood on the precipice of a mountain, gray and white rock beneath their feet, rolling hills of green forests spreading out in the distance, fog lying in the folds.

Neither were smiling.

Nora and the woman in the picture could have been mirror images of each other, if not for one thing: the eyes. The woman in the picture stared back with no emotion. In her eyes was a cold-burning fire that nothing could extinguish.

Maria glanced between Nora and her father.

Robert walked to the corner of the office, studying Nora, his expression one of confusion and, Nora thought, possibly hurt. Or perhaps he was dreading what came next.

When they locked eyes, he motioned to the sheaf of papers on the desk, as if saying, *Go ahead, take a look.*

The top page was a cover page for a book:

THE BIRTHRIGHT:
HOW HUMANITY CAN SURVIVE WITHOUT THE SUN
BIOLOGICALLY & PSYCHOLOGICALLY
Dr. Nora Brown

Unable to resist, Nora flipped over the first page and read the opening line:

Humanity has a bright future. But we have a dark past. The mistake we have made is assuming the darkness is over, that we have advanced beyond it. We have assumed our base nature no longer exists. That is the foolish assumption that has doomed us.

But for the brave—those capable of confronting truths and embracing true science—there is a future. It awaits, but the darkest chapter of humanity lies between it and where we are now, a darkness only found beneath the surface, where we will be tested and where we will triumph.

The Pax has lost the war on the surface. We cannot defeat our enemy, but we can use their weaknesses against them. And we can hide. If we are strong enough to survive—and wait long enough—we will inherit the Earth. It is our Birthright.

Nora had thought that nothing could rattle her more than her father's speech in the auditorium. She was wrong. The manuscript on the desk turned her world upside down. Her counterpart on this world wasn't simply an aghast observer. She was a collaborator. A partner in the Poseidon project, though it was clear that her father had kept the exact details of the plan from her. She knew they were going to ruin the surface of the Earth, but for the sake of keeping the details from the Covenant, she hadn't been told the details of exactly how.

The idea that some version of her was capable of such darkness terrified Nora.

When she looked up, the father she had never known was standing in the corner, his hands clasped behind his back, watching her.

"I'm going to ask you some questions," he said quietly. "And I want you to answer. I don't want this to become unpleasant."

"How did you know?" Nora asked.

He cut his eyes to Maria. "At first, I thought it was part of some ruse for her benefit. I assumed she was part of some follow-up operation you were planning. Or perhaps some ploy to set up a Pax Arcology in South America, a refuge or something." He smiled. "The look on your face when I brought you down here... you're a great operative, but that was real. You were shocked. But you've been down here many times. And you've known we were planning the final assault on the Covenant—just not the details. I saw the horror on your face in that auditorium. The other curiosity is the two men who were with you. One of our rover bots saw you with one of the men. But you've never mentioned them. We know one is a Covenant military officer. And finally, as if there was any doubt left, you didn't even know your own office."

"It's true. I'm not the daughter you know."

"Where is she?"

"I don't know."

"You're lying."

"It's true. Based on what Commander Matthews told me, she's still there, in Reich Europa, perhaps at Peenemünde. She was captured there during her operation."

"If that's true, who are you?"

"I'm... I'm who she could have been."

70

Robert considered Nora's words for a moment. "You're who she could have been... if what?"

"If a thousand things—a million things—had gone differently."

"What things?"

"To begin with, the Axis powers losing the Covenant War— what we call World War II. In my world, Britain never fell during the Blitz. America rose in the wake of the war. There was a true, long peace after. A world without the Covenant."

"What are you talking about? Where are you from?"

"A world far different. More kind. But with its own problems."

"Assuming I believe you—and I'm not saying I do—what are you doing here?"

Nora couldn't help but smile and shake her head. "Honestly, I don't know."

"*How* did you get here?"

"That's an even stranger story."

"What do you want?"

"This morning, I wanted to save a dying man who was in my care. And beyond that, I wanted to go home. I still do. But right now, I'm wondering if I'm here for another reason. If I have a purpose here. I have a friend who thinks we're here for a reason. I thought it was a crazy idea until I saw your presentation."

"Now what do you think?"

Nora studied the copy of her father, this dark counterpart in a ruined, evil world. The weight of the conversation fell upon her then—the idea that her next words might change the fate of this world forever.

And as she contemplated what to say, she also wondered what the Pax had done with Ty and Kato. Were they dead?

What would become of her and Maria now that this man knew they didn't belong here?

Nora also realized that within her mind, she had a tool that she had sharpened over a lifetime, but never used in such a way: psychology. Almost by instinct, she began building a profile of this Robert Brown, looking for facets and threads that could be pulled upon. It came naturally to her, and when she spoke again, it was with a new confidence in her ability to save not only herself and Maria but Ty and Kato, and perhaps help heal this wounded world. For the first time, she saw her role in whatever was happening here.

"You think we don't know each other. In a way, it's true. But it's also true that I know a version of you very well. The father I grew up with disappeared when I was eighteen. I see a lot of him in you. If I'm right about that, then I know that you don't really want to release that pathogen into the seas. The Robert Brown I know wouldn't have killed something he loved so much— something so many depend upon, something that gives life to billions of innocent people. Children and mothers and fathers and sons and daughters."

"You're a Covenant agent, sent to make me second-guess what I have to do."

"You know that's not true."

"What do you *want*?"

"I didn't know it until now, but I want to help you. I want to help return your daughter to you—the one you know. And save Dylan and Allie and Wyatt."

"How?"

"I don't know yet. But I've very recently begun to agree with my friend. I think I'm here for a reason, on this world at this moment for some purpose. I have a role to play. I don't know what it is. But right now, I think I'm meant to be in this room with you, because you need my help. And I need your help."

"Help with what?"

"I need to find my friend. His name is Ty, and he was nearby when you found us. Another friend was with him: Kato Tanaka. You mentioned them just now."

Robert studied her. "Yes. We have them. One of our combat spiders lanced them, and a team captured them."

"What did you do to them?"

Robert inhaled sharply. "Ty wasn't in our files. Tanaka is a Reich Europa intelligence operative. One based in Peenemünde."

"The man in your custody is not in any way connected to the Covenant or Reich Europa. Before yesterday, he had never heard of either. Like me, he's a... visitor here."

"This is insanity."

"I think, deep down, you know it's true. It's the only reason we're in this office and not in a prison cell."

"The only reason," he said slowly, "you're not in a prison cell is *how* you're different from her."

"How am I different?"

Robert stared at the floor and shook his head.

"How?" Nora asked again.

"Her heart is a lot harder than yours."

Nora saw it then. The opening. "But that's not why I'm here. I'm here because you wish her heart wasn't that hard. And seeing me tells you it's not too late for her. Or for your grandchildren."

71

Ty lay on the thin mattress, trying to think of a way to escape this prison.

Like the hidden compartment in Lars's truck, there was no way to mark time. There was no clock and no view of the sun outside. Only hunger and the weariness it brought with it. He wondered how long he had been here.

The door lock slammed open, and footsteps sounded in the hall. The door to his cell swung inward, the faint light that had shown through the small square now pouring in, almost blinding Ty as he sat up and stood on wobbling legs he hadn't tried to use in some time.

He squinted and watched as a figure strode through the doorway. Ty couldn't see her face, but he knew who she was by her outline.

Nora.

Upon seeing him, she quickly closed the distance between them and pulled him into a tight hug, her warmth pressing into him, the closeness, the feel of her even more satisfying than the water his dry mouth craved, and the food his body yearned for.

Her voice was sharp and commanding, its force surprising him. "Unchain him!"

She moved her hands to his face, thumbs running across his cheeks like windshield wipers, clearing away the dirt and grime.

Her lips were inches from his, her voice a whisper.

"Are you hurt?"

"No."

A guard came in and unlocked his hands, and the second the cold metal was taken away, Ty rubbed his wrists, incredibly glad to be free again.

"What happened?" he asked.

Nora glanced at the guard outside the door. "I can't tell you here. Come on."

She took his hand, and Ty squeezed hers tight, feeling the softness. At that moment, he never wanted to let it go.

In the corridor beyond the cell, Maria was waiting, arms folded at her chest. She was scowling, but at the sight of Ty, she uncrossed her arms and smiled slightly.

Beside her stood a man Ty hadn't seen in seventeen years.

"Dr. Brown," Ty whispered.

"Do I know you?"

Ty shook his head. "No. I guess not."

"Come on," the man said, leading them out of the corridor and down another, then another where the cells were different, more like interrogation rooms.

In the second one, Kato was seated at a table, hands chained to a ring in the center, feet shackled to the floor. He was hunched forward, head lying on its side on the table, facing the door, eyes closed. A dark bruise covered his cheek. His hair was soaked, Ty assumed, from sweating.

The sight stopped Ty in his tracks. He felt his stomach drop as he watched, waiting, hoping Kato would take a breath.

He was still.

Nora didn't hesitate. She rushed forward and pressed two fingers to his neck as she looked back and called, "Release him! And give me some water and a med kit."

Kato stirred at Nora's touch, and Ty let out a breath he hadn't realized he was holding. The other side of Kato's face wasn't much better. Through eyelids that seemed too heavy to hold open, Kato peered up at Nora, and the very slightest of smiles formed at the corner of his bloody lips.

72

Ty sat in the club chair, trying to organize his thoughts. On the coffee table in front of him, a pile of empty cups and plates was stacked up like scrap in a demolition yard. He hadn't been the only one hungry.

In the cramped lounge, he and Kato had eaten like wild animals while Nora and Maria had watched and taken their bites with more grace.

When the food was gone, the four of them sat on the couches and chairs and took a moment, all seeming to contemplate their dilemma. And Ty had to admit: it was a dilemma of unimaginable proportions.

As the food digested, Ty's mind began working better. To him, their situation was nothing more than a puzzle that beckoned, waiting to be solved. Mentally, he began arranging the pieces. But there were several that didn't fit.

The Covenant.

Ty's mother.

Nora's father.

And, somehow, even though he didn't exist in this world... Ty's father. He was certain Richter was connected somehow. Or was Ty projecting that onto the situation? Because he wanted him connected. He had always yearned for that connection. At the DARPA facility, for a brief time, he had experienced it.

But Richter wasn't the most concerning issue. Ty sensed that there was still a piece of this puzzle that he was missing.

His gaze settled on Maria, who was sitting alone on a worn fabric couch, staring off into the distance of the small staff lounge. It was her. *She* was the missing piece. But how?

Nora got up from her club chair and walked over to the couch where Kato was sitting alone, hands steepled at his nose and lips.

"How do you feel?"

Kato didn't look up. "Fine."

"Do you need another painkiller?"

"No."

"It has to hurt."

"I've been punched in the face before."

Silence stretched out. Kato seemed to realize the others were uncomfortable with what he had said.

He looked up. "Thank you, Doctor, but I want to keep my mind clear." He locked eyes with Ty. "I believe we're about to decide what to do. I'll bear the pain to be able to think."

"Okay. But do me a favor? Call me Nora."

Kato nodded.

Above, the air conditioning vent rumbled to life and warm air flowed down. What impressed Ty most was that this facility had power at all. Based on what he had read of the history of this world—and what Nora had just filled them in on during the meal—electronics had been nearly eradicated in the Pax. But not below ground, and that was the key. His guess was that this was an old government facility in the DC area. The furniture reminded him vaguely of the decor at the DARPA facility. Or maybe it was the fact that he felt equally as trapped.

"I'll ask the obvious question," Kato said. "How do we get out of here? How do we get home?"

Maria was still staring into the distance, unfocused. "I second the obvious question."

"The obvious fact," Ty said, "is that the Pax still has our quantum radio medallion." To Nora, he asked, "Did you ask about it?"

"I did. They have all of your belongings—the gun, the medallion, et cetera."

"We need the medallion back," Kato said.

"They won't give it back." Nora cut her gaze to the door. The meaning was clear: *they're listening.*

Ty had assumed as much, but he appreciated the reminder and it being impressed upon Kato and Maria.

"They're still suspicious," Nora said. "They think we might be Covenant agents."

"Clearly, we're not," Kato said.

"Yes, but it's hard to prove in a world where information moves at the speed of an airship."

Kato nodded slowly. "So we make a plan to get the radio medallion back."

"It doesn't help us," Ty said, not looking up. "We had the radio medallion before. We know the problem there—we don't know what to dial."

"It's obvious," Kato said, "that no one else here does either. Might as well get it and risk it."

"I don't like that risk," Ty said. Then he addressed Nora. "There's another risk—that they dial it. Do you think they will?"

"I doubt it. As I said, they think it's Covenant technology. A bomb. A surveillance device. Or something worse. Experimenting with it—possibly setting it off—is the last thing they want to do."

Nora clasped her hands together. "But I don't think we should be focused on the radio medallion at this moment. If we leave this world, we leave it to die. The Poseidon pathogen will effectively end life on the surface of the Earth. Not tomorrow or next month, but in the years that follow."

Since Nora had described the plan, Ty had considered it. He knew that perhaps the most significant development in Earth's history was the Great Oxygenation Event that occurred several billion years ago, when cyanobacteria began releasing copious amounts of oxygen into the atmosphere. Before that, Earth's atmosphere had likely been mostly dinitrogen and carbon dioxide.

What the Robert Brown on this world was proposing was a great de-oxygenation event, essentially Earth's planetary evolution reversing itself. It was terrifying.

"Not our problem," Kato said. "I took an oath to support and defend the Constitution of the United States of America. This is not that USA. It barely exists here."

"We have a higher oath," Nora said. "To human decency."

Maria held her hands up. "Can we back up a second?"

When no one said anything, she continued. "What happens if we do get the radio medallion back and it doesn't work?"

At the silence that followed, she pressed on. "What happens then? We stay here, in the Pax? We live underground with them?"

"It's the obvious option," Nora said.

"I can't do that," Kato said.

Maria's voice was quiet and hesitant. "I'm assuming they don't have any sort of treatment for... opioid addiction."

"No," Nora said quietly. "But there could be natural remedies."

Maria closed her eyes and shook her head. "Forget it. I'm done. Anything but that." She cut her eyes to the door, as if silently reminding herself. "I'm open to *any* options at this point."

"What we know," Ty said, "is that this world will effectively end in less than a week. The Covenant rockets will fall on the Pax. Or the Poseidon pathogen will be unleashed. Possibly both. What I didn't realize until this second is that we have—in this room—the ability to prevent both events. And I think that's why we're here."

73

"How?" Nora asked.

"First off, we have the pieces to stop the Covenant's rocket launch." Ty motioned to Kato. "In this world, Kato Tanaka is a Reich Europa intelligence operative. What's more, he's based at the Peenemünde facility."

"How does that help us?" Kato asked. "If he's already there, how would I even get inside the facility? They'd know I was a fake the moment I arrived."

"Not if we change your appearance." To Maria, Ty said, "You recently told us something about your past. What you did as a child when your mother had a bruise. And what you did before becoming a singer."

"I was a makeup artist," Maria said. She studied Kato's bruised, swollen face. "Sure. Wouldn't be hard to disguise him."

Nora bunched her eyebrows. "Yes, but why would they even let us in to begin with?"

"Same answer," Ty said. "Maria. She's the missing piece. She's performing in Peenemünde at the A21 missile launch ceremony."

Maria's eyes went wide. "Right. *That* Maria. Not *me*."

"They don't know the difference."

Kato stood. "It could work."

"This is crazy," Maria said.

"I'm skeptical too," Nora said, "but I want to hear more."

"Where does the Maria on this world live?" Kato asked.

"Argentina," Nora replied.

"Neutral territory," Kato said, pacing now. "I assume the Pax Humana has an embassy in Argentina?"

"I could ask my father, but I think it's a safe bet. Why?"

"We could use the embassy as a staging ground for an

operation to kidnap this world's Maria Santos. We simply hold her at the embassy, which, if it works like our world, is sovereign national territory. No one will report her missing, because we'll replace her with our Maria. No one will even know the real Maria Santos is gone."

"Then what?" Ty asked, thinking he knew where Kato was going but not certain.

"Then, we start the more difficult part of the operation."

Kato motioned to Nora and Ty. "We pose as Maria's entourage as we all fly to Peenemünde for the launch ceremony. Inside the facility, we'll each have a role. Maria gets us in and gets us access. I'll say I'm her security detail. Ty can be technical—lights and audio-visual. Nora will be hair and makeup."

Kato paused for a moment. "The trick will be the second replacement: finding this world's Kato and... subduing him so that I can slip into his role."

"How does that help us?" Nora asked.

"If I'm right, he'll have unrestricted access to the facility. At that point, I can try to find the rockets and destroy them."

"I see a better alternative," Ty said. "The rockets are likely guarded against someone trying to take them out."

"I agree," Kato said. "But what options do we have?"

"Instead of destroying the rockets," Ty said, "Kato and I could find the launch control area and change where the missiles are supposed to land."

"What would the new target be?" Nora asked.

Kato held his hands out. "I see two options. The most benign would be to have them land in an unpopulated area. The northern region of Greenland, for example. The other option would be to target Covenant military capabilities. Their rocket-building facilities. The Seawall. Bases."

"That might take a lot of lives," Nora said quietly.

"It might," Kato agreed. "But it would also change the balance of power in this world forever. It would give the Pax an opening to rebuild, to get back onto equal footing and give their society a chance at a real future."

"For now," Nora said, "let's simply assume we alter the rocket targets away from the Pax." She glanced at Ty. "Then what?"

"We exit. No one will suspect Maria Santos and her entourage of being connected to the malfunction," Ty said. "When we return to the Pax, we ask for the radio medallion back, then we decide what to do. We study it. Maybe there's even some information about it in the Covenant files, which we can access in Peenemünde."

At that moment, Ty sensed a presence in the room. He jerked his head and looked over at the folding tables and empty metal chairs where the staff took their meals. But there was no one there.

"What is it?" Nora asked.

"Nothing." Ty rubbed his temple. "It's nothing. What was I saying? Oh yeah, we get back here, get the radio, and go from there. We'll have time at that point, with no impending rocket strike, and we will have built trust with the Pax."

"There's one thing we're missing," Nora said. "The other Nora. If she's at Peenemünde, we should try to rescue her. And the members of her team."

"It might make getting out more difficult," Kato said.

The door opened, and Robert Brown stepped in and closed it behind him.

"You *will* rescue her. That's part of the deal."

"You've been listening," Ty said.

"To every word. You people are either crazy, or I'm going crazy, and frankly, if all of this was *slightly* less crazy, I'd just throw you all in a prison cell on the surface and forget about the whole thing. But what you're talking about might be crazy enough to work."

He studied the four of them. "We haven't had a chance to change the balance of power like this in a long time—not without doing something as damaging as Poseidon."

"So you'll help us?" Nora asked.

"We'll get you to Argentina. And we'll send a diplomatic pouch with orders for the special operators stationed at the embassy to help you with the Santos op in country." He paused. "But we have one more condition."

Ty waited, knowing what it was, watching Nora, wondering how she would feel.

"Our last condition is that those rockets need to fall on a specific list of Covenant military facilities. That's non-negotiable. If you say no—or if those rockets don't hit the target list we supply—you'll never again see that... radio device you seem so obsessed with."

74

The airship sailed through the sky, the winds buffeting it but never dragging it off course.

In the dining compartment, Ty sat with Nora at a table by a window, peering down at Florida. It was an odd thing, seeing the beaches so empty. Sand stretched out, and blue-green water crashed upon it. There was no sign of humanity. It was as though the land had returned to a prehistoric time.

They had been told that the flight time to Argentina was approximately sixty hours. Ty estimated that the ship was traveling at around ninety miles per hour—about the speed of the Hindenburg and airships of that era.

The big question was whether Maria Santos would indeed be in Argentina when they arrived. They had no way of knowing. If she was gone—if she had already made her way to Reich Europa—the entire operation was likely finished. If that was the case, Ty didn't even want to think about what would become of them.

There was nothing he could do about it now. They were fourteen hours into a sixty-hour journey. Obsessing over that now would do nothing to help them. There was something calming about that. He could enjoy this journey and rest his mind a little.

Ty needed it. The last few days had been the most intense of his entire life.

After breakfast, a waiter came and collected the plates and brought a pot of tea and set a deck of playing cards on the white-linen-covered table. Nora glanced at them with a smile.

"Rummy?"

Ty smiled theatrically. "You couldn't beat me before—in our

youthful, carefree years. What makes you think you can best me now?"

She stared off and tapped her chin with her pointer finger, playing along. "If memory serves, one of us rescued the other from a dingy dungeon outside DC. So who exactly is the master of strategy here?"

Ty laughed as he picked up the deck. "Let's find out."

They played cards and laughed and occasionally glanced out the wide windows as the coastline of Florida disappeared, and Cuba loomed on the horizon and then slipped under them and away.

As the day went by, the sun shifted around them. It shone through the far windows at breakfast, directly overhead at lunch, and right in their eyes at dinner—at which time Ty pulled the shade, making the space feel even more intimate.

The food was excellent. For Ty, the time with Nora was even more enjoyable. Here in the sky, he felt something he hadn't in a long time: what he'd felt on that blanket on the National Mall when they were eighteen, the day Nora's father had disappeared.

It amazed him how time could change so many things—except how you felt about someone. He realized then that how you felt must be imprinted somewhere deep down in a mind, in a place not easily overwritten.

For him, being with Nora was effortless. It brought him a sense of calm and clarity that he needed now.

They both declined coffee after dinner, but Nora didn't rise.

She rolled up the shade and glanced at the setting sun over the thin strip of land that separated the Atlantic and Pacific oceans, the bridge between North and South America.

Her voice was barely a whisper.

"It was so strange seeing him."

"Your father?" Ty asked.

"Yeah."

"I know exactly how you feel," Ty said. "In fact, I might be the only one. Seeing my father recently, after so long... it was jarring. It turned my world upside down."

"He was so different, and yet still the man I knew. It's amazing how a person's environment can shape them."

"In the end, he helped us."

"At a price." Nora stared out the window again. "If we let those rockets land in the Covenant, how many will die?"

"How many will die if we don't?"

"None, if they detonate in Greenland."

"Not today. But what about the future? If we leave the Covenant military intact, they can still destroy the Pax."

A few silent moments passed before Nora said, "I should check on Kato."

Ty rose to join her, and they strode through the halls with stained wood panels and art hanging on the walls.

The vessel was like a cruise ship from another time, a gilded age of luxury in the sky. It made sense to Ty. This was the only way for dignitaries and celebrities from the Pax to travel. Perhaps it was the last vestige of opulence left in the wilting nation. Transporting the team this way was a cover, to be sure, but Ty felt very special to be seeing it.

At Kato's door, Nora knocked, and he called quickly, "Come."

Nora turned the handle and pushed the door inward. The stateroom was tidy. The small bed had been made, and the only thing out of place was a rolling cart with a half-eaten plate of food by the door.

Kato clearly hadn't lost his discipline. He sat cross-legged on the floor, his bloodshot, watery eyes peering up at them with a placid, laser-sharp focus.

"I came to check on you," Nora said.

"I'm fine."

"I'm across the hall if you need me."

The smallest of smiles formed on Kato's lips, a genuine gesture. "Thank you," he said, voice filled with feeling.

At Maria's door, Nora knocked again, but no response came. She knocked once more, concern growing on her face.

After a few seconds, she pushed the door open and strode to the narrow bed by the window where Maria lay on her back,

A.G. RIDDLE

sheet pulled up to her neck, eyes wide open, beads of sweat on her forehead, shivering slightly.

Nora knelt beside her. "Maria, can you hear me?"

The woman turned her head, blinked heavily, and nodded.

"You need to take a pill."

She shook her head. "Need to ration them. Don't have... that many left."

"Can I do anything?" Ty asked.

"We'll be fine," Nora said. "Just give us a little space."

Back in his stateroom, Ty lay on the bed and stared at the ceiling and listened to the hum of the airship. His mind wandered and eventually it focused on his mother. She would be in Peenemünde. Well, not *his* mother. The woman waiting for him was the mother he'd never had. In a way, she was like what Nora had faced in the Pax: a father from another world, who made different choices.

There was a soft knock at the door.

A very Nora-like knock.

Ty smiled. "Come in."

The door swung open, and she stepped inside, a slight grimace on her face. "Sorry if I snapped at you back there."

"You didn't. I understood." Ty sat up. "Is she all right?"

"She's scared. She wasn't doing that great even in the museum. She knows she'll have to perform in Peenemünde, but she doesn't even know the songs. And she's dealing with the physical addiction. She's scared of that too."

Ty could see the exhaustion weighing on Nora. Seeing to Kato and Maria's needs had drained her. He scooted back on the bed and patted the space beside him.

"Take a load off."

Ty stretched out next to the wall, Nora lying alongside him, both staring up at the ceiling.

"You've got your hands full with the three of us," Ty said.

"Since the police came to my door that morning in Oxford, it's been exhausting. But it's also been exhilarating. Taking care of the three of you... it's been so fulfilling for me, in a way teaching wasn't. Don't get me wrong, I loved it, but somehow, I feel like this is where I should be right now."

For a while, they listened to the carts rolling by outside the door and the airship's engines rumbling beyond the window. Every now and then, the ship shuddered from the force of the wind.

Nora's voice was reflective and light when she spoke. "What's going to happen, Ty?"

"I don't know."

"You really think there's something else going on here? Some greater plan at work?"

"I do."

He was about to say that the Covenant being in both worlds was a factor he couldn't reconcile, but that he was sure it was significant. Before he could elaborate, he felt the soft touch of her hand on his. His hand was palm down on the bed, and she covered it with hers.

"What do you think it means that we're both part of this?"

"As in..."

"We're the only two of the four who knew each other before."

"I don't know. But I think it means something."

Nora tightened her grip on Ty's hand. "When my dad disappeared, I was really lost. I wasn't myself. It broke my heart."

"It broke mine too."

"But I think," Nora said slowly, "I think mine's starting to heal now."

"Mine too."

75

Kato woke covered in sweat. Last night's dream lingered in his mind like a bad taste he couldn't wash out of his mouth.

He rolled out of the narrow bed and stumbled to the bathroom. At the faucet, he turned on the water and let the cold stream run into his hands until he had a nice pool, which he splashed on his aching face.

He straightened up and studied himself in the mirror. His cheeks were red and swollen and a little blue where the bruises were fading. With the help of Maria's makeup, he thought he would look almost normal by the time he reached Peenemünde for the ceremony.

The punches he had taken in the Pax interrogation room weren't the worst beating he had ever received. But combined with being in this place—and being away from his family—it had unhinged him. He thought that it stung worse because before he had come here, he had felt so close to getting Joan and Akito back. He had unfinished business at home, and he was going to get back there. One way or another. At any cost.

That thought stopped him cold.

At any cost.

That sort of thinking was how good men did bad things.

He knew what he needed now: distraction. He needed to do something productive. He saw a way to do both—and practice for what was coming.

He dried his face and exited his room and crossed the hall and knocked quickly at Maria's door. He hadn't checked the time, but down the hall, in the dining compartment, the morning sun blazed through the wide windows.

The door opened and Maria peered out at him, deep bags

under her eyes as though she hadn't slept a wink. A layer of sweat coated her forehead.

"You okay?" Kato asked.

She smiled, and a small laugh escaped her. "Not really. You?"

"Same."

"You need help?" she asked.

"This is going to sound crazy—"

Maria held up a hand. "Hey, *nothing* sounds crazy when *everything* is super crazy. So just stop saying that. Crazy is like, our specialty."

Kato laughed. "Right."

Maria swung the door open wider. "Come on in."

When she shut the door, Kato continued. "Before we left, they gave you what you needed to disguise us, right?"

Maria pointed to a suitcase in the corner. "Yeah."

"How are you going to disguise me?"

"Well, your counterpart wears his hair like yours—close-cropped, military style. Since you're posing as a private bodyguard, I was going to fit you for a long-hair wig, use makeup to lighten your skin tone slightly, not enough to clash with your hands, and add a birthmark to your face. You'll wear glasses and contact lenses that alter the color of your eyes. It would have been nice to have some sort of dental device to alter your smile and even voice a bit, but we don't have anything that would work."

Kato marveled at her. "That feels like more than standard hair and makeup expertise."

"I've had a lot of odd jobs. One was makeup for a private detective agency. It paid the bills." She studied him. "Why do you ask?"

"I was wondering... if you wanted to practice. To alter me now."

Maria nodded. "Sure. One condition."

Kato waited.

"You help me put my disguise on too. I don't like what I see in the mirror these days."

With those words, Kato felt a little less alone in the world.

76

When Ty woke, the morning sun was shining through the stateroom window like a bomb blast, achingly bright against his eyes, even through the sheer curtain. Nora's arm was draped across his chest, her soft skin warm against his, her gentle exhales blowing against his ear.

Ty didn't remember going to sleep the night before. But he remembered the words he had said. And what Nora had said. And what it meant.

He felt his heart beating faster as he replayed the conversation in his mind.

Nora stirred, as if the increase in his breathing was a wake-up alarm for her.

The night before, they hadn't discussed her sleeping in his room. They hadn't discussed sleep at all. Somewhere in the conversation, one of them had slipped off to sleep, possibly him, possibly her—he couldn't exactly remember.

It was as if a haze surrounded the night. On the other side was this perfect, light-drenched moment when she opened her eyes and stared at him, and a smile formed on her lips. It was the most beautiful thing he had seen in a very long time.

She didn't say a thing. Neither did he.

They lay there, listening to the wind roll over the airship and the engines hum.

She moved first, dragging her arm over him, her hand pausing on his chest to give him a light pat before she rose and turned.

"Hungry?" she asked.

"Yeah. I can get up and bring food back if you want to stay."

"No. I'm up. I want to change clothes and check on Kato and Maria."

When they had both changed out of the clothes they had slept in, they stood outside Kato's door, Ty knocking. After the third attempt, he turned the handle and they ventured in. Kato was gone.

They checked the dining compartment then, but neither Kato nor Maria was there.

At Maria's door, Ty heard laughter. When he knocked, she yelled, "Yeah!"

He pushed the door open and stared in awe at the long-haired man standing next to Maria. It actually took Ty a few seconds to fully realize that it was Kato. The transformation was that drastic.

"She's good," Kato said, smiling.

Maria was beaming, clearly proud of her work—and perhaps to have had something to do, to take her mind off the demons she was running from.

Ty thought then that there was something magical about this voyage in the sky, that it was like a sort of crucible in which the hard elements of their team were melting together, becoming more than they were alone. And he thought, some of what was burning away in that crucible was the poison of the past each of them hadn't been able to rid themselves of alone.

"I want to be next," Nora said.

Ty stepped toward the door. "I'll bring breakfast."

By dinnertime, Maria had perfected their disguises.

Ty and Nora once again dined at the small table by the window while Kato and Maria remained in their staterooms.

After the meal, he ordered the deck of cards and offered to deal, but Nora simply smiled.

"Let's play in the room."

Almost against his will, he read more into it. He wanted to think she was feeling the same thing he was. But still he wondered—until she took his hand as they walked out of the dining compartment. He was sure of it then.

Inside his stateroom, he set the deck of cards on the small

table by the window, but Nora didn't sit down. She stood there, staring at him, a knowing smile on her face, as though she had just learned a secret, one so juicy she knew it wouldn't keep.

Ty stepped toward her.

She didn't move. Only stared.

He took another step.

Her smile grew.

He leaned in.

She closed her eyes and his lips touched hers, and he wrapped his arms around her and pulled her in tight. Ty felt as though time itself stopped and the whole world exploded.

The moment he'd activated the quantum radio had nothing on what he felt right then.

He didn't know how long the kiss lasted. A second. An hour. A year. It was as though time and space had been obliterated, as though they had slipped into a pocket universe where only the two of them existed. In that kiss was seventeen years of longing and unfulfilled love, things left unfinished and things he'd never thought would be possible again.

When it ended, his chest was heaving. Hers was too.

He swallowed, fear now mounting inside of him. Instinct and pure desire had brought him here, but now his rational mind fought him.

"We shouldn't," he whispered.

Nora sighed. "No, we shouldn't. I'm your doctor. And us being together will complicate the mission. It's irresponsible."

"Selfish."

"You're right," Nora said. "We really shouldn't."

She leaned forward and pressed her lips to his, and Ty felt his body going nearly numb. Nora brought a hand to the back of his head and ran her fingers through his hair, gentle at first, then digging her nails into his scalp and pulling as their tongues met.

They only broke the kiss to take a breath.

"Nora," Ty said, gasping, "I want to, but—"

"No buts." Her eyes twinkled in the soft yellow light. "I don't know what's going to happen, Ty. That is probably the only thing I know for sure. For us, it could end in Argentina.

Or in Peenemünde. Or a million other ways. But we have here and now, on this ship, in this room." She swallowed hard. "I've missed you. I've regretted what happened. I shut you out then because I couldn't deal with what happened to me, and I was scared I would drag you down too, and I didn't even know who I was anymore."

His heart was beating fast as he processed the words, listening, hanging on every one.

"I know who I am now, Ty. And I know my life is changing again. I'm scared, just like back then, and I don't know what's going to happen next, but I'm not going to make the same mistake I did before. I'm not going to shut you out this time. Because I think we're stronger together."

77

The next morning, Ty lay in bed after he woke, watching Nora sleep. Her face was nuzzled into the crook of his neck, her breath nearly silent, tickling his skin under the covers, which were piled high upon them. There was a slight chill in the stateroom (the airship's heating and air conditioning was a minor shortcoming that they had easily overcome the night before).

They had left the shade up. Ty knew the heat and light of the rising sun would wake Nora soon, but he wanted to let her rest. He wasn't sure when their next good night of sleep would be.

Soon, she opened her eyes and looked up at him.

"You let me sleep."

"Yeah."

"You always let me sleep. On top of you. Trapping you."

"I don't mind it. I like it."

She pushed up off the bed, taking a sheet with her to cover her body.

Ty rose, went to the bathroom, and returned with a towel wrapped around him. Nora sat at the small table, pulling her clothes on.

He felt the ache and fatigue that he usually experienced in the mornings, though the time and stress in that prison cell in the Pax had made it worse, he thought.

The bottle of pills was by the bedside, and he wanted to reach out and take one—but not in front of her.

To his surprise, Nora seemed to read his mind. She grabbed the pill bottle, unscrewed the top, and tilted it until one slid into her hand. She held it out to him. "You need this, right?"

He took the pill and swallowed it down with some water from the glass by the bed.

"It's okay," Nora said. "You shouldn't feel sheepish about taking those pills in front of me."

"I don't like you seeing my flaws."

Nora stood and took his face in her hands. "It's not a flaw."

Ty laughed. "What is it then?"

"The most natural thing in the world. Every human being alive takes actions to care for their own health." She nodded at the pill bottle on the bedside table. "One of your health routines, right now, is to take those pills. Maria takes a prescription medication for her health too. In the past, so have I."

Ty bunched his eyebrows and opened his mouth to ask about that, but Nora waved him off. "And no, I'm not going to tell you about it right now, because right now we're talking about you."

Ty smiled.

"For now, I'm your doctor too," Nora said. "You have to be able to talk to me about your health. The entire team is depending on you."

"All right. But I'm not going to like it."

Nora laughed. "Of course. That's your right—do logical things for your health and not, for one single second, like it."

"I'm glad we're on the same page."

"Well, then, Mr. Not-happy-about-improving-his-health, how have you been feeling?"

Ty turned. "Honestly, pretty good." He pointed to the pill bottle. "I don't know what's in those pills, but they work. Better than the combination I was using before. And frankly, I'm a little nervous about what I'll do when I run out. My father wasn't exactly forthcoming about what was in it."

"You're not the only one with that fear."

"Maria."

"Yes. But we'll figure that out after Peenemünde."

Ty shrugged. "If there is an after Peenemünde."

She grabbed his chin and gently lifted it and smiled at him. "Hey. No negativity. This is going to work. Believe it. And then we make it happen."

A knock at the door drew their attention. Ty reached down

and tightened the towel around his waist before opening the door. A young, uniformed staff member stood in the hallway, eyes alarmed at Ty's partial lack of clothes.

"Sir, we're on approach. We'll be moored in about two hours."

"Thank you," Ty said as he closed the door.

Nora's expression grew serious. "Are you ready?"

Ty nodded. "I'm ready." He shrugged. "Well, as ready as one can be to infiltrate a Nazi weapons facility in an alternate universe."

"You know what I feel like?"

"What?"

"Like I'm on a roller coaster. That moment when it's been tossing you around but you're okay, and then it slows down and it's climbing the final hill for something that is about to get totally out of control, and you get this nervousness that won't go away."

Ty smiled. "Yeah. I get that feeling too."

"You know what else I'm feeling?"

Ty squinted. "Unsure about what happened last—"

"No. Not one bit. I've never been so sure of anything in my life." Nora smiled. "The other thing I'm feeling is hungry. Let's get breakfast."

A few hours later, Ty, Nora, Kato, and Maria were standing in the office of the Pax ambassador, inside the Pax Humana embassy in Buenos Aires, Argentina.

A special forces operative stood beside the ambassador's large mahogany desk, reading the paper they had brought. The man squinted, shook his head, and then looked up at the group.

"Is this a joke?"

"It's not a joke," Ty said.

"You want us to kidnap a South American citizen who is not a known Covenant operative, who is in fact a global celebrity that everyone would listen to about being kidnapped—abduct her from her home—and simply keep her here until you tell us to release her?"

"That's accurate, Major," Kato said. "Do you have a problem with that?"

The man sighed heavily.

"We don't really care how you get it done," Kato said. "Buenos Aires is your theater of operation, and you have the local expertise. I would suggest acquiring her tonight and being very careful that she doesn't know that it's the Pax behind it. Obviously, within an hour of taking her, you should smuggle our version of Maria into the residence so that she can resume the real Maria Santos's life."

When everyone else had left the ambassador's office, Nora closed the door and turned to the woman, who looked to be in her sixties. The ambassador had white hair that was tied in a bun and wore glasses that were perched near the tip of her nose.

"There's something else this mission needs," Nora said. "It wasn't in the briefing."

"Go on," the ambassador said.

"Have you ever heard of a medication called methadone?"

"No."

"It may be called something different here."

"What is it?"

"It's an opioid."

It was clear to Nora that the woman knew what that was. Her eyebrows bunched together, and she studied Nora more closely.

Maria had spent an hour with Nora on the airship, applying makeup and cutting and dying her hair. Nora was also wearing large non-prescription glasses, but the way the ambassador was looking at her it was clear she saw recognition there. Did she know this world's Nora?

"While it's in the same category as heroin and opium," Nora pressed on, "methadone can also be used as a cure for addiction. It blocks the high from other opioids while giving a similar feeling, alleviating withdrawal symptoms and cravings."

"It's for the singer? Or you?"

"I can't say."

"Why not?"

"It's part of my job."

The ambassador studied her again. "Are you related to Robert Brown?"

Nora inhaled. "Distantly."

"This business of yours, this mission, it's a strange affair. One I don't understand. But I also know that the Pax is dying. Without a change, and a big change, we will be wiped from the map. I'll try to find this medication for you. And if I can't?"

"I'll make a list of alternatives, like suboxone and naltrexone. Thank you for any help. This could save someone's life."

Six hours later, Nora sat in the basement of the embassy, staring at a video feed of this world's Maria Santos pacing in a holding room, yelling at the ceiling, "What do you want from me?"

Their operation to stop a war that could destroy the entire world had officially begun.

78

Maria wandered through the massive house. It felt like a museum to her.

The gallery hall off the foyer was filled with breathtaking art. Small couches with no backs lined the walls like sitting benches waiting to assist patrons who were tired of walking.

The great room was like the lounge of a hotel, with seating groups scattered across the vast space, near the fire, at the window, and a few floating in the room. Maria imagined that parties with hundreds of people had been hosted here.

She found herself in the grand two-story foyer, with its curved staircase. In the distance, she heard Nora, Ty, and Kato searching the home.

She was searching too, but she had to admit, she was nearly too dazed to process what she was seeing.

Outside the great room, she walked down a narrow hall, where she found a powder room with a large common space with three sinks and four enclosed toilet compartments. The bathroom was bigger than any bedroom she had ever had at a homeless shelter.

The master bedroom was even more breathtaking, like something out of a magazine, with beautiful furniture and draperies that were like masterpiece paintings in textile form, bright and swirling and captivating.

Beside the bed was the biggest shock of all: a picture of Maria and her mother standing together on a beach, both wearing floppy linen hats that looked as though they were blowing in the wind.

The Maria Santos she saw in the picture was happy and healthy and all the things Maria wasn't. That she owned a house like this was mind-boggling to her. Maria had never even stepped foot in a place like it before.

Yet she and the woman in the picture were the same. Same parents. Same DNA.

Choices.

That was the only thing that separated them. Choices and their environment.

She realized someone was in the room, watching her. She jerked around, startled.

Kato stood there, his wig and makeup on, looking like a completely different person. In a strange way, Maria felt pride at his transformation—she had *done* something creative for the first time in a long time.

"Basement's clear," he said.

"What did you find?"

"A recording studio—with no notes or relevant data. A movie theater. A gym with an emphasis on cardio equipment. A wine cellar—"

Maria broke into a laugh. "Of course you did. Just like my place."

He studied her. "You doing okay?"

"Aren't we all?"

Her laugh died down, and still, Kato stared at her.

More quietly, she said, "I'm okay. It's just... seeing this, it really lays it out. How thoroughly I screwed my life up."

"You didn't—"

"I did," Maria said, nodding.

"Well, it's not over."

"It almost was for me, once."

"You know what I think?"

"Of the things I know, what you're thinking isn't one of them."

"I think this whole thing—whatever is happening here—it's like one big do-over."

Maria cocked her head at him. "How do you figure?"

"I can't say exactly. It's just a feeling I get."

"Can't exactly take that to the bank."

"My instincts have saved me a million times in the field."

Maria considered that for a moment. Then she said the thing that scared her most in the world. "I'm not her."

"You don't need to be her."

"You don't understand. If she's sung a song a hundred times, and I take the stage and try to sing it, someone will know it's off."

"We'll tell them you have a cold."

Maria closed her eyes. "It's more than that. More than how you sound. It's how you command the stage. Your command of the audience. *She* has it. I did once. Now... I don't know."

"It doesn't have to be perfect." Kato took a step toward her. "It just has to be the best you can do. That's all any of us are doing."

Ty appeared in the doorway to the master bedroom. "What's going on?"

"Just clearing the room," Kato said, his tone changing, more matter-of-fact. "Nothing so far."

Ty turned away. "Well, we have found something."

79

Maria climbed the opulent marble staircase, gripping the steel rail, the crystal chandelier buzzing overhead, her footsteps echoing around her.

At the top of the landing, there was a wide cased opening that led to a gathering room with a wet bar. Floor-to-ceiling windows looked out onto a well-lit, manicured backyard. A pool spread out to the right, the water rippling slightly in the wind, the moon and lights from the tall security wall reflecting across it.

Maria realized she had stopped to gawk at it when Ty said, "This way."

He was already marching down the hall, Kato behind him. They were less star-struck by the lavish home. In a strange way, that made Maria feel like even more of an outsider in the group.

Nora was waiting in an office with a simple white wooden desk with open legs. Two large club chairs sat in front of it. A couch, a coffee table, and comfy chairs sat in the corner.

A large laptop sat on the desk, the brand name SIEMENS stamped across the back.

"Get this," Ty said, spinning the laptop around to face Maria and Kato.

"The operating system is called LinOS." Ty pointed to the logo, which was a man's face with longish hair and a faint smile. "As in Linus Torvalds. That's crazy, right?"

Maria eyed the others. They were as lost as she was.

"I'm not sure we're following," Nora said.

"You know, Linus Torvalds, the inventor of Linux. Didn't any of you ever use Red Hat Linux or another distribution?"

The silence gave him his answer.

Finally, Kato said, "I'm not familiar. Why? Is there a login vulnerability? Can you hack it?"

Ty shook his head. "No, I just thought it was interesting. Like Bill Gates might not even exist in this world. Linux—and its successor—clearly became the standard OS for consumer computers. Torvalds might be the richest person in this world."

"Do you know him?" Kato asked.

Ty shook his head. "No. I don't know him. I just thought it was cool. Let's move on." To Maria, he said, "Any idea what your password might be?"

"Valentina," she said, almost without thinking.

Ty keyed it into the laptop. "Wrong. What else?"

Thus began an hours-long process of Maria guessing passwords, Ty tapping on the laptop keyboard, and Nora and Kato sitting on the couch, bored. Finally, Kato rose and walked to the door. "I'm going to do a security sweep."

Maria figured he was simply tired of sitting there playing guess the password. She didn't blame him.

"I'm going to get food from the kitchen," Nora said. "Any requests?"

When Nora returned with sandwiches, Ty and Maria were still at it.

They had tried everything. Maria's birth date. Favorite color. Father's name (even saying it sent anger through her). She kept coming back to Valentina. Her mother's name.

Kato strode in and laid a stack of crumpled pages on the desk. "I found these in the studio. They're about the only papers there."

The top page was a draft of a song that was partially completed. It had a typed heading and lyrics that had been marked through with a pencil. Handwritten notes lay between the lines and in the margins.

Maria read the title:

"A Hymn for The World After"

Holding her breath, Maria moved down the page, scanning the lines.

In the dark forest of our world
I heard the drumbeats of war
Beating in the night
Counting down to the end of all things

And in the darkness, I saw a light
Twinkling in the night
Shining all around me
Counting down to the end of all things

Reading the words gave Maria chills. It was her voice. Her rhythm. Lines like she might write, as though she had created this and forgotten it, as if she were an amnesiac retracing steps she couldn't recall.

After Ty read it, he handed it to Nora. "Dark stuff."

"It implies," Kato said, "that this Maria Santos might know something about what the A21 rockets are carrying and what the Covenant's plans are."

The words hung in the air.

"Obviously," Kato continued, "we should have the Pax spec-ops team interrogate her. I imagine she'll talk after even light coercion—"

"No," Maria whispered. She closed her eyes. "Please don't."

She could feel all of them looking at her.

"I can't explain it," she said, "but please don't harm her. Nothing traumatic. I know we have to hold her until this is over, but I just... I don't want to be part of anything that could harm her enough to derail her life."

Kato reached out and put a hand on her upper back. "I'm sorry. I didn't really think about that. It was just instinct."

"I understand. This is... all new. I know I don't know her, and she's not me, but—it's hard to explain. I just don't want her to be hurt."

Kato jerked his head suddenly, pausing as if listening through his earpiece. "Surveillance team outside says someone is approaching the residence. On the sidewalk, dressed in a uniform. A female. Latin American. Looks to be in her fifties."

Kato paused. "She's at the door. She's got a key." To Maria, he said, "Get out there—to the foyer."

"And say what?"

"Get rid of her."

Maria bolted out of the office and out onto the landing. She gripped the rail and was about to descend the curved staircase into the foyer, but stopped.

She looked almost exactly like the other Maria Santos, with a few small exceptions: her face was slightly more worn, with more worry lines and sun damage. It was nothing makeup couldn't fix. The other thing was the look in her eyes. Staring in a mirror, Maria had to admit that she had a sort of wounded, guarded look. And for good reason. In the photos scattered about this palatial home, this world's Maria Santos stared out with a twinkle in her eye, the almost mischievous, playful glint of a woman ready to drink the world from a cup and howl at the moon.

Maria wasn't that person, though she had been a few years ago. A friend or close acquaintance could tell the difference. They would be able to tell that something was wrong.

She lingered at the balcony overlook in the foyer, hoping the distance and darkness would hide the differences.

Below, the door swung open, and a heavyset woman shuffled in and immediately turned to close and lock the door. She was wearing a maid's uniform and her hair was in a tight bun.

"Hi," Maria called from above.

The woman jumped and spun, backing up into the door, a hand held to her chest. "Ma'am..." she said in Spanish. "You scared me."

Maria held up her hands and answered in Spanish. "Sorry!"

The woman eyed her. "Is everything all right?"

Maria spread her hands out, mentally cringing the moment she did it, knowing she was overselling her casual act. "Fine. All good."

The woman nodded slowly. "I see."

"What are you doing here?"

"Ma'am?"

"I mean. What's… on your schedule today?"

"I was going to start the laundry and make you breakfast of course." She studied Maria again. "Did you have trouble sleeping before your trip? Shall I make something different?"

"No. No, not at all. I've just been working."

"The nerves."

"Yes, my nerves. Always before a performance."

"Are you still leaving today?"

Maria's heart beat faster. "Yes. Still today. In fact, I need to focus on getting ready. Why don't you take the day off? I need a little space to work and think."

The woman nodded. "Very well, Miss Santos. Good luck, dear."

With that, the woman left, and Maria exhaled so hard she almost collapsed.

Back in the office, she opened her mouth to speak, but Kato cut her off. "We heard. Leaving today." He turned to Ty. "We really need to get access to that laptop."

80

Ty bit his lip. "I have an idea."

Nora blew out a long breath. "It makes me nervous when you say that."

"Don't worry," Ty said. "It's not a crazy idea." He smiled. "When I'm going to do something crazy, I'll say, 'Hey guys, watch this.'"

Nora slowly closed her eyes and shook her head as she suppressed a laugh.

Ty leaned over and typed quickly on the laptop's keyboard, then grimaced.

"It didn't work," Nora said.

Ty typed again, concentrating on the next combination. "I'm not done yet." It failed, and he mentally grasped for the next possibility. There were only a few left.

On the next attempt, the login screen disappeared. "We're in."

"How?" Nora asked, rounding the desk to stare at the screen.

"Maria's first idea was actually correct, as first ideas usually are. Where we erred was not developing that idea enough. The password *is* Valentina."

"Why didn't it work the first time?" Kato asked.

"Because I simply typed in the word. Well, with a few variations on the capitalization. Then I gave up. But the idea was right. It just needed to be tweaked."

"For security," Nora said, seeming to realize the key.

"Correct," Ty said. "The actual password is Valentina with an uppercase V, the numeral one where the 'l' is, and a plus sign where the 't' is. It's a strong password—with uppercase letters, lowercase letters, a number, and a special character. It's also easy for Maria to remember. I bet when the system made her change

365

it, she replaced letters with numbers or special symbols, like using the at sign for the letter 'a'."

Ty used the track pad to begin exploring the interface, which the geek inside of him was loving.

"Here's the email app," he said. "It's called GotMail. That's clever."

Until the sun came up, they poured over the emails and documents on the computer. What they revealed was both surprising and promising.

Most of the communications between Santos and the Covenant had occurred on a secure network called ReichNetz that was only accessible via a Virtual Private Network—or VPN. There, they found the details they needed.

First, Santos had been hired to perform a single song—and not any of the songs in her current catalog. The Covenant had commissioned her to write an original song, and in those details, Ty got his first glimpse of what the Covenant was planning.

On the screen was a private message from Dr. Helen Klein. Even seeing his mother's name here sent a chill through Ty. He dreaded reading it but knew he had to. He wondered if she would be in Peenemünde. He soon saw the answer.

Sehr geehrte Frau Santos,

Vielen Dank once again for agreeing to perform at The World After ceremony. Though the audience will be smaller than the crowds you are accustomed to performing for, I assure you that this will be, quite possibly, the most momentous performance of your life, one that will be remembered and written about in history books for generations. I'm sure that seems a bit hyperbolic to you now, but I am confident that time will prove those words true.

But first, a word on procedure. We require that you arrive the morning prior to The World After ceremony in order to rehearse and to ensure that all equipment functions properly.

Travel arrangements may be left to you, or the Wehrmacht can arrange transport. We have no preference, but please inform us of your choice as expediently as possible.

You may bring a limited number of support staff—four at most. Please bear in mind that, by law, Pax citizens are not allowed anywhere inside the borders of the Covenant, including Reich Europa. South American citizens, such as yourself, are more than welcome. With that said, all members of your party will be required to present their SA ID cards, and their identities will be verified. This is standard procedure at all Covenant military facilities.

Please also be aware that no electronic devices will be allowed inside the facilities at Peenemünde, including mobile phones, smart watches, and smart bands. Any such devices will be confiscated at the security checkpoint at the airfield and held until your departure.

Additionally, members of your party will be searched upon arrival. As I'm sure you're aware, narcotics are strictly forbidden throughout the Covenant. The mandatory sentencing guidelines inside the Reich are quite severe for illegal possession of restricted substances or medications without a proper prescription. I say this not to accuse but in hopes of avoiding any unpleasantness.

We request that you perform a single rehearsal the night before the ceremony so that we may test the technical equipment. Peenemünde is a large facility that has grown over the last hundred years it has been in use. The World After ceremony will occur at the old power plant, which now serves as the administrative office for the Aggregat program and conference center. You will be performing in the turbine hall, and I do hope you will find the acoustics suitable.

With that, I turn now to the main event, if you will: our humble request for a song that we hope will become a classic for the ages.

What we envision is a sort of anthem for a turning point in human history, a hymn celebrating an event that will forever mark the transition from decades of war to everlasting peace, a song to celebrate a technical achievement and a new dawn for humanity.

It should be a somber piece. We see The World After as humanity's destiny, but one we will buy with the greatest price of all: human lives. It is a peace we have paid for with blood and time and lost futures. It is a peace only achieved on the other side of war. The song we request is in that vein: of a people striving for an end to hostility and being brave enough to pay the price for it, of a world with a single society and purpose, forged in fire and inseparable forevermore.

You were selected by our committee because your *Worlds & Time* album encompasses so many of the themes of this night, of the dawning of The World After. So many of your songs and lyrics speak to our struggle and what's ahead.

I hope that you will find inspiration in the guidance I have provided, and I so very look forward to meeting you in person.

With great admiration and very best wishes,

Helen

Ty read the letter through again, lingering on his mother's words. It was so bizarre to see a window into such a dark version of the woman who had been the only constant in his life, a shining beacon of light in the dark periods of his youth. And here she was, in another world, with values so different. Or were they? Was the version of Helen Klein he knew still somewhere inside of her?

He would know soon—and time was running out. In the office, the four of them set about working to prepare.

Kato radioed the Pax security team outside and had them convey a series of requests to the embassy. The first priority was finding three South American citizens who were close in appearance to Ty, Nora, and Kato.

Next up was logistics. It turned out that Maria Santos had her own plane, but she had a contract with a group called Aeromericas to house the plane, maintain it, and provide a pilot and flight staff.

Maria phoned them and informed them that she would provide her own staff and pilot for the flight to Peenemünde, and they agreed without protest. Apparently, this Maria Santos had the option of supplying her own personnel and simply using the company for maintenance and storage.

Next, they tracked down all of the actual staff that were slated to accompany the singer. Ty could tell Maria was nervous as she called them, but what she related to them was a highly plausible cover story: that Reich Europa security was now insisting that they alone select who accompanied Maria to the private ceremony. Thanks to the Reich's apparent reputation, each person Maria called accepted the explanation without complaint.

The doorbell echoed through the house. On the laptop, Ty pulled up an app called HomeCentral, which offered access to the house's speakers, automated shades, lights, thermostat, and cameras.

On the security feed, he watched from the front door camera as a delivery man from Andeso Inc. walked away from the front porch. A package sat on the mat.

"I bet it's from the embassy," Kato said, and slipped out of the room. Soon, Ty saw him on the camera opening the door and snatching the package.

The box held the rest of what they needed for the mission: directions to the private airport in Buenos Aires where Maria's plane was waiting, South American IDs for the individuals Nora, Ty, and Kato would impersonate, and aerial maps of Peenemünde.

Ty assumed the maps had been bought from freelance spies or Covenant insiders at an enormous price. The Pax was trying to do whatever they could to help the mission. With their nation's very survival on the line, no price was too high to pay.

There were also photos taken from the air of military installations across the Covenant. There were twelve in all, and each location was like a mega military base, a small city with high walls and training grounds, sprawling barracks, and an airport. From the scale in the photos, each of the sites had to be capable of housing millions of people. Ty's best guess was that he was looking at a group of facilities that together held anywhere from twenty to fifty million troops.

"Incredible," Kato said. "Why would they need such a large army?"

"Especially," Nora said, "if they have a missile that can obliterate their enemy without a ground invasion. They must have a force half the size of the remaining Pax population."

"And," Kato said, "the Pax is the Covenant's only enemy. It's not like the troops are for some other conflict."

Ty pointed to the twelve images. "One thing is certain: these are the targets the Pax wants the Covenant missiles to hit. I think this is why they risked the mission to Peenemünde with this world's Nora. The Pax knows it can't win a conventional war. They're vastly outnumbered. And by showing us these photos now, the Pax is making it clear that if we simply destroy the missiles or land them in unpopulated areas, the Pax will still fall. The Covenant will still have its invasion force."

Nora closed her eyes. "This is too much. The thought of directing those missiles at these bases..."

"We don't have a choice," Kato said. "This is war. We're going to do what we have to."

"And while we're doing it, we should look for an alternative," Nora said.

"Yes," Kato agreed. "But I can't see it right now."

As the sun rose, shining through the windows of the office, the four of them turned their attention to the photos and maps of the Peenemünde Army Research Center. The facility was situated on a peninsula that projected into the Baltic Sea, near where the border of Germany and Poland had been in Ty's home world.

To him, the complex seemed like a mix of a military base and a NASA launch complex. Along the sea, there were large launch pads. At the end of the landmass was a large airstrip with two long runways and hangars. Near the center, what looked like a small city spread out. The streets were arranged in a grid pattern, with buildings that could have been shops or apartments or warehouses.

Railroads crisscrossed the island like stitches across the land. Most ended at large industrial buildings that Ty assumed were manufacturing facilities.

On the left-hand side of the island was a narrow strait separating it from the mainland. There were two harbors there. One was near the old power plant where the ceremony would be.

From the sky, Peenemünde looked like a maze. In a sense, it was. Soon, they would have to find a way to what was at the center of it—the command center where they could disable or redirect the rockets. If they didn't, this world would fall, one way or another.

81

At the private airport, Ty had asked Kato, "Are you sure you can fly this thing?"

Kato had replied instantly, "I can fly anything."

In truth, he hadn't been so sure. But he had always believed that the first rule of piloting was: don't crash. And that the second rule was: never let your passengers doubt you can fly the plane. He planned to observe both rules, no matter what universe he was in.

In the cockpit, he had puzzled over the instruments only a moment before realizing it was actually an Embraer jet similar to the ones from his world, albeit with a much longer range.

At cruising altitude, he had activated the autopilot and waited in the cockpit, half expecting something to go wrong. Thankfully, it hadn't.

In the main cabin, he had settled down on a couch and begun meditating, observing his breath flowing out of his nose, the soft tickle on the skin there.

Soon, his eyelids were heavy. Sleep tugged at them, and he knew he needed to rest before they landed. Now was the time, while the plane was flying itself.

Yet his mind drifted to what waited for him at their destination. His greatest enemy in life: himself. A dark version of himself.

Kato had spent his entire professional life in hostile environments, in places where everything could kill you. The people you passed on the street. The people you paid to help you. The people you bought secrets from. The water. The food. The snakes in the jungle. And most of all, the people with guns and knives drawn in the shadows, creeping up behind you.

This world was a different kind of theater of operations

altogether. It was more dangerous than any place he had ever encountered, for one reason—the most dangerous threats weren't the ones you expected. In Kato's experience, the things that got a good operator killed were those they never expected. Things you weren't afraid of, that you didn't see, that snuck up on you and took your life before you even knew it.

He had already seen one such threat, at the cavernous home in Argentina when it had been time to interrogate this world's Maria.

Interrogating the woman had seemed a natural next step to Kato. Their Maria wouldn't stand for it. Kato hadn't anticipated that, though he understood it now, why Maria couldn't bear seeing a version of herself tortured, possibly mentally scarred forever.

Kato understood it. Every person had had their feelings hurt at some point. That was life. Emotional harm always left scar tissue. Sometimes it was a thin scar. Sometimes it was thick, making it harder to feel again. And sometimes, a hurt deep enough changed a life forever.

Something like that had happened to their Maria. And she couldn't bear to let it happen to this version of herself.

At that moment in Argentina, when Maria pleaded for the safety of her counterpart, Kato had realized that he would soon face the same decision—how much he could harm another version of himself. There was no doubt in his mind what the answer was: he would do *whatever* it took. If possible, he would incapacitate his counterpart. If required, he would end him. He would do that to protect the three people on the plane. He would do it to protect the starving and dying people of the Pax, even though they had locked him in a basement cell like an animal. Their government had done that. The people were innocent.

Most of all, he would do it so that he could see his wife and son again.

He wondered what kind of Kato Tanaka was waiting for him in Peenemünde. Had he discovered the darkness within his heart as Kato had? Was he in control of it? Was he as strong as Kato? As fast? Had he trained as hard?

Kato also wondered what dealing with his counterpart would do to him; if the looming fight to come would dredge up the darkness he had managed to keep under control for so long.

82

The plane flew through the night, against the sun, across the Atlantic, bound for the heart of Reich Europa.

Nora couldn't help but watch Ty. Since takeoff, he had been sitting in one of the plush chairs on the aircraft, staring down at the printed pages—the pages of the email messages from this world's Helen Klein.

Nora knew he was nervous about seeing her. And what he might have to do.

She felt a connection with him, like an invisible cord that pulled tight whenever they drifted apart, a link that time hadn't degraded, only buried. It had been resurrected by these circumstances, and she hoped it would never be buried again.

The bond between them wasn't just the night they had spent on the airship. It was deeper than that. The connection between them had always been strong, ever since childhood. The strands of the tie that bound them were made of hardy fibers—the strength of which she hadn't realized until now.

To Nora, she and Ty were like two bodies with one soul. She had never felt so safe or so comfortable with anyone in her entire life. Words couldn't describe it.

Circumstances had torn them apart. Fate had brought them back together. Now she felt the urge to wrap him tight and never let him go again. Given the opportunity, she wouldn't.

But what they were involved in was madness. And somehow, with him in her life, it hardly mattered. In him, she had found a piece of herself that had been missing—the last part of a puzzle that was her life.

When she wasn't pondering the reentry of Tyson Klein into her life, Nora's mind drifted to another person who loomed on the horizon: the other Nora. Was she still being held in Peenemünde? This world's Nora was a dark mirror of her, someone who had grown up in a world filled with war and hate. And it had shaped her thinking.

What would she be like? How would she react to Nora?

Answers awaited in a few short hours.

Most of all, she felt a deep sense of responsibility to the other three individuals on the flight. They were in her care. They were her responsibility. That thought was like a vine of steel wrapping its way around her spine. It gave her strength. And purpose. There was a deep well of power in that, one she'd never known existed.

At the same time, her life and future were in their hands. In the power of Ty's mind. In Kato's instincts. In Maria's voice.

Ty had been right: they were four corners of something. Of what, Nora didn't know. But she knew it was something wondrous, something with the power to change this world.

83

Kato exited the cockpit and strode down the aisle. Nora sat at a club chair, seeming lost in thought. Maria was at the back of the plane, at a table, scribbling on the pages of the song she had been frantically working on.

Ty was sitting at the other table in the cabin, staring out the window. Kato plopped down across from him.

"You know what this feels like?"

Ty raised his eyebrows. "As in?"

"An impossible mission to take out some Nazi big guns. With history hanging in the balance. Led by a ragtag team thrown together."

"What exactly are we talking about here?"

"We're talking about an epic World War II film featuring a wall that seems impossible to climb."

Ty nodded solemnly. "Oh yeah. I know exactly what we're talking about." He paused. "We're talking about *The Guns of Navarone*."

Kato leaned back in the seat and exhaled theatrically. "Nailed it. You just earned yourself a hundred dad-joke credits."

"Now who's the one with the big guns?"

Kato closed his eyes. "Ninety-nine left."

"Worth it," Ty whispered.

On the couch, Nora leaned forward. "Are you guys talking about a World War II film?"

"Not just any World War II film," Ty said. "*The Guns of Navarone*. With Gregory Peck."

"Why do guys love World War II films so much?"

"When you see it," Ty said, "you'll get it."

"Will I?"

"Tell you what. If we live through this, we'll watch *The Guns of Navarone.*"

Nora smiled. "All right. It's a date."

At the table at the back of the plane, Maria stared at the pages of the song, "A Hymn for The World After." It was unfinished and marked up, like a treasure map that had been torn in half.

When she had learned that this world's Maria Santos had never sung the song she was to perform in Peenemünde, she had been relieved. Soon, though, reality had set in: the downside was that she had to finish the song and perform it for the first time.

In hours, the plane would land. She would need a finished song then. She was the only one on the plane who could write it. But all their lives depended upon it.

It gave new meaning to the word deadline.

She had expected to be falling apart, stressed out, and completely unable to cope.

Instead, she felt alive. She felt a passion for the work, not just the urgency born of need that had burned inside of her in the homeless shelter in Nashville, but a true connection to the theme of the song.

A changing world was something she knew all too well—a life that could slip away before you knew it.

She clung to that feeling, the kernel of an idea. In her mind, the words flowed. Her pen moved, scratching out the verses and chorus and bridge, marking through words and writing in the space between the lines and in the margin.

When she was done with the draft, she stared at it, amazed, almost in shock, a part of her wondering where it had come from. That was the magic of art—creating something you weren't even sure you were capable of creating. It was a transcendental experience, one that, once experienced a single time, some artists chased for a lifetime.

Maria realized something then, the truth of how she had climbed this ladder—she knew how high it went. She had seen what a version of her had been capable of accomplishing, how high that Maria had been able to climb. She saw the art that Maria had created. And now she knew *she* was capable of it.

She wondered what every person could do if only they were sure of what they were capable of. Some part of her had believed that her failure was simply her destiny, that it wasn't within her to succeed, that her momentary rise had been a blip, a lucky break in a career destined for failure—or mediocrity at best.

Now she churned out the lines like what she knew herself to be: a star. And she couldn't wait to take the stage and hear the words in her own voice.

At the same time, that thought terrified her. She hadn't felt that way in a long time—that mix of excitement and fear—and it made her feel more like herself than she even thought was possible. Best of all, while she had been thinking about the song, she hadn't once thought about the bottle of pills.

Ty watched as first Nora, then Kato, then Maria surrendered to sleep. He spent his watch rereading the pages of the messages from his mother's counterpart.

What bothered him the most was the voice in the messages. The tone. The cadence. It was the same as his mother, as though she herself had written the messages. Except for the content, which still disturbed Ty deeply. In his mother's counterpart, he saw what Nora had seen in her lost father: a good person turned around by an evil world.

He wondered if there was a way to save her, as Nora was hoping to do for her father. They were on opposite sides of the same war. In a way, they were playing the same role: the scientist charged with using their field to end the conflict, deploying technology to change the world forever, in their cause's favor. Was there a solution that saved both of them?

As the plane flew through the night and the time ticked down to their arrival, Ty couldn't see that solution.

Another problem ate at him: the quantum radio medallion. Even if things turned out as he wanted them to in Peenemünde and the Pax returned the device to him, then what?

If that occurred, it would mean that they'd saved this world, but they would also be in the same place they were in at the National Museum of Natural History: lost in the vast wilderness of the multiverse with no way home.

84

An hour before they landed, Ty watched as Maria spent time touching up the makeup and disguises for all of them.

He had to admit that they didn't look precisely like the South American citizens they were impersonating, but they were close. He was thankful that South America had become a melting pot similar to the United States, with citizens from so many races. Without such an abundance of Asian and Caucasian citizens, it would have been hard to find a match.

When she was done, the four of them sat in the plane's cabin, Maria and Nora on a plush leather couch that ran along the wall, Ty and Kato in chairs at a square table across from them.

"I think we should review our plan," Ty said.

"Don't get killed," Maria said.

Ty held a finger up. "That's step one. The rest gets more complicated."

"It always does," Kato said.

"I'll just state the obvious," Ty said. "I think I should do most of the scouting at Peenemünde. There is no Ty Klein in this world—that we know of. Maria will be busy—and conspicuous if she were trying to get into guarded areas. We know Kato and Nora have counterparts, and they're likely both at Peenemünde. You two should stay out of sight to minimize risk as much as possible."

"I agree," Kato said. "But I'll have to come out eventually to replace the other Kato. I also need to observe him some so that when I do replace him, I can try to imitate some of his mannerisms."

"All fair points," Ty said. "But let's back up and state our priorities. First and foremost, we need to find the launch control facility for the A21 missiles and change their targeting."

"Easy to say," Kato muttered.

"Hard to do," Ty said, completing the thought. "It's true. But I think once Kato replaces his counterpart, we should have free rein of the facility."

"The real issue I see," Kato said, "is timing. I think there's only so long I can fake being him. I don't know Reich Europa military protocol or anything about his command. Eventually, someone is going to get suspicious."

"I agree," Ty said. "We need to do some surveillance and wait for our moment. Also, if we change the missile coordinates too early, someone is going to know."

Maria took a sharp breath, clearly a little nervous. "Can I ask what might be a dumb question?"

Ty held his hands up. "In the multiverse, there are no dumb questions."

"I don't speak German," Maria said. "My Spanish is pretty good, Portuguese is okay, but I doubt that is going to help us in Peenemünde."

"I thought about that too," Ty said. "I speak somewhat fluently, if a little awkwardly."

"To be fair," Nora said, "that's also your situation in English."

Ty laughed. "Touché. But unlike my English, my German was getting better. French is pretty common in Geneva, but there were also a lot of German speakers at CERN. How about the rest of you?"

"I spent some time at US military facilities in Germany," Kato said. "I picked up a bit of the language, enough to get around, but I'm guessing my German is a pale shadow of my counterpart's. It would be the first giveaway. Mandarin and Japanese, I'm good. Same for Arabic. Farsi I'm passable but not quite fluent."

Ty eyed Nora. "Nur ein bisschen," she said with a smile. *Just a little.*

"Well," Ty said, "the emails to Maria's counterpart were in English. I think our best hope is that the Covenant has adopted

English for events with multilingual attendees. If not, this is probably over pretty quickly."

"Let's assume," Nora said, "that we succeed. We need to figure out where we're going to redirect those missiles."

"I've been thinking about that a lot," Kato said. "This is a war, but it's not our war. I think we should use an unpopulated area as the target."

The silence in the cabin told Ty that everyone agreed.

"The risk," Kato continued, "is that they won't give us back the radio when we return. But I think it's a risk we have to take."

"I agree," Ty said. "Let's just hope we get the chance to make the change."

From the cockpit, Ty heard Kato communicating with the tower at the Peenemünde airport. Soon the plane's wheels touched the tarmac with a squeak, and it came to a stop in the shadow of the air traffic control tower.

A stair truck sped out of a hangar and gently docked to the plane.

Ty stood by the door, peering out the small window. A delegation of about twelve people was walking from the terminal toward the plane. When they arrived, he pulled the outer door open and walked onto the stair landing, feeling the cool breeze from the Baltic Sea blowing across him. Below, he got his first up-close glimpse of the welcoming committee.

At the front was Lars Jacobs. Somehow, he looked ten years younger than the truck driver Ty had met in his world. His eyes twinkled with confidence and positivity.

Beside him stood Helen Klein. She was, in all appearances, a clone of Ty's mother. Except for her eyes. They were hard and piercing, like a predator on the prowl, reminding Ty of Richter.

What he saw next took his breath away. Hanging around her neck was a small round metal object. It was hollow in the middle, with an outer ring featuring twelve symbols that appeared to be star clusters.

There was no mistaking what the device was.

This world's Helen Klein was wearing a quantum radio medallion around her neck.

85

Ty descended the steps, toward the tarmac and the waiting delegation. Peenemünde's small airport terminal and tower loomed behind them.

He was first to reach the bottom of the stairs, followed by Kato. No one in the delegation paid any attention to them. Their eyes were fixed on the jet's outer door, waiting for Maria to emerge.

Ty couldn't help staring at his mother. She stood stock still, eyes fixed on the open door. It was so strange for her not to acknowledge him. It hit him then that she truly was a different person—perhaps the same in many ways, but a person who had absolutely no idea who he was.

When Maria emerged and stood at the top of the stair landing, the audience lit up like a cluster of stadium lights.

Helen Klein began marching forward as Maria descended the stairs. They met just as Maria reached Ty and Kato.

Still Ty's mother didn't acknowledge him. She smiled at Maria. "Miss Santos, it's nice to finally meet you in person. Welcome to Peenemünde."

A strong wind blew across the tarmac as Maria spoke, drowning out her voice, which was already shaky and weak.

"Thank you." Maria swallowed. "It's an honor."

Ty thought Maria was hating the attention and scrutiny. He had gotten to know her well enough to have a good idea of what she was thinking at this moment. Nora was standing behind her, and Ty could almost sense her wanting to reach a hand out and place it on Maria's back to give her a silent show of support.

Kato was scouting the terminal and buildings beyond like a bird of prey searching for threats.

Ty marveled at how in tune he had become with his three fellow travelers in such a short amount of time. It was like they shared a connection, one that grew stronger with each passing minute.

"Let's get you to your accommodations," Ty's mother said, turning and holding a hand out to guide Maria.

They walked away from Ty, Kato, and Nora, ignoring them.

Ty had always thought being attacked by someone you loved and trusted was one of the most unsettling things a person could endure. At that moment, he realized there was something worse: being ignored by someone you loved and cared about. He knew it wasn't the fault of this world's Helen Klein—she had no way to know who he was. Still, the experience unsettled him, and as he followed the group, he tried to process the emotion, the wind from the Baltic Sea whipping across him.

He sensed someone to his left, standing on the tarmac, but when he looked, there was no one there.

Nora came to a stop beside him. "What is it?"

"I thought..." Ty stared at the emptiness, at the inlet with its scattering of sandbars and the vast harbor beyond. "It's nothing," he said, continuing toward the airport terminal.

Inside the small airport, Reich Europa security personnel searched Ty, Nora, Kato, and Maria thoroughly, including their bags.

On the wall behind the security station, there were four photos. The first was Adolf Hitler. The second was Reinhard Heydrich. Ty didn't recognize the other two people, though he assumed they were the subsequent supreme leaders of Reich Europa.

The security guard studied Ty's South American ID, then set it on the counter and typed at the SIEMENS computer terminal. Finally, the man handed the card back to Ty and waved him on.

A tram transported them from the airport to the old power

plant, and as Ty stepped off, he found another surprise waiting for him: Penny Neumann stood at the main entrance to the power plant, holding a clipboard to her chest, smiling bright enough to light up half the world.

86

Penny stepped forward and extended her hand. When she spoke, her German accent was thicker than that of the Penny Neumann Ty had known on his home world.

"Miss Santos! I'm a huge fan. It's really quite an honor to meet you."

Maria stepped off the tram, and as she did, Penny seemed to think better of the offered hand, as if it would be beneath Maria or too presumptuous of Penny to assume that the woman shook hands. She pulled it back in and clutched the clipboard to her chest, knuckles turning white.

"I'm glad to be here," Maria said, still sounding nervous.

Penny turned and escorted them into the building as several staff members unloaded their bags from the tram.

The power plant was clad in red brick with tall steel windows. The lines were sharp, and the proportions seemed exactly right to Ty, the massing striking without being over the top. Inside, the facility was reminiscent of old warehouses and industrial buildings that had been converted to condos. There were exposed brick walls everywhere, steel beams running vertically and horizontally, and lots of glass, including big windows and skylights above.

Penny gave them a short tour of the facility before leading them to the residential wing. Ty thought it felt like a boutique hotel, with comfortable but not lavish accommodations.

He and Kato were assigned to share a room. It had a door to the adjoining room, which Nora was assigned to.

Maria's room was separate from the other two. It was on a corner of the building and far larger, with a sitting area, a half bath off the common area, and a bedroom suite with a king bed and a well-appointed full bath.

In the living room of Maria's suite, Penny smiled and said, "Well, I'll let you all get settled in. Just a reminder, rehearsal is in four hours."

Ty could almost see the color draining from Maria's face, but she held it together until Penny strode out and the door closed behind.

"Well," Kato said, his voice abnormally formal and put-on, "I'm sure you want to get some rest, Miss Santos. Can we get you anything before we leave?"

Maria seemed to get his meaning—*they're likely listening to us.*

"I'm fine. Thank you."

Back in the room he shared with Kato, Ty plopped down on one of the beds and pondered their current dilemma: they needed information. Specifically, they needed to know where the rocket control room was.

Penny. She was the key.

Ty had to go talk to her. He knew her—or he knew a version of her. He could use that. In much the same way as she had used him on his home world, he was now being forced to use her in this world.

Strangely, the situation gave him an insight into the Penny he had known on his world. For the first time, he felt like he understood the situation she must have been in. And finally, unexpectedly, he forgave her, fully and completely, and the most surprising thing was how good it made him feel.

Ty woke to a tug at his foot. He stirred, opening his eyes, realizing that he had drifted off to sleep on the bed, still wearing his clothes. It had been hard to sleep on the plane, and this brief nap in the hotel room had actually made Ty feel more tired.

Kato was looming over him.

"What?" Ty croaked.

Kato stomped over to the window and motioned to the entrance of the power plant.

At the window, Ty immediately saw what had drawn Kato's attention: his counterpart was exiting the tram. This world's Kato wore a black uniform adorned with medals, rank insignia, and patches Ty didn't recognize. His posture was rigid, his march faster than a walk, his piercing eyes straight ahead.

"I'm going to go stretch my legs," Kato said.

He turned and exited without another word, leaving Ty to wonder if this world's Kato would recognize his counterpart, even under the wig and makeup. Their operation was about to face its biggest test yet.

87

Kato was standing in the power plant's turbine hall when his counterpart entered. A small entourage of Sicherheitsdienst officers followed the man, all lower in rank than him. Kato's counterpart scanned the room and immediately, Kato tensed at the gaze. He made a mental effort to make himself look natural as he advanced across the far wall, inspecting the windows for security flaws he knew weren't there.

His counterpart marched deeper into the room, barking questions in German to his subordinates. The sound of his voice was different from Kato's—and it wasn't just the foreign language. His speech was more clipped. If Kato was being generous, he would call the tone efficient. Being less generous, the man came off as impatient and harsh, as though the next thing he said would be a criticism.

Another Sicherheitsdienst officer entered the room and raised a straight arm salute and yelled, "Sieg Heil!"

The words made Kato's skin crawl. They echoed in the hall as his counterpart shouted "Sieg Heil" back. That made Kato even more uncomfortable. He would be glad when this was over.

They discussed the entrances and exits to the room and how many attendees would be present during the ceremony. They were about to discuss the countersurveillance measures present when Kato's counterpart abruptly cut off the conversation. What he did next was the sum of Kato's fears: he marched directly toward Kato.

The footsteps echoed in the vast space, bouncing off the brick walls and tall glass. Kato made no reaction. He studied the window in front of him and began moving to the next one.

"Was machen Sie hier?" Kato's counterpart spat out.

Kato let his nervousness show—it wasn't a hard act. He also tried to alter his voice to sound higher. "Es tut mir Leid, Herr Sturmbannführer, aber mein Deutsch ist nicht so—"

Kato's counterpart exhaled heavily and held up a hand. He spoke slowly, chopping out each word and pausing, like one might speak to a child. "What. Are. You. Doing. Here?"

"A security check."

The man snorted. A small, unkind smile formed on his face.

Kato pressed on. "I work for Maria Santos. As personal security."

"Miss Santos is in no danger here. You are wasting your time. And mine. Leave."

Kato hesitated—but only for a fraction of a second. Leaving so easily could have made him look guilty.

"I'm paid to do a job," he said. "And I must do it. I have my orders."

That seemed to resonate with his counterpart. Following orders would be something he understood all too well—and could respect, even if he thought the man was wasting his time.

"Very well. You may return to this room in one hour—after we are done. Understood?"

Kato nodded.

His counterpart jerked his head toward the door, silently dismissing him.

Kato was exiting the room when the man called to him. "Wait!"

Kato stopped in his tracks and turned slowly. His counterpart was squinting.

"What is your name?"

Kato supplied the name from the South American identity he was using.

"Have we met?"

"No," Kato replied. "I don't think so."

"Have you always lived in South America?"

"Yes."

With each answer, the scowl on his counterpart's face deepened. Kato could feel a thin layer of sweat forming on his forehead, the pores welling up, not breaking out in beads yet, just enough for the cool air conditioning blowing down to tickle at his skin.

Kato wanted to swallow hard to make his voice sound more natural—and wipe the sweat from his face. But he forced his body to appear relaxed. His gaze was slightly to the right of his counterpart, not daring to look him in the eyes.

"Dismissed," the man said, the word uttered like someone might spit out a bad bit of food.

As Kato exited the hall, he felt the man watching him. He was suspicious now. Would he do a deeper background check? Have someone watch Kato?

Kato would do those things.

The launch was in twenty-six hours. Kato wondered if he had that much time left.

88

Maria couldn't keep her palms dry. She kept wiping them on the white dress, which, mercifully, didn't show the stains.

She sat on a folding chair on the stage in the power plant's turbine hall. It was half filled. At least two hundred people were here, mostly staff for the event: waiters, security, the orchestra members, and the assistants to the VIPs.

At the back of the room, Ty, Kato, and Nora stood by the double doors, watching her. She had to admit, having the three of them here gave her some comfort. They were like an anchor for her in these violent seas.

One of the waves that could sink them stood nearby—Kato's counterpart. It was so strange seeing him in the Reich Europa military uniform. When his gaze hit Maria, it felt as though she had mistakenly opened a meat locker, the frigid air making her shiver.

Helen Klein stepped to the lectern and cleared her throat.

"For those of you who are visitors, welcome to Peenemünde. For the staff here, thank you for your work to date. It has been exemplary. I know you've put a lot of effort into this event in a short amount of time. Rest assured, your suffering will end tomorrow night."

Forced laughter rippled across the room.

"Tonight is a simple rehearsal. I'll give my remarks, and then our special guest, Maria Santos, will perform a song written especially for this momentous occasion."

Helen looked back and smiled at Maria. She forced a smile that she knew looked awkward, but Helen didn't seem to notice. She refocused on the crowd.

"Before we begin, a word on security. I want to thank the

Peenemünde site security, as well as the SD—who have graciously agreed to increase the counterintelligence measures here at the base to ensure that this event is not disrupted. As some of you know, we've already had one attempted incursion on this facility by Pax operatives. We don't know how much they know about what we're about to do here, but we know they're trying to stop us. As I speak these words, they may be trying again to stop us. This is a pivotal moment in Covenant history—and human history. But it can all be derailed if we aren't careful. I'm asking each of you to remain vigilant, especially for the next twenty-four hours. If something looks off, report it. If you see something, say something. No observation is too small. No question invalid."

Maria watched as Kato's counterpart scanned the room. His gaze settled on Kato a moment before staring back at Helen Klein, who was unfolding a sheaf of papers and placing them on the lectern.

"With that, I'll begin my speech. Which, mercifully, is short."

Muted laughter again echoed in the hall.

Helen's voice was louder, more formal as she began her speech.

"How do you end a war? That is the question that was put to my organization—the Darwin Program. We are scientists. Rational people. For us, negotiation and compromise seem the obvious solution. But we all know that won't work. For decades, our approach to the Pax was simple: if we use non-lethal force to limit their ability to develop offensive weapons, they will eventually come to the table and talk terms—they will come to their senses. They have not. They fight on, even when we don't. We've built a seawall to keep them out. Yet they have gone to great lengths to get around it. In submarines and planes and hidden boat compartments, they have tried to land teams of counterinsurgents in our homeland, to try to gain some advantage in the war. Why? They must know it's hopeless. In the years that separate our civilizations, have we drifted so far apart that we no longer understand each other? Are we even the same type of humans anymore?"

Helen paused, letting the crowd consider her words.

"The military has offered the obvious solution to ending the war: overwhelming force, occupation, and eventual assimilation. Their solution, in a word, is messy. It is also impractical. It would cost the lives of Covenant soldiers. It would drain resources—money and time that could be spent building schools and hospitals and high-speed rail lines that enable families across the Reich to spend the holidays together, safely. And the question that must be asked, if we were to conclude this war in a conventional way, is to what end? What does the Pax have that helps the Covenant? Unfortunately—or perhaps fortunately—the answer is nothing. We don't need their citizens. They have no technology. We are rich in natural resources. What we want, simply, is to be left alone. But they won't. Even in the face of a hopeless, unwinnable war, they fight on. And they force our hand."

Helen shuffled to the next page.

"So, I return to the original question. How do you end a war with an enemy that fights on when there's no chance of winning? They fight just to fight. Well, frankly, there's only one way to win that war: you have to change their minds. You have to make them not want to fight. Tonight, that is what we will do. How, you might ask? Science. In a way, we return to the science that ended the last war."

Helen flipped to the next page.

"In 1940, the Reich launched a series of A4 missiles at Great Britain. Those rockets and the payloads they carried ended the brief European conflict that preceded the unification of Reich Europa. We used science—not boots on the ground—to end that conflict. Tonight, we once again turn to science to give us peace and an end to a terrible war. In particular, we once again rely on the rockets developed here at Peenemünde. This time, we won't be destroying military bases or burning cities to the ground. We have come a long way since then. Our intention is that there won't be a single life lost in tonight's solution. We are going to launch the final salvo in the Pax war. It will end the war in the only way possible—it will change their minds. Peace will follow. With that, I welcome you to The World After, and I'd like to ask our very special guest, Maria Santos, to perform the anthem of this new era."

Helen turned to Maria and smiled and held out a hand.

Maria stood and swallowed and walked to the microphone stand to the left of the lectern. Behind her, the orchestra struck up, and she sang the first verse of "A Hymn for The World After."

In the dark forest of our world
I heard the drumbeats of war
Beating in the night
Counting down to the end of all things

89

That night, after the rehearsal, Ty went through the door to Nora's adjoining room and, for the sake of anyone listening, made small talk like what they were posing to be: Maria Santos's audio technician and hair and makeup artist.

After, they lay in the bed, whispering in each other's ears, hoping it was too quiet for any surveillance device to hear.

"How was it," Nora said, "seeing your mother?"

"So weird."

"It's jarring."

For a moment, they lay in silence, Ty feeling her warm breath on his ear.

"I didn't expect to see Penny here."

"Does she seem similar to the one you knew?"

"Not sure. She looks the same. Same mannerisms. But it's hard to know what she's like. I do know this: we need information—on where your counterpart is being held and where missile control is. I think she's our best shot."

"I think our best chance is Kato replacing his counterpart."

Ty sat up and gave her an exaggerated frown, then leaned close and whispered, "You don't trust my covert agent skills?"

"No offense, but you're the most honest person I know."

Ty fell back to the bed. "I just feel like I need to try—to have a backup in case Kato fails."

"Be careful, Ty."

The next morning, Ty got up early and went down to the boiler house café. He got a coffee and a scone and sat in the corner, staring out the tall steel window, watching the sun come up. It was amazing how many of the staff were up early. Based on the activity there, he would have thought it was midday.

Ty was just starting to contemplate what he would do if Penny didn't show up when she walked into the café. Like the woman Ty had known in Geneva, her eyes were puffy in the morning and her hair was in a tight ponytail.

She ordered a coffee and a blueberry muffin and, at the end of the counter, turned to find a table. Ty stood up and waved.

She bunched her eyebrows—only for a slight second of confusion—but then seemed to recognize him.

"Hi," she said when she reached him.

"Hi. We met yesterday. I handle AV for Maria Santos."

"I remember. It took me a minute."

"I don't want to interrupt your day, but I was wondering—if you have time—if you'd join me."

She shrugged. "Sure."

When she sat, he said, "This is my first time visiting the Covenant, so naturally, I'm a little curious."

She carved off a piece of the muffin with a fork, like an iceberg calving, and chewed it quickly, in sharp, small motions. "What would you like to know?"

Ty tried to sound nonchalant. "Nothing in particular." He wasn't sure he had succeeded.

"Well," she said, carving off another bite, "we're at a Reich military research facility. It isn't much like the Covenant at large."

"Even more interesting."

"It is," she said. "But assuming things go to plan, there won't be a need for places like this anymore. Or even a military."

There was an opening here—Ty could feel it—but try as he might, he couldn't assemble the words to get through it. He was nervous. Even more nervous than the first time they had met in that coffee shop in Geneva's Old Town.

The stakes were far higher now.

Not sure what to say, Ty asked, "Are you a student?" The question sounded lame even to him.

Penny cocked her head. "I was. I recently graduated with a master's from Heidelberg University. I had considered doing a

PhD in international relations at the University of Geneva, but I applied for this job as well. I didn't think I would get it, but I did. I wanted to work in the realm of international peace efforts. In a way, that's what I'm doing here. Though, it's nothing like I expected. It's funny how things turn out."

Ty sipped his coffee. "Yes, it is. So what are your plans for the day?"

"I was going to go for a walk to rehearse my tour for the people arriving today."

"Could I walk with you? I'd love to get some fresh air. And you could practice your tour on me."

She raised her eyebrows. "Sure."

Outside the power plant, they strolled along a paved walking path, the sun rising in front of them. Behind them, Ty heard a plane landing.

"So," Ty said, "did you grow up in Germany?"

She frowned at him.

Instantly, he realized what he had said. "I mean, did you grow up in the Reich?"

"Yes," she said quietly.

To their right was a long, one-story building with a low-pitched roof. The stench coming from it was intense. Desperate for any change of subject, Ty motioned to it. "What's that? And what is that smell?"

Penny grinned. "It's the primate facility."

"*Primate* facility?"

"Yes. This is one of the sites for the Reich's comparative genomics project."

Ty must have looked confused.

"Come on," Penny said, taking the path toward the building. "I'll show you. It's part of the tour for some of the scientists visiting today."

Inside, the building was much like a horse stable. There was a small office near the entrance where a tired-looking man in a non-military uniform was sipping coffee. He hit a button, and the door buzzed open as he waved Penny through.

The main part of the building had a single lane down the

middle and stalls for the primates on each side. They were spacious, and inside, Ty recognized chimpanzees, gibbons, gorillas, and orangutans.

"They're using them for experiments?" Ty asked.

Penny nodded.

"What kind?"

"I don't know exactly, only that it's part of the Darwin Program, specifically, the comparative genomics project. It's aimed at understanding how we can share so much DNA with primates but be so different."

Outside the primate building, they strolled along the path, Ty deep in thought. Were the primates connected to the A21 missiles? Or a completely separate project that just happened to be housed in the same location?

When they reached several larger buildings that were five or six stories, Ty said, "What are those?"

"Barracks. And the one on the right is the SD station here at Peenemünde. They operate some of their Baltic operations here."

Ty nodded. If he had to bet, he would wager that Nora's counterpart was being held there.

"The missiles launch from here, right?" Ty asked.

"Yes," Penny said, resuming the stroll along the path.

"So is there a building that is dedicated to rocket control or operations?"

Penny studied his face for a moment. When she spoke, her voice was strained. "It's not really my area."

90

Ty burst into his room, searching for Kato. He was gone. But where?

Ty beat his fist on the door to Nora's adjoining room. He heard the pitter-patter of her feet, and the door slowly creaked open, revealing her tired, pale face. She had still been asleep. But she looked almost sick to Ty.

"You okay?"

She nodded, eyes half closed. "I think the time zone change and stress is finally catching up to me."

He pushed the door open and hugged her and whispered in her ear, "Where's Kato?"

"I don't know."

"I found it. Where I think they're holding your counterpart."

That seemed to wake Nora up. She stared at him.

"We've got to find Kato," he whispered. "Quickly."

In her room, Maria sat on a plush sofa, staring at the sun through the tall window. It was like an executioner's blade, rising. When it fell, and night came, she would have to take the stage and perform.

She knew if she thought about it too much, it would get her too worked up. She would spiral. She needed distraction.

She set about practicing her performance of "A Hymn for The World After." After three full renditions, her nerves still wouldn't settle.

She knew what she needed. The bottle of pills was hidden on the plane. Bringing the drugs with her would have raised questions at the security checkpoint—namely, how a physician in Nashville, Tennessee could have prescribed methadone for her. Especially given that Nashville, Tennessee was uninhabited in this world and had been for a long time. But she could always say she forgot something on the plane, return there, and take a pill. That was the backup plan she'd made with Nora.

The pills waiting there beckoned to her. They would chase the demons away, leaving calm in their wake. For a while.

The pills would also sedate her. If she was too sluggish for the performance, someone might suspect she wasn't the real Maria Santos.

She knew the fear of being caught was driving some of her nerves—almost as much as performing in front of the crowd.

But there was another fear. If she was caught, it would put the whole team in danger. She didn't want to let them down. That terrified her as much as the stage. And the demon inside of her.

One pill would make the cravings and fear back away.

Or maybe half a pill. That was the answer.

No.

The answer was neither. She had something she didn't have before. Something more powerful to give her calm and confidence.

She exited her room and walked down the hall. At Nora's door, she knocked and waited.

Nora was still in her pajamas when she opened it. Ty was there too, by the window, looking out as if searching for something. Or someone.

Maria entered and motioned Nora to the bathroom, where she closed the door and turned on the shower, the soft noise distorting their voices for any listening devices that might be present. "I was thinking about going to the plane. For the pills."

Nora studied her face. "You can take a half if you need it. It should wear off by tonight."

Maria shook her head. "I don't want to take any chances. I don't want to let you guys down. I just... needed someone to talk to about it."

★ ★ ★

In the hallway outside the power plant's foyer, Kato watched his counterpart march into the building. Two Gestapo personnel were waiting for him. When he came to a stop, they raised a straight-arm salute and barked, "Sieg Heil!"

He returned the salute, and they began what was clearly another tour of the facility, with an emphasis on the hour-by-hour activities of the day.

There was tension there between the Gestapo officers and Kato's Sicherheitsdienst counterpart. It was likely a matter of pride. And perhaps rivalry to some extent.

It wasn't clear to Kato exactly how the Reich Europa armed forces were organized, but on his home world, the Gestapo and Sicherheitsdienst had both been groups within the Schutzstaffel, or SS. The SS itself had originated as a group of Nazi party volunteers called the Saal-Schutz, or Hall Security. In the early 1930s, the Saal-Schutz was charged with securing meeting locations for Nazi party gatherings. As the SS grew into a major paramilitary organization, it was integrated with the German armed forces.

Here, it was clear that the Gestapo had been charged with securing the location, but the Sicherheitsdienst was conducting the counterintelligence operations. The recent incursion by the Pax operatives had probably encouraged them to be extra cautious.

Kato waited as the three men passed by, talking in a strained conversation. Some of the words Kato didn't recognize. Maybe they were names of places here at Peenemünde. Either way, he needed to brush up on his German. Assuming he lived through this.

The group kept referencing the "Bunkier," which translated to bunker. Was that where the missiles were controlled? If so, where was it? There was talk of the chapel, oxygen factory, and raid shelters.

Suddenly, the group doubled back. Kato didn't dare alter his course or react. He marched straight ahead, not avoiding eye contact but not focusing on his counterpart, who was barreling toward him.

The man threw up a hand. "Halt."

Kato stopped, keeping his distance from him—and mentally preparing to fight.

"Are you following me?"

"I'm doing my job," Kato said. Saying "no" would contradict the accusation and invite conflict.

"Security," his counterpart spat out, "is our job."

Kato nodded.

"From here out, you are to remain in the common areas or your room. Is that understood?"

"Yes."

"Go."

Kato turned and walked away, feeling the man's eyes upon him.

He had been caught—and he was certain that his counterpart was even more suspicious now. Worst of all, his movements were now confined. Making his assault on his counterpart would be more difficult. He would have to wait until he was in the common areas—if he ever ventured there.

But time was running out for him to make the swap. It was already afternoon, and to make matters worse, his counterpart was suspicious. He needed to replace him soon.

Kato sat down at a table in the boiler house café and watched the foyer, waiting, hoping his counterpart would come through again.

Out of his peripheral vision, Kato spotted his counterpart moving past the boiler house, down a long corridor that led deeper into the power plant. The two Gestapo agents were still with him.

Three against one. Those were bad odds—especially since one of the three was a clone of him.

But Kato sensed that this was his last chance to make his move.

He watched as his counterpart was about to turn down a corridor leading away from the boiler house. He stopped and spun and locked eyes with Kato. For just a small fraction of a second, the man's face changed. Kato saw a flash of alarm. The man had seen him. Not just seen that Kato was there in the café watching—he had *seen* him. It was the eyes. Before, Kato had made an effort to keep his gaze passive and nonthreatening. Now his counterpart had seen something else: a predator. He had seen *his own* eyes staring back at him.

He knew.

91

For a long moment, neither Kato nor his counterpart moved. They merely stared at each other.

Behind his counterpart, one of the two Gestapo officers said something Kato couldn't hear.

The man barked a reply.

Kato thought his counterpart was going to charge toward him. To his surprise, the man turned and walked away.

Kato rose and pursued him, down the hall. There was no hiding now. He had to replace him immediately—or risk being exposed himself.

The three men turned a corner. Kato quickened his pace. When he turned the corner, the two Gestapo officers were standing on the right with their backs against the wall. Kato's counterpart was gone.

Was it a trap?

Kato slowed his pace.

Alarm bells were ringing in his head.

Neither of the Gestapo men looked at him. They only stared straight ahead. Both wore sidearms at their hips.

On the left side of the hall, Kato saw a sign for a bathroom. On instinct, he pushed the door open. Immediately, he heard his counterpart's voice. It was quiet, but direct, issuing orders in a hushed tone.

Kato let the door close behind him and locked it immediately. At the sound of the click, his counterpart stopped talking.

Kato's heart beat faster, the sound echoing in his ears, a *thrum-thrum-thrum* that hammered out of control.

His fists closed. Ready.

He stepped forward, rounded the corner and crept into the bathroom's open area.

His counterpart stood there, a small radio held to his mouth. He smiled. "I've already reported you. A security team is on its way here now."

Kato swallowed. He couldn't fight him here—not with reinforcements coming. And the Gestapo already outside. He was trapped. His mind went into overdrive.

"You're right. I have been following you."

His counterpart cocked his head, but remained silent.

"I wanted to talk to you."

"Why?"

"I have information."

"What kind of information?"

"About the Pax. And the A21 launch. I want to trade it for Covenant citizenship."

"I am not an immigration officer."

"But you are an intelligence officer. One with rank. You can help broker a deal if the information is valuable—and it is."

"Tell me."

"No. I need to show you. I brought it with me. Photos and documents."

"You're lying."

"I'm not. I know that the Pax sent a team here to try to destroy the A21 missiles. You stopped them. You still have one of them. A woman named Nora Brown. What you don't know is that they haven't given up. They're planning another attack. Today. I have the details. You need them right now."

His counterpart studied Kato's face, as if searching for cracks in the story—or perhaps to confirm whether they were indeed the same person.

The light in the bathroom was dim. That was good. The man probably couldn't see the makeup Kato was wearing, likely couldn't tell the hair he saw was a wig.

"Please," Kato said. "Take a look. You won't be sorry. It's in my room." He motioned to the bathroom door. "You have two men with you. I'm a simple security guard. You can't be afraid of me."

His counterpart snorted. "Very well. Show me. But—we are going straight to your room. And the Gestapo outside will search it before I enter."

"Of course." Kato motioned to the radio. "But at least call off the team coming here. I don't want people to know I'm defecting."

Kato's counterpart eyed him a long moment, then raised the radio to his mouth and spoke quickly in German. When he was finished, he nodded to the door. "Proceed. And be quick."

92

Kato walked in front, his counterpart behind him, the two Gestapo officers bringing up the rear.

They weaved through the halls and up the stairs. At Kato's door, he paused. It could end right here. If Ty was inside and his disguise was off, Kato's counterpart could recognize that he had altered his appearance. Same for Nora if she was in the room.

"Halt," Kato's counterpart said. He motioned to one of the Gestapo officers. The man stepped forward, scanned what must have been a master key card at the door, and stepped inside, leaving the door ajar.

The room looked empty.

Quickly, the officers scanned the room and pushed open the doors to the bathroom and small closet. The Gestapo officer peered out at Kato's counterpart and nodded.

The man stepped into the room as the Gestapo officer exited.

Kato stepped inside and gripped the door to close it.

"The door stays open."

Kato hesitated. "This information is sensitive." He glanced at the two Gestapo officers. "For your eyes only."

His counterpart exhaled heavily. "Very well."

Kato closed the door.

His counterpart stepped deeper into the room, putting distance between them, staring at Kato, studying his every move, his body bracing like a snake coiling, waiting to strike.

"There is no intel, is there?"

"There's a team here in Peenemünde."

"Liar."

Kato knew he would get one shot at this. He knew that if he lost the upper hand, he might lose the fight. He needed a weapon. But he didn't have one. He couldn't reach for one. Not quickly enough.

His only advantage was the element of surprise. That would be hard to achieve. His adversary was backed up to the wall. And judging by his stance, he was ready to fight.

"Where is it?" the man asked.

"On a data drive."

"Where?"

Kato pointed at his wig—at the long blond hair. "It's here."

His counterpart squinted. "What?"

Kato inclined his head, but not low enough that he couldn't see his counterpart, who was squinting, leaning forward to see, slightly off balance.

Kato reached a hand into the long strands of the wig and ran his fingers through it, as though searching for something. He gripped it and tugged hard, ripping the wig off and throwing it in his counterpart's face.

The action served its purpose. The man instinctively reached up to catch the wig, confusion clear on his face.

Kato took a long stride and lunged, slamming the man into the brick wall behind him, hoping to knock the wind out of him so that he couldn't cry out.

But his counterpart was fast. He twisted slightly before hitting the wall. He rolled off of it, gripping Kato's shoulders and pushing him away, into the bed nearby.

As his head hit the mattress, Kato felt his counterpart pounce on top of him, right arm raised. Kato was off balance and barely had time to turn his head to the side before the fist hit him, the blow as hard as a sledgehammer.

Kato dug an elbow into the mattress and rolled.

His counterpart kept pummeling him, driving both fists into his head and torso.

The man was strong—and fast. Stronger and faster than Kato. He knew that, in these brief moments of hand-to-hand combat, it was clear who had the physical advantage.

And his counterpart was on top. Kato was pinned down.

He was losing this fight. And ultimately, would lose this fight.

Kato knew it.

He again tried to roll, to get free, and finally, he managed to get onto his stomach. He was about to push up, hoping to propel the man off of him, when a sickening blow landed on the back of his head, at the base of his neck.

What felt like an electric shock went through Kato. His body seemed to go numb. He lost control of his limbs as he collapsed to the bed, unable to move.

93

Still face down, his head turned to the side, Kato watched as his counterpart rose off of him. The man stared down at Kato, hate in his eyes, and a grin forming on his lips.

With each passing second, feeling was returning to Kato's body, as if the blow had sent a shock down his spinal cord that was fading.

The man studied Kato's face, and his eyes went wide. Without the wig, he could see that Kato was a near mirror image of him. He swallowed, and the smile vanished. "What are you?"

The door that led to Nora's adjoining room swung open, and Ty stepped in. He glanced at Kato, who was struggling to get up off the bed, then at his counterpart. The man reached for the sidearm at his hip.

Ty did something that surprised Kato: he jumped at the Sicherheitsdienst officer, colliding just as the man's fingers touched the gun. The man having one hand preoccupied with reaching for the gun gave Ty just enough advantage to overpower him. They collapsed onto the wood floor with a loud crash, but that was the end of Ty's assault.

Kato's counterpart moved his hand off the gun, giving up on drawing it. He rolled easily on top of Ty and was raising a fist to strike when Kato sprung from the bed. Seeing his teammate—and friend—about to be pulverized had unlocked a deep reservoir of strength.

He took his counterpart from the side, wrapping an arm around his neck, his legs clamping around the man's abdomen, his other arm holding his counterpart's left arm. On the floor, he held tight, like a crab trying to squeeze the life out of its prey.

The man writhed and choked, but Kato held on. His

counterpart punched behind him with his free hand, the blows landing on Kato's side. The first two hurt. The third almost made him lose his grip. The fourth shook him loose, but Kato held on, feeling his grip slipping away.

The man was *strong*.

From a seated position, his counterpart leaned forward and arced backward, trying to bash Kato's head into the hardwood floor.

Kato leaned his head forward to avoid the impact and tightened his arm around the man's neck, bringing a gurgling sound from him.

His counterpart drew his arm up to do another backward punch, but Ty caught the man's arm and pinned it to his chest, above where Kato's legs were wrapped around him. Ty leaned in, putting both his hands on the arm and applying all his weight. It was enough to stop him—even Kato's counterpart couldn't push through the force.

Kato squeezed harder on his neck, tightened his legs, and held the man's other arm.

He was weakening.

His breathing was ragged.

Kato heard footsteps at the door that led to Nora's room. He looked over to see Maria and Nora in the doorway, staring, aghast.

Kato held tight, feeling the life flowing out of his counterpart. It was sickening—the act and the feeling. But he held on. He had no choice.

Ty was panting hard, still holding the man's arm. He looked up at Kato, silently asking, *Are we really going to do this?*

Kato gritted his teeth and squeezed tighter, until his counterpart wasn't moving anymore. When he released his lifeless body, Kato felt an emptiness he had never known. Sitting on the floor, with the man that was him in another life lying in his lap, he sensed a dark feeling flowing into him. It wasn't fully remorse. Or rage. Or fear. It was a cloud of something new, an utterly disorienting, oppressive sense of darkness.

The room was quiet. Everyone was still.

Then, a knock at the door broke the silence.

94

Another knock echoed in the room.

Kato didn't move. He sat on the floor, cradling his dead counterpart.

Ty rose and stepped quickly to the peephole and looked through.

Penny stood in the hallway, glancing back at the two Gestapo officers nearby. They were talking into their radios, but Ty couldn't make out the words. Had they heard the fight inside the room? Probably. But why was Penny here?

He turned to Kato. "Should I answer it?"

"No."

Through the peephole, he watched Penny knock again.

A few seconds later, one of the Gestapo officers walked over and spoke to her in German. Ty thought he was telling her to leave, and apparently, he had. Penny walked down the hall, then hesitated.

She stepped to Nora's door and knocked.

Ty turned to Kato, who was still staring down at his counterpart, seeming in a state of shock.

"She's at Nora's door," Ty hissed.

"Just…" Kato shook his head. "Get rid of her. Lead her away if you have to."

Ty went through the door to Nora's room and closed it behind him.

He opened the outer door to Nora's room, just a crack, cognizant of the Gestapo men watching down the hall. One cocked his head when he saw Ty.

"Hi," Penny said, seeming nervous.

"Hi."

She leaned to the right, trying to see into the room. "Am I interrupting?"

"No," Ty said, too quickly, awkwardly. "Not at all."

Penny bit her lip. "I was going to go for another walk. I was just... I was wondering if you might want to join me? The ceremony is in a few hours, and it's probably my last break."

Ty nodded. "Sure. Okay."

He slipped through the door and closed it quickly behind him.

The Gestapo officer squinted at him. Ty thought he was going to ask a question, but Penny turned away from them and strode off, Ty close behind. He expected the officer to call out. But he didn't.

In his mind, Ty arranged the questions he wanted to ask Penny. He needed to find out where the missiles were controlled. This might be his last chance.

"So where are we going?" he asked as they descended the large metal staircase.

Ty thought she seemed nervous when she answered, "I thought we might visit the primates again."

Kato laid his dead counterpart out on the floor.

"Maria," he whispered. "I need you to make me look exactly like him. *Right now.*"

Maria blinked hard twice, as if the words had snapped her out of a trance. "The makeup is in Nora's room. I'll get it."

To Nora, Kato said, "Help me get his clothes off."

Kato unbuckled the SD officer's belt and threaded it out of the loops and removed the gun as Nora began unbuttoning his uniform.

Another knock came from the door, a pounding this time, far less delicate than Penny's soft raps.

Kato dropped the SD uniform and rushed to the peephole. One of the Gestapo agents stood there, leaning toward the glass eye to try to peer in.

Kato covered it with his thumb and cleared his throat. Mentally, he tried to modulate his voice to match his counterpart's. His

German would likely sound different from the other man's. Saying a lot would be a risk.

"What!" he shouted in German, infusing the world with annoyance.

"Everything okay?"

"Ja!" he yelled, hoping the sharp response would make the Gestapo officer back off.

He peered in the peephole and watched as the man paused, looked back at his colleague, and shrugged. They mumbled to each other, but Kato couldn't make out the words. The man wandered away from the door, still talking quietly with the other Gestapo agent.

Kato returned to his dead counterpart and finished undressing him and jerked the Sicherheitsdienst uniform on. He stuffed the dead man in the closet and fidgeted while Maria smeared makeup on the scar on his face and the new bruises from the fight. When she was done, she glanced between the corpse and Kato.

"We have a problem."

"What?"

"Your hair is slightly shorter than his."

Kato put his counterpart's hat on. "It's close enough."

"What are you going to do now?" Nora asked.

"I need to find your counterpart."

"Ty took a walk with Penny this morning. There's an SD building near here. She's probably there. If not, you might find the location in the files in the building." Nora grabbed the notepad on the bedside table and quickly drew a crude map to the SD building. "It's here."

Kato nodded. "Okay. Sure. What could go wrong?"

Ty could tell something was off about Penny. She wasn't like she'd been this morning—upbeat and reflective. She was guarded now. Hesitant in her responses.

"Everything all right?" he asked as they strolled along the path.

"Yes," she said, a little too quickly.

Behind them, the red-brick building of the power plant loomed, the late-afternoon sun already behind it. Around them, trains full of cargo and personnel rolled on the tracks and trams ferried more attendees about the sprawling base.

"Did I say something wrong this morning?"

Penny picked up the pace. "Not at all."

"Why are we going back to the primate building?"

Penny didn't slow. Or make eye contact. "I thought you liked it."

"I did."

She swallowed. "Good."

Ty's instincts told him to turn back, but how would that look? What could he do?

Penny pulled the door to the building open and held a hand out to Ty.

He stepped inside, bracing himself, but it was the same entry room he had seen before. The guard was even the same. And he was still drinking coffee and looking tired. He barely glanced at them before waving them on.

Penny opened the door to the animal wing and Ty stepped through, focused ahead on the pens, which looked the same.

"Don't move," a man said. He spoke English with a German accent.

Ty froze. He heard the door close behind him.

Penny shuffled around him, keeping her distance, tears welling in her eyes.

On the other side, a Gestapo agent sidestepped into view. His eyes were hard, and he held a pistol that was trained on Ty.

"Get inside the pen. Don't try anything. I *will* shoot you."

Ty stepped slowly toward the cell. "You have me mistaken."

"Do not bother lying. We have already checked your identity. The person you're impersonating is in Brazil right now, at a Covenant consulate."

To Penny, the Gestapo officer said, "Inform Dr. Klein that we have a security breach. We need to notify Miss Santos as well. Have them send someone to her room to search it."

95

Kato looked down, inspecting the SD service dress uniform one last time. It was fine. His German was the problem. He needed to say as little as possible. One mispronounced word could sink the entire operation.

He pulled the door handle with a snap, stepped into the hall, and quickly jerked it closed.

The closest of the two Gestapo officers turned to him. "What did—"

"I need to make a report."

The Gestapo officer frowned. "Should we guard the door?"

Kato saw an opportunity there.

He nodded once. "Yes. No one in or out."

The guard nodded slowly.

"Including you two," Kato said.

Before they could say another word, he spun and marched away, the boots pounding on the wood floor.

Ten minutes later, he was scanning his counterpart's wrist badge at the SD building Nora had identified. As he walked in, he kept his eyes fixed ahead, staring impassively, as though he had walked this route a thousand times.

Beyond the guard desk, there was a touchscreen wall directory. He didn't dare stop or interact with it—he couldn't give any indication that he didn't know the building's layout. Out of the corner of his eye, he scanned the listing and identified the one he found most promising: "observation area" in subbasement two.

In the elevator, he pressed "U2" but it wouldn't light up. The car didn't move. He swiped his wristband on the magnetic reader and hit the button again. This time it lit up, and the elevator dropped.

It opened onto a room with concrete walls, beady lights above, and a floor-to-ceiling glass security divider. Several armed SD soldiers stood behind the glass, watching. Upon seeing him, they made no reaction.

Kato strode to the card reader by the glass door, held his breath, and scanned the wristband. The door popped open, and Kato strode past the armed guards and through an unlocked door, into a small reception area with a wide wooden desk. A rotund SD soldier sat there, staring at the screen, smiling as though he was watching a video. When he realized Kato was standing before him, he ripped off his headphones, stood straight up and raised a salute.

"Sieg Heil!"

Kato returned the salute. "Sieg Heil. I need to speak with the Pax agent, Nora Brown."

The man glanced down at his screen, "You are not on the schedule, Herr Sturmbannführer."

As a student of military history, Kato had studied the Nazis extensively. One thing he knew from that research was that the Third Reich fostered a respect for authority—almost to a point of unquestioning adherence to orders from above. He could use that. In fact, his rank was perhaps the only thing that might save him in this high-risk mission.

"Scharführer, listen closely. The schedules are made by Sturmbannführers." He held his hand straight out to the door that led out of the room. "Take me to her. Right now."

The color drained from the man's face. He scurried around the desk and swiped his wristband at the door. He almost stumbled as he waddled down the corridor.

He opened the cell door, and when he lingered, Kato shouted, "Dismissed."

Inside, Kato saw what, at first glance, looked like a carbon copy of Nora.

She stood in the middle of the ten-by-ten cell. It had a narrow bunk, a metal toilet and sink, and a stack of books by the bed. Where Nora's eyes were bright and kind, this woman stared back with unbridled rage.

For a moment, Kato thought she was going to rush him. Her posture was that of a feral animal ready to pounce. Instead, she spoke in a voice that was slightly rougher than Nora's.

"Have you come to execute me, Sturmbannführer?"

Kato answered in German-accented English. "Only to ask you some questions."

"I know how the SD asks its questions. Let's skip to the execution."

"This isn't what you think it is."

"Says a man who lies for a living."

"Come with me. It is very important. Time is of the essence." Kato stepped closer and spoke more quietly. "I know you don't wish to be underground. Here, or at home—permanently. Let's see if we can prevent that."

For a split second, her eyes flashed in shock, but she quickly regained her composure.

Kato stepped out of the cell and held an arm out. "I do not wish to talk here. Please. Accompany me."

The woman clenched her teeth and marched out of the cell.

At the guard desk, the man rose. "Herr Sturmbannführer, are you..."

"I will be conducting this interrogation off-site."

The man reached for the phone.

"Halt." Kato's word was like a whip hitting the man. "This is an active operation. Time is of the essence. As is secrecy."

"But it has to be cleared."

"*I* am clearing it. If I have to remind you of my rank one more time, Scharführer, it will be the last time. Is that understood?"

"Yes, Herr Sturmbannführer."

"Hand me those restraints and the key."

Kato handcuffed Nora's counterpart and connected the cuffs to another cuff on his left hand. The three-foot tether between them might draw attention, but he didn't see a way to avoid it.

As they rode the elevator and marched out of the building, Kato mentally prepared to be caught for removing her from the site without authorization. But no one said a word.

On the walking path outside, the woman said, "Where are you taking me?"

"Somewhere we can talk."

"About?"

"I can't say right now."

"Why not?"

"You'll see. And when you do, it's important that you don't say a word. Do you understand?"

"Believe me, not talking to you is something I fully intend to do."

In the power plant, Kato and his prisoner drew a few stares and frowns, but no one stopped him. No one questioned a high-ranking SD officer escorting someone in plain clothes.

At his room, the two Gestapo officers were leaning against the wall by the door. They stood up straight at the sight of him and scowled when they saw Nora.

"Herr Sturmbannführer..."

"I'll be interrogating the prisoner here. Maintain your post. No one in. Or out."

Before they could ask another question, he swiped his wrist at the door lock, ushered Nora inside, and slammed the door shut.

The passage to Nora's room was open, and she was standing at the threshold. She had recently taken her wig off and washed the makeup off her face. Without the hair and makeup, Nora looked like an almost exact copy of her counterpart, who gawked at her for a long moment, then shuffled away from Kato until the tether pulled tight.

"What is this... you're replacing me?"

Kato dropped the German accent and returned to his natural voice. "It's not what you think."

"Where's Maria?" he asked Nora.

"It's almost time. She had to go to her room to get ready." Nora glanced around at the room. "Can we talk here?"

"Yes," Kato said. "After what happened—and what we said before—I don't think they're watching. Or listening. Must be a privacy thing for visitors. I imagine it would cause a major issue if they surveilled VIPs in their rooms."

"Makes sense," Nora said.

"What's happening here?" her counterpart asked, voice quivering.

"Where's Ty?" Kato asked.

"Still with Penny," Nora replied.

Kato stepped to the closet and opened it, revealing a wadded-up pile of white bedsheets. He pulled them off. His counterpart sat against the back wall, unnaturally pale, wearing only his underwear.

Nora's counterpart staggered back, head whipping between Kato, his counterpart, and Nora.

"What is this? Some SD mind trick?"

"We need your help," Kato said.

"With what?"

"Stopping the missile launch."

"Who are you?"

"I know this is going to be difficult to hear," Kato said, "but we are from another Earth. Another world in the multiverse."

The woman grimaced, and Kato thought for a second she was going to laugh. Her lips trembled as her body began shaking, and her eyes rolled back in her head.

Kato placed his hands on her arms and felt the strength leaving her body.

"Is she having a seizure?" he asked Nora.

"I don't know."

The woman collapsed to the floor, lurched forward, opened her mouth, and emptied the contents of her stomach on the floor.

96

Standing in her bathroom, with her hair styled and makeup on, Maria saw a stranger in the mirror. The person looking back at her now positively glowed. It was a version of herself that might have been if she had made different choices. A version of her that might still be. If she was strong enough. If she ever got off this bizarre world and returned home.

She wondered what the audience would see. This world's Maria Santos? The superstar? Or would they see through the mascara and foundation and concealer and hair spray? Would they realize the lie? It wasn't enough to simply look the part. Her voice would have to convince them.

A pounding at the door made her jump.

She rose and peered through the peephole. Helen Klein stood there. Two Gestapo agents loomed behind her.

Maria swallowed hard. Maybe they were here to escort her to the turbine hall for the ceremony. She glanced at the clock. It was too early.

She cracked the door.

"Miss Santos," Helen said. "May we come in?"

Maria let the door swing open and watched as they strode in. The Gestapo agents fanned out, visually searching the room but not going as far as opening doors or unzipping her suitcases.

Helen gently closed the outer door and clasped her hands behind her back. "We have a security breach, Miss Santos."

Against her will, Maria inhaled sharply. "Oh?" she managed to say, not trusting her voice.

"One of your employees is not who they say they are."

"How?"

"This person is using a real South American identity, but they are not that person. The actual South American resident is still in Brazil. We're holding the impostor."

"I see."

One of the Gestapo men cleared his throat. "The question, frankly, is how in the world you could not have known that this man was an impostor."

Gently, Kato helped Nora's counterpart to the bed. She sat there, swaying, listless. The news of who Kato and Nora were had hit her like a knockout punch in the boxing ring.

"Focus," Kato said. "We need your help."

The woman looked at him through teary, bloodshot eyes filled with fear and confusion. "What?"

"Where is the missile control room?"

She shook her head, as if resisting.

"Think," Kato whispered. "Why would I need to know where that room is if I really was an SD officer? I could find out any number of ways. I'm telling you the truth. I'm trying to help the Pax."

Nora bent down, her face inches from her counterpart. "Tell him. What do you have to lose? Think about it."

"All right. It's in the Bunkerwarte control room. It was used as an air-raid shelter during the war. It also housed the power plant's control room. The walls are two meters thick. The ceiling is reinforced concrete."

Without a word, Kato uncuffed himself from Nora's counterpart, covered the dead body in the closet with the sheet, and exited into the hall.

The two Gestapo men there wore looks of alarm now. One was talking into a handheld radio.

"Herr Sturmbannführer, we have a problem."

"Not now."

"Herr Sturmbannführer, it is urgent. We have an intruder."

Kato spun. He knew he would get one chance at this. And he knew the only way out. "Do you not think I know that? Why do you think I came to this room? With the prisoner? I am one step ahead of you. You are slowing me down." He pointed to the door. "Guard that room and keep your mouth shut and do only as I say, or you will face the consequences."

Kato didn't wait for a response. He turned and barreled down the hall and turned the corner before letting out the breath he had been holding.

Maria swallowed hard.

Being a drug addict had derailed her life. It had taken so many things from her. What she didn't know—until that moment— was that it had also given her one ability that might just save her life here and now: the ability to lie. Drug addicts, if they used long enough, eventually had to become skilled liars.

"I didn't know he was an impostor because I had never met him until this trip. He was recommended to me. I changed my team recently because of... a betrayal of my trust by people close to me. I don't wish to say more than that. The media will know soon enough, but I prefer my privacy as long as it will hold."

The Gestapo man glanced over at Helen, who squinted at Maria. "Do you know where the members of your team are now?"

"No. I went to my makeup artist's room a while ago and left when she was done. I assume she's still there. There were two army men guarding the room next door."

Helen appraised her again. "From here out, we will be detaining all members of your party."

Maria nodded. "I understand."

"You will accompany this Gestapo officer to the turbine hall and give your performance, then you will immediately leave the Covenant. Do you understand?"

"Yes."

With that, Helen marched out of the room, one of the Gestapo agents following close behind her. The other stared at her with cold eyes.

"Let's go, Miss Santos."

★ ★ ★

In the hallway, Kato saw Maria's door open and Helen Klein stride out, a Gestapo agent behind her.

She scrutinized his face but walked right past.

At the stairs, Kato gripped the rail and descended three and four at a time, leaping, his boots echoing up the stairwell.

He slowed his pace at the ground floor landing and waltzed out casually, on his way to the missile control room.

97

When Nora had finished putting on her wig and makeup, she sat on the bed next to her counterpart, an arm around her, comforting the woman. She wasn't sure what to say. It seemed her counterpart didn't either. They simply sat in silence.

For Nora, seeing her double had been more jarring than she imagined.

But the revelation of who Nora was—the idea that she was from another universe—had completely rattled this world's Nora Brown.

Nora was wondering what to say to the woman when she heard the door to her room fly open. Nora rose and walked over, peering through the connecting door into her room, where a towering Gestapo agent strode in, gun drawn, two more troops behind him, also raking their guns left and right. The lead man pointed his gun at Nora through the doorway.

"Don't move."

Another Gestapo agent opened the door to the bathroom and charged in, gun first. The third man went through the connecting door into Ty and Kato's room and began searching it, ignoring Nora and her counterpart. For now, the wig and makeup she was wearing were working. Nora wondered how long that would last.

The Gestapo agent took a step toward the closet.

Nora drew a breath in.

The man held his gun in one hand and with the other, jerked the closet door open. Nora hoped he would stop at the sight of the crumpled pile of sheets.

If so, she might still get out of this. She had done nothing wrong.

The man reached out, fingers closing around the sheet, and pulled it toward him, revealing Kato's dead counterpart, lying with his back against the wall, skin ashen and rubbery, dressed in a white tank top and underwear.

The man spun and pointed his gun directly at Nora as he took out a radio and began barking orders into it. When he was done, he called through the doorway.

Helen Klein strode into the room. She cast a glance at Kato's dead counterpart lying in the closet. Recognition seemed to dawn on her face. She turned and glowered at Nora.

"Who are you?"

Nora stared at the woman she had known all of her life— her best friend's mother, the lady next door who had been like a second mother to her. Here, in this world, she appeared so similar, but the differences were there too— subtle but important.

Nora wasn't sure what to say. Helen didn't ask another question. She stepped forward, scrutinizing Nora. She reached out, grabbed the wig, and ripped it off.

Kato marched down the corridor toward the double doors to the Bunkerwarte control room. They were giant iron slabs that loomed like the gateway to an impenetrable bunker.

Kato stopped at the doors and swiped his wristband on the magnetic pad. The light flashed red. His counterpart clearly didn't have access to this room.

He was at a dead end.

Kato wished Ty was there with him. He would likely have some brilliant idea to get inside.

Since Ty wasn't there, and Kato's adrenaline-fueled mind couldn't come up with any bright ideas, he did the only thing that seemed obvious to him: he raised a fist and knocked on the door.

He heard a mechanical whirring and looked up to see a camera panning toward him.

"Why are you here?" a voice asked.

"I need to get inside."

"Why?"

Kato noted a few things. They hadn't addressed him by his rank. And there were voices in the background—shouting. His every instinct told him to flee. But he couldn't. This was his last chance to stop the launch. He had to try—he knew if he lived through this, he would regret it if he didn't.

"I have information you need."

"Regarding?"

"The launch. Open up."

In the corridor behind him, Kato heard boots pounding the concrete floor. He pivoted toward the sound.

Over the speaker, the voice switched to English with a heavy German accent. "Remove your sidearm from the holster and lay it on the ground. Do it now, or we will shoot you."

In the distance, the troops were growing closer. He wasn't going to be able to shoot his way out of this one.

Kato drew the gun and set it at his feet.

"Now kick it away."

The pistol clattered across the concrete floor, into a wall.

A dozen SS soldiers turned the corner, pouring into the corridor, submachine guns trained on Kato.

The iron doors parted and slowly drew into the wall. The control room was quite large, with at least ten stations where men and women were hunched over their computers. Kato counted eight armed SS troops gathered just inside the door, guns held at the ready.

Kato realized the truth then. He'd never had a chance of getting inside the control room. And even if he had gotten inside the room, he wouldn't have gotten through the security and been able to alter the launch.

It hit Kato then how futile the mission had been.

As the hope drained out of him, an officer with a rank directly above his counterpart stepped forward. The Standartenführer sneered at Kato. "Whoever you are, you have killed a Reich Europa Sturmbannführer. For that, you will pay a heavy price. For a very long time."

98

In the turbine hall, Maria sat on stage, nerves frayed, heart thundering in her chest.

A man in a white suit stood at the lectern, addressing the crowd in German. She didn't know what he was saying.

The Gestapo agent that had escorted her to the venue sat in the front row, watching her with barely concealed contempt.

He didn't buy her story.

Maria wondered what use they would have for her after she sang the song.

In the primate complex, Ty stared at Penny.

"I'm not who you think I am."

She snorted. "Apparently. I told them you were asking questions. They tell me you're an impostor."

"It's complicated, Penny."

"It's a complicated world."

"Let me explain."

"Explain what? That you came here to make war."

"I came here to stop one."

"Says a liar."

"I need your help."

"I can't." Penny swallowed, fear rising in her voice. "And I don't believe you."

A strange sensation ran through Ty, a feeling of things coming full circle—of seeing a revelation that was hidden before but now shone as bright as the rising sun.

Ty walked to the steel bars and wrapped his fingers around them.

"I think you do, Penny. You're just too scared to trust me. I don't know what's going to happen, but I do know this: there is a much stronger person inside of you, waiting to come out. You'll be surprised. But don't let that person change who you are."

The Gestapo agent beside the cage shook his head. "Enough!" He held a hand out to Penny. "Visiting hours are over. Vielen Dank für Ihre Hilfe, Frau Neumann. Gehen Sie, bitte."

When she was gone, the Gestapo officer grinned at Ty. "The previous team that assaulted this facility killed seven of ours. Naturally, there is a desire to square that particular account. However, we did not expect you to be foolish enough to try again so soon. As such, we are thrilled at this *opportunity* you've given us."

Helen examined Nora's wig for a moment, then let it fall to the floor. Her gaze shifted between Nora and her counterpart sitting next to her.

"So the Pax has perfected cloning?"

"No," Nora said.

Helen exhaled heavily. "Do not bother denying it. We've caught your clone of Sturmbannführer Tanaka—outside the missile control room. Twins of someone from the Pax is unremarkable. A copy of a Covenant citizen and Reich Europa military officer—that could only be the work of cloning."

"It's not. There's something even more strange and wondrous going on here. You sense it, don't you? That's why you're talking to me now. You know something is happening here that is important—something your scientific mind is urging you to investigate."

She studied Nora a long moment, then turned away. "It won't matter soon. We've captured the audio-visual technician accompanying Miss Santos. We know he's an impostor. Or perhaps another clone. We're not sure yet."

Nora's heart sank. They had captured Ty too. Maria was likely trapped in the turbine hall. They had failed.

Yet, in that dark moment, Nora saw a hope, the same one she had latched onto when this world's version of her father had cornered her in the bunker below Camp Shenandoah.

Ty.

And Helen.

They were the key to everything.

"You want to know what's happening here?" Nora whispered.

"Very much."

"I'll tell you something I can't possibly know: that the medallion hanging around your neck is a quantum radio."

Helen's eyes bulged. She staggered backward as though she had been struck by an actual blow.

"It's capable of communicating between worlds."

"How do you know that?"

"I know that it has changed the course of history here. I was being truthful with you: we're not clones."

"What are you?"

"You want answers?"

"Yes."

"Ask the young man who was posing as Maria Santos's audio technician. His name is Ty. It's short for Tyson Klein. Talking to him might save your life and the lives of everyone you know. Please hurry."

99

In the turbine hall, the man at the lectern switched from German to English.

"Unfortunately, Dr. Klein has been detained tonight. Such a shame. She put so much effort into this event, and I know her remarks would have been far better than my rambling."

Tepid laughter rippled through the hall as the man glanced back at Maria.

"However, things are about to get better. To officially start the launch sequence, we will be serenaded by a performer who needs no introduction: Maria Santos. We have the distinct pleasure, here tonight, of witnessing a song that she wrote specifically for this occasion, a piece she calls 'A Hymn for The World After.' And now, let us welcome Miss Santos."

Maria's heartbeat pounded in her ears as the applause thundered in the room. She felt herself rise and approach the microphone.

A bead of sweat formed under her armpit. Another on her forehead.

Behind her, the orchestra struck the first note.

She stared at the crowd as the music filled the hall.

For the first time in years, she opened her mouth and began to sing for an audience.

In the dark forest of our world
I heard the drumbeats of war
Beating in the night
Counting down to the end of all things

As the first line escaped her, an almost magical thing happened:

all of her fears melted away. Every other thought in her mind faded. For that brief moment, as the lights shone down on her and every eye in the room bored into her, she seemed to exist out of space and time. Alone and at peace.

Maria Santos hadn't felt this good in a long time. Not without drugs.

In the primate facility, the Gestapo agent paced in the central corridor. It was unnerving to Ty. Apparently, it had the same effect on the animals. Many of the primates had started whooping and screeching.

One of the animal trainers had to come in to calm them, but their efforts had been only partially successful.

The door opened, and, to Ty's surprise, Helen Klein strode in, a digital tablet in her hand.

She said a few words in German to the Gestapo agent, so soft Ty couldn't make them out. When he replied, she hit back with a sharp retort that struck him like a slap. Ty wished he knew what the word meant. Whatever it was, it sent the man stomping away.

She didn't smile at Ty. She examined his face, and he had an idea of what she was seeing: herself. Ty's facial features had always favored his mother.

Her scowl softened slightly. "I want answers."

"You deserve them."

"Who are you?"

"I've never been great at speeches." Ty got up off the ground. "In fact, as a kid in school, I always dreaded giving presentations. To the point of faking sickness."

He snorted. "My mom was pretty good at seeing through that act. She was also good at recognizing my limitations—and helping me understand them and deal with them. When I was terrified of public speaking as a kid, she explained it with science. She told me that we humans evolved to be afraid of a room full of eyes staring at us. As hunter-gatherers, our ancestors who realized eyes were watching them usually got eaten not long after. We evolved with that experience haunting us. We evolved to have a fight-or-flight response at the moment we see a group of eyes staring at us. Today, in a civilized society, our rational minds can overpower that deep-rooted instinct, but it takes practice. She taught me a trick to help make that happen: harnessing kindness to control our instinctive fight-or-flight reaction. Science. She was very good at it—and using it to explain the world to me. I was a strange kid, but I really won the lottery when I got her as a mom."

Helen's chest was heaving now.

Ty reached up and tore out a few hairs. "Like I said, I'm not one for speeches. I'm going to let science do the talking. That's a language you understand. One neither of us can dispute."

He held the hairs out, through the bars. "I assume, in this comparative genomics facility, you have a DNA sequencer?"

Helen nodded.

"Here is one of the answers you're looking for. Sequence my genome and compare it to your own."

100

As Kato marched down the hall, the chains that bound his hands and feet clinked. The jingling was the only sound, and with that melody calling out, gut-wrenching questions weighed on his mind.

He wondered if he would ever see his wife and child again, if he would grow old and die on this bizarre world, this battlefield he couldn't have even imagined a few days ago.

Would his family look for him?

Would they be told what had happened to him?

Would his son grow up without a father?

In the turbine hall, the band played, and Maria sang the second stanza of "A Hymn for The World After." Singing again was bliss, but she knew that with each line, this world crept closer to oblivion.

And in the darkness, I saw a light
Twinkling in the night
Shining all around me
Counting down to the end of all things

In the primate facility, Helen marched out with Ty's hairs, and when she returned, she seemed more composed.

"The results will take a minute or two. In the meantime, I have questions."

Ty nodded. "I bet."

"Who are you?"

"One of the ways men and women are different—one of the many ways—is that a woman can't have a child without knowing it. Well, unless her eggs are removed, and people are generally aware of that. Which begs the question: if you're confronted with DNA results that confirm you have a thirty-five-year-old son, what does it mean?"

"Indeed. What would that mean?"

"It would mean that the son you're staring at right now was born to a Helen Klein very, very similar to you in an alternate universe."

"Impossible."

"The DNA sequence will confirm it."

"How is this possible? How are you here? Why?"

Ty pointed at the quantum radio medallion hanging around her neck. "On my world, I made a discovery: that there was quantum data being broadcast into our universe. The data stream included schematics to construct a quantum radio—one very similar to the one hanging around your neck. I used that device to travel here with three others."

Helen stared at him, eyes wide.

Ty pressed on. "In the world I'm from, I grew up in Washington, DC, in a quaint neighborhood where my single mother raised my brother, my sister, and me. She was a very hard-working woman. A professor at Georgetown—of evolutionary biology. The Helen Klein that raised me had a lot of rules in her house, but there were a few above all others. One: you treat people the way you want to be treated. And two: if you do something wrong, that's on you, and if you see something wrong and don't tell someone or do something about it, that's on you as well. I'm betting that there is some part of those principles in you. If not, I fear for this world. Those values might be the only thing that saves us."

Ty smiled. "You just asked me why I'm here. Until a few minutes ago, I didn't know exactly why my quantum radio brought me to this world. I thought there was a reason, but I couldn't quite see the whole picture. But I see it now."

"See what?"

"I see a way to save your world."

"*My world* is in no danger."

"It is. You think the Reich's A21 missiles will end the war, but you're wrong. The Pax has a superweapon too. A biological one. They're ready to release it. You can't stop it. Not with missiles. Not with any army. And certainly not in the time you have. Maybe not ever."

"What do you want?"

"I just told you. My mother taught me that if I see someone doing something wrong, it's my responsibility to stop it or report it. I'm here to stop it. I didn't know it until now, but *I* am here because of you. If I'm right, you're the only person in this entire world who can stop what's about to happen. Our mission here was about one thing: this moment. Me reaching you in time to stop a mistake that can't be undone. A mistake you can prevent."

In the turbine hall, Maria sang the next stanza, her eyes moving across the enraptured audience.

A true north calling us home
Out of the shadows of The World Before
Crumbling all around us
Counting down to the end of all things

101

Helen Klein's tablet dinged, and she glanced down at it. The edges of her mouth curled up.

"DNA results?" Ty asked. "It confirms that I'm your son. But I think you knew that was true before you even saw it."

Helen stared down the corridor of the primate facility. Nearby, two of the chimps were beginning to chatter.

She motioned to her tablet. "I've turned surveillance off here. So let's talk. What are you asking from me—specifically?"

Ty sensed that he needed to explain more before making his request. Springing the question too soon might spook her. He needed her to believe him, but he also knew that time was running out.

"A few days ago, someone tried to kill me. They sent a bomb to my apartment. I got out. But they didn't stop. They sent a man to kill me. I was lucky. Someone who cared about me saved me both times."

Ty paced in the cell, his gaze fixed on the ground. "What I learned after that was that an organization called the Covenant was responsible for those attempts on my life. In my world, the Covenant exists only in the shadows. I had never even heard of them. When I arrived on this world, imagine my surprise when I discovered that the Covenant rules entire continents. Why?"

"You believe it's the same Covenant?"

"Occam's razor."

"The simplest explanation is usually the right one," Helen said. "But is that the simplest explanation?"

"The only alternative is coincidence—that there are two separate organizations that just happen to have the same name. I'm a scientist. I don't like coincidences."

"What are you saying?"

"I'm saying that I believe what's happening on our worlds is connected somehow. I believe that's why the Covenant tried to kill me. And I'm asking you to trust me enough to answer a few simple questions."

Helen inhaled and nodded.

"How did you develop the quantum radio? When?"

"In the twenties, in the ruinous years after the Great War, during the Weimar Republic, a package was delivered to my grandfather. He was a professor at the University of München. Back then, quantum physics was in its infancy, and the university and its alumni played a major role in developing it. Max Planck, the originator of quantum theory and a Nobel laureate in Physics in 1918, was an alumnus of the University of München. Werner Heisenberg and Wolfgang Pauli, who were practically the founders of quantum mechanics, were also associated with the university."

Helen reached up and touched the quantum radio medallion hanging around her neck. "The device my grandfather received came with a key that decoded two-letter combinations of the twelve symbols into alphabet letters and numbers. The radio medallion began receiving signals soon after he unwrapped it. Symbols on the dial would light up, and he would transcribe the messages using the key code."

Helen smiled. "He thought the transmissions were a prank at first. Perhaps some trick from another physics professor who was using magnetics to manipulate the device. What changed his mind was the messages he received: predictions of future events, predictions that were right every time."

"And then they started making requests, didn't they?" Ty asked.

"No. They began making *suggestions*. Those suggestions were ignored—at first. And then a few were undertaken. With those moves, our fallen nation began to rise again."

"Let me guess: one suggestion was to focus on building rockets in the 1930s."

"Correct."

"On my world, Germany lost World War II. That's what we call—"

"The Pax War."

"Regardless of what the war is called, the Covenant changed the course of history on this world," Ty said. "Why do you think that is?"

"One of my team's greatest debates is who created the quantum radio medallion—and why it was given to us."

"They never told you?"

"No. The Covenant said only that it was our benefactor—an organization dedicated to safeguarding our future. And it seemed they were. Indeed, our working theory is that the Covenant is actually a group in our future, sending messages back in time to change the timeline. To correct the past. Or an extraterrestrial species capable of modeling our future."

"I don't think they're either."

"What are they?" Helen asked.

"I don't know exactly. Not yet. But I think a better question is: what do they want?"

"We don't know."

"What have they asked—" Ty caught himself. "What have they *suggested* you do?"

"The comparative genomics project, for one."

"What's the project about?"

Helen ventured over to one of the cages, where two chimpanzees were huddled together, chattering quietly.

"It's about one of science's greatest mysteries."

"What makes us different from them," Ty said.

Helen's head snapped back to stare at him.

"My mother was interested in that too. Did you find it?"

"We did. A very small number of genes control intelligence— human-level intelligence."

"How does that information help the Covenant?"

Helen turned away from the chimp cage. "Via radio broadcasts, the Covenant suggested that the knowledge could help us end the war. The premise of what they suggested was the same as what we had pursued for the last seventy years: an enemy that is incapable of fighting will never be a threat."

"What are you telling me? What's in those rockets?"

"In a strange twist of fate, our weapon is biological too."

"In your speech, you said you were going to change their minds."

"Precisely. The A21 missiles don't contain any incendiary ordnance. They contain a bioweapon that operates at the epigenetic level. It essentially switches off a small number of genes. Genes that control intelligence. The change will not kill anyone in the Pax. But it will render their intelligence level comparable to that of the chimpanzees in these cages."

Maria's voice filled the turbine hall, booming like bombs dropping.

And that star asked a price
For the light of everlasting peace
Shining all around us
Counting down to the beginning of all things

And we paid it
With blood and time and hearts forever lost
Beating all around us
Counting down to the beginning of all things

102

Ty shook his head. "You don't want to do that. You don't want to take the humanity away from those people."

"What choice do I have? They want war. They won't stop."

"They will."

"How do you know?"

"I've seen it. On my world, Europe and Asia have been at peace with the nations of the Pax Humana for seventy-five years. It's possible." Ty nodded. "Sure, there was a very tense period—a long Cold War—where everyone thought the world could end at any given moment. Both sides were armed with weapons that could wipe out the other side. Just like you and the Pax are right now. In my world, that mutually assured destruction terrified both nations. In fact, I think maybe it was the key to peace. You don't realize it, but what you have now is what you've always wanted: a real chance at peace. It's peace or annihilation. The only thing you have to do is trust that the other side wants to see their children have a future. They don't have one now. And because of that, they have nothing to lose. If you study them a little closer, you'll realize that they aren't so different from you."

"What *exactly* are you proposing?"

"Peace. That's why we came here—to make sure both sides have a future, one way or another."

"What does peace mean to the Pax?"

"They know you've built massive military bases with millions of troops."

When Helen said nothing, Ty continued. "I bet the Covenant *suggested* you build those bases and assemble such a large army."

"What are you saying? What are you asking me?"

"The Pax made a simple demand of us: to change the coordinates of those A21 missiles to hit your massive military bases. They want to eliminate the missiles and the troops."

"Out of the question. Those troops are Covenant citizens. They are sons and daughters and mothers and fathers, brothers and sisters."

Ty held his hands up. "I'm just conveying their orders to us, letting you know what they're thinking."

"I won't do it. Not to my own people."

"To be honest, our team wasn't willing to do it either. Our plan was to make the missiles land in Greenland or somewhere they couldn't harm anyone. Our goal was simply to disarm you. But even with the missiles gone, the troops will remain—and they'll be a threat to the Pax." Ty paused a moment. "The troops are a curious aspect of all of this, don't you think?"

When Helen said nothing, he continued. "Answer me this: if you had the ultimate weapon of peace, why would the Covenant instruct you to assemble millions of troops?"

Helen turned away and paced. "We assumed it was a backup. In case we weren't able to create the bioweapon successfully."

"But that theory doesn't make sense, does it?"

"No," she said quietly.

"Because if they know the future, they would know that you would succeed in building the bioweapon. You wouldn't need millions—tens of millions—of troops."

"True."

"I think that's what the Covenant is after. If I had to guess, I would bet it's all been to that end: a troop build-up for some purpose that has nothing to do with the Pax or Reich Europa or possibly even this world."

"Even if you're right, I can't use our weapon on them. I won't."

"You don't need to. There's another way."

"Which is?"

"Right now, both the Covenant and Pax are scared. You each see a predator across the sea—eyes upon you, waiting to pounce like our ancestors did. You're being driven by your fear, your fight-or-flight instincts. But you don't have to be. There's a very easy way to overcome that fear. Kindness. You taught me that—another version of you did."

"It's a beautiful thought, but kindness can be seen as weakness. The truth is that we live in a cruel world where the kind don't always survive."

"You'd be surprised. Here's what I'm asking you to do: see if the other side is willing to be kind too. If both of you are, this entire world will have a brighter future."

Helen squinted at him. "I wouldn't even know where to begin. Who to even talk with in the Pax."

"It just so happens the exact person you should begin with is very close by."

Helen frowned at him, clearly confused.

"Dr. Nora Brown," Ty said. "Her father is a high-ranking Pax official. And the scientist who controls their superweapon. In a way, he is your counterpart. Both of you have your fingers on the weapons that can end the world. And I think neither of you really wants to press those buttons. Make a deal with her. You want peace? You won't get it by fighting. But you could by talking."

Helen considered his words for a moment, then tapped on the tablet and spoke in German.

"What are you doing?" Ty asked.

"Bringing her here. Along with the other prisoners."

"Good."

They waited in silence for a while, Ty mentally struggling with what else he could say to change her mind. He knew time was slipping away.

"In your world," Helen said, "what happened after the war ended?"

"Germany was split into four occupation zones, each administered by a different nation: the US, Great Britain, France, and the Soviet Union. Berlin, the capital, was divided in half. The US, Britain, and France combined their zones. In the US, there was something called the Marshall Plan, which gave billions in aid to Europe to help it rebuild. It took a long time. To this day, the US still has massive military bases in Germany."

"Interesting."

"You need to cancel the rocket launch. Whatever you do, if you launch, and those rockets land in the Pax, it's over. This world is over."

Helen stared at him.

The door opened, and four Gestapo agents strode in, guns in hand. Nora, Kato, and Nora's counterpart trudged in, followed by four additional Gestapo agents.

Helen motioned to the pen where Ty was being held. "Uncuff them and put them in with him."

When they were in the cage and the door was locked, Helen dismissed the agents.

She glanced between Nora and her counterpart, studying them, finally settling her attention on this world's Nora Brown.

"I'm told the Pax has created a superweapon."

The woman stared defiantly. "If you try to strike us down, it will be the last thing the Covenant ever does."

"She wants to help you," Ty said.

"I don't believe it."

Helen stepped closer to the metal cage separating them. "In addition to the A21 rockets, we have a standing army of almost thirty million."

Nora's counterpart didn't blink. "The size of your army won't matter against what we've built."

"You miss my point," Helen said. "It seems we have a knife at each other's throat. The wrong move ends things for both of us. What I'm proposing is the other road: we both keep our weapons. But we empty our military bases. We send our troops to the Pax and help you rebuild your society. We enter a new era of cooperation."

Nora's counterpart snorted. "An invasion by any other name."

"No," Helen said. "Not an invasion. Or an occupation. A humanitarian mission." Helen locked eyes with Ty. "An act of kindness. Our troops would be unarmed. Only a small number would come at first. Engineers. Construction crews. Advisers. *When* we build trust, more will come. And some—who want to—might even stay. And integrate. We will also open the Covenant to citizenship for Pax residents."

"Those are some very, very big promises. Prove to me that you can deliver."

Helen raised the tablet at her side and tapped it. "I just canceled the missile launch. Next, I'm going to get all of you—and Maria Santos—back to the plane you arrived on."

"What are you asking from me?"

"Only one thing: to take my offer back to the Pax."

"How do we know you can do what you're promising?"

Helen reached up and touched the quantum radio medallion. A smile formed on her lips. "For a very long time, almost a hundred years now, my government has relied on my department to tell them what strategic moves to make to ensure our future. They follow our directives without question. They have learned to. Simply put, if I tell them we have to do something to ensure our future, they do it."

To Ty, Helen said, "You were right. I am the only person who could make this happen. And in a strange way, you were the only person I would have believed."

She held the medallion up and glanced at it. "At first, my ancestors were skeptical of this device. Then, when we discovered that what it told us was the truth about the future, it gave us the key to a better future. And so, we trusted what it told us. Without question. That changes today. Going forward, we're going to start thinking for ourselves—and creating our own future."

Helen studied Nora's counterpart. "Do we have a deal? Will you take the offer back to your people?"

"Yes. I will."

103

In the turbine hall, Maria stood at the microphone, smiling at the crowd, singing the final lines of "A Hymn for The World After."

And that star gave us The World After
With all its light
Shining all around us

A new dawn
Beyond the darkness
Where peace has no price
And no end

The last note echoed in the hall. The band fell silent.

The crowd rose and clapped. The pounding applause reached her like an ocean wave crashing onto the shore.

She swayed, feeling the afterglow of the performance, a sensation of pride and accomplishment and self-worth that her bad decisions had deprived her of for so long. It reached down and soothed the hurt deep inside her wounded soul.

In her peripheral vision, she saw Helen Klein step to the lectern. She was clapping too.

When the applause abated, the woman spoke in a clear voice that rang through the vast room.

"I suspect Miss Santos's performance here tonight has been far more transformative than any of us suspect. Let's have another round of applause for her."

The ovation started up again, and Maria glowed in the adoration.

When it receded, Helen spoke again. "I have one small alteration to tonight's agenda: the launch viewing outside the power plant has been canceled. Instead, we'll skip directly to the reception. But rest assured, The World After has begun. It's not the world we expected. But I believe it's going to be far better."

A more muted applause filled the room.

In the front row, the Gestapo agent stood up and motioned to Maria, pointing toward the exit door to his right.

She scanned the room, searching for Kato, Ty, or Nora. But she didn't see any of them.

With a sinking feeling in her stomach, she trudged off the stage. Another Gestapo agent was waiting at the tram. Her bags were already loaded in the back. Still, there was no sight of Kato, Nora, and Ty.

The lights of the tram carved into the night as it careened toward the airstrip. Maria racked her mind, trying to think of a way to help her team. Her friends. She didn't even know where they were. But the missiles weren't launching. That was something. What did it mean?

At the airstrip, the Gestapo officers ushered her toward the waiting plane. She climbed the staircase, her suitcase in hand.

The moment she stepped inside the cabin, she saw Kato and Ty sitting at a table, playing cards. Nora was lounging in a club chair nearby. Beside her was a woman who looked almost exactly like her. Almost. Her counterpart wore a stern, wounded expression, like a wild animal that had just been freed.

Ty set down his cards and rose from the seat. "Heads up! We've got a celebrity on board!"

Maria smiled. "Haha. Very funny."

"How was the show?"

"Good. But it seems like I've missed the real show. What happened?"

Ty shrugged. "Things didn't go as planned."

"Understatement," Kato muttered, also rising from his chair and moving to close the plane's outer door.

"To be precise," Ty said, "things didn't go as planned. But in the end, they turned out better than we could have planned." He smiled at her. "You were part of it. How do you feel?"

"Better than I have in a long time."

PART III

THE LOOKING GLASS WORLD

104

The plane flew toward Buenos Aires.

In the cabin, Ty sat in a plush chair, gazing out the window, deep in thought.

He looked up when Nora plopped down across from him. Her counterpart was snoring softly on the couch. Maria was asleep in a club chair. Kato was in the cockpit, the door closed, seeming to want time to himself.

"This is the first chance I've had to really talk to you since Peenemünde," Nora said.

"Yeah. It was pretty crazy at the end."

"What are you thinking about now?"

"Unanswered questions."

Nora laughed. "Which ones?"

"Several. But mainly, who brought us here? To this world?"

"Who says it was someone? What if it was just chance?"

"I'm a scientist. I don't believe in chance. Or coincidence. There's something else going on here. And I want answers."

It was night when the plane landed in Buenos Aires.

A strong gust of wind blew across the tarmac as Ty stepped out onto the stair landing and descended. Kato, Nora, and Maria were close behind, followed by Nora's counterpart.

At the bottom of the stairs, Nora's counterpart pulled away from the group and walked ahead, making a beeline for the terminal. Ty knew she couldn't wait to get in touch with the Pax embassy and relate what had happened in Peenemünde—and the offer the Covenant had made.

The glow of the moon mixed with the floodlights from the

terminal and the round beady lights embedded in the ground, creating a strange confluence of illumination.

Ty thought he sensed something to the right, but when he turned, the tarmac was empty. It was that same strange feeling he had experienced since coming to this world. He stopped and stared at the point where he felt it strongest.

Kato stopped too and stood beside Ty. "What is it?"

The light in the air where they were staring rippled.

"I don't know," Ty whispered.

Nora and Maria turned and backtracked to join them.

"What's going on?" Nora asked.

The light bent and seemed to suck inward.

"We should go," Kato said, voice strained.

Ty was pretty certain they couldn't outrun whatever was about to happen. He inhaled and watched, waiting.

Maria's voice was shaky. "I don't like this."

Ty felt Nora's fingers intertwine with his and squeeze.

On the tarmac, four human figures appeared where the ripples had been. They wore black outfits made of nonreflective material that fit loosely. Every inch of their bodies was covered. Their helmets featured mirrored visors that covered their entire faces. To Ty, they looked like astronauts in slightly less bulky suits.

There were no markings on the outfits—no words, no flag, no logo. Each of the figures had a small metal ring mounted in the center of their chests. It was a quantum radio medallion, and the symbols on the dial were the same as the ones on the medallion Ty had used to bring them to this world.

The figure closest to them reached up and tapped the dial on the medallion mounted on their chest, four quick pecks.

In the blink of an eye, Buenos Aires disappeared.

In the next second, Ty, Nora, Kato, and Maria were standing on the edge of a cliff, the wind blowing across them. Ahead, red and brown canyons and mountain ridges stretched as far as the eye could see.

The four figures stood nearby, facing Ty's team, unmoving, as if waiting for Ty and the others to adjust to the new world.

Ty knew instantly they were on another Earth within the

multiverse. It was night, and the moon shone brightly in the sky, casting shadows across the rocky expanse. The air was crisp and cool but not frigid. It smelled clean and fresh, as though nothing man-made had ever touched it.

The only sound was the wind. Above, the stars in the night sky were breathtaking, a masterpiece of light and color.

Ty expected one of the four suited figures to speak, but they didn't. Their mirrored helmets merely focused on Ty, Nora, Kato, and Maria, waiting as the team took in this strange world.

"Who are you?" Ty asked, his voice distorted in the blowing wind that lashed the cliffside.

The voice that replied was like a human voice that was being disguised by a mechanical device. "You already know, Ty."

"You're the ones who've been watching us. Since the museums at the National Mall. And after. I felt a presence."

"That's right."

"Why?"

"To observe you."

"Why?"

"You know, Ty."

Nora tightened her grip on his hand.

"Who are you?" he asked again, voice quavering in the relentless wind.

"You know, Ty."

"You sent the quantum broadcast I found. With our genomes. And the schematic for the quantum radio medallion."

"Correct."

105

On the cliff, the wind blew through Ty's hair and tugged at his clothes. He stared at the four figures.

"Why did you send the broadcast?"

"You already know, Ty."

"You needed our help."

The figure inclined its head slightly.

Ty pressed on. "You needed us on that world—to stop the Covenant."

"Correct again."

"Why can't you do it yourself? You clearly have far more advanced technology than we do."

With the previous questions, the figure had answered instantly. Now the group fell silent, the only sound the howling wind whipping across the rock face.

Behind them, the air changed. It rippled and coalesced.

A figure appeared, also wearing a suit with a mirrored helmet, except the material of the newcomer's suit was gray.

One of the four suited figures who had brought Ty to this world quickly brought a hand up to the quantum radio medallion on their chest and dialed.

Once again, the world disappeared.

In the next second, Ty was standing in a forest with massive trees. They were wider and taller than any redwood he had ever seen but with similar bark, leaves, and cones.

Unlike the cliff where they had been a second before, it was quiet except for the creaking of the forest as a twig or branch fell. Fog drifted among the trees like groups of ghosts parading through.

In the distance, there was a soft boom. The ground trembled.

The four figures stood near one of the towering trees. Ty could still feel Nora's hand gripping his.

In his peripheral vision, he saw Kato spinning around, taking in their surroundings in every direction. Ty assumed he was scanning for threats.

Maria was breathing rapidly. Nora reached out and took her hand, silently trying to calm her.

"What was that?" Ty asked.

"Covenant agents," the closest figure replied.

"They're hunting us?"

"Yes. But we're dealing with it. We may have to change Way Stations again."

"Way Stations?"

"A world like this one. An Earth without humans but with a breathable atmosphere. There are no threats to you here."

"Except the Covenant."

"Only if they find us."

"Back up," Ty said. "Who are you?"

"You can call us quantum historians."

Ty squinted, unsure what to ask next. "Where are you from?"

"We're from the same place as you, Ty."

"Earth."

"Correct. But the Earth we evolved on is different from yours. Not radically different, but different enough to matter quite a bit. Our civilization was slightly more advanced than yours in one important way: when your world was developing the atom bomb, we were experimenting with quantum technology. Our world was one at peace. A single global society with a shared purpose: to use science to unravel the greatest questions of human existence. In the subatomic world, we saw the thread that we could pull to unravel these mysteries that haunted us. What we didn't know then was that our discovery would be our undoing."

In the distance, the booming started again, growing closer. The figure ignored the sound.

"Our great discovery was that via particle collisions, we could make the membranes between universes porous. At first, we sent other subatomic particles through."

"Like you did to our world," Ty said. "The quantum radio broadcast."

"Precisely. We used what you would call entangled particles. We sent one of the entangled particles through the pores between the universes and kept the other on our end. When we manipulated the particle in our universe, it changed the state of the entangled particle in the other one. This process required an exceptional amount of computing power and energy, but it worked."

The ground trembled again, and Ty, Nora, Kato, and Maria all turned to look, but there was only a cloud of fog moving across the trees.

"Pay no mind to that," the figure said. "It's no threat to us."

"What *is* a threat to us?" Ty asked. "Why are we hiding in this Way Station?"

"You've seen already. On the A21 world. And your own. And just now."

"The Covenant."

"Correct."

"Who are they? What are they?"

"They are not so different from us. Or you. We found them by accident. As I said, we began our venture into the multiverse through a series of entanglement experiments. Soon, they grew tiresome. The answers they yielded were less profound. We wanted to know more about the multiverse. To observe and explore. And importantly, we had no fear of what we might find. Scientifically, we had no equals. We were sublimely clever, but we had a disastrous flaw."

"You were naive."

"In the extreme."

The figure who had been speaking paused, as if listening, then turned to one of the other figures and froze.

Ty assumed they were communicating via some wireless mechanism in the helmets. It looked like an argument.

The lead figure turned again and resumed speaking, the grating, computerized voice a sharp contrast to the serene forest.

"We soon discovered that with the right collisions and particles, we could vastly enlarge the pores between the universes, dilating them enough to send matter through. We sent rovers. We lost more than we could count. We soon discovered that across the multiverse, life on Earth was the exception, not the rule. And so was an atmosphere survivable by humans. Yet we persisted. We made a sort of map of the multiverse, marking the Earths that were hospitable to human life. They were rare too. And on those habitable Earths, every now and then, we found one populated by humans."

The figure paused. "You might think that means there aren't that many inhabited Earths. But the nature of infinite numbers dictates otherwise. While only a very small fraction of these worlds were inhabited, there are an infinite number of universes, and because even a small fraction of an infinite number is itself an infinite number, there are, thus, an infinite number of inhabited human worlds, more strange and varied than you can imagine. And some so similar to your own that you'd have to study them a lifetime to find even the tiniest difference."

The figure took a step deeper into the forest, toward the nearest cloud. "In the multiverse, we found our purpose. We saw a role we were singularly qualified to perform: cataloging the quantum realm. We were scientists. We are *still* scientists. We set about taking a scientific inventory of the multiverse, observing and documenting all of the habitable Earths and the humans that lived on them. The ranks of the quantum historians grew as more members of our society used quantum radio medallions to port to unexplored worlds. We had a rule for any historian traveling the multiverse: never interfere. We were—and remain— observers only. We saw no other way."

A cloud of fog drifted between the two groups. When it had passed, the figure spoke again.

"For years, we believed that we were the only ones to discover the door between universes. A few of the human-populated worlds we encountered were more advanced than us in other fields: medical technology, nanotechnology, space exploration, artificial intelligence, immortality, telepathy, and telekinesis. We had our strengths. They had theirs. Our particular ability simply allowed us to visit them. In fact, we found worlds with technologies and wonders so breathtaking I cannot now describe them to you—for your own sake. But no matter how advanced or different from us, we never met another human society that was our equal in the quantum sciences."

The historian paused. "As such, we assumed we were the only humans moving across the multiverse. And no world was ever able to detect our presence. This was the case for years, until a team of quantum historians was observing a world populated by Neanderthals who had built an advanced society. The Neanderthals couldn't detect our presence, but the team quickly realized that there was another group of observers on the planet— using technology similar to ours. At first, they thought there had been a scheduling error—that there was simply another team of quantum historians present. But when they made contact with the other team, they quickly learned the truth: they were not from our world. For the first time, we made contact with a civilization capable of traveling the multiverse like us. Another group of observers. It was an incredible discovery."

Ty swallowed. "Let me guess: this other group was the Covenant."

The figure inclined their head slightly. "Indeed. Whereas we called our teams quantum historians, the Covenant called their teams quantum agents. Our activities, however, were much the same: mapping the multiverse and cataloging the vast eventualities of human possibility. In the Covenant, we believed we had finally found a kindred spirit, another ship in the night, an equal to share the joy of exploring the multiverse."

The ground trembled again. Three booms sounded, closer now. Ty wanted to look back, but he found himself captivated by the quantum historian's story.

"We visited the Covenant world, and there we saw what appeared to be our mirror world. It was something we had long sought—a world we thought we could learn from. And we did. What we didn't know then, in the joy of meeting them, was the heavy price we would soon pay."

"What kind of price?" Ty asked.

"The ultimate price," the historian answered. "Lives. And possibly, the future of our society."

"What happened?"

"As I said, in the Covenant, we believed we had found a kindred spirit. A society with our quest for discovery and knowledge—and quantum technology as advanced as our own. Together, we traveled the multiverse, making observations and returning home to share our discoveries with a waiting public that was fascinated by the findings. We shared our data with each other like two friends with the halves of a treasure map, embarking on the ultimate adventure together. What we didn't realize was that the Covenant was different from us in a small but important way."

Behind Ty, the booming sound grew louder. The cadence of the pounding had stopped before, but now it persisted, growing closer, louder, the ground shaking.

Nora squeezed Ty's hand.

They turned in unison just as a cloud of fog cleared. The trees towering above swayed as the giant beast came into view.

The animal had four legs like tree trunks, round, stubby, and heavy. Its body was covered in leathery brown skin. It must have been three hundred feet long, with a tail a third of the length of its entire body and a neck about half that. Its small head turned lazily to look at the eight small figures standing in the forest below.

Ty stared up in awe at the dinosaur.

Brontosaurus: that was the name his mind supplied, but he knew this dinosaur was likely different from the one that had lived on his Earth so long ago.

The magnificent creature raked its eyes over the group on the ground and merely glanced away, as if it had seen a few bugs. It marched forward, chewing a mouthful of plants, the ground shaking less as it moved on.

The quantum historian spoke again, drawing everyone's attention.

"What we didn't realize was that the Covenant saw the multiverse differently than us. As I said, we were naive, and at first, this nuance in their perspective wasn't apparent. And we didn't know to look for it. To us, we were simply a pair of vessels upon the quantum sea, charting a course together, sharing in the discoveries. But where we saw the islands and the animals and the fish in the ocean as things we would never interfere with, the Covenant saw something entirely different. We only learned what they saw after an event on the Covenant home world we call the Cataclysm."

The historian spread their hands. "After the Cataclysm, the Covenant ventured out into the multiverse not as explorers, but as exploiters. In the worlds of the multiverse, they saw their only means to save their homeworld. Their voyages became not missions of discovery, but missions of change—efforts to alter worlds in ways that could help them overcome the Cataclysm."

"That's why the Covenant is interfering in our world," Ty said.

"Yes."

"And the one you brought us to."

"Also correct. They are preparing both worlds for harvest."

"Harvest of what?"

"It varies by world—and in truth, on some worlds, we're not quite sure what the Covenant is doing. On the world you just saved, their objective was clear."

"The troops."

"Correct. They were building an army—we assume to bring through to another world for warfare. You stopped that."

The Brontosaurus's footfalls were faint now, the cadence regular as it paced away. Ty let a few of the booms echo in the forest, and then asked the question that was bothering him. "Which brings us back to my previous question: why didn't you? It's clear you have the technology to stop them. If you've visited countless worlds in the multiverse, it seems like you're a good bit more qualified than the four of us to stop a world war."

"We can travel across the multiverse, and we can alter entangled particles on a small scale, but it's not enough to stop the Covenant."

"Why?"

"For one, countering Covenant operations requires understanding what they're trying to do. But it's more than that. Effecting change on a macroscopic scale requires direct intervention."

Ty smiled. "You seem as capable as us."

"In many ways. Physically. Scientifically."

Kato spoke then: "You didn't want to get your hands dirty. Or, in this case, bloody."

"Those are not the words we would use," the figure said.

"But it's the truth, isn't it?" Kato asked.

Ty took the silence as confirmation by the historians.

"Why lead us to the A21 world?" Ty asked. "Why not send us a message asking for help?"

"Consider it a moment, Tyson, and you'll see the answer."

"You were testing us."

"We were. The world you just left, the A21 world, was a test of your abilities, and most importantly a test of your morality. We wanted to know what you would do when a dying man was laid at your feet. And how you would react when you knew that you were the key to saving a world that wasn't your own. Would you risk your own lives for them? For strangers? You could have tried to use the radio to get home, but you didn't. You were disciplined, and you worked together as a team. Even in the face of long odds, you took risks to save those strangers, and you stopped the Covenant on that world."

"Again, all things you could have done yourselves," Kato said.

"We are pacifists. We have been for a very long time. Recruiting quantum intervention agents from our world would violate the core beliefs of our society."

"But it doesn't bother us," Ty said. "We grew up in a world of both violence and peace. You need us because we're capable of doing what you can't—stopping the Covenant and making a mess in the process if that's what it takes. In a way, we're the middle ground between your society and the Covenant. We're capable of changing worlds, like the Covenant, but we care enough to save them—like you. That's really why you need us."

Before the historian could answer, waves formed near one of the giant trees and the air began sucking in. Just as a Covenant agent appeared, the forest vanished.

106

The forest was replaced with a sheet of ice that stretched to the horizon. Only one thing jutted out of it: the dome of the US Capitol building.

Overhead, the sun was dim.

Ty exhaled a breath of white steam, and the world disappeared again.

Next, he was standing atop a stack of metal shipping containers on a massive cargo ship. In every direction, ocean spread out around him.

Ahead, a metal object protruded from the sea. Ty recognized it. It was the top of the Eiffel Tower.

The world vanished, and Ty found himself standing in a space station in front of a wide window that looked down on the Earth.

For a moment he was mesmerized by the view. For Ty, going into space had been a lifelong dream. Now he was here—just like that, in the blink of an eye. In the Way Stations they had just transited, he had gotten a very small glimpse of the wonder of the multiverse. Seen and gone in the blink of an eye. Would this Way Station disappear too? Ty hoped not. He wanted to stay here, to drink in the view and explore this place. He realized it then: he was much like the quantum historians. To him, the multiverse was the ultimate frontier, an endless expanse of possibilities in science and history and human potential. And for some, as he had seen on the A21 world, it was also a place of great misery.

Kato glanced around at the metal walls and hatch that led out of the room. The four historians were standing near the large window.

"Won't the station personnel detect us here?" Kato asked.

The historian's computerized voice was loud in the space.

"This facility has been abandoned for a long time, though the environmental systems still work. This Way Station should be safe for a while."

The historian turned their helmet downward, toward the Earth, the view reflected in the mirrored visor. "When you first arrived on A21, all of you made it clear that you wished to go home. You could have gone home at any time. To the exact place you left. And you still can. Right now."

The historian reached inside a hip pocket on the suit and drew out a quantum radio medallion that was identical to the one on their chest. The historian tossed it to Kato. "All you need to do is dial the sequence you dialed to leave your world: the third symbol, the fourth, seventh, and eighth. This will be the last time you can dial that sequence to go home."

Kato looked down at the medallion.

"However," the historian said, "we have an offer to make you. An offer that could save your world from whatever the Covenant is planning. I hope you will stay a little longer, to hear us out."

For a long moment, no one said a word. Ty finally broke the silence. "We're still here."

The quantum historian walked away from the wide window, deeper into the room of the space station. There were benches near the window and couches beyond that. This place must have been some sort of lounge.

The historian turned to them, and the speaker on the suit rang out in the vast room. "With every passing second, the Covenant grows stronger. Their army gets larger. They conquer more worlds. They have an advantage: they have the map of the multiverse we created together, and a lot of data about populated worlds to work from. We know they're conducting experiments on hundreds of worlds—and advanced operations like the one you stopped on A21. We must stop them. And we need help. We need a team to do exactly what you've just done on A21: serve as *our* quantum agents. To put it simply, we need you to travel across the multiverse and prevent the Covenant from achieving their goals."

"And why exactly would we do that?" Kato asked.

"For your own self-interest," the historian replied.

"I'll decide my own self-interest," Kato shot back. "And before I do that, I want to go home. I want to see my family again."

"You can. But as we speak, your world is being manipulated by the Covenant. The changes to your timeline have impacted each of your lives. I believe you have some idea of just how different your lives *should be*. What we offer is simple: a trade. If you help us stop the Covenant on worlds less fortunate than your own—like the A21 world—we will help you repel the Covenant from your world."

"How would it work?" Ty asked. "We can't rewrite history. Our lives are already... changed."

The quantum historian cocked their head, allowing the silence to stretch out.

In that quiet pause, Ty realized the answer to his question. "Wait. The quantum radio doesn't just broadcast across the universe. It *can* cross time, can't it? I thought so. The medallion could take us back."

"Space and time are simply two sides of the same coin. Your world is on the verge of learning that. What we offer is what you describe: the ability to rewrite the history of your world. To correct the past. To remove the Covenant from your timeline. When those changes are gone, you will be living in your true world, what we call your Looking Glass World. It's a world that knows about the multiverse—the dangers of it and the promise of it—and celebrates each of your roles in saving it."

Ty's mind was racing. Before he could ask one of the twenty million questions running through his head, Kato's voice rang out in the room.

"Show us."

Ty, Nora, and Maria turned to him, and Kato pressed on.

"Show us the world you're offering. Prove it. *Prove* that it exists, or my answer is no."

"We expected this request. And have prepared for it. What you see next is a glimpse of your Looking Glass World. It is what's waiting for each of you at the end of this road."

107

In the Looking Glass World, Nora walked down the street, grocery bags in her hands. On the sidewalks and in the small front yards, children were laughing and playing. Adults and older children passed by on bikes and scooters in the dedicated lane beside the road.

At her home, Nora pushed open the white wooden gate and walked up the bluestone path to the front door. A small package was lying on the porch by the welcome mat. She picked it up and tucked it under her right arm and stepped closer to the door, which clicked open thanks to the camera's facial recognition.

In the kitchen, she set the bags on the island and ripped the package open.

Inside was an author's proof copy of her book: *The Birthright: Life Lessons from a Thousand Worlds.*

She ran her hand over the book, feeling it. For her, there was something transcendental about holding the tangible result of a project she had worked on for so long, a book she believed would touch so many lives.

She opened to the first page and read the opening lines.

You have a birthright. That birthright is to be happy and healthy. Not all of us claim that birthright.

To me, that is the greatest human tragedy. This book is about ending it. It is about helping you understand your own mind and the people around you. Ultimately, that is the lever of your destiny: understanding yourself and the world around you.

This may sound strange to you, but right now there is a version of you living a very similar life on a very similar world. Let's call that person your counterpart. The only difference between you and your counterpart is that they have discovered the principles of *The Birthright*. That other version of you understands their own mind. They understand how their decisions impact their life. They understand the people around them. These things are as vital to you as the air you breathe.

I believe a life is built a day at a time. Our days are numbered, like the pages of a story we write with the decisions we make. Decisions are forks in a road we travel through the multiverse. They determine where you end up in life—and how happy you are.

Our minds are what steer us along this road. The trouble is, we're never really given a map of the road or a manual for our minds. Most of us feel, for so much of our life, like we're lost, or only possibly on the right track.

This book is about helping you find your way. It's about how to operate your mind. It's a map of the roads you will encounter. And ultimately, it's about arriving at the destination that is your birthright: happiness and health. Let's begin.

Nora set the book down. Her gaze settled on the refrigerator. Written there, on the digital whiteboard, in her neat handwriting, was a grocery list. Beside it was a weekly schedule. As she read the names of the people in her life, a smile spread across her face.

Ty stood in an auditorium. It was similar to the one he remembered at CERN, with slight changes. This place was a little larger, with seats that looked more comfortable and wood-paneled walls. It was, in a word, plush. The CERN facility had been more utilitarian.

The audience was different too. About fifty young men and women sat quietly in the rows of stadium seating. Most were college age, or a bit older, as though they had just graduated.

On the screen behind Ty, white letters on a blue background read *Welcome to the QDA*.

Ty stepped to the podium and scanned the crowd. What surprised him wasn't what he saw. It was what he felt. The nervousness that had consumed him at CERN was gone. He felt confidence born of a deep sense of peace and kindness. His voice boomed in the auditorium.

"Welcome to your first day at the Quantum Defense Agency. Today, you join the ranks of thousands of individuals working with a single purpose: to protect our world from quantum intervention. Our enemies are, for the most part, flesh and blood like you and me. But the tools they use are subatomic. Unseen. But that doesn't mean they're not there. Trust me, they are. At this very moment, they may be trying to infiltrate and alter our world."

Ty paused. "The potential damage they could do is limited only by your own imagination. Or rather, their imagination. Imagine, if you will, a world where the United States never entered World War II, where Britain lost the war, where bombings in the US homeland were a daily occurrence. Consider the possibility of even stranger worlds, where ice covers the Earth. Where water covers the planet. Where dinosaurs walk among humans, hunting us. Where Neanderthals are fighting a war against humans like us."

Ty studied the crowd. "But I submit to you that those are not the scariest worlds one can imagine. What terrifies me the most is a world suspiciously like our own but with debilitating problems the population has lived with for so long they've stopped trying to fight them. Imagine a world where hate is spewed online and in person every minute of every day. Imagine a world where politicians gain power by setting us against each other. Consider a world where hunger and disease are so common people accept it, where only a small percentage are trying to end it."

Ty let those words sink in. "I know that world exists, because I was raised in that world, not the one you know. At the QDA, we're fighting the most important war in human history: a war to protect the world we've built—to protect our timeline and the quantum integrity of our universe. We're fighting for the future. We're fighting for the past. We're fighting for the very lives of each of us living right now. We can't lose. We have to win every day. Because if we don't, we lose everything."

Ty smiled. "No pressure."

At the back of the room, the door opened and Ty's twin brother, Tom, stepped inside. This version of Tom was a near mirror image of Ty. His face looked fresh—not worn or aged by the stress of prison. An employee ID badge for the QDA hung around his neck.

When Ty's talk was over and the new employees were filing out of the auditorium, Tom made his way to the stage. He smiled at Ty.

"Giving them the ole 'Welcome to QDA—don't screw up or the world is over' bit?"

"I like to start with the easy stuff."

"You're an inspiration, Ty."

"How's it looking today?"

"Quantum traffic is low. Zero interdictions in the last forty-eight hours."

"What I like to hear."

"They actually sent me to tell you that you're coming up on mandatory time off in the next few days. Apparently, the GovAI thinks you might be on the verge of working too hard. You've got to take a half-day either today or tomorrow. It has analyzed your schedule and strongly suggested you take a half-day today."

A few minutes later, Ty was sitting in the back of a self-driving car, watching the pristine streets of Washington, DC go by. There were no homeless people, or individuals shouting and holding signs on street corners or in front of government buildings. He saw a city in harmony.

The screen on the back of the front seat came to life and a message flashed, "Incoming Call. Helen Richter."

Ty tapped the accept button and his mother appeared on the screen. She was standing in her kitchen. A plume of steam rose from a pot on the stove behind her like a volcanic eruption.

"Hi, sweetie," she said, leaning forward.

"Hi, Mom."

"We were wondering if you all want to come for dinner tonight. We're inviting Tom and Sarah too."

"I'll check, but that sounds fine to me."

Ty's father leaned into view. "And don't be late like last time."

They set a time, and Ty asked what they could bring, expecting his mother to refuse any help—which she did.

As the call ended, the car pulled onto Ty's street, rolling through the shadows cast by the old trees that loomed above.

The garage door lifted as the car approached and closed the moment it was inside.

Ty stepped out and into the mudroom and listened, hearing rustling in the kitchen. A woman's voice rang out.

"Ty?"

He stepped into the kitchen. "The one and only." He shrugged. "Well, technically, one of an infinite number of possible Tyson Richters across the multiverse—"

She held a finger to his lips. "Why are you home?"

"My AI overlord is worried I'm working too much. So I couldn't stay at work. And I came home because... well, I thought you might like me being at home."

"You thought right."

Kato awoke in a large bed with a woman sleeping beside him, her arm across his stomach, her head lying on his chest. He glanced down and realized that it was his wife, Joan, sleeping peacefully.

To his right, morning light streamed in through the sheer curtains.

Kato inclined his head, trying to get a better look around the room. Joan inhaled sharply and turned away from him, freeing Kato to rise from the bed.

At the window, he saw a faint reflection of his face. It was cleanly shaven. And the scar was gone. So were the shallow lines that had begun forming on his forehead.

But that wasn't the biggest change. The biggest change wasn't how he looked at all. It was how he felt. When he stared at the morning sun, a warm sense of calm settled over him. *This* life was one he looked forward to every day. It was a life where demons didn't hide in the recesses of his mind, waiting to emerge around every corner. It was a life where he could become the most important thing he was ever meant to be: a good father and husband.

Through the window, he watched snow fall on the backyard. The swings of a child's play set swayed gently in the wind.

Beyond the bedroom door, the pitter-patter of little feet grew louder.

The handle turned and Akito burst through, followed closely by a girl a few years younger than him.

Both yelled, "Daddy, Daddy!"

"Come see what Santa brought!" Akito screamed before turning and rushing out of the room, his younger sister chasing after him. Kato started after them, eager to see Akito—and the daughter he had never known—but stopped in his tracks when Joan sat up. She squinted at the light through the windows and rubbed her puffy eyelids.

A silent moment stretched out for what seemed like an eternity as he waited, wondering what she would say, wondering what their relationship was like in this Looking Glass World.

When she smiled, it felt to Kato like it was warm enough to melt all the snow for miles.

"Hi," she said, yawning.

He let out the breath he had been holding, carrying with it a single-word reply, "Hi."

Joan closed her eyes. "I need you to get me a last-minute Christmas present."

"Anything."

"Another hour of sleep." She yawned. "Can you watch them? Please?"

He swallowed hard as tears welled in his eyes. "Yeah. I can watch them. For as long as you want."

Maria sat in a salon chair in the dressing room, staring at a mirror surrounded by light bulbs. The counter was covered in makeup and hair products. Brushes coated in powder lay atop round tins of foundation and blush.

The woman Maria saw in the mirror was her—the most beautiful version of herself she had ever seen. Here, in this dressing room, she glowed brighter than the lights around the mirror.

Beyond the door, the crowd roared, singing along to the song performed by the opening act. When the music ended, they began chanting for Maria to come out.

What surprised her most was not what she saw or heard, but what she felt: calm. In that dressing-room chair, she felt a sense of joy and serenity she had never known. She felt as though an invisible sun were burning inside of her—one that bad decisions had once nearly put out, but now shone again, a force of nature only she could stop.

The door opened, and a woman wearing a yellow polo leaned in. "Ready when you are, ma'am."

Maria rose from the chair and strode out into the corridor, security falling in beside her. The coliseum staff and event workers stood aside as she passed, all eyes on her, everyone smiling, some clapping, the sound drowned out by the thundering crowd that grew louder with each step.

At the entrance to the stage, the lights were blinding. Maria paused a moment, letting her eyes adjust. After a few seconds, she was able to make out the massive letters on the screen above the stage:

Maria Santos
Worlds & Time Tour

The chanting grew louder, the sound beating in her chest harder than her own heart.

She climbed the first step, then another, and on the third rung, the crowd caught a glimpse of her. Those who weren't already wearing their augmented reality headsets slipped the eyeglasses on, ready for the groundbreaking show that was redefining live musical events.

The eruption of sound that came then was nearly enough to bowl Maria over. It flowed around her like a wildfire carried by the wind: untamed, searing and unstoppable. It seemed to combine with the invisible sun inside of her, giving her even more strength, a force she didn't even know was possible.

She glided out to the center of the stage, took the cordless microphone from the stand, and paced before the raging fans, hearing the cheers building, waiting for it to ebb. Some performers liked singing into a headset. Maria had always preferred a handheld microphone: it was how she started, in those dive bars, and it always reminded her of how far she had come. And besides, without it, she wasn't sure what to do with her hands.

At the first break in the cheers, her voice rang out loud and clear in the massive stadium. "Thank you. Thank you so much. Tonight, I'm going to begin with a song that's very special to me. It's about some of my very best friends in the universe. It's about figuring out who you are and overcoming the challenges in your life. It's about learning to love and to trust, and when you must, to fight with everything you have. And win."

She took a deep breath as the crowd started up again. "It's a song called 'The Heroes of a Thousand Worlds,' and it's based on a true story."

108

Once again, Ty was standing in the observation room on the space station. Through the floor-to-ceiling glass window, Earth loomed below.

The glimpse of the Looking Glass World was fading now, but Ty's mind clung to it. He liked that world. More than that, he liked how it had made him feel.

He wondered what the others had seen. Glancing back at Nora, Kato, and Maria, he saw no clues. But each of them seemed deep in thought.

The four quantum historians moved away from the glass, toward the room's only door. One stopped and looked back. "We'll give you some time to consider."

In the historian's mirrored helmet, Ty saw himself standing in front of Kato, Nora, and Maria, nodding.

When the four historians were gone, Kato paced away from the group. "Let's start with the obvious: I liked what I saw. I liked it very much."

"Same here," Maria said.

"Me too," Nora said quietly.

"Same," Ty said.

"Is it real?" Maria asked, staring at Ty. "I mean, can they really do it? Or is it... some trick?"

Ty peered down at the Earth below. "It's real."

"How do you know?" Kato asked.

"I know because there's something I didn't realize until now. A piece that never fit before."

Nora studied his face. "Your father."

"That's right," Ty said. "Somehow, he knew our world was

being manipulated. He's part of this somehow… in a way I don't understand yet."

"Can we trust them?" Kato asked.

"I don't know," Ty replied. "I think we can only trust what we've seen: the quantum historians are trying to save worlds. The Covenant is trying to destroy them—or at least, use them for their own benefit. I know what side of that war I'm on. And if it means risking my life, I'm willing to do that."

Ty walked along the glass window, mentally arranging the words he wanted to say. "When I made the discovery at CERN— when I identified the quantum radio transmission—I thought it could change the world. I thought it would help us unravel the greatest mysteries of the universe and human existence."

He nodded to the Earth below. "And it has. What we've found is different from what I expected. It's also more amazing. We have the opportunity to solve some of the greatest scientific mysteries of all time. And probably ones I can't even imagine right now. Honestly, just for that, I'm in. But for what's waiting on the other side… it's an easy decision for me. But I think we should all make our own decision."

"I can't go home," Kato said quietly. "I thought I could, but now that I've had a little time to consider it, I know I'm not ready. Not like I am right now. What I had to do in Peenemünde… it changed me. I need to decompress. To recenter myself. And what I saw in the Looking Glass World—that's the life I want. I'm willing to do a tour of duty in the multiverse for that. I'm in."

Nora locked eyes with Ty. "So am I. Wherever this road goes, I'm in. I know what's waiting on the other side."

"I am too," Maria said. "I also like what I saw in that… whatever it was." She glanced at Kato. "I also see what we're about to do like a tour. In a way, it's similar to my last tour. Different places. Different people. Different challenges. I just hope it doesn't end up like the last time I was on the road, and what happened to me. I want to say that upfront, for all of you to know: I have a demon that I've been struggling with my whole life—my anger. I've used drugs to help me control it. And that's only dug me in deeper."

Maria took a deep breath. "When this all started, I was on my way to beating the drugs. Or I thought so anyway. But the stress of what we just did was hard on me. I almost didn't make it. I would understand if you don't want to take me along. And I won't go without being honest about what I'm dealing with."

"We all have demons," Nora said. "Of varying sizes."

"We're standing on a space station," Ty said. "If they can take us here, the historians ought to be able to help you, Maria. I think we should make it part of the deal."

"I agree," Kato said.

Nora nodded. "So do I."

Ty glanced at Kato. "I'm going to ask them to help you as well."

Kato gazed out the wide window, into the black of space. His head dipped slightly, making the smallest of nods.

"I think," Nora said carefully, "that we should ask them to resolve all of our outstanding health issues—mental and physical—before we embark on this... tour of duty." She kept looking at Ty, and he took her meaning.

"All right," he said. "Anything else?"

When no one said anything, Nora asked, "Who's going to talk to them?"

"Not it," Kato said. "I typically negotiate using a gun or my fists. Doesn't feel like that kind of negotiation."

"Also not it," Maria said. "This is way over my head."

"Ty should do it," Nora said.

"Me?" Ty laughed. "I'm the guy who pays the asking price when I buy a used car."

Nora laughed. "True. But I don't think this is that kind of negotiation either. And plus, I believe you have questions you want to ask them."

"Ask them why they wear those suits," Kato said. "It's been bugging me since Buenos Aires."

"Got it," Ty said. "Anything else?"

Nora walked over to him and put a hand on his back. "Just be yourself. Good luck."

109

Ty exited the observation room in the space station and stepped into the corridor.

The passageway was narrow, just wide enough for four people to pass if they were standing shoulder to shoulder. The walls were bare. Ty had expected to see directional signage, but there was none.

The hallway had the same artificial gravity as the observation room. Ty was amazed by that—and the space station in general.

Growing up, he had harbored a lifelong fascination with the International Space Station. But compared to the facility he was standing in, the ISS was like a tree house. This was a mansion in space: roomy, luxurious, and polished.

A part of him wanted to explore every inch of it. He sort of hoped the direction he had chosen outside the observation deck was wrong. He wouldn't mind seeing more of the place.

The corridor curved slightly, and after a few seconds the left-hand wall opened up to a room that looked like a cafeteria, with tables attached to the floor and a serving bar at the back.

Where the walls and ceiling of the corridors were light gray, this room was white, with even brighter lights. The four quantum historians stood in the middle of the room, facing each other.

At Ty's arrival, they all turned to him.

"We've discussed it," he said.

The four mirrored helmets stared at him, showing his reflection. None of the historians responded, which was a little unnerving.

Ty pressed on. "We accept your offer. But we have some conditions."

"State your conditions."

"First, we'd like medical treatment for each member of the team."

"Elaborate."

"Maria has been trying to overcome her substance addiction. She needs help."

"We can treat her here on the station in the med bay. We can expedite the alleviation of her physical dependence. But her mental challenges will remain. A mind is far harder to fix than a body."

Ty nodded. "Kato needs help too. What he had to do in Peenemünde has had an effect on him."

"As we said, we can heal his wounds from the fight, but fixing his mind will take time—and we don't have technology that can do it."

"You can't help him?"

"No. But Dr. Brown can. And like the rest of you, some of the answers you seek, you'll find in time, on the worlds of the multiverse."

Ty considered that for a moment.

"Do you have other requests?" the historian asked.

"Before we came to A21, my father gave me a medication that has helped me to function. I assume you know about my condition?"

"We do."

"I only have so much of the medication he gave me. I don't know what it is. I need more of it. Or a cure."

"We can provide neither."

"Why?"

"Because we're not entirely sure what your condition is. It's a type of quantum sickness, a category of disorders that is new to us. We are studying it, and have been for quite some time."

"Why?"

The historian cocked its head. "Ask the other question you came to ask."

He took a step deeper into the cafeteria. "On my world, before we came here, it was clear to me that my father knew more about what was happening than he told me. He had the medication I needed. He knew a lot about the Covenant, and what was going to happen. How?"

"It might be better if you don't know. We offer you this opportunity to withdraw the question."

"I want to know. Have you already interfered with our world? Are you responsible for us being here?"

"We made the decision, that if we arrived at this juncture, we would allow your father to tell you."

The words echoed in the cafeteria.

Ty blinked, mentally trying to catch up. "I want to see him."

"Very well."

110

In the cafeteria on the space station, an image appeared on one of the long white walls, as though a movie projector was shining onto it.

The image was of Ty's father. He sat in a chair in front of a triple window that looked out on a small, well-manicured yard. He was young, slightly younger than Ty was now, perhaps in his mid-to-late twenties.

"What is this?" Ty whispered.

"A video your father filmed a very long time ago—in the event you required an explanation."

Ty walked closer, studying the image. "Video of what?"

"We should let him tell you. Are you ready to proceed?"

"Probably not. But play it anyway."

In the video on the wall, Gerhard Richter fidgeted in the seat. "Shall I proceed? Do I simply speak?"

"Yes," a man said. Ty tried to place the voice, but couldn't from such a small amount of sound.

"Two days ago," Richter said, "a man and woman came to my home here in West Germany. They made an extraordinary assertion: that the history of the world was not correct, that our timeline has been manipulated. It's something, frankly, I and others have speculated about for some time. To be perfectly honest, I considered it a fantasy: a conspiracy theory we merely wanted to be true because we didn't want to place blame for the state of the world on our ancestors."

Richter paused, seeming to consider his words. "As such, I asked them to leave. I assumed they were running some sort of elaborate scheme. A confidence trick, perhaps. I thought the dismissal would be the end of the affair. However, in my mailbox that evening, I found a letter describing twelve events that would happen the following day."

Richter looked out the window, composing himself. "I'm making this video now because everything on that page came true. And because of the other predictions they've made—in the event that they come true as well."

He inhaled sharply. "In the interest of being unambiguous, I should add that I consider the odds of their predictions coming true to be quite low. But the gravity of what I've been told compels me to take the forecasts seriously. Even if there is a remote chance the events will come to pass, precautions must be taken."

Richer crossed his legs. "Today is New Year's Day, 1983. My visitors tell me it's a flag day because of what they assure me is a very important event: in the United States of America, a group operating within the Department of Defense called the Advanced Research Projects Agency—or ARPA—will begin requiring all computers connected to its ARPANET to use TCP/IP instead of NCP. I'm told that TCP/IP, or the transmission control protocol and internet protocol, will eventually become the standard for how computers communicate with each other. They tell me that it seems like a small change now but that the interconnection of computers will change the world, like a ripple in the sea that will eventually become a tsunami that touches every nation. Today, hardly anyone realizes how important connecting computers over vast distances will be. But those who recognize the gravity of this development—and invest accordingly—will reap immeasurable rewards."

Richter scoffed. "Two days ago, I would not have believed it. But as I say, my visitors have already proven that they know the future. At least in the very short term. It would be… unprofitable to ignore their long-term predictions."

Richter took a deep breath. "My visitors have shared several other predictions about the future of our society—which, if true, put me in a position to make investments that will make me a very rich man. After enumerating these predictions, they asked something of me, an act I have refused. The price is not worth any information about the future."

Richter clenched his jaws and exhaled. "My visitors insist that I am integral to stopping the interference they claim is happening in the world. They believe that soon my wife and I will move to the United States, that she will be given a position at Georgetown University in Washington, DC, and that eventually, she will give birth to twin boys, followed by the birth of a daughter a few years later. They have further predicted that one of our boys will one day make an incredible discovery—a breakthrough with the potential to right the wrongs on this world, to save the lives of countless people and end the suffering that will occur on this planet."

Richter paused. "What disturbs me is what they've asked of me. A sacrifice. I have been told that the only way for my son to make this discovery is for me to leave home before his fifth birthday. They tell me that my absence in his life will have a profound effect on him. Naturally, it will make him curious about what happened, about why I left, why I refused to be part of his life. My absence will leave him with an emptiness that words can't describe, a certain... desire to prove himself, that he is valuable. Most of all, he will wonder about the great questions of existence, the deep mysteries of the universe. That desire—and emptiness—will be the key to his greatest achievement."

Ty felt dizzy. It was as though his father's words—and the revelations—had sucked the oxygen out of the room like a hull breach on the station.

He staggered away from the screen, and with each step, his legs felt weaker until the floor was rushing up toward him.

111

Strong hands caught Ty, breaking his fall.

The quantum historian dragged him to a chair and propped him up. The person squatted down, their mirrored helmet close to Ty's face. He saw a warped reflection of himself, which fit this moment perfectly. He felt as though the video was like walking through a house of mirrors: seeing the world in a warped way and then finally striding out into the light and seeing the truth—what had actually happened to his family.

As his senses returned to him, he managed to speak.

"You lied."

The computerized voice echoed in the cafeteria: "About?"

"You said you never intervened in worlds. You only observed."

"That's true."

"You intervened in ours. In my life. In my family."

"*We* are not the ones who visited your father."

Ty squinted. "The Covenant."

"No."

"I don't understand."

"You will." The historian's helmet focused on Ty, seeming to stare at him. "Do you want to see the rest of the video?"

"No. But I need to. I need to know what happened. Play it."

On the wall in the space station, the video of Gerhard Richter sitting in the chair began playing again.

"I have refused this request. I will not desert my wife or my children. I do not care the cost. I will face the future with them or not at all."

Richter paused. "They have told me that certain events in the near future will change my mind. I do not believe it. Nothing will change my mind. I grew up with only half of a family in a

488

ruined world. My children won't endure the same thing. I want something better for them."

In the video, Richter stared straight ahead.

"Is that all?" he asked.

"Details," the voice said.

Again, Ty tried to identify the person speaking, but couldn't.

Richter exhaled. "Very well. This entire matter is bizarre beyond words, but I will indulge you—on the off chance this becomes relevant to the future."

He pinched his bottom lip, seeming deep in thought for a moment before resuming his speech.

"Again, what my visitors have told me is quite familiar to me: that my son, without a father figure in his life, will develop... a certain hunger, a drive to prove himself. That quest will lead him to a discovery that has to do with subatomic particles—quantum technology. The role they've asked me to play, beyond deserting my family, is to make investments that might support that discovery. It's absurd. They have urged me to partner with the American group previously mentioned—the Advanced Research Projects Agency within the Department of Defense—to develop quantum technology. It all seems far-fetched to me. In fact, I had to ask what the word 'quantum' meant. It's a fancy way of saying very small. I hardly care. As with so many things, time will tell."

Richter fell silent.

"Details," the voice said again.

Richter exhaled. "My visitors have informed me that my son's discovery will result in the creation of a device—one integral to humanity's future. I don't quite understand the details of what I've been told, but they insist that when the device is completed, it's imperative that he gain custody of it—him and no one else. I've been told that I will have to help my son escape with it from a facility in the United States."

Richter stared at the camera. "Is that sufficient? I'm growing weary of this."

The image on the wall faded.

Ty looked back at the four suited figures.

"Where's the rest?"

"That is the entirety of the video."

"What happened?"

"You know what happened."

"He said he wouldn't leave us. He did."

"Things happened after the video. Things that changed his mind."

"What things?"

"This is not the time."

"Make it the time."

"Time is a force of nature. None of us control it."

Ty brought his fingers up to his temples and massaged them, willing his mind to work, to process what he had just learned.

"What's happening here? I know it's more than you're telling me."

"We are telling you all we can."

"You're not," Ty said.

The quantum historian was still, the mirrored helmet reflecting Ty's face. "Worlds and time hang in the balance, Ty. This is the end of what we can tell you at this juncture. Now, we need your answer. Do you still accept our offer?"

"They're still in," Ty said. "And so am I."

"Very well," the historian said. "It will take us a few hours to treat Miss Santos. We will do so in the med bay. The rest of you may roam the station. I believe it's of interest to you."

"Extremely. But there's one other thing I want. It's sort of a strange request."

"It's the multiverse, Ty. Everything is strange, and anything is possible."

"On our world, there was a movie made in the 1960s. It's a World War II film called *The Guns of Navarone*. Do you know it?"

"We are familiar with *The Guns of Navarone*."

"Would it be possible for Nora and me to see that movie?"

There was the briefest of pauses, then the historian nodded once. "It will play on the far wall of the observation deck when you give the voice command 'play movie.'"

"One last thing," Ty said. "Kato wants to know why you wear the suits."

"Kato will get his answer in time."

Ty let his head fall back. "I knew you were going to say that."

112

In the space station's med bay, Maria settled into the chair and waited as the two quantum historians worked at the console nearby. They never touched her, but she drifted off to sleep.

When she woke, it wasn't how she felt that struck her. It was what she didn't feel.

The cravings were gone.

Her mind was clear—clear in a way it hadn't been in a long, long time.

Kato wandered the halls of the station. He visited the mechanical area, the bridge, a science lab, and ended up in the crew quarters.

The door to a stateroom opened as he approached, and he stepped inside. There were bunks on the left and right walls and desks against the far wall, with a small window above them.

Carpet covered the floor—likely to deaden the sound of any bunkmates coming and going.

Kato lowered himself to the floor, crossed his legs, and began to meditate. In the silence and the stillness, he observed his breath flowing over the edge of his nose. The meditation was like treading water, the darkness inside of him like a weight pulling him down toward the abyss.

He had been in these waters before. The meditation strengthened him, but as he focused on his breathing, he wondered how long he could keep his head above water.

In the observation lounge, Ty settled down on the couch next to Nora. Through the floor-to-ceiling window, Earth loomed below.

She smiled and shook her head. "This. Is. Crazy."

Ty shrugged. "It's the multiverse. Everything's crazy."

"It's also kind of wonderful."

"Yes. It is." Ty leaned back and put his arm around Nora. "Play movie."

On the far wall, the opening credits of the sixty-year-old film began playing.

For the next two and a half hours, Ty and Nora lounged in the room, watching the movie, as if they didn't have a care in the world—or worlds. For the first time in quite a while, Ty didn't think about anything, and he didn't worry about anything. He simply existed in the story, watching the characters travel across a war-torn land with only their instincts, skills, and friendships to see them through.

When the movie ended, Ty turned to Nora. "Well, what did you think?"

"I... liked it."

"Really?"

"It was good, but I think maybe you and Kato would have enjoyed it more." She smiled. "I enjoyed the company though."

"Me too."

Nora's smile faded slightly. "Ty, I want to say something."

Her tone immediately gave Ty pause. This sounded like the beginning of bad news. "Okay," he said cautiously, mentally bracing.

"If we were home right now, I would love to see where things go between us. Actually, I'd like nothing more in the world."

Ty swallowed, now knowing precisely where this was going, not trusting his voice to speak.

"Back on the A21 world," Nora said, "when you were fighting with Kato's counterpart... for a minute there, I shut down. I was terrified. I thought I was going to lose you. And it just..."

"Wrecked you," Ty said.

"Yes. It did. It was like nothing I've ever experienced. Except." She inhaled, and once again Ty completed her sentence: "Except when you lost your father."

"Yes, it was like that, all over again. Paralyzing. Terrifying.

I think I have this lingering fear from that—of loving someone completely and losing them. I thought I was over it. I thought it had been enough time. That I was ready to love with my whole heart again. What I didn't know—until I thought I was about to see you die—was that..."

"Was that you're not over it."

Nora held her eyes closed. "Please don't hate me."

Ty took her hands in his. "I don't. I understand."

"I just think us being together while we're doing this—traveling through the multiverse—will make it more difficult for us. It might cloud our judgment. Or put the mission at risk—or Kato and Maria. We just..."

"I know," Ty said. "You're right, but I don't like it."

"I don't either," Nora said. "It's not a *no*. It's not *never*. It's just not right now."

"It gives me something to look forward to."

"Me too."

113

After the movie, Ty and Nora sat in the observation lounge and talked for a long time.

To Ty, it felt like those afternoons they had spent together so many years ago on the National Mall as teenagers.

They talked about nothing and everything and whatever entered their minds. And he loved it. If given the chance, he would have stayed in that moment forever, safe in the space station, looking down on Earth, pondering ideas big and small.

But he knew they had to go.

Maria returned first, and Ty immediately saw a difference in her. She was glowing. There was, he thought, a sort of inner peace about her now, a quiet confidence that seemed to flow from the core of her being.

Kato returned next, and to Ty, he seemed like a dark mirror of Maria: serene on the surface but suppressing something darker deep inside.

The four quantum historians strode into the room and stood, their mirrored helmets showing a warped reflection of Ty, Nora, Kato, and Maria.

"Before you depart for your first official quantum mission, we have a gift."

Each of the four historians stepped forward and held out a hand, palm up.

Ty hesitated a moment, then extended his left hand, palm down, and grasped the historian's hand. Around him, Nora, Kato, and Maria were doing the same.

Ty felt a slight tickling in his fingers, then in his palm, and finally in his forearm, as though ants were crawling under his skin. He shivered.

The historian released him.

Ty glanced down at his forearm, where a symbol was appearing on his skin. It looked almost like the dialog box on a computer.

Ty looked over at the others. Nora, Maria, and Kato also had the Gestalt menu on their forearms.

"What is the Gestalt?" he asked.

"On the worlds of the multiverse," the historian said, "we can offer you very limited support. As you've seen, Covenant agents are hunting quantum historians. Our presence draws them. Our communications draw them. But the Gestalt is the one tool we can provide you. It is a foundational technology on our world, one given to all adolescents and adults. Think of it as a sort of... evolution of the internet. The Gestalt stores data in your DNA and is capable of data communication across vast distances. In your case, the Gestalt has been loaded with the sum of knowledge from your world—history, science, and more, instantly available and searchable. It also contains a translation library that will enable you to understand all the languages we have observed across the multiverse—and speak them, though your accent will come across as neutral."

"That's helpful," Ty said. He hadn't even considered the language barriers they would encounter in the multiverse.

"Allow me to demonstrate its operation," the historian said. They reached forward and lifted up Ty's left arm, then brought the thumb of his right hand to the heel of his left hand and pressed.

The Gestalt menu disappeared. Once again, Ty's skin was unmarked.

"The Gestalt reads your fingerprint at the activation point to ensure someone else can't open it. All you do is hold your thumb there for two seconds and the Gestalt will activate."

The historian pressed Ty's thumb into his hand again, and the Gestalt menu materialized.

"We have also taken the liberty of adding four other items to your local Gestalt storage: each of your great works. For Miss Santos, *Worlds & Time*—including everything from her notebook. For Miss Brown, the manuscript of *The Birthright* and her research notes. For Mr. Tanaka, *The March of Humanity*. And for Mr. Klein, his quantum research."

"That's much appreciated," Ty said, "but how do we add to our work?"

"Simply write into the Gestalt—either with a closed pen or your finger—which you'll get used to."

Maria was already navigating the Gestalt, pulling up her songs. "Yeah, this is definitely going to take some getting used to," she said softly.

"The Gestalt has another vital function," the historian said. "Data collection and transmission. As you observe worlds across the multiverse, the Gestalt will automatically gather data—including everything you observe and learn. That data will not be communicated to us in real-time. As I said, Gestalt transmissions can be traced. As such, during your quantum missions, the Gestalt will operate in offline mode—it will collect data and you will have access to data, but nothing more."

"When does the data get transmitted?" Ty asked.

"When your mission is complete."

"How does it know that?" Ty asked.

"For each world you visit, the Gestalt will receive an encrypted mission profile and desired outcome."

"Like a smart contract," Ty said.

The historian cocked its head. "An apt, though basic, analogy."

"Thanks," Ty said. "I think."

"Once the Gestalt detects that the mission outcome has been achieved—via some event you observe or information you collect—it will execute the departure protocol, which begins with uploading the data from your time on the world and any changes you made to your work or notes. The Gestalt will then receive an encoded transmission with the dial code for the next world you've been assigned to, as well as a clue about your mission there and the corresponding encrypted mission outcome."

"Wait," Ty said. "We only get a clue about what we're supposed to do?"

"We can't broadcast your mission in clear text via the Gestalt. The data could be intercepted by the Covenant."

"But you can send an encrypted smart contract for the mission outcome," Ty said.

"The programmatic trigger offers greater security—which the Covenant can't break. We must assume that they can decrypt standard data. As such, a clue is all we can offer you. If the Covenant knew your mission objective, it would put you in danger—and allow their agents to counter your actions."

"Assuming they even know we're operating in the multiverse."

The historian paused. "A fair point. But given your actions on A21, they will know soon."

"And they'll begin hunting us then," Ty said. "Like they're hunting you."

"Yes. They will."

The historian's helmet panned across them. "This is important: when the Gestalt identifies that the mission is complete and reveals the dial code for the next world, you should dial as quickly as possible. The broadcast from your Gestalt to us will be like a homing beacon for your location in the multiverse. The moment it transmits, the Covenant could become aware, and they may come after you—or direct their agents on the local world to your location."

A long silence stretched out.

"Any further questions?" the historian asked.

"Just one." Nora held up the quantum radio medallion. "On A21, you said we could have dialed our birthday symbols at any point to go home. Can we still do that—enter that code and go home?"

"No. From here out, that code is disabled. Dialing anything other than the codes we supply would risk jumping you to an uninhabitable world. Instant death."

"Well, since you put it that way," Ty muttered.

"Are you ready?" the historian asked.

Ty took a deep breath. "Yes."

On his forearm, the Gestalt activated, and in the center of the box, a sequence of four symbols appeared.

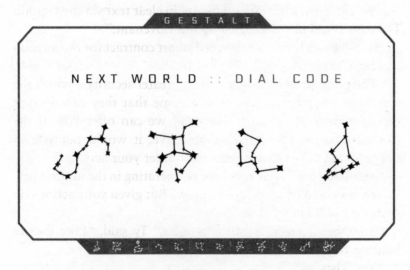

Nora held up the medallion. "Should I dial?"

"We dial this one together," Ty said. "Ladies first."

Holding the medallion in her left hand, Nora reached out with her right and keyed the first symbol. Maria hit the second one.

Kato made eye contact with Ty, nodded, and walked over and pressed the third symbol.

Ty glanced back at his forearm, at the fourth symbol that would transport them to another world in the multiverse.

He reached out to Nora, to the medallion, but stopped, hand hovering above it.

"One last question," he said to the historian. "What are our chances out there? Of coming home?"

"If you work together, and believe in yourselves, nothing can stop you. If you don't, nothing can save you."

Ty nodded.

The quantum historian stepped closer to Ty. The garbled, computerized voice was softer when it spoke.

"But I'll tell you, Ty, sometimes it's going to feel like you're going around in circles."

For a moment, Ty was transported back to Geneva, to the little coffee shop in the Old Town, six months ago, sitting at the table with Penny, where he had said the words *Some days it just feels like we're going around in circles.*

Ty smiled at the historian. Yeah. He knew it.

He pressed his finger onto the quantum radio medallion, and the world disappeared.

Author's Note

Thank you for reading *Quantum Radio*.

This is one of my longest books (second only to *Pandemic*) and certainly one of the most complex (which, I feel, is saying something, given my previous work).

It's a book I was passionate about writing. I penned the first draft during the Covid pandemic, in large part as a method of escape. And to me, that's what the novel is about: escape. It's about other worlds, like ours, where things turned out differently. It's about worlds where anything is possible (both good and bad). It's about big ideas in science and history, which I've always been drawn to (and part of why I began writing).

Quantum Radio is about people who want to change the future. They just have different ideas about what that future should look like. And, to a certain extent, different ideas about what to sacrifice in order to create that future. Looking at this work from the outside, more than eighteen months after I finished the first draft, it's easy for me to see how it was influenced by the event occurring in our world. I hope it's given you some escape—and perspective.

Quantum Radio is also a novel about families and friends who have been separated and are finding their way back to each other. I actually wrote this novel before *Lost in Time*, but the two stories share common themes (derived, no doubt, from my own life at the time).

As you probably know by now, my taste in fiction—both as a reader and an author—is quite eclectic. Some of my novels are more expansive than others, but I'll say that *Quantum Radio* spans more genres than perhaps any of my past work. It's a novel with quite a bit of science and history in it. And historical fiction, alternate history, a love story (or two), family dramas (three or four of those, actually), and elements that one could argue are more fantastical than anything else I've written.

I had hoped these elements would add up to something new and wonderful. But I also long ago accepted that not every book I write will be a hit with every reader. As such, at the end of the novel, I wanted to provide a glimpse of how it will all end up, in the event that some of you might want to get off the ride there (and wait for the next series or standalone, which might be more to your taste). The reason is simple: maintaining my relationship with you—my reader—is ultimately the most important thing to me.

I don't know how long this series will be. This is a fairly large story, and my track record isn't great at predicting how many pages (or books) a story will take to tell. But I hope you'll stick around for it. There are some great surprises in store and stories that I hope will inspire your imagination, curiosity, and appreciation of the world around you.

I have to thank some very special people who worked incredibly hard to help bring this novel to you: Sophie Whitehead, Ben Prior, and Nic Cheetham at Head of Zeus; my agents, Danny Baror and Heather Baror, Gray Tan and Brian Lipson; my wife, Anna, who wears more hats than I have words for; and my in-laws and our help at home. Novels take a village these days, and I'm proud to be part of a great one.

And finally—and most importantly—my thanks to you, my reader, for once again coming this far. I wouldn't be writing without you.

See you in the Multiverse,
Gerry

About the Author

A.G. RIDDLE spent ten years starting and running internet companies before retiring to focus on his true passion: writing fiction. He is now a *Sunday Times*, Amazon and *Wall Street Journal* bestselling author with nearly five million copies sold worldwide in twenty languages. He lives in North Carolina.

Visit agriddle.com